Catherine Jinks is the author of many children's and YA books as well as several novels for adults. She has been writing for over fourteen years and enjoys commercial and critical success across a wide range of genres and age groups. *The Dark Mountain* is her ninth novel for adults. Catherine lives in the Blue Mountains of New South Wales with her husband and daughter.

www.catherinejinks.com

To Kim Johnston

With gratitude

The
DARK
MOUNTAIN

WHAT KIND OF SECRET IS WORTH
A LIFETIME OF BETRAYALS?

CATHERINE
JINKS

ALLEN&UNWIN

First published in 2008

Allen & Unwin
83 Alexander Street
Crows Nest NSW 2065
Australia
Phone: (61 2) 8425 0100
Fax: (61 2) 9906 2218
Email: info@allenandunwin.com
Web: www.allenandunwin.com

National Library of Australia
Cataloguing-in-Publication entry:

Jinks, Catherine, 1963-
  The dark mountain / author, Catherine Jinks.

  ISBN: 978 1 74114 995 1 (pbk.)

A823.3

Set in 13/16 pt Adobe Jenson Pro by Bookhouse, Sydney
Printed and bound in Australia by Griffin Press

10 9 8 7 6 5 4 3 2

Oh! The light from the mountain is fading away
And the shadows creep over it chilly and grey,
I see the dark rocks in their sternness and pride,
But the flowers are hidden that grow by their side.
The tall trees are tossing their wild arms on high
As the shriek of the curlew goes mournfully by,
The cold night is coming it will not delay.
For the light from the mountain is fading away ...

Louisa Atkinson Calvert, c. 1850

Acknowledgements

Kim Johnston first introduced me to Oldbury, and without her this book would never have been written. However, I also wish to thank Linda Emery, of Exeter, New South Wales, for her invaluable help, as well as the staff of the Orange Public Library.

My main source of written information was Patricia Clarke's *Pioneer Writer: The Life of Louisa Atkinson*. Linda Emery's *Tales from a Churchyard* and James Jervis's *A History of the Berrima District* were also crucial texts.

It was my intention to write a novel in which nothing could be disproved. Nevertheless, there were many gaps that had to be filled, and I filled them using my imagination. If I have overlooked or misinterpreted anything, I should very much like to hear about it. Because this is a story that deserves to be told in full.

August 7th, 1905

Dear Aunt Charlotte,

I do hope that you are not offended by my addressing you in this familiar way, but I am quite *convinced* that you are my mother's eldest sister, and consequently, my aunt. Having read your letter in last week's *Evening News*, I know that it must be so. You named your father as one James Atkinson, senior, of Oldbury, Sutton Forest. It happens that my mother, Mrs Louisa Calvert, was James Atkinson's youngest daughter.

I never knew my mother. As you are no doubt aware, she passed away two weeks after I was born. When my father followed her I was only twelve, and although your brother, Mr James Atkinson the younger, invited me into his home at Oldbury for a short time, he too died before I reached my fourteenth birthday. At that age I was too young to be taken into the confidence of my elders, and am therefore not well acquainted with the events that unhappily severed the connection between your branch of the family and mine. But I have *long deplored* this sad estrangement, and would very much like to mend the breach.

The fact that you were writing from Orange startled me, for I lived there myself not long ago. Have you recently arrived in town?

Or can it be that we used to pass each other on the street, all unknowing?

I am also puzzled by one portion of your letter, in which you described the notorious convict John Lynch as having escaped from Cockatoo Island after his arrest for the murder of a fellow convict, Ned Smith, at Oldbury. Your brother's widow once related to me an account of this affair, and it was her recollection that John Lynch was actually *acquitted* of the murder, owing to the drunkenness of the chief witness against him—a certain George Barton, Oldbury's overseer. Can this be true? I must concede that my aunt was not, perhaps, the most *reliable* informant, having previously suffered a severe stroke. No doubt it affected her memory.

Please forgive my blunt approach, which I trust is not unwelcome. If there has been any delay in the delivery of this letter, you may blame me *entirely*; the *Evening News* mentioned only that you were Charlotte E. McNeilly of Byng Street, Orange, so I was forced to use an incomplete address.

I remain most respectfully yours,

(Mrs) Louise S.A. Cosh

I am found out.

Mrs Louise S.A. Cosh has caught me in a lie, and now I must confess to it—or even worse, admit to being mistaken. I should never have written that letter. I certainly should not have posted it. As always, my pride has been my downfall.

Whatever shall I do?

My intentions were good. It was for Edwin's sake that I wrote the letter, for he is taken entirely too much for granted, in my opinion. He is as much the town's son as he is mine, striving ceaselessly for its betterment, yet there is a certain attitude that I have noticed among various gentlemen hereabouts—a certain *benevolence* which I find hard to stomach. 'Good old Ted', they say, as if he deserves no higher compliment. I felt constrained to remind them that, although his father worked as a carrier and his sister married a blacksmith, Alderman Edwin Thomas McNeilly is directly descended from one of this country's finest pioneers.

How many people know, for example, that my late father, James Atkinson, was a founding member of the Agricultural Society of New South Wales? Or that he was the first to venture into the unexplored gorges of the Shoalhaven? Or that he wrote that well-regarded study, *An Account of the State of Agriculture and Grazing in New South Wales*, which, when published in London, attracted many highly respectable settlers to this country in its earliest days?

When I consider Edwin's civic pride, and his charitable kindness, and his untiring labour on behalf of his fellow man, I am reminded very much of his grandfather. If not for the misfortunes that have blighted this family, I truly believe that Edwin's name—like my father's—would now be widely known in far more exalted circles. I truly believe that Edwin would have risen to even higher ranks of government, and accomplished greater things. 'Blood will out', as the saying goes. Why—only see how promising my grandchildren are! Look at Flora's boy, Hubert: how well he conducted himself in the war! And darling George, though barely two, is already speaking quite clearly.

But here I am, a doting fool, letting my pride rule my pen again. With the result that I am now exposed to the prying attentions of Mrs Louise S.A. Cosh, who seems to share her mother's penetrating eye for detail. What shall I say to Mrs Cosh? That the past should not be dissected like one of my sister's freshly killed specimens? That there are shadowy places in the history of this bloodline that will not bear close examination? Or should I simply remain silent, as I did before?

The fact is, I was *not* 'all unknowing' when I passed Mrs Cosh in the street. She was Miss Calvert at that time, of course. (She must have married since, and not in Orange either.) But back then—it would have been ten years ago, at least—I saw her often enough buying worsted at Dalton's, or visiting the Post Office. I shall never forget my first glimpse of her, on the footpath outside the Davis Bros. Furnishing Arcade. Mrs Dunstan was with me; she took my arm, and was very concerned.

'Why, Mrs McNeilly,' she said, 'are you ill?'

I was, for an instant. I thought that I should faint, because I had seen an apparition: I had seen my sister, or so I believed, though she had been dead for all of twenty years. I had seen her slight figure and her dark curls—even her large, clear eyes and heavy chin. As she passed from my sight into the depths of the Drapery Department, I said to Ms Dunstan: 'Who—who was that lady?'

'Which lady?'

'The lady who just crossed our path. The very young lady in green, with dark hair.'

'Oh!' Mrs Dunstan seemed confused, but not for want of information. 'I think you mean Miss Calvert?'

'Miss Calvert?'

'Mr Richards pointed her out to me, yesterday. She is the new children's nurse at his school.'

'How very—how very interesting,' I said, through trembling lips. 'Miss Calvert? I thought I knew her, but I was mistaken.'

'Such a *nice*-looking young lady,' Mrs Dunstan added, in a tone of slight concern. 'It hardly seems right that she should have studied to be a nurse, does it?'

I later discovered that Miss Calvert had in fact studied at the Royal Prince Alfred Hospital in Sydney. This titbit, however, did not come directly from Miss Calvert herself. It was gossip that circulated throughout the town, as gossip always does at the arrival of a new face. I myself was never formally introduced to Miss Calvert. The truth is, I took care to avoid her. It was fortunate that Edwin, in marrying Annie, had adopted the Methodist form of worship, because Miss Calvert forced me to abandon Holy Trinity when she joined its congregation. I caught a glimpse of her one Sunday in the back pews, and had no wish to find myself chatting with her on the porch, or over tea at the rectory. So I threw in my lot with Edwin—much to Annie's delight—and suffered no pangs of conscience as a result. Why should I have?

'Temperance' has always been the Methodist rallying cry, and I hold very firm views on abstinence myself.

Besides which, I have no patience with this precious emphasis on religious *forms*, which seems quite out of place in the modern world. As my sister Louisa once wrote, *'If those forms be not in opposition or perversion of His Revealed Law, they are nothing, only servants to assist and prevent confusion in our devotions.'* Wise words from the Oracle. Do you know, I believe that I might even have inspired them? For I do recall speaking very passionately on the subject, years and years ago. 'True religion is the worshipping of God in spirit, not in forms!' was my plaintive cry.

A young girl will say absolutely anything, when she is in love.

Be that as it may, however, I deserted the Reverend Dunstan's congregation for my own tranquillity of mind. And yet what tranquillity can there be for one such as myself? I could never be at ease—not while Miss Calvert was in town. And then, on one memorable occasion, Edwin himself finally spoke to her. It was a few months after the birth of James Atkinson McNeilly, whose name was chosen solely to please me, I am sure. Edwin was parading down Summer Street with his bonnie new son, fending off the boy's many admirers, when he was stopped by Miss Louise Calvert.

I am grateful that I was not present to witness this encounter. If I had been, I should certainly have died of an apoplectic fit. As it was, I only heard about it when Edwin returned home. He came into the sitting room, where I was smocking a little jacket, and surrendered James to his mother.

'Wet through,' he declared. 'At both ends.' Then he threw himself into his leather-cushioned chair, as Annie whisked her damp, wailing bundle out of the room. 'You will go blind, Mother—you should light a lamp,' he said.

'At this hour?'

'I saw Frank Mulholland outside Plowman's.' (Every word is seared into my memory.) 'He seems well again.'

'Good.'

'James tried to steal his fob. I swear, that child was born to be hanged—though he seems very popular with the ladies.' Edwin reached for the latest *Western Advocate*, which was sitting on top of Annie's workbox. 'Did you know that Richards has bought the Wolaroi Mansion?' he continued. 'I did not.'

'To live in?' I inquired, astonished.

'For his school. He must be doing well with it, don't you think? I had the news from one of his staff—the children's nurse, Miss Calvert. She was with Mrs Dunstan, and stopped to lavish praise upon His Royal Highness. A very nice young lady, I thought. Mother? Is something wrong?'

'No. No, not at all.' How unconvincing I must have sounded! 'Did you—did you mention his name?'

'Whose name?' Edwin frowned. 'Jimmy's?'

'His full name. Did you mention it?'

'Why, no.' By this time Edwin was clearly puzzled. 'Should I have?'

'By no means.' I think I may have laughed, then. 'Just a silly fancy! Of no real consequence. You mustn't mind me . . .'

'Are you all right, Mother?'

'Perfectly. Thank you.' Seeing his fair, guileless face all creased in concern, I was smitten by the most terrible pangs of guilt. It seemed so *wrong* that he should be kept in ignorance—that he and his cousin, each as innocent as the dawn, should be passing each other like strangers. For one moment I was tempted to speak. I actually opened my mouth. But then it occurred to me: what should I say? How could I possibly narrate, in a few simple words, all the misery and passion and deceit that brought me here, to this place? How could I possibly unpick the dense and matted fabric of my life, with little James whimpering in the next room, and a pudding on the boil nearby? I do not believe that Edwin has ever beheld such murky depths as the ones that haunt me. He has grown up buoyant and sunny, skimming the bright surface of the world like a kingfisher. He knows nothing of what lies beneath. Nothing.

How could he even begin to comprehend?

So I closed my mouth and was silent. Until now. Or rather, until I took up my pen and wrote to the *Evening News*, like a fool. I have opened Pandora's box. I have unlocked the family vault. It therefore behoves me to explain, as best I can, why Edwin McNeilly and Louise Calvert had to meet as strangers, so many years ago.

For their sakes, and for the benefit of all my descendants hereafter, I offer up a true account, with nothing omitted, of the ruin occasioned by one event that took place on the thirtieth of January, 1836, in the Belanglo Forest of New South Wales.

Be ye merciful, as your Father also is merciful.

One
1836

The day itself was hot and sultry. A late storm threatened in the slow gathering of dark clouds to the north, but from sunrise it was evident that there would be no early relief. I remember so clearly every passing minute of that day, though all the days before it seem a golden blur, with here and there a break in the mist: the vivid image of a forty-pound turnip, displayed in the milking yard and encircled by exultant men; my newly christened brother, a mass of lace, cradled in my father's arms; a pink cockatoo trapped in the nursery, flapping from corner to corner, its drifting feathers later retrieved from inside the grate. Even my father's death seems to have cast no great shadow—not one, at least, that I can discern from this distance—though I know (for I was told) that it was terrible and protracted; that he was deprived of all his faculties by the fever and the pain; and that Louisa's crying tormented him so much that she was removed from his presence. Perhaps the rest of us were, also: I cannot tell. I recall nothing of his deathbed. Nothing of his rapid decline. My memories of my father are in every instance suffused with happiness, for he was a good man, kind and just, as all who dealt with him are pleased to testify.

There was at least one neighbouring family which owed its complete happiness to my father. Long before I was born, it was Papa who noted the anguish of his convict servant, John Hollands. It was Papa who arranged that John's wife Mary and their five children should be brought from England to New South Wales. Through my father's patronage, Mary Hollands received a grant of land in Sutton Forest, and her husband was assigned to her. Thus was the family reunited, to my father's eternal glory. In this, as in every other facet of his life, he displayed the generosity of spirit, the radiant common sense and the patient determination that earned him the general respect of the colony.

It seems to me now, looking back, that his noble influence could be felt even after his death. Or was I too young to retain any ominous impressions? I was six years old when my father died. Between that date and the incident at Belanglo, I experienced nothing that left me with any lasting sense of dismay. I saw pigs feasting on wheat stubble. I picked peaches and chased hens. I scolded my sister Emily for playing near the creek, and overturned one of the pans in the dairy. Not once was I beaten. Not once did I run away and conceal myself.

Yet the storm clouds must have been gathering long before that fateful day in 1836. For George Barton was among us—and John Lynch, too. It seems incredible now, but they have left no mark on my early recollections, though I know that they were about. My mother told me so. She told me that my father had hired Barton as overseer; that she herself was not responsible. And she told me of an event which occurred not one week after my father's death, when John Lynch disobeyed a direct order.

'His character was always bad,' she announced, as much to distract me as anything else. (This must have been in Sydney, for she was poring over a newspaper article about Lynch's execution for mass murder.) 'Had we only known then what we know today!' she said. 'But I never liked him. He was lazy and insolent. Even at that time, before he committed his most heinous acts, his disposition struck me as being utterly flawed. He refused to yoke the bullocks. When instructed to take a dray out to Bargo Brush, he refused to yoke the last two bullocks—I don't know why.'

For his refusal, John Lynch received a sentence of fifty lashes from the magistrates' bench. This, at least, was my mother's story, and I have no reason to disbelieve it. I must admit, though, that it does give me pause. Perhaps my father did *not* extend his influence from beyond the grave. Had he done so, I doubt that John Lynch would have been brought before the local magistrates. Very few of the convicts under my father's protection ever were; his strength of character was such that, on those rare occasions when his assigned men did misbehave, he dealt with them in his own fashion, firmly but fairly, and never in contradiction of the laws of the land.

If more settlers had been like Papa, this country would have had a much happier birth.

Needless to say, I saw nothing of John Lynch's punishment. I was blind to any discontent among the huts that stood behind our great house. If the assigned men were disrespectful or if they suffered any unfair usage at the hands of their overseer, I did not witness it. Like any young child, I saw only what lay directly in front of me: the plum pudding dispensed at Christmas; my cambric muslin frock; the candle moulds; the grindstone; the smooth, alluring handrail on Oldbury's staircase, which curled at the end like the spiral shell of a triton. My interests were narrow but keen. I loved my mother's sketchbook and her camel-hair paint-brushes. I enjoyed mounting a stick, and racing against Emily when she was similarly mounted. I adored the skittish young kangaroo who came to be fed every evening near the stockyard. Upon waking, I would throw off my covers, eager to greet the day.

On this particular day—January the thirtieth, 1836—I rose early, roused by the clatter of buckets and the warbling of magpies.

At the time, Oldbury's nursery was positioned directly over the front portico, facing south-west; therefore no pearly fingers of sunlight were creeping through the window shutters. I did not share my bed, then, for Emily had her own (as did James), and Louisa, though nearly two, still slept beside my mother, who was concerned about her health. Louisa was a sickly child, who grew into a frail adult. I don't believe that Mama ever ceased to fret over her, from the very moment of her birth. Indeed, there are children who seem to enter this world reluctantly, and whose grasp of life remains weak for as long as they might live. Louisa was one such child.

The same could not be said for the rest of us, however. We were all sturdy enough. Being raised on a farm must have constituted some advantage, in this regard; we were not so exposed to the epidemics that swept through Sydney, and our food was almost always fresh. Furthermore, our supply of water was very good. From the window of the nursery I could look out across the gently sloping front garden—over its picket gate and incipient hawthorn hedge—towards the creek, which never ran dry. Not ever. Even during the great drought of 1839, the creek at Oldbury continued to flow. No doubt this is why my father chose the spot, for in other respects Oldbury could, perhaps, have been better situated. It was so very *crammed up* against the foot of Gingenbullen that one felt perpetually encroached upon—since Gingenbullen, though hardly more than a hill (and a flat-topped hill, at that) still possessed a powerfully solid presence. It was impossible to ignore. Cloaked in dark, dull foliage, and crowned with certain mounds or tumuli left by ancient native tribes, it was altogether too close for comfort.

So was the creek. During heavy rains, the low ground could get very boggy. As a child this did not concern me—in fact I delighted in mud at that age—but now I wonder if it was entirely healthy, living pinched between a steep rise and a sodden morass. Not that anything was sodden on that day in January. It had been dry for some weeks. Pulling open a shutter, I found myself peering out at a parched and dusty scene. Even in the softening light of sunrise, the grass in the pastures beyond our front garden was leached of colour, pale and crisp. The sky to the west was cloudless.

'What are you doing?' Emily whispered. She had swept aside her white bed-curtains, and was struggling to disentangle herself from her twisted sheets. (Emily always slept as if being tossed on a griddle.) 'Where are you going?'

'Shh!' I closed the shutter. 'You'll wake James!'

'Is it time for breakfast?'

'Shhh!'

I had already learned to dress myself, for with three younger siblings, I had been given little choice in the matter. Emily was not so well trained. She needed help with her buttons and her shoes—help that I gave her, though grudgingly. Only her hair was beyond my skill. We both wore our hair in rags when we went to bed, Emily because her hair was dead straight, and myself because my hair was inclined to frizz unless carefully tended. Looking at the crop of blue cotton sausages that dangled from my sister's head, I felt as helpless as a landsman confronted by a tangle of ship's rigging.

'We'll brush our hair later,' I hissed, and crept out of the nursery onto the landing. To my surprise, I saw that Mama's bedroom door was standing slightly ajar, and I wondered if Louisa had been sick during the night. But my train of thought was suddenly interrupted, for Emily had slipped past me and gained the stairs; she had taken the lead in a way that I found unacceptable. Who was the elder of us, after all?

'Wait!' I commanded. 'Wait for me!'

She obeyed at once, as was her nature. At that age Emily was highly biddable, and I do not believe that she changed very greatly over time. Of the four of us, she was the most easily led, and remained so until her death. She was also the fairest. At six, her hair was still light—far lighter than mine. I have always resembled my mother, having inherited her dark hair and eyes. The others, to varying degrees, were more our father's children.

'I'm very hungry,' Emily murmured, as I took the lead. 'Do you think Robert will give us some milk?'

'Not if Mama is awake,' was my reply.

'Is Mama awake?'

'Perhaps.'

Together we padded downstairs to the hall, and from there into the dining room, which was still handsomely furnished. (The sideboard, the carpet, the silver candlesticks—all were later sold.) Standing just inside the door, we could see into the adjoining breakfast room, where Jane was arranging cutlery. In 1836 there were five domestic servants at Oldbury, all but two of them assigned; Jane was one of the free servants. She was very young— about fourteen, I should think—and not well trained, placing each fork so carefully and nervously onto the cloth that she might have been laying out a corpse.

I could hear my mother's voice from the kitchen.

'Mama!' exclaimed Emily, rushing forward. I followed at a more sedate pace. The kitchen occupied a separate stone building, close to the breakfast room and directly accessible from the back veranda. The dairy, an identical structure, stood opposite the kitchen like a mirror image. There were bread ovens in the kitchen, and larders leading off it, all of them locked. The curing of ham and bacon was accomplished further from the house, as was the laundry. In an establishment the size of Oldbury, one is not forced to hang wet clothes over sugar bags, or store soap and tallow beside dressed meat. There is a proper place for everything, and nothing goes to waste.

'You must take all you want now, for I will not be here to unlock the larders,' my mother was saying. 'Do you hear me, Bridget?'

'Yes, Mam.'

'Think very carefully about what you might need. You will need jam for the pudding. You will need salt for the meat. I do not want to hear complaints about insipid dishes, because you have not had the forethought to plan for dinner.'

'No, Mam,' Bridget replied. Though I doubt that she understood the meaning of 'insipid', she could not misread my mother's tone. I should point out that my mother's patience had been sorely tried, over the years, by the measures that had to be taken on the Oldbury estate to protect our supplies of food and drink. Stolen linen cannot easily be concealed; stolen food, on the other hand, always disappears quickly. Tea and coffee, sugar and treacle, rice and brandy, cocoa and arrowroot—all of it had to be secured behind locked doors, or chained to the wall in barrels, or kept under my mother's watchful eye. She was heartily sick of being summoned to the kitchen, at regular intervals throughout the day, because our cook needed currants, or almonds, or something else of great importance that had been forgotten the last time my mother unlocked the storerooms. One might ask: 'Why not, in that case, simply find another cook?' But competent servants of good character were not readily available at that time, in that part of the world. Though Bridget might have been dull-witted in some respects, she was honest, loyal, sober, and reasonably clean. I was never informed of the crime for which she had been transported, but she had received her ticket-of-leave while my father was alive.

Jane, the young housemaid, was her daughter.

'I shall also need some light provisions,' my mother continued. 'The rest of the salt beef, wrapped in a cloth; the usual tea and sugar; perhaps a little dried fruit.'

'There's tart, Mam. From yesterday.'

'Leave the tart for the children. I'll tell Eliza.'

'Where are you going, Mama?' I felt impelled to speak, for I did not like it when my mother left us. 'Are you going to Sutton Forest? May we come too?'

My mother turned. She was all of forty in 1836, but did not look it; her hair was still raven, her figure still neat, her constitution still vigorous. Though small in stature, and clad for the most part in widow's weeds, she managed to present a forceful appearance.

That morning, I noticed, she was dressed in her old riding habit.

'Charlotte,' she said. 'Where is your brother?'

'Asleep.'

'*You* should be asleep.'

'Where are you going, Mama? Are you going to church?'

'I am going to Belanglo,' she replied. 'With Mr Barton.'

'May we come too?'

'No, you may not.' Looking down at Emily, who was clutching at her skirts, my mother said: 'You must brush out your hair, both of you. I don't want you running around in such a state.'

'I am very hungry, Mama,' Emily declared, and my mother lifted an eyebrow.

'In that case you should brush out your hair at once,' she said, 'because you cannot recite your morning prayers looking like a sea-urchin—and you cannot reasonably expect breakfast until you have said your morning prayers!'

'But Mama—' I began.

'Ask Eliza to help you,' my mother interrupted, and turned back to address Bridget.

So we were forced to retrace our steps, Emily and I: across the back veranda, past Jane in the breakfast room, through the dining room and up the stairs. Here we met my brother coming down, for he had recently awakened. He had also made a feeble attempt to dress himself, but being only four, he had not achieved the kind of results likely to satisfy Mama. He had simply pulled his little breeches on over his nightshirt.

'James!' I said. 'You can't come down like that.'

'Where's Eliza?' he lisped.

'I don't know. Perhaps with the baby.'

Eliza was our nurse—the latest in a series of nurses whose failings were a constant trial to my mother. Thanks to the colony's acute lack of respectable female domestic staff, my mother had been forced to lower her very high standards with regards to the care of her children. No sooner did she find an acceptable freed or freeborn nurse than this paragon was certain to be carried off by some local farmer or shopkeeper in need of a wife. Alternatively, when driven to choose from a selection of assigned convicts, my poor mother had to cope with secret drinkers, savage tempers, slow wits or careless dispositions. A bright and merry girl might prove to have a fatal weakness for male company; a stolid and reliable one might be absolutely impossible to wake at night. Eliza, for her part, was rather timid, and almost incapable of exacting obedience from a strong-willed child. On the other hand, she was quiet, neat, patient, and extremely good with babies.

She doted on Louisa, beside whose crib we found her sitting, with a small, embroidered cap in her hand and my sister perched on her knee.

'Look!' she said, when she saw us standing on the threshold. 'Where's Charlotte? Where is your sister?'

'Charla!' Louisa crowed, pointing one pudgy finger at me. But I ignored it.

'Mama says, will you help us to brush our hair?' I said to Eliza. 'And James needs dressing.'

'Aye,' our nurse answered softly. 'I'll do that.'

I am not sure why Eliza was transported to this country. No doubt her crime was some minor theft, for my mother would have been loath to employ a prostitute. All I knew about Eliza was what she had let fall herself: she spoke often of her younger sisters and brothers, who had frequently been left in her charge when she was 'no older than Miss Charlotte'. Perhaps her dreamy and placid disposition stemmed from a nostalgic tendency, together with a firm refusal to dwell on more recent events in her life. At any rate, she never referred to her 'lagging', or to anything associated with it.

Possibly she had received firm instructions from my mother on the subject, and had not the courage to defy them.

She was a pleasant-looking girl, with a weak chin, a rather high colour, and nimble fingers. Her plain and fancy work were equally good; my mother often gave her lace to mend, and our daintier garments to repair. She therefore made quick work of my hair rags, and of James's innumerable buttons. But she was constitutionally incapable of persuading him to stop throwing his marbles at the wall. When she tried, he simply bade her to 'return to her work'—in exactly my mother's tone and manner.

I was the one who had to make him mind: who wrested the marbles from him, told him that he was as stupid as a goose, and warned him that I would tell Mama. Then I propelled him from the nursery, and together we proceeded back down to the breakfast room, with Emily following close behind.

My mother was waiting.

'Much better,' she declared, upon examining us. 'I saw a pair of rough-headed savages in the kitchen earlier, but now my dearest daughters are returned to me.' And she led us all through our prayers, taking particular care with James, who still found them a struggle. Though he could recite the Lord's Prayer, the Morning Hymn was quite beyond his powers.

After prayers, Mama gave us our bread, butter and tea, telling us that we had to be good while she was gone, and urging us to mind Eliza—who by this time had joined us. 'I shall set you each a task that must be completed before I return tomorrow,' Mama said. 'James, you are to find me three native leaves, each of a different shape, and sketch them in your book. Emily, you have still to finish your reading. Charlotte, you are to write me a short essay on the manufacture of a batter pudding, from the ploughing of the sod to the consuming of the finished product. This afternoon,' she added, 'I want you all to find at least two new specimens for our seed pod collection.'

My mother, I should explain, was a tireless and indefatigable teacher. She had always undertaken to educate every one of her children without the aid of either school or governess; she taught drawing, writing and botany particularly well. Of late, however, her time had been very much given to the management of Oldbury. Her duties as a mother had been progressively overtaken by her duties as a landholder.

I had noticed this change, and resented it.

'Could *I* not come with you, Mama?' was my plaintive request. 'After all, I'm a big girl, now.'

'You are,' my mother agreed, retrieving Louisa's spoon from the floor. 'Which is precisely why you must stay here, and take care of the others. It is your duty, Charlotte—your duty as the eldest. Could she be teething, do you think?' (This to Eliza.) 'Her gums seem rather red.'

'Aye, Mam. They do.'

'Poor poppet.' Mama laid the backs of two fingers against Louisa's pale cheek. 'You must wash her mouth out with rosewater, and if that fails, I shall boil up some poppy heads. Yes, James, what is it?'

'I'm finished.'

'Are you, indeed? Then what do you have to say for yourself?'

'Uh . . .' He screwed up his face in thought. 'Thank God for my good breakfast!' he finally exclaimed.

'Well done. Down you get.'

'And me, Mama?'

'You too, Emily. Only don't go far, if you please.'

I would have stayed, given the chance. But I was sent off to watch the others until it was time to say goodbye. By then the sun was up, though the shadows were still long. James retrieved his little wheelbarrow, and occupied himself with transporting stones from one pile to another, while Emily begged some new milk from our dairyman, Robert. At last two saddled horses were brought around to the back veranda, and they proved to be a magnet for every child within hailing distance. I begged a carrot from Bridget, and was given a handful of oats instead; the oats were carefully apportioned; the horses, Angel and Toby, were fed and stroked, under the single eye of Henry the ostler, as various cloth-wrapped bundles were loaded into saddlebags.

Finally, my mother emerged from the house. She was accompanied by Eliza, Louisa, and our overseer, George Barton; she had donned a hat, and was pulling on her gloves. I had eyes for no one else, at that moment. It was my custom to disregard Eliza, who occupied a curious position in my mind, halfway between the family and the household furnishings. Louisa, too, was of little consequence. (She couldn't really talk, after all.) As for George Barton, if I had noticed him in the past, it was only as a kind of extension of the estate—his barking orders, delivered high over my head, were of a piece with the cracking of stockmens' whips or the scraping of blades on our grindstone. To me he was little more than a gruff voice and a pair of heavy riding boots.

Even now, I cannot tell you exactly what he was to my mother, at that time—though I have my suspicions.

'Give me a kiss, my darling,' Mama said, pressing her lips to Louisa's cheek. 'And James, too. You must be a good boy, James.'

'I will do my drawing, Mama.'

'Of course you will. Charlotte will see to it, won't you, Captain?'

'Yes, Mama.'

'And I have told Bridget that you may have some raspberry tart, today.'

'Hurrah!'

James threw his arms around Emily, and together they jumped up and down. My mother mounted her horse. George Barton was already in the saddle, silently waiting. It never occurred to me that there should have been other men, on other horses. I rarely questioned anything about my elders' actions, before that day.

'Step back now, please,' my mother ordered. 'Eliza! Get them out of the way.'

'Aye, Mam. Come along, Miss Charlotte, Master James.'

Herded onto the veranda, we watched our mother turn her horse. Others watched with us. There was a curious lack of movement, in fact: an unusual absence of cheerful cries from the convict huts and busy clatter from nearby outbuildings. Bridget was watching from the kitchen door, with her daughter beside her. Robert was watching from the window of the dairy. Someone watched from the kitchen garden, and someone else from the path near the fence.

In hindsight, I can only deduce that this general scrutiny stemmed not from a conspiratorial sense of anticipation, but from sheer astonishment. It is evident to me now that my mother had never previously ridden out alone with one of her employees. Had she been making a habit of it, she would not have occasioned such a deal of unspoken surprise among the rest of her staff.

Why she should have chosen to do so that particular day is a question that will forever remain unanswered.

'Quickly!' I exclaimed, as my mother blew us a kiss. 'We can wave from the front door!'

And this is exactly what we did. With Eliza loping along behind, carrying Louisa, I led Emily and James back through the house and onto the porch. From this vantage point we had a good view of my mother when she came around the side of the main block and headed for the gate. We waved, and cried out. Since Henry was already at the gate, holding it open, we refrained from approaching it ourselves.

Henry frightened us a little, because of his empty eye-socket.

'Mama! Mama! Goodbye, Mama!'

My mother waved back at us jauntily. George Barton preceded her through the gate. The trees along the fence were not so well grown, then—the elms, in particular, were only saplings. Nevertheless, the sight of Angel's glossy rump was soon screened by foliage. When it again became visible, my mother was merely a distant silhouette, riding west towards the Belanglo wilderness.

'I wish she wouldn't go,' said Emily, with a sniff.

Then we all went inside the house again.

Two

The rest of the day passed as follows.

Firstly, I helped Jane to make curd cheese. We tied up the curds tightly in three pieces of old Holland cloth, which we thereafter hung in the dairy to drain. James and Emily also begged to 'help', but they were not at all useful, being mostly engaged in hitting each other with the skimmers. After that, Eliza took us for a short walk in search of leaves and seed pods. To do this we were obliged to pass near the convict huts, but I recall nothing untoward about them: no huddled groups of whispering men, nor sidelong glances from the few men who *were* about. James and I squabbled over a parrot feather. Emily scratched herself on a fallen log. Louisa watched us silently from Eliza's hip, round-eyed, her thumb wedged firmly in her mouth.

The leaves that we found were quite diverse: a length of Settler's Flax, a sprig of *casuarina*, and something we thought to be of the pea family. Our seed-pod search was not particularly successful, since we found only one that was strange to us. On our way back to the house, on the flats, we stopped to watch a team of bullocks dragging a grating roller over some clods. I knew the ploughman by sight, though not by name; there were at least a dozen convicts ssigned to Oldbury, and I had little truck with those not engaged around the house. The men who yoked and drove the bullocks, who cleared the fields and ploughed them, who roped and branded the cattle, who worked as shepherds on our far-flung sheep stations—these men, on the whole, were strangers to me.

Upon returning home, we ate a mouthful of bread with cheese, and some raspberry tart. Then Louisa was put to bed for a few hours, while the rest of us toiled over our books at the breakfast table. Having arranged his leaves, James began laboriously to sketch them. Emily plodded through lesson five of *A First Book of English Grammar*. I made a plan of my essay on batter pudding, carefully numbering and briefly summarising each of the points that I wanted to make. My mother, in teaching me the art of composition, had always stressed the importance of preparing one's ground before building one's edifice. 'Picture yourself setting out on a journey,' she had said to me. 'If you don't draw a map first, how can you be sure that you will reach your intended destination?'

1. The grain, I wrote. *Ploughing, sowing, harvesting, grinding.*

'Eliza,' I said (for she was sitting nearby, mending a Guernsey shirt), 'how do you make batter pudding?'

'Why, Miss, 'tis aisy enough,' she replied. 'You must take batter, and bile it at a gallop in a floured cloth.'

'Yes, but what is *in* the batter?'

'Flour,' she answered. 'Salt. Eggs and milk.'

'Thank you.' *2. Eggs*, I wrote. *Laying, collecting, breaking.*

James completed his drawings long before I had finished my essay, and went to help Jane clean the lamps. Then Emily came to the end of her lesson; I saw her through the window shortly afterwards, throwing a stick to an old collie. Louisa woke at about two o'clock, her cries filtering down to the breakfast room, whereupon Eliza immediately got up to fetch her.

I was left alone for some time.

It was Emily who came to me at last, and said: 'Is Mama home yet?' She was very dirty. I told her, 'No', then glanced into the dining room—where a mosaic of sunlight lay on the floor, having fallen through the little panes of glass in the window. 'Mama will not come back until tomorrow. Have you forgotten?'

'I wish she was home,' Emily whined. 'I'm *so* hot.'

'You should go down to the cellar,' was my advice, but she shook her head.

'The cellar is locked.'

'Oh.' Of course. Mama had taken the keys.

'Will you play with me, Charlotte?'

'All right.' I was glad of an excuse to leave my employment, which was proving rather dull. 'Let us play Shipwreck.'

So we played Shipwreck for a while in the front garden. I filled the role of the Captain, Emily was the Captain's Wife, and James was the Bloodthirsty Savage. We played until we heard the pounding of hooves on dry soil, and looked up to see a foam-flecked stockhorse canter past us, heading for the house.

Its rider was unknown to me.

'Who is that?' said Emily, in wondering tones. 'Is it Mr Barton?'

'No,' said I. 'James, wait!'

But James had already hurried after the new arrival, who was vanishing around the side of the house. This fact in itself seemed strange to me. Why not dismount at the front door, like a proper visitor? Taking Emily by the hand, I followed my brother, suddenly aware of how late it was. Shadows were creeping across the parched front lawn. It was breathlessly warm, and unbearably sticky. Big clouds were building in one corner of the sky.

'There will be a storm soon,' I observed, as we passed between the main house and the kitchen. But when we reached the veranda, the scene unfolding in front of it drove every other consideration from my mind.

Eliza was there, with Bridget and Robert and Henry the ostler. There was also a man pouring sweat, dressed rather like a drayman in a round blue woollen frock and cabbage-tree hat. I recognised him as our visitor, and wondered who he could be. Not a gentleman, at any rate. That much was apparent.

So too was the general feeling of alarm. Though our visitor spoke quietly, to a tight-packed cluster, I could see clearly from a distance the effect of his words: the wide eyes, the pursed lips, the furrowed brows. Robert was shaking his head, in concern or disbelief.

I started forward, dropping Emily's hand.

'What is it?' I demanded, in a loud voice. 'Has something happened?'

They all turned as one, but only Eliza responded. She broke away from the main group, moving towards me and blocking my path.

'No naid to fret,' she assured me, though her expression was troubled. 'Why not take the little ones to wash their hands, now?'

'Is Mama all right?'

'As right as ninepence.'

'How do you know?'

'Because your Mam is at Mereworth, Miss. We have heard it from this lad they sent.'

'But how can that be?' I was amazed. 'How can she be at Mereworth, when Uncle John will not speak to her anymore?'

'Oh, Miss,' said Eliza, as she cast a distracted eye towards the steel-grey clouds rolling over us, 'there might be strong faylings, but Mr Atkinson would never turn a lost soul from his door, let alone his own brother's wife.'

And with this assurance I had to be satisfied, for Eliza would not discuss the matter at any length. She said only that Mr Barton had been taken ill, and was resting at my uncle's property a few miles away. No doubt he and my mother would both return in the morning.

'But what if Mr Barton is still sick in the morning?' I wanted to know.

'Now, now,' Eliza said maddeningly. 'Don't fret your head, Miss. George Barton can take care of hisself, and there's no call to afright the little ones. Go now, and wash your hands for dinner.'

I looked towards the other servants, but their faces wore the habitual blank expression that I had often encountered among the assigned staff. Facing it, one was often put in mind of sheep or cattle; there were some who took it as a manifestation of intense stupidity. Even at that age, however, I realised that it was a symptom of concealment. Having lost almost everything else—including their freedom—most convicts were anxious to keep their thoughts (at least) well sequestered.

Thunder rumbled in the distance.

'Is my mother ill too?' I asked. 'Is that why she went to Mereworth?'

'Bless you, Miss, there's nowt to fear for the leddy,' our visitor declared, removing his grimy hat. 'Not a scratch on her, I swear.'

'Not a *scratch*?'

'Mr Barton had an accident,' Eliza explained quickly. 'And is ill on account of it. Go now, Miss, afore them chops get cold.'

So I went. Though uneasy, I could see no point in staying—and as Eliza said, I did not want to 'afright' the little ones, who were too young to be burdened by any fears that I might have entertained. My mother, I knew, was relying on me; she called me 'the Captain', and I staunchly lived up to this cognomen, shepherding James and Emily to the kitchen, seeing that they washed their hands, and dragging them off to the dining room—all in a bluff and encouraging manner that concealed my inner qualms. It must have been all of five o'clock, by then, and we were accustomed to dining a good deal earlier. James, especially, was in a snappish and querulous mood.

He would not eat his stewed onions.

'But you liked them last time,' I pointed out.

'No I did not.'

'Yes you did. I remember.'

'Did *not!*'

'Ah, let him bay, poor lad,' said Eliza, with an exaggerated sympathy that chilled me to the bone. She had brought Louisa to the table, and was trying to persuade my youngest sister that a little potato mush might be to her taste. 'Would you care for some tart, Master James?'

I was not at all sure that my mother would have allowed two servings of tart in one day, but I remained silent. While the others enjoyed their treat wholeheartedly, I was barely able to swallow a mouthful of mine; it had exactly the same effect on my spirits as baked funeral meats. After we had finished, Emily begged to feed our little kangaroo friend, Bunny. But by this time the thunder was very loud, and a few heavy drops of rain were falling. Eliza would not let us out of the house again.

'When the storm hits,' she said, 'you'll want to be safe inside. Just like your Mam.'

I tried to comfort myself with thoughts of my mother at Mereworth. As rain drummed on the shingles above our heads, Jane filled the nursery basin, and we all washed—with varying degrees of enthusiasm. James simply dabbed at his dirt. Louisa nearly overturned the basin. Emily was so attentive to her hands and feet that her face was wholly neglected, until Eliza attacked it.

As for me, I was of an independent disposition, and would not let Eliza touch me—not, at least, until it was time to roll up my hair. I had no choice then.

'What time will Mama be back tomorrow?' I asked her, grimacing at every tweak.

'That I can't say, Miss.'

'In the morning?'

'Perhaps.'

'I wish Mama was here now,' Emily piped up. 'To read us a story.'

'Not tonight, Miss.'

'But I want a story!' James's bottom lip began to tremble. 'I want Mama to read us a story!'

'Be quiet, James!' My nerves, at this point, were sorely tried. 'You *know* that Mama is not here, so how can she possibly read you a story?'

'But I *wa-a-ant* one!' he wailed.

'Then I will tell you one,' said Eliza, and launched into the tale of a certain English highwayman, renowned for his brutal crimes, who was cursed by one of his dying victims. Shortly afterwards, one dark and stormy night, he accosted a jet-black coach drawn by four jet-black horses. 'Bail up!' cried he, all unaware that beneath the coachman's huge, three-cornered hat, no face was visible.

'And when Blunderbuss Jack threw open the door of the coach, he saw the Devil a-sitting there,' Eliza finished matter-of-factly, tugging James's nightshirt over his head. 'And the Devil rayched out his hand—which was all bone, no flesh—and grabbed Blunderbuss Jack by his wicked throat, and pulled him inside. And the door slammed shut, and the coachman's whip cracked, and away went the coach. And that was the end of Blunderbuss Jack the Highwayman. Only sometimes, late at night along that same stretch of road, you can still hear him scrayming.'

If Eliza was meaning to subdue us with this fable, then she succeeded—for we said our prayers very quietly, and went to bed without protest. But I do not believe for one moment that this was her intention. To formulate such a plan would have required some imagination, and Eliza had none.

'Eliza,' said James, as she made to withdraw, 'was Blunderbuss Jack in the Bargo Brush?'

'No, no,' I answered, before Eliza could. 'He was in England, silly.'

'And England is a very long way away,' Emily added, from behind her bed-curtains.

'Aye, Miss,' said Eliza. 'A very long way.'

Then she left the room, shutting the door behind her.

I remember lying there, listening to the birds calling each other home, and waiting for James to speak. I knew exactly what thoughts were churning around in his head. At last he murmured: 'There are highwaymen at the Bargo Brush.'

'Not highwaymen. Bushrangers,' I replied. 'Bushrangers are different.'

'Why?'

'Because they are.' I had decided that there must be a distinction of some sort, though I had no idea what it might be. 'Now go to sleep.'

He promptly obeyed me, for he was very tired. Emily began to snore soon afterwards. But my own mind was unsettled; I tossed and turned. Though I make no claim to any great perspicacity, all this talk of bushrangers had filled me with dread. Unlike James, I knew that bushrangers did not confine themselves to Razorback and the Bargo Brush. My mother had spoken of bushrangers. I had heard her talking to some of the other settlers after church: she had spoken of cattle killed, and huts plundered, and men roaming through the forests like packs of wolves.

I could imagine a yellow-eyed bushranger creeping up to our house with his pistols cocked, while all inside were sleeping. Try as I might, I was unable to expunge this picture from my thoughts. Even while I slept it haunted me—for my dreams that night were frightening.

Not for one moment, however, did I entertain the idea that the bushrangers had already struck.

Three

Our dray was sent to Mereworth the next morning, to collect my mother.

I did not understand why a dray should be necessary, until it was explained to me that Mr Barton's injuries prevented him from riding—or from sitting up in the gig. When I asked what those injuries might be, I received no firm reply. 'Mebbe it's his back,' said Eliza, vaguely.

We had wandered out to the stockyard to watch the bullocks being yoked. It was always a sight worth watching. I never ceased to marvel at the way those massive, horned beasts could be shoved this way and that, at a whim (though some of the men were more skilled in their handling than others). The mighty creatures having been yoked to their shaft, there would follow a great straining and creaking, and a shifting of weight that could be felt through the soles of one's feet, and the wheels of the dray would slowly begin to turn. The effect was powerful, like a rainforest eucalypt being torn out by its roots. James, in particular, always liked to be about when the dray set off.

On this occasion, we followed it down to the creek before retracing our steps. Eliza then took us inside to eat breakfast. It seems incredible now, but I distinctly recall mentioning George Barton in my morning prayers. I asked the good Lord to 'Please make Mr Barton well', or something to that effect. I should have asked, instead: '*Break thou the arm of the wicked and the evil man.*' I prayed for Mama as well, of course. And for our dear Papa in heaven—which I imagined to be like an enormous church, with God at the pulpit, and angels singing in the choir.

After breakfast, I helped Jane to salt and press the curd cheese, while Emily attended to her sewing, and James to his wheelbarrow. But we were restless, and disinclined to settle. Our ears were pricked for the rattle of the dray—though we knew full well that we could not expect to hear it *very* soon. James was quite maddening in his impatience. 'When will Mama come?' he kept asking. 'Why is she not yet come?' At last Bridget was forced to stuff his mouth with dried figs, to buy us all a little peace. Or to 'tip 'im a sweetener', as Bridget put it.

As the day warmed up, we retreated from the kitchen and sought shady nooks within the house. Though locked out of the cellars, we found some refreshment in the sitting room, because it received next to no sun in the morning. Oldbury, I should mention, was not like Throsby Park, or Regentville, or most of the other big houses built between Sydney and Goulburn around that time. No veranda graced its front or sides like a species of hat-brim; there was only a modest portico shading the main entrance. My mother always told us that the house was built in her honour, as a wedding gift, so perhaps it was for her sake that the front veranda was omitted. I am led to believe that English houses do not normally boast verandas, and my mother must have been homesick for England when she first arrived in this country. Perhaps my father built her a familiar sort of house, in which she could feel entirely comfortable.

At any rate, we were in the sitting room when my mother returned. Even Louisa was present, squatting on the floor with a selection of spoons. I had pulled a chair up to my father's campaign chest, the top drawer of which folded down to make a little shelf, or desk, revealing a series of pigeon-holes and small drawers. (This chest, like most of our other fine pieces, was later sold.) As I struggled to complete my essay on batter pudding, I would glance out the window, eager to catch a glimpse of any approaching vehicle.

The human eye, however, has not the penetration of the human ear. Our dray was still out of sight when we were alerted to its proximity by the crack of a whip, and the distant urging of a teamster. Immediately, we all rushed to the western window; even Louisa joined the throng, and was nearly trampled by her heavy-footed siblings.

'There! There, I can see it!' Emily cried.

'Where?' For I could not. 'Show me.'

'*There!*' She pointed. 'Look!'

'Mama!' shouted James, and ran to the door.

My mother was not mounted. That much was instantly apparent, and it unnerved me, though I could not have said why. She was sitting up on the dray beside the driver, while another man led her horse. Perhaps for this reason she was no longer clad in her riding habit. Instead she wore an unfamiliar morning dress of shirting stripes, and a straw bonnet.

It was not until I had almost reached the dray that I noticed Mr Barton lying behind her. He was stretched out under a blanket, and must have endured a very uncomfortable ride. Drays are not ideally suited to the transport of passengers. Even goods, when fragile, rarely survive them unscathed. I have heard a joke about a dairywoman sending milk by dray, and finding that it has reached its destination as butter.

'Stand clear, children!' my mother exclaimed. 'Stay away from the bullocks! Eliza, make sure they keep their distance.'

Quite a crowd had gathered by the time the dray creaked to a halt. All the domestic servants were there, as were two or three assigned farmhands in duck trousers and neckerchiefs. Some merely stood watching, while others stepped forward to help. Henry offered his hand to Mama, whereupon she took it and dropped to the ground, her wide skirts bobbing like one of the transparent jellyfish that we saw much later around the wharf-piers at Port Jackson.

I ran to her, but James reached her first. She stooped to gather him up, and stretched out an arm for me. 'Oh, my loves,' she said, pressing us close. 'Oh, my darling children.'

My mother was not much given to emotional outbursts, nor to wild expressions of devoted attachment. Normally hers was a more temperate affection. So while gratified by her trembling voice and flushed cheek, I was also alarmed—especially when I saw a very thin scratch under her eye that had not been apparent the previous morning.

'You have hurt yourself, Mama,' I said. 'You have scratched your face.'

'Just an ugly old ironbark,' my mother replied, scooping Louisa out of Eliza's arms. 'It tried to snatch off my hat as I rode past. How is she, Eliza, is she well?'

'Well as I ever saw her, Mam.'

'Good,' said my mother—but her voice was faint, and her tone distracted. Mr Barton was being helped from the back of the dray. I could see at once that there was nothing wrong with his legs. It was the upper portion of his body that seemed to pain him. He moved stiffly, with many an involuntary wince and suppressed groan. Having reached the ground, he shook off his attendants, as if the touch of their hands was entirely too much to bear.

My mother went to him, still carrying her youngest daughter. For a moment they stood together, and my mother's hand was on his arm, and his head was bent close to her ear. Something about this attitude bespoke an intimacy that I had not hitherto suspected.

Indeed, the contrast between his expression as he spoke to my mother, and his tone as he addressed the hovering servants, was startling. 'Would you be flogged for yer idleness?' he suddenly demanded, turning on them with a violence that must have jolted his wound. For he grimaced, and my mother winced in sympathy.

She watched him head for the veranda, as if concerned that he might stumble. Only when he had glanced back, and reassured her with a crooked smile, did she finally attend to her children.

'Mama,' said Emily, 'did you see Uncle John?'

'I did,' my mother replied, her thoughts clearly pursuing another course. 'Eliza!' she went on. 'Tell Jane to make up the bed in the guest-room.'

Eliza nodded. James, who was holding my mother's hand, asked if there was to be a visitor.

'Mr Barton is our visitor,' my mother informed us, moving towards the house. 'He is too ill to return to Swanton just yet.' (Swanton, the overseer's cottage, lay about half a mile to the east.) 'We must make him comfortable here until he has recovered. You must all be very good, and leave him alone, and not make much noise.'

'What happened, Mama?' I thought it high time that some explanation was offered. 'Did Mr Barton fall from his horse?'

It is fortunate that our overseer did not hear this artless question. He was already inside the house; we had still to reach the veranda. My mother stopped. She took a deep breath, as if to steady herself. But all she said in reply was: 'Have you eaten your dinner?'

'No, Mama,' said James.

'No, Mama,' said Emily.

'Then go and wash your hands, and I will speak to you in the dining room. Go. Quick march. I shall be with you directly.'

If this was a promise, it was soon broken. My mother did *not* appear in the dining room directly. Though our salt beef arrived, and our poached eggs, my mother kept us waiting and waiting. Eliza was there, and she offered one mild explanation after another: Mama was washing, or resting, or perhaps attending to Mr Barton.

'But what about our lessons?' Emily protested. 'We have missed our morning lessons.'

'They'll keep,' Eliza replied, though she was hardly qualified to judge. At last she went to seek direction from my mother, returning with Mama's apologies. My mother had a headache, and would speak to us when her health improved. In the meantime, we should be very quiet, and very good, and not stray too far from the house. 'Mebbe later, if she wants some tay, you can take it to her,' Eliza promised.

To our disappointment, no demand for tea was forthcoming. My mother kept to her bed all afternoon, forcing Louisa to take her afternoon nap in the nursery. The rest of us were forbidden to go upstairs in case we woke Louisa, or disturbed my mother, or worried Mr Barton, who was currently occupying one of the back bedrooms.

For a while we drifted about, peeling bark off eucalypts and digging holes in the dirt. At last I went into the kitchen, where Bridget was assembling a tray for Mr Barton. He was hungry, she said; he wanted white bread, and some brandy in his tea. Upon asking if I might take up the tray, I was denied this honour. ('Wit *dose* little arms, Miss? Oh, no.') So I gathered some flowers for a small bouquet, and insisted that they be taken up with the tea. 'Because we are very sorry that Mr Barton is ill, and wish that he was better,' I explained.

I also racked my brains for something that Mama might appreciate, wishing that I had a pot of calf's-foot jelly or a pair of embroidered slippers to give to her. In the end I concluded, glumly, that keeping the others quietly occupied would be the most useful gift of all. So I played the Captain's part until bedtime, when my mother finally emerged from her room.

We children were in the nursery, having our faces washed and our hair attended to. Perhaps we were a little noisier than we should have been; the sight of my mother standing in the doorway, with her finger to her lips, immediately silenced us. She was wrapped in a plaid shawl, and her face looked pale and bruised.

'Hush, my dears,' she murmured. 'Remember that we have a sick guest.'

Emily clapped her hands over her mouth. James ran to Mama, and buried his head in her skirts. My mother nodded at Eliza, who immediately withdrew, bearing Louisa on her hip.

'Will you say our prayers with us, Mama?' I asked.

'Yes, indeed.'

'Will you tell us a story?' James begged, his voice muffled by layers of wool and cotton.

My mother hesitated. She disengaged herself from James and went to sit on his bed. All the while her brow was working; she seemed to be settling a point in her mind. I did not like to see her so irresolute. It was contrary to her nature, and it scared me.

At last she spread her arms, inviting us to sit beside her.

'I *shall* tell you a story,' she said, 'but only because I want you to know the truth. You might hear the servants talking, and no doubt they will say all manner of foolish things, which will frighten you, and I don't want you to be frightened.'

'Frightened of what, Mama?' said Emily.

'Frightened of bushrangers.' My mother took a deep breath. 'You see, children—poor Mr Barton was attacked by bushrangers yesterday.'

I felt deep within me a sudden lurch of fear. James, however, seemed almost excited.

'Like Blunderbuss Jack?' he inquired, and my mother blinked.

'Like what?' she said.

'Oh, don't pay him any mind,' I interrupted. 'Please tell us what happened.'

'Yes, tell us!' cried Emily.

'Shh.' My mother was frowning. She spoke less firmly than usual; there was a strained and almost startled look in her eye, which, along with her slightly abstracted manner, seemed to suggest that she had not properly come to grips with recent events. 'You see, children—it was very bad, of course—very bad—but I am quite safe. And Mr Barton, too,' she added. 'Mr Barton will recover. So you must not be frightened.'

'They did not *hurt* you, Mama?' Emily wailed.

'No, no.' My mother swallowed, pressing her close. 'They hurt Mr Barton.'

'Oh, Mama!'

'Shh. Don't cry, Emily. It serves no purpose. I am well, as you can see.'

'But poor Mr Barton!'

'Yes. Poor Mr Barton.'

'Did they shoot him?' asked James, whereupon my mother flinched. Visibly, she flinched.

It should be understood that my mother *never* flinched. She would snap, and even shout on occasion, but she never flinched.

I was so shocked to observe it that I lashed out at my brother in fear.

'Be quiet, James!' I snarled, at which my mother urged us all to calm ourselves.

'Now, you must be sensible,' she said. 'There is no need to fret, because the police will catch these men.'

'Have you *told* the police, Mama?' I wanted to know.

'We have sent a message to Bong Bong. The Chief Constable has been informed.'

'I hope he shoots them!' This was not my better self speaking, but I was very angry and frightened. The thought of my mother being threatened by bushrangers was more than I could bear. 'When he catches them, I hope he shoots them!'

'Charlotte, this is not helpful. You are alarming your brother.' It was true. James had begun to cry. 'Come, be still. Listen to me.' Though Mama's voice cracked, she cleared her throat and pressed on bravely. 'What happened was very bad, I cannot deny it. We were bailed up, Mr Barton and myself, by two absconders with guns. And they struck Mr Barton, and they took our money. I tell you this, children, so that you will know the truth, and not be misled. Also, I want you to realise that, while our sufferings were great, they would have been much worse had we not prayed to God for deliverance. God is our refuge and our strength, my loves. We should never despond, however painfully we may be situated— because God can, when he sees fit, extricate us from the greatest of calamities. As He did with Mr Barton and me.'

'I love God so much, Mama!' Emily sobbed. 'I love Him because he saved you!'

'And you should thank Him for it, Emily. We should all thank Him, from the bottom of our hearts.'

We then knelt together in thanksgiving, my mother guiding us through our prayers. It made us more tranquil, I think. It certainly calmed *me*. Yet for all that, we were loath to let my mother go after we had crawled into bed. James begged her for a song, and Emily for another kiss, and I sought reassurance.

'Where was it, Mama?' I demanded. 'Where did it happen?'

'A long way from here,' she replied.

'But how far?'

'They will not come to the house, Charlotte.' My mother spoke firmly. 'You can rely on that.'

'But—'

'You have nothing to fear. It is all over. Now go to sleep.'

She was wrong, of course. It was *not* all over. And we had everything to fear. Even now, I don't know if she was lying or simply mistaken. My mother often lied, though more often than that she simply omitted. Hers was the art of deceitful silence. One of her favourite Proverbs was: 'Even a fool, when he holdeth his lips, is counted wise.'

She certainly never spoke of the attack again—not to me, at any rate. She simply refused to discuss it.

There were many, many things that she refused to discuss.

Four

So there you have it: a full account of those two fateful days. I believe my memories are so detailed because within months—even weeks—I was reviewing the content of both days, over and over again, in a vain effort to detect some kind of hint, or clue, or *explanation*. But what, after all, could my memories tell me? I had seen nothing. I had been told nothing. Therefore I knew nothing—far less, it transpired, than most of the educated people in Sydney, who were unacquainted with Oldbury but who were nevertheless free to read the *Sydney Herald*.

I was not free to read the *Sydney Herald*. Though my mother subscribed to several newspapers, they were not left about in piles for me to leaf through. On the contrary, my mother would read aloud to her children only selected and 'improving' portions, lest our wandering eyes snag on stories of assigned convicts murdering their masters. These, she thought, would alarm us. She had no objection to our becoming acquainted, through the agency of newspaper reports, with the wages of sloth, greed or drunkenness. In her opinion, there was a moral to be learned from the sad tales of bankrupt gamblers, or hanged bushrangers—just as there were lessons to be learned from less bloody extracts concerning the tea trade, or agricultural pests. But she did not want us to fret about the assigned men at Oldbury.

It seems rather ironic, now. All things considered.

I cannot say whether my mother received a copy of the *Sydney Herald* for the eleventh of February, 1836. If she did, she made no mention of it. Quite probably she destroyed it. I know for a fact, however, that this particular edition was widely read among the literate families of Bong Bong and Sutton Forest. They would have received it around the eighteenth, meaning that they would have been well primed for the Sunday service two days later. It was only then, outside the little weatherboard chapel on the Argyle Road, that I even began to understand the full implications of what had happened to my mother in the Belanglo Forest. Until that time I was still living in a dream.

Not that the dream was an altogether happy one. Between the incident at Belanglo and the Sunday service three weeks later, I felt a growing disquiet that could probably be attributed to several sources (the visit of the constabulary, for instance), but which primarily stemmed from Mr Barton's presence in our house. For he stayed, you see. He stayed in the back bedroom, even after he could move about freely again.

He seemed to take up residence.

It is difficult for me to describe George Bruce Barton with any kind of honest detachment. To conjure up his image is to conjure up such a host of vile memories that his features are instantly distorted by them—made monstrous and inhuman, like a savage mask. Nevertheless, I shall try to do him justice, however little he might deserve it. I shall concede that, in those days, he was not an ill-looking man, before the depredations of strong liquor were quite so evident in his mottled complexion and swollen lineaments.

He was fairly short, with a fine head of thick, light, wavy hair. Beneath these heavy locks his face was shaped like an axe-head, bisected by a slightly flattened nose. He had fair, freckled skin—

heavily tanned—and blue eyes set in such a morass of seams and wrinkles that he could have been peering out of a pair of unmade beds. His teeth were crooked, but otherwise quite good—large and a little brown, like tombstones. When unshaven, his beard glinted gold and grey against the heavy line of his jaw.

There. I have set down my description, and it is not a bad one. It is reasonable. Objective. Yet my hand trembled as I wrote it; I felt ill and faint just contemplating those teeth—that nose. I know now why Louisa was so intemperate when she wrote her novel *Myra.* That was in '64, a good twenty years after her final encounter with George Barton, but her feelings were still as strong as they had ever been. I saw this at once, the moment I came upon her villain, Guy Kershaw. '*To others Guy Kershaw was repulsive; not bad looking, perhaps, but badly and coarsely featured; not stupid, but with low sharpness.*' This was a delineation from his early life; as the novel unfolded, Guy's appearance did not improve. '*A rather short man,*' Louisa wrote, '*with a low, bloated face, a face on which gross sins and brutal selfishness had left their indelible stamp—such a drear waste of sin and vulgarity, with a glaring masquerade of gentility about it.*'

It warmed me, to some extent—this torrent of rage and disgust. It confirmed me in my own beliefs. Louisa might have been young when the curse of George Barton descended upon our heads, but she wasn't too young to remember. No doubt he haunted her dreams for years, much as he did mine.

But Louisa's earlier memories must have been warped by her later ones, for George Barton was not so 'badly and coarsely featured' in that first year. Though his *manner* may have been wanting, his appearance was unexceptionable. Had it not been, I would have shown myself less eager to approach him with my good wishes for his improved health. I would have run from him, as I later did. I would not have thought him such a romantic figure.

Or perhaps 'romantic' is not precisely the word. Perhaps the word 'pitiable' is more correct. At eight years old, I had not yet stuffed my head with the rubbishy extracts to be found in journals such as *The Mirror*. I was not inclined, therefore, to cast George Barton in a role for which he was most ill suited: namely, the role of wounded hero. At that age, I pitied him for the hurt that he had sustained. I did *not*, however, see anything Byronic in his situation, nor admire the pallor of his cheek, nor regard his morose fits as in any way intriguing, or suggestive of hidden depths. An older girl might have imagined some sort of bush duel, or perhaps a brave act of chivalry. I did not. I merely felt sorry for Mr Barton because he was so evidently unwell.

He did not even rise from his bed until the day after his return—and then only for a short time. It was at about eleven o'clock. I was in the breakfast room with James and Emily, hunched over a botanical sketch, when Mr Barton appeared in the doorway. He looked ghastly: his face was rigid, his eyes were bloodshot, and his hands were covered in scabs and bruises. But he had taken some trouble with his clothes, and had combed his thick, wavy hair down flat.

'Oh! Good morning, Mr Barton,' said I, upon observing him.

'Morning,' he rumbled in response, his gaze flitting around the room uneasily.

'Good morning, Mr Barton,' James and Emily chorused, eager for any distraction that might present itself. George Barton did not reply. He seemed at a loss. Pushing an errant lock from his forehead, he finally said: 'Is yer mother not here?'

'Mama is unwell,' I explained. It was true; my mother had spent the greater portion of the last day in her bedroom.

'Ah,' he said. Then he turned on his heel, and walked back upstairs. As he did so, I noticed something that was to haunt me for some time afterwards.

A spot of blood had seeped through the back of his shirt.

That afternoon, two mounted police arrived from Bong Bong. They caused great excitement at Oldbury. James was almost beside himself, while many of the assigned men seemed to melt into the thick bush that cloaked Gingenbullen. In contrast, we children were not backward in coming forward, though I was slightly alarmed to learn that one of the policemen was Chief Constable Cheater. I had always thought it an odd name for a police constable, and was worried that James might laugh. James, however, did not see the irony of Mr Cheater's name. He was far too engrossed in Sergeant Quigley's pistol.

The two policemen were conducted into the sitting room, where tea was served while they waited for my mother. She finally came down with Mr Barton, who was a truly pitiful object. His colour was shocking. I noticed that his hands shook.

My mother also seemed distressed. Her voice was faint as she told me to take James and Emily off somewhere to play. I was *most* disappointed. But my mother would brook no argument; I could see it in the flint of her eye. So I obeyed, reluctantly, and heard nothing of what passed between the four adults in the sitting room. Eavesdropping was quite impossible, I fear, partly because James could not be trusted to keep silent, and partly because the wooden boards in the vestibule *creaked* so.

The policemen departed about an hour later. I did not see Mr Barton again until the following day, when I glimpsed him several times. I saw him talking to my mother outside the kitchen; I saw him smoking a Dudeen pipe on the veranda; and I saw him watching a team of assigned men yard the more recently acquired cattle. If you know anything about cattle, you will know that yarding them—and in particular, counting them through the gate—is an accomplishment that requires some skill and concentration. It is also a fine sight, in its way, and will often draw an audience. But I was struck by the intensity of the overseer's regard. He did not attempt to direct or interfere with the proceedings. He simply stood there, motionless, watching with narrowed eyes.

Even I could see that his silent presence was having a bad effect on the men. Though they did not look his way, they seemed acutely conscious of him; they were tense and nervous. At the time, I assumed that he was merely doing his job as an overseer. Now I wonder if he was searching their faces for signs of guilt.

By the third day, Mr Barton was looking much better. He must have been feeling much better as well, because I heard him haranguing the assigned men at intervals throughout the morning. I realised, then, that the rough edge of Mr Barton's tongue had been an integral part of Oldbury for some time—that his volleys of abuse were as familiar as the singing of magpies and the lowing of cattle.

He also joined my family for dinner. It occurs to me that this might not have been an unprecedented appearance. For all I know, he had joined us for dinner before, on occasions that have slipped my mind. If so, he cannot have said much. Or perhaps what he did say was of such little interest that I simply disregarded it.

This time, however, I paid more attention. I was even slightly wary. My mother was still recovering from her ordeal, and I had seen little of her. I was therefore reluctant to share her with any intruder, no matter how unfortunate he might have been. The very fact that Mr Barton was present, sitting at the other end of the table, meant that my mother's attention was divided between her children and her guest. Indeed, her whole manner changed. She became skittish and distracted. As for Mr Barton, his manner was downright odd. Between long spells of silence, he would suddenly erupt into short bursts of what might almost be described as *banter*. When my mother asked him how he liked his pork, he replied: 'I like it better now than I did when it was alive. For that pig was allus a vicious beast, and I'd rather eat it than it should eat me.'

Emily looked at our guest with a kind of horrified condescension.

'Oh, Mr Barton,' she said, 'pigs don't eat *people*.'

'Do they not?' he rejoined, in a jocular tone, but with narrowed eyes. 'Then what of the fellow I knew in Sydney, who slept one night in a gutter, dead drunk, and woke up with half his face eaten off by stray hogs?'

'Dear me,' said my mother, with an awkward laugh. 'I protest, Mr Barton, you will put us all off our food.'

'No need for that, Mrs Atkinson,' was his response. 'For this pig on our plates was never fed a face in its life. Though there's many hereabouts you might *think* had been sharpening its teeth on their heads, just to look at 'em.'

My mother smiled. Emily, however, was not so amused. Seeing her puckered brow, I declared: 'You must not worry, Emily. If pigs are properly fed, they will not eat people. And our pigs are properly fed.'

'Yes, indeed,' said my mother. 'Your dear father raised his experimental peas here solely as pig food. And of course they receive all our scraps.'

'But not the *pork* scraps, Mama!' Emily exclaimed. 'We do not feed them to each *other*, surely?'

'Never fret yerself, Miss Emily,' Mr Barton answered before my mother could. 'A pig's flesh is more tender than its feelings. It'll not jibe at week-old horse, so why should it turn up its snout at its own dear mother? Given the chance, a pig would eat off its own tail. That's my experience. You're wasting your pity on a pig.'

Perhaps he was right. Perhaps a pig's flesh *is* more tender than its feelings. But the same could not be said for my sister Emily—nor, indeed, for the rest of us. My mother had seen to that. From our earliest years we had been taught Dryden's little rubric '*Take not the life you cannot give/For all things have an equal right to live*'. In obedience to it, we had often carried beetles away from carnivorous ants, and placed them in the boughs of small trees.

As a consequence, we were not at all happy to hear Mr Barton speaking thus.

'Why, a farrowing sow will eat her own offspring,' Mr Barton continued, almost with relish. 'Is that not so, Mrs Atkinson?'

'I believe it has occurred,' my mother was obliged to concede, for she had a great respect for the laws of Nature. 'But I hardly think it a topic suitable for children.'

Whereupon Mr Barton subsided, with a rather graceless shrug. It seemed to me that my mother had put him in his place. Later, however, I saw them pass each other on the stairs. As they did so, Mr Barton stopped to whisper in my mother's ear, and press her arm above the elbow. She responded with such a long, earnest, compliant look, before nodding, that I felt a pang of something very like jealousy.

The following day our overseer went to Swanton, but returned in the late afternoon. And on the fourth of February he was present at our house to welcome Mr Charles Throsby, who was then a local magistrate.

You should understand that my family had been acquainted with the Throsbys for some years. My father had also served on the Sutton Forest bench. In 1826, he and my mother had crossed to New South Wales on the same ship as Mr Throsby's sister. It was only a few hours' ride to Throsby Park up the Old Argyle Road from Sutton Forest, so the Throsbys were our neighbours, in a manner of speaking. Mr Throsby was even a Trustee of the Sutton Forest chapel, though he later built his own church at Bong Bong. I was distantly acquainted with his children, and with their governess, Miss Mary McRae.

Since my father's death, however, there had been less communication between our two families. The Throsbys did not much care for my mother. At the time, I did not quite know what to make of this, and wondered if the Throsbys' objections had to do with my mother's outspokenness. It was not until much later that I discovered the truth behind my mother's cool relations with the Throsbys. Here was yet another subject that she refused to discuss, except in the most general terms. 'Mrs Throsby,' she said once or twice, in her most ironic tone, 'is very much taken up, these days, with all her children and her Sydney guests.'

This is not to accuse the Throsbys of being uncivil. Mr Charles Throsby, in particular, was never cold or snubbing. It was not in his nature to concern himself with social pettiness of that kind, for he was a very active, busy man, morally upright and practical-minded. In those days, before his stroke, he was still fit and able, though slight of build; his large mouth and wideset eyes were enormously expressive of good sense and determination. When he arrived at Oldbury that Thursday morning, he positively leapt from his horse, and greeted all the children by name—even Louisa. He was short with the servants, but not impolite. His movements were swift and contained as he removed various writing implements from his saddlebags. One got the impression that, while concerned about my mother's state of mind, he could afford to waste no time on idle chit-chat.

Within minutes he had summoned Mr Barton, accepted an offer of tea, and disappeared into the sitting room with my mother—who impressed me as being rather reluctant to accompany him. There was a short discussion on the veranda about the necessity of her presence. 'Mr Barton,' she protested, 'was the injured party.'

But Mr Throsby held firm, and the three of them were soon closeted away together. Once again, I heard nothing of what was said. Not that I really needed to. What was said soon became widely known, and even now I cannot tell you why. I understand why the statement was taken, for Mr Throsby had a job to do. Presumably, the document was required by the Colonial Secretary, to whom it was eventually dispatched. My question is: why did it end up in the *Sydney Herald?* And for what *possible reason* was my mother's name included at all?

I still think that Mr Throsby could have exercised discretion, with regard to my mother. Had he really no idea of the scandal that would follow?

Or was it that he simply did not care?

Five

My uncle, John Atkinson, arrived in this country just two years after his older brother. For a while he and my father lived in the same house. Then my father put at his disposal a portion of the Oldbury estate, which John renamed Mereworth. A house was built on Mereworth, but after my father's death there was some confusion as to Uncle John's entitlements. His grant had not been made final, you see. The whole business had been conducted with a carelessness that was uncharacteristic of my father. What's more, both brothers were known in the relevant documents, ambiguously, as 'J. Atkinson'. Therefore Mereworth was returned to my father's estate, leaving Uncle John in straitened circumstances.

I know all this because my mother explained it to me, years after the fact, when we were living in Sydney. She described herself as 'perfectly blameless' in the affair, and my uncle as 'unreasonably intransigent'. According to my mother, the villains of the piece had been her co-executors, Mr Alexander Berry and Mr John Coghill. It was *they*, she said, who had thrown up objections to Uncle John's inheritance. She herself had always regarded John as the true owner of Mereworth. 'And yet he took against me,' she declared, 'believing that I wanted it all for myself. When I could *not* have been more sympathetic.' Thanks to Messrs Berry and Coghill, my mother lost forever the loving support of her brother-in-law—or so she claimed.

Perhaps it was the truth. I really cannot tell. For all I know, my uncle never liked her, and was freed from the obligation of dealing with her when my father died. Or perhaps his relations with my father were already strained. (This would account for the sloppy handling of my uncle's grant, and the fact that he was not appointed executor in my father's will.) It is also possible that my mother disliked Uncle John. She was certainly outraged when he built an inn near Mereworth, and secured a licence for it. On the one hand, it is possible that there was a family history of jealousy and bad feeling with which I am entirely unacquainted. On the other hand, Messrs Berry and Coghill were just the sort of men who, upon finding someone objectionable, would have worked tirelessly in the pursuit of that person's utter ruin—as my mother soon came to realise on her own account.

Whatever the cause of the estrangement between my mother and my uncle, it had already occurred by February 1836. As a result, I only ever saw my cousin John at church on Sundays. He was four years my senior, and far more worldly: his confidence far outstripped mine, for he was already imbued with a certain kind of authority that stemmed from long acquaintance with the stockhorse, and with stockmen. Perhaps you are not familiar with this peculiar brand of confidence, which displays itself less and less, nowadays, as the wild interior of this country is progressively parcelled up and covered over. Once, you would have come upon it at every station, inn and waterhole; the colony was then well supplied with innumerable young men—the sons of settlers and squatters both—whose lives were entirely devoted to pursuits that revolved around the driving, yarding, tracking and branding of cattle.

Louisa was always ready to condemn such an existence. In book after book, she warned against its perils: against the 'mere animal existence' of constant activity and motion; against the development of physical as opposed to moral strength. While she acknowledged the stockboy's 'iron power' and skill, she deplored his want of spiritual culture, which restricted him to conversations about wise dogs, brave horses, sturdy bullocks and fierce bush cattle. *'Their one enjoyment a race, their occupation stock-keeping, their conversation horsey, their social value nil,'* was how she put it.

In this last instance, she was speaking through the mouth of a concerned father, as delineated in *Tom Hellicar's Children*. But I recognised Louisa's voice—or rather, I recognised the voice of my mother, who had nothing but contempt for the sort of mind that found stock work congenial. They used to tire me, the pair of them, with their talk of 'hurrying lads to ruin' and 'monotonous occupations removed from all thought'. As if cutting out a couple of head from the drove could be accomplished just as easily with a carved block of wood in the saddle!

To do my sister justice, she never made the mistake of assuming that intelligence is confined to the higher orders. As I recall now, she made mention of those who, though gentlemen, are of a 'low type naturally'—and claimed (on at least one occasion) that there is no position, however humble, from which men may not rise if they have a mind.

Which is all well and good. But her mistake lay in classifying the stockman's position as humble—for a less humble breed I have rarely encountered. What poetic figure is conjured up when one views a mounted bushman cracking his long whip overhead, urging his dogs to attack as he dodges the charge of a wild herd? Not that of a tradesman or labourer, certainly. Rather, one is reminded of a scene from Sir Walter Scott, save that the knight wears no mail. You might argue that there can be no comparison: that a man who earns his keep with a dog, a horse and a bullwhip cannot hope to emulate a man 'valiant and virtuous, full of haughty courage/such as were grown to credit by the wars'. But there is no confidence like the confidence of a man whose greatest desire is to have his horse killed from under him by the horns of a savage beast, that he may boast about it at night around a camp-fire.

This, at any rate, is my opinion. And it is based on careful observance, for I have *some* familiarity with a stockman's life. I have even tasted the fierce exultation of a headlong ride or two. There was a time when I spent many hours of the day on horseback—when I sought the limitless freedom of plains and forests as an antidote to the restrictions of a hopelessly confined social existence. Therefore I have some sympathy with stockmen. I even admire them. And I would never make the mistake of underestimating either their cleverness or their hard-won fortitude.

John Atkinson, I believe, felt the same. What twelve-year-old boy would not? I have some notion that he grew up listening to tales of mustering, and of horse-breaking, and of 'real Russian' bulls which—though legged, thrown and tied fast—will yet break three strong ropes, one after the other, before charging everyone in the branding yard and leaping over a six-rail fence. Without doubt he must have had good grounding in the bushman's art. I was told years later that he took a herd from Bong Bong to Moira Station, on the banks of the Murray, when he was only nineteen.

But I digress. In 1836 John Atkinson was still aspiring to the stockman's life. At that time he had mastered only the requisite cool-headed swagger, which he practised upon me with great enjoyment. He was already sprouting up towards the sun like a beanstalk, and had left me far behind; from his lofty vantage point he gazed down with a kind of benevolent condescension that I found *most* trying. Even so, I revered him. I could not help myself. For while his father's manner was ponderous, as deficient in verve as it was richly endowed with unbending dignity, John Atkinson the younger had *charm*. This could not be denied. My mother called him conceited—and I suppose he was. But he had reason to be, because he possessed the sort of bright, avid gaze and clear-cut features that wring indulgent smiles from even the most hardened acquaintance.

And I was not the least bit hardened, in those days.

Picture me, then, in front of the Sutton Forest chapel at eleven o'clock on a Sunday morning. At that time Sutton Forest was barely extant. Beside the shabby weatherboard chapel stood the Anglican school, which comprised two neat little whitewashed cottages. Across the road could be seen Mrs Davey's General Store, and the house of old Mr Wright, who at eighty-seven was still spry enough to attend the Sunday service. To the north, down the dusty ribbon of the Argyle Road, lay Captain Nicholson's estate, which he had called 'Newbury'—no doubt because my father had called *his* estate Oldbury. To the south, not far from the church, a small group of buildings clustered around the road: the Talbot Hotel, the Harp Inn, and a handful of slab huts. Beyond these dwellings, Sutton Farm and Payne's Creek marked the end of Sutton Forest.

Hardly the 'busy haunts of men', as you must agree. Yet this pitiful outpost was my notion of a metropolis. I had seen no larger settlement in my life. And I could imagine no happier excursion than a trip to Sutton Forest, unless it were a visit to Bong Bong. If I yearned for the Sunday service, it was not because I enjoyed the Reverend Vincent's sermons on the Life Everlasting. It was because I wanted to press my nose against the window of Mrs Davey's store, and admire the Throsbys' horses, and hear the latest news from my cousin John.

John, you see, had his ear to the ground. Though not a lover of books and learning, he was knowledgeable about the world in which he lived. Somehow he contrived to read newspapers. From an early age he had also developed a taste for the company of hired hands, spending much of his time listening to gossip in kitchens and stables and stockyards. By this means he had acquired a degree of bush lore that made him useful about the farm, even though he was still young; on more than one occasion his father—who could ill afford the array of staff that we supported at Oldbury—had been obliged to send John on various errands to Bong Bong, Berrima and Throsby Park. John had friends scattered about the countryside. My mother often said that John was running wild, and would bring much sorrow to his family if continually indulged. 'I fear for him,' she would sigh. 'I fear that his spiritual education will be neglected, and that he will come to grief.'

Personally, I entertained no such fears. It seemed to me that John was far better equipped for life than *I* was. He knew absolutely everything, and was happy to impart what he knew. No doubt he liked to impress his little cousin, but I will say this for him: having no imagination at all, he was never tempted to embroider his facts with fantasy. Nothing that he told me, to the best of my knowledge, was a lie. Indeed, for a boy so deficient in 'spiritual education' he was remarkably truthful. Perhaps he realised that the truth was all he needed to tell. My own acquaintance with the world was so limited that it required no wild flights of fancy to persuade *me* of my inferior status.

Being the supplicant in our acquaintance, I did not wait for John to approach me. Instead, upon being released from the musty confines of the chapel that February morning, I charged ahead of my mother and ran straight up to my cousin, who was standing a little apart from his family, hands in pockets, surveying the nearby school grounds. John was at that time reed-thin. He was dressed neatly, but his clothes showed signs of wear—such as can be seen in the wardrobe of any active boy whose parents are beginning to feel pinched for cash. Only his hat looked new. It was a cabbage-tree hat, of the type then fashionable among country folk, and woven very fine.

'Hello, cousin!' I exclaimed. 'You have a new hat!'

A strange expression crossed my cousin's face. I do not believe that I had ever seen it there before. Though fleeting, it was easily identified as embarrassment. My instant reaction was to ask myself: why is John embarrassed? Surely he is *proud* of his new hat?

'Yes,' he replied, after a moment's hesitation. 'Yes, I got it yesterday.'

'Can you roll it up, and put it in your pocket?'

'I can.'

'Show me.'

Obligingly, he removed his hat and rolled it up, to demonstrate how delicate the texture was—while all the time glancing over at his parents. I found this odd, because my cousin normally liked to emphasise his independence by ignoring his mother and father, unless they addressed him by name.

'Very nice,' I admitted, peering back at my own family. Sure enough, James was moving in our direction. I did not want him to spoil our chat with his tedious and noisy interruptions about scabs and dead beetles. I wanted my cousin all to myself. 'Quickly,' I said. 'Come around here. I have to tell you something.'

'Oh, yes?' John sounded sceptical. But there was a glint in his eye, and after one final glance at his parents, he followed me to a sheltered corner of the churchyard, sauntering along with his hands in his pockets, the bright new hat once again on his head.

'You will never guess what happened,' I announced, hanging off a fence-post as I eagerly addressed him. 'The police came to our farm. And Mr Throsby, too.'

'Because of the bushrangers?' said John.

'Oh.' My heart sank. It seemed that I would *not* fill the role of herald, after all. 'Did you hear about the attack, then?'

'Of course.' For some reason John cast a quick look over his shoulder. When he turned back, I could not read his face. The emotions written on it were complex—too complex for me. They belonged to the realm of adult concerns. 'It was in the newspaper,' he added.

'The *newspaper?*'

'The *Sydney Herald.* Didn't you know?'

I shook my head, speechless with astonishment.

'They printed Mr Throsby's official report,' my cousin went on. 'About Mr Barton and the flogging.'

'The flogging?' I was confused. 'What do you mean? Were the bushrangers flogged?'

John stared at me for a moment. 'Not the bushrangers,' he said at last. 'I mean Mr Barton's flogging.'

'Mr *Barton* was *flogged?*'

'Shhh!' Once again, John looked over his shoulder. 'If your mother has kept it from you,' he said quietly, 'maybe she doesn't want you to know.'

'Know what? What did it say in the newspaper? *Tell* me—you must tell me!'

He hesitated. I still cannot be sure if his hesitation stemmed from a real concern for my peace of mind, or whether he merely wanted to savour my pleadings. Both, perhaps.

'Hurry!' I exclaimed. 'Before James comes!'

'I only know what I read,' my cousin replied, with an elaborately careless shrug. 'Your overseer was out riding with your mother, and they were set upon by two bushrangers, who stole their money, gave Mr Barton thirty stripes with a bullwhip, and put a gun to your mother's head.'

'Oh!' This was a painful revelation indeed.

'Was no one else there?' John continued, lowering his voice and leaning forward slightly. His eyes were narrowed. 'It seemed from the newspaper that your mother and the overseer were by themselves. But maybe that was false. Surely Mrs Atkinson took other men with her?'

'No. I don't think so.'

'They were alone, then?'

'Yes.'

John grunted. His eyebrows went up. Sensing trouble, I quickly asked: 'Why? Was that wrong?'

Again, John shrugged. He had the grace to look slightly abashed.

'If there had been more people, would the bushrangers have stayed away?' I pressed him, alert to something odd in his manner. 'Is that what the newspaper said?'

'Of course not. It was just a report.' He began to retreat. 'Your brother is kicking Will Throsby—look,' he said.

'John, wait!' I grabbed his sleeve. 'You didn't tell me!'

'Tell you what?'

'The *rest*.' I refused to let him go. 'What else did it say in the newspaper?'

'Nothing.'

'*Tell* me!'

'Calm down,' he said irritably, shaking me off. 'It said that Mr Throsby's stations had been robbed by two armed bushrangers in the last few weeks. And your mother's, too. That was all.'

'Do you think she should have stayed at home? Because of the bushrangers? Is that what you think?'

'Charlotte, you are *far* too young to know what *I* think,' John rejoined, in patronising tones.

'I am *not* too young!'

'At any rate, I have to go,' my cousin added. 'Mama is calling me.'

Was it delicacy or cowardice that drove him away? To this day, I have no idea. All I know is that he left me there to puzzle over his strange reticence. He had been hiding something. That I *did* understand. For he had demonstrated far less interest in the flogging than in the fact that my mother had been riding alone with her overseer.

Why?

I was only a child, then, and very innocent. I could find no answer in my heart. Yet as I wandered back towards the church, I began to sense a curious restraint among the familiar congregation. At first glance, nothing appeared to have changed. Mr Throsby was talking with my uncle about the magistrate's court. The Reverend Vincent was complaining about the shortcomings of his parsonage to Mrs Williams. Mrs Throsby and Miss McRae were both struggling fruitlessly to keep the seven Throsby children from running amok. Yet it was almost as if these people drew away from me as I passed. No one greeted me, or smiled at me, or commented on the new silk ribbon that trimmed my Tuscan bonnet. Instead, I noticed curious pauses in the conversations that were being conducted far above my head. When I caught the eye of old Mrs Wright, she turned her face quickly.

In the midst of all these people, my mother stood alone. Wearing her dark widow's weeds, she looked stark and sombre against all the fluttering, sun-bleached ginghams and tarlatans. She smiled bravely as she held James's hand and balanced Louisa on her hip. Yet the space around her was empty.

I ran to her, filled with a sudden protective instinct.

'Mama,' I said. 'Where is Emily?'

'Is she not with you?' my mother asked. 'Perhaps we should form ourselves into a search party.'

'There she is,' said James, pointing. And there she was: a woebegone figure dragging her feet, with wet cheeks and a distraught expression on her face. The crowd seemed to part before her, yet no one bent to offer comfort. Later, when I was more conscious of our plight, I could not recall any hostility in the air. There was more a sense of confusion. Or so I thought.

Emily approached us, and buried her face in my mother's skirts. She would not tell us what ailed her.

'Never mind,' Mama said. 'It is very hot, and you must all be hungry. I have some peaches in the gig for my darlings. Who wants to go home? Yes?'

So we departed from Sutton Forest, and did not return until ten days later—when my mother married George Bruce Barton.

Six

An interlude

Why did my mother marry such a man?

This question tormented me for more years that I care to acknowledge. Looking back, I can see now that I was never free of it. Sometimes it became an obsession, filling every waking moment and many dreams as well. At other times it was relegated by more urgent questions to the darkest corners of my mind, where it festered like a corpse. Once or twice it thrust itself upon me when I was frantically busy, with little time to spare for idle speculation. (How I would curse my own wayward thoughts!) This only occurred, however, when new evidence slyly presented itself, in the form of newspaper extracts or chance meetings. Then the old, bitter question would spring back to the forefront of my mind, dragging with it all its associated resentments and complexities.

Take Charles Throsby's report, for instance. Many long years passed before I finally read it—some *twenty-five* years, in fact. I was on my way to Goulburn from Berrima, with my husband and children. It was a cold, wet winter's night. We had stopped at a species of inn that you will find nowhere, these days: a subsiding slab hut, propped up by many flimsy additions that served as cellars, larders and private rooms. This hostelry may have been at Marulan, though I can no longer be sure. After forty-five years, my memories of it are not as clear as they should be.

Wherever it was, and however humble, still we were glad of it. How relieved we were to be enjoying a roof over our heads! For we had been travelling by dray, exposed to all the elements; the day had been blustery, and the road very soft. Perhaps for this reason, there were not many travellers abroad. We practically had the whole inn to ourselves, and were easily able to secure a private room—which, though not luxurious, was at least big enough to contain us all. The publican, moreover, was a kind and decent man, who made us very welcome. He apologised for the lack of fireplace in our room. His wife brought extra blankets for the children, and stewed up a beef broth especially for little Ernest, who was feverish. I cannot remember this good couple's name, unfortunately. I only recall that they were both Irish.

For that reason, my husband sat up late in the public room. I did not. (It is my belief that a lady of proper upbringing can never feel really comfortable in any hotel, however lavishly appointed.) So I retired to our bedroom, where I sat amongst my slumbering children, listening to the rain and watching for leaks. I had been alerted, you see, by the stains on the walls. They were reddish stains—almost blood-coloured—and they suggested to me that some missing roof-shingles had been replaced by slabs of bark overhead. It was hard to tell how recently this might have occurred. While new sap will often give water that peculiar reddish tint, there was no knowing how long the stains had been present. Perhaps the damage was old, and the roof had been repaired. Peering closely at the sheets of newspaper with which the walls had been lined, I saw that many of them were of considerable antiquity. The *Illustrated Australian Magazine*, for example, was a journal long defunct. So was the *Illustrated Sydney News*. The *Sydney Herald* had for the past eighteen years been known as the *Sydney Morning Herald*; it was odd to see the old masthead again.

I was studying it idly when my gaze slipped down past the advertisements to another page, which was plastered almost at eye level. And suddenly my own name leapt out at me.

Atkinson.

I never paused even to take note of the honorific placed before it. Instead my gaze travelled swiftly back up to the headline, which had been set in capital letters.'*FLOGGING OF AN EMIGRANT SETTLER BY RUNAWAY CONVICTS*', it read. And in smaller type, beneath: '*The following statement was sworn before me at Oldbury on the 4th of February, 1836.*'

I turned away, gasping. It was as if someone had kicked me in the chest; I could hardly breathe. I rose and moved towards the mean little window, fleetingly conscious of a need to fling it open. Of a need to escape, perhaps? Yet for all that, I was drawn inexorably back to the grimy newsprint—which had been waiting there patiently for so many years.

This is how, after a quarter of a century, I was finally able to acquaint myself with the content of Charles Throsby's report on the incident at Belanglo.

The report itself was quoted in full. In the words of 'George Bruce Barting' (*sic*) it described how, about ten miles from Oldbury, 'the deponent' had been going down a steep mountain, leading two horses, when he was stopped by a pair of armed bushrangers who sprang out from behind a rock. They told him to set loose his horses. When he refused to comply, they ordered him to remove his jacket and hand over all his money. Barton then surrendered both the jacket and twenty-one shillings.

'*The man who acted as leader, told the man with the gun to keep it levelled at the deponent, and to fire directly he gave the order,*' I read. '*He then took deponent's handkerchief from his neck, and proceeded to tie him to a tree; this he would not submit to until persuaded by Mrs Atkinson, who was with deponent at the time . . .'*

Who was with deponent at the time. Such innocent-sounding words, are they not? Yet I could have scratched them from the wall.

The account continued with a description of how Barton's waistcoat and shirt were torn off his back. Whereupon the leader of the gang proceeded to flog him with an 'uncommonly thick' stockman's whip, very short in the thong, made of green hide and exceedingly heavy. When asked by the deponent how many stripes he was to expect, the flogging bushranger replied, 'Thirty', and made good his promise. Apparently it was his declared intention to give Barton ten minutes' rest after this, followed by ten more minutes of punishment. However, *'through the intercession of Mrs Atkinson'*, this scourging was not inflicted.

Instead, the lead bushranger turned on my mother. After directing her to untie Barton, he put a large pistol close to her face, while his companion brandished the whip over her head. Although he had never struck a woman, he announced, he had a good mind to serve her as Barton had been served, because she had allowed the men to be *'treated so very bad'* in her establishment. According to George Barton, my mother took issue with that. She denied it to the bushranger's face. She defied him to name any man who could lay a complaint against her.

A groan escaped me, at this point. Then I covered my mouth and looked around quickly, for fear that I had woken the children. I had groaned because, all at once, the whole scene at Belanglo had come alive in my head. Before that, it had been merely faded words on yellowed paper. But now, through the dry cadences of Mr Throsby's magisterial style, I could plainly hear my mother's voice. *'I defy you to name any man who could lay a complaint against me!'*

She would have said it, without a doubt. Despite the whip, despite the pistol, she would have said it—for all that her lips might have been shaking, and her tongue might have been dry.

She would have turned up her dark eyes and swallowed her fear, and she would have demanded that her assailant give a full and thorough account of himself.

There, beneath the silent, watching eucalypts—with George Barton's blood soaking into the dusty earth—she would have refused to plead or grovel. Pride and anger would have come to her aid.

There was truth here. I knew it. But the rest of the report puzzled me. This flogging bushranger had replied that his information came, not from my mother's servants, but from a gentleman, Mr Munn, who was supposedly 'the son of the professor of that name in Edinburgh'. Who was Mr Munn? A settler, perhaps? A *former* Oldbury convict? And why would the flogger go on to say that Barton was not the only one to be served in such a manner, since he (the flogger) considered it his duty to flog all the Gentlemen so that they might know what punishment was? George Barton was not a gentleman. As far as I was aware, he had been a humble miller before arriving in New South Wales. And it was my experience that even the most base convict retained a fine sense of the distinction between *real* Quality and the kind of common man who rose to colonial prominence through the exercise of wit or cunning.

Then there was Barton's vagueness about the men themselves. No descriptions were offered, though there was a long digression about Mrs Atkinson's sheep stations, which in the past twelve months had been robbed ten times 'by the same party'. How could Barton have known this? Moreover, according to the report, he felt satisfied that there were other bushrangers in the gang who did not show themselves—'one of whom was called Simmons'.

Now what, I asked myself, was this all about?

If the others did not show themselves, how on earth could George Barton have identified one of them as 'Simmons'? How would he have been familiar with the name at all? Had Simmons escaped from George Barton's Belanglo property? (The name certainly struck no chord with *me*.) Or had this Simmons fellow been identified in the past as one of the bushrangers who had robbed our sheep stations?

I was deeply troubled as I read the report, for it seemed to throw up more questions than it answered. Of course, George Barton was a liar. I knew that all too well. He had lied to me in the past about Belanglo. He had told the most obscene, disgusting lies. In fact I could sense him in the background of this measured report, struggling to present himself in the best possible light as he blamed others for his misfortunes. His claim was that he had refused to submit to being tied 'until persuaded by Mrs Atkinson'. The implication was clear: it was my mother's fault that he had been flogged. And these alleged, mysterious bystanders who had not shown themselves: could they have been placed at the scene by George Barton, lest anyone doubt his manhood? He would have identified an insult in every question put to him by Charles Throsby, I am sure. 'Were there only two?' Mr Throsby would have asked—purely in the interests of exactitude—and Barton would have hastened to justify himself. 'Only two that I saw,' he would have replied, 'but there were more, oh yes. Waiting with their guns trained, ready to blow holes in us both if I resisted.'

I could see it all, just as if I had been there in the room with him.

I read through the article again and again, with a growing sense of frustration and despair. It told me nothing of importance— certainly nothing that illumined my mother's part in the incident, though at least it did not confirm Barton's later accusations against her. There was no suggestion of complicity between any of the parties involved; no proof that a deal had been struck as a life-saving measure. Nor was there any real proof that the flogger had held a personal grudge, since he had spoken of punishing *all* gentlemen. Nothing had been said about the men themselves—only about their whips and their firearms, which were described in great detail.

Did this mean that Barton had no memory for faces? Or did it mean that he was *trying* to conceal the identity of his attackers, lest it come out that they were former employees, tyrannously used and eager to exact vengeance for the torments he had inflicted on them? Could the two names mentioned—Munn and Simmons—have been invented by Barton? Certainly they were unknown to me.

As for the infamous John Lynch—who later loomed so large in our imaginations—he made no appearance whatsoever.

Slowly, carefully, I peeled the strip of paper off the wall. In the public room my husband was laughing. Outside, the rain was beginning to ease, though the wind had picked up. It whistled through cracks and rattled doors. It even disturbed the flame of my lamp, making my task more difficult. But I persevered until the paper came away, torn in parts though still legible. Disappointing as it was, it nevertheless represented to me another precious piece of the puzzle that lay at the centre of my life.

If there *had* been other men lurking in the bushes, could one of them have been John Lynch?

Perhaps. Perhaps not. Years after his ordeal, George Barton would insist that Lynch had been somehow involved—though the extent of this involvement would change according to my stepfather's state of mind. But if Lynch *had* been present at Belanglo, then Barton cannot possibly have seen him there. For Barton knew him. Barton could have identified him. And yet John Lynch was still working at Oldbury a month after the event, obscure and unregarded, exhibiting no hint of the unspeakable passions that later distinguished him from the common mass of humanity.

Poring over the fragile newsprint, straining my eyes in the dim light, I cast my mind back to those dark days of my early youth, when nothing had made sense and everything had conspired to keep me at a disadvantage. George Barton, I was aware, had become more and more obsessed with John Lynch. Progressively, John Lynch had assumed monstrous, almost fantastical proportions in my stepfather's mind. As his condition deteriorated, George Barton had begun to blame Lynch for countless offences—including the scars etched across his shoulders. And no one had questioned my stepfather's veracity, because John Lynch was easy to blame. You can accuse a mass murderer of just about anything.

Yet Barton had *not* accused him. Not four days after the event, at least. No one had been accused, and no one arrested. I knew that well enough. No one has ever been charged with holding a gun to my mother's head.

No one has ever been convicted of saving a poisonous seed in my life.

Seven

My mother gave us little warning.

One afternoon she gathered us together in the sitting room: myself, James, Emily and Louisa. It was a wet sort of day, and we had spent most of the morning inside. Consequently, James was restless. He had to be restrained from kicking a chair leg, and from unpicking the loose stitches on his cuff.

'Children,' my mother said, 'I have something very important to tell you. James? Are you listening? Because this concerns everyone, and if you have any questions, I want you to ask them now.'

Obediently, we waited. The gravity of my mother's tone alarmed me somewhat, as did her slightly forced smile. This news, I could see, was supposed to be good. Yet my mother was concerned about our response to it.

'Children, I have decided to marry Mr Barton,' she announced. 'Tomorrow, at Sutton Forest.'

Presented with such little ceremony, this staggering communication was greeted by blank stares. Its full import was not immediately apparent. Louisa was too young to understand. James had no interest in marriage whatsoever; he was immediately distracted by a sharp curse uttered by some frustrated convict at work outside. Emily looked confused. Clearly she found it impossible to reconcile the word 'Barton' with the word 'marriage'.

I said: 'Why?'

'Why have I decided to marry Mr Barton?'

'Yes.'

My mother took a deep breath. 'Because you need a father,' was her reply.

This was the most ridiculous explanation that I had ever heard. 'But we already have a father,' I objected. 'In Heaven.'

'And do you see no need for another on earth?' was my mother's response. 'Someone to look after us all, and work for our comfort, and share our happy life?'

While I thought about this, Emily spoke.

'How can you marry Mr Barton, Mama?' she inquired. 'He is not a gentleman.'

My mother's lips tightened. That I *do* remember—most distinctly. She may even have flushed.

'You are not fit to pass judgement on your elders, Emily,' she rejoined, and Emily subsided. But I was not so easily overborne.

'If you marry Mr Barton, Mama,' I said, 'will you become *Mrs* Barton?'

'Of course.'

'Oh.' This I did *not* like. It seemed disloyal to my father. In fact the marriage itself seemed disloyal to my father. 'It would be better if you didn't marry Mr Barton, Mama,' I declared. 'He could still visit us, and eat dinner with us. You don't have to marry him.'

'But I choose to marry him, Charlotte,' my mother said gently. She put her arm around my shoulder. 'I still love your father, of course I do. And we shall all be reunited in Heaven. Until that time, however, I must struggle on here as best I can—and Mr Barton will help me. He will help us all.'

The laughter of the Gods! I can almost hear it as I recall my mother's words. Perhaps I caught a faint echo of it even then, for I said sceptically: 'How will he help us?'

'In many ways.'

'How?'

'By taking some of the burden from me. So that I may spend more time with you. This farm is too much work for me, Captain.'

'Is it?' I found that hard to believe. My mother had always seemed a tower of strength, clever, energetic and plain-spoken. For two years she had managed the Oldbury estate without suffering any strain that was at all apparent to me. Why this sudden need for a husband?

I wondered if the incident at Belanglo had shaken her.

'Are you afraid of the bushrangers, Mama?' was my next question. 'Are you afraid that they will come here?'

'Of course not.' My mother's tone was sharp. No doubt she had seen James turn his head at the word 'bushranger'. No doubt she had heard Emily gasp. 'Don't be foolish.'

But it seemed to me a logical conclusion to draw. Of course my mother was afraid. I myself was afraid sometimes, at night, when the creatures of the bush were making strange sounds outside my window. 'Mr Barton can still sleep in the house with his gun,' I said. 'Even if you don't marry him.'

'Mr Barton has a double-barrelled percussion gun,' James interrupted brightly. 'He killed a kangaroo with it.'

'He beat a dog with it,' Emily added, her brow creasing in dismay. 'I saw him.'

'Sometimes dogs must be beaten, Emily,' my mother said. 'It is a sad fact, but there are wicked dogs in this world who understand no other form of reproof, and are a threat to both man and beast. Now . . .' She drew Emily closer. 'You are all to attend the wedding, so you must look your best. I thought that we might take out the silk frocks, and see if they still fit you. If not, then Louisa will wear Emily's, and Emily will wear Charlotte's.'

'And what shall I wear, Mama?' was the question that sprang to my lips.

'You may be obliged to wear your cotton velvet,' my mother replied. 'And we must pray that the weather doesn't turn, or you will be too hot. Now why don't you fetch your workboxes, and if alterations are required, you can help me to make them.'

'What about me?' asked James, who had no workbox. 'What shall I do, Mama?'

'Why, you must play with Louisa.'

James stuck out his bottom lip.

'And I shall tell you a story while I sew,' my mother went on. 'The story of a terrible shipwreck, and the poor little girl who survived it.'

My mother had a huge fund of shipwreck stories, which we greatly enjoyed—perhaps because we had never ourselves put to sea. In later years, our particular favourites were the wreck of the *Joseph Forbes* and the wreck of the *Stirling Castle*, complete with bloodthirsty natives, dangling skulls, and the torture of poor Captain Fraser. (The suspended hand never failed to thrill us: I remember Louisa asking if it was the hand of a white person, and the thrill of horror we all experienced when my mother replied, in grave tones, 'They could not tell, my dear. *For the sun had completely blackened it.*') On reflection, however, I am not sure whether these maritime tragedies preceded 1836. If not, then the tale we heard as we let down our silk frocks was probably something like the wreck of the *General Boyd*, which was not so much a wreck as an ambush. We were particularly interested in this story because one of the four survivors of the dreadful massacre was a little girl called Elizabeth, who was later rescued by Mr Alexander Berry, my mother's co-executor, and grew up to marry Mr Charles Throsby.

I had always envied the Throsby children their mother's adventurous past. Still, I found it hard to believe that placid Mrs Throsby had once spent three weeks among the savage inhabitants of New Zealand. And I could never quite bring myself to share Mama's low opinion of Mr Alexander Berry. For all his misguided persecution of my mother, he was also the man who, with a bold party of sailors, had captured two Maori chieftains and kept one of them as hostage while sending the other off to retrieve the suffering infant Elizabeth.

You may be sure that my mother stopped telling this story soon after Mr Berry began to make himself disagreeable. Nevertheless, the damage had already been done. I am sure that we were none of us as rude to Mr Berry as our mother may have wanted us to be.

In any event, the day before the wedding was spent in quiet pursuits: sewing, singing, story-telling. I saw Mr Barton only twice—at dinner and shortly before bedtime, when I was sent with Emily to make my curtsey to him as he smoked his pipe on the veranda. He was also nursing a small flask, and I recognised the smell that hung around him. Some of the assigned men would go about smelling the same when they were in a particularly loud or cheerful mood.

Mr Barton certainly seemed happy. He greeted us with a broad grin that remained plastered all over his face as we said good night, one after the other.

'And are you going to be good little daughters for yer new Pa?' he asked jauntily.

'We shall be stepdaughters,' I replied in a dignified manner. 'Not daughters.'

'True enough.'

'And we always try to be good,' Emily added. 'Because God expects it of us.'

'I don't know about God,' said Mr Barton, 'but *I'll* be expecting it, right enough. I'll not take kindly to scamps in *my* house, and will deal with them directly.'

'Your house?' I was confused. 'You mean Swanton?'

Mr Barton uttered a short bark of laughter.

'Swanton? Not likely. I mean this house.' His eyes narrowed to slits as his grin widened. 'This will be my house tomorrow. Once I marry yer Ma.'

'Oh no, Mr Barton.' I could contradict him on this point with utter confidence. 'This house belongs to James. Mama has said so.'

'Not until he comes of age, lass.' Mr Barton leaned back and stretched out his legs, as if disposed to settle himself comfortably before explaining to us a tricky point of law. 'Until then, it will be my house. To manage as I think best.'

'And Mama's too,' I hastened to remind him.

'Oh, aye. And yer Ma's too.'

His tone had become dreamy. When he lapsed into silence, Emily and I took our leave. I seem to recall that we included him in our prayers that night. But he occupied far less space in my mind than my silk frock, which Mama had lengthened by adding several insets of pink ribbon at the hem. Truly, I considered his role a minor one—as if the wedding would have continued whether he was present or not. Perhaps it was a failure of imagination. Not being able to envisage how he would insert himself into our little family, I took it for granted that he would not. Not, at least, in any noticeable way. I assumed that life would continue as before, with Mr Barton making occasional appearances at dinner.

It never crossed my mind that he would lay claim to my mother's bed.

The next day we all went to Sutton Forest. Mr Barton rode one of the horses, while the rest of us—my mother, myself, James, Emily and Louisa—went squashed together in the gig. It was a subdued and modest wedding. The Reverend Vincent officiated. Miss McRae was present, and signed the parish register as a witness. There were some others, too, but whether they had been formally invited, or whether they were simply villagers eager for distraction, I have no way of knowing.

My uncle did not appear.

The ceremony itself proved to be rather a disappointment. I believe that I must have expected something more splendid, or at least more joyful. But my mother and Mr Barton looked very strained throughout. Mr Barton, his hair slicked down with oil and his best boots polished up, was so nervous that he dropped my mother's ring. As for my mother, though she had shed her widow's weeds in favour of an old gown of cinnamon-coloured silk, her appearance was not much improved by this change of costume. On the contrary, her cheek was pale and her mouth set. Perhaps she was conscious of a malicious air among those who gathered, rustling and nudging, in the rear pews. Or perhaps she was simply annoyed by the Reverend Vincent's quite evident desire to be elsewhere. Our rector, I should tell you, was not a very *amiable* man. Though tall and handsome, with a devoted wife and eight healthy children, he was often to be heard complaining about his health, his house, his servants, and the distances that he was required to travel. No doubt he viewed the wedding (like almost everything else) as an imposition. I know that he was a firm supporter of banns, for I had heard him moaning about special licences, and about the 'lawless' speed with which a marriage might be accomplished if a special licence were employed. Maybe *that* is why he looked so discontented. My mother, you see, was married by special licence.

Our dinner after the wedding was far more enjoyable than the event it honoured. There was roast fowl, currant cake, and ginger beer even for the children. Bridget and Jane had decorated the dining table with sprigs of gum blossom and late China roses. Mr Barton drank quite a lot of wine. After dinner, we all went out to the convict huts, where rum was distributed to toast the health of the happy couple. My mother was then presented with a painted tin containing a specimen of mimosa—in deference, no doubt, to her botanical interests. The domestic servants had also made an effort, producing a pair of embroidered handkerchiefs. The atmosphere was fairly muted, however, and even after sunset there were no boisterous dances around the camp-fire. The best that could be said for the day is that we children enjoyed currant cake twice: once at dinner and again with our tea, before bedtime.

I think of that cake as being a species of Last Supper. For as we climbed the stairs, wiping crumbs from our mouths, my mother said: 'Louisa will be sleeping in the nursery tonight.'

I could not have been more astonished. As you know, Louisa was accustomed to bedding down near Mama. Never before had she been allowed to try her luck in the nursery.

Emily clapped her hands.

'Oh, good!' she exclaimed. 'Louisa! You will sleep with us tonight!'

'But not in *my* bed,' said James, with a touch of alarm. 'She won't be sleeping in *my* bed, will she, Mama?'

'Of course not.' Pushing open the nursery door, my mother explained that Louisa's cot had been placed between Emily's bed and mine. Sure enough, there it stood: Louisa's cot, all made up, with her knitted yellow duck sitting on top of it. Louisa looked confused.

'You will have fun with us here, Louisa,' I said, feeling all the obligations of an eldest sibling. 'You are *much* too old to be sleeping in Mama's room.'

'If you want, I shall sing you a lullaby,' Emily added.

'And I will give you my soldier to sleep with—just for tonight,' said James.

At first, Louisa seemed quite happy. She accepted our tributes with a queenly air, and was eager to be placed in her cot. But after the lamp was extinguished, and the door closed, she began to whimper. She began to call for Mama.

Nothing that I did or said made the slightest difference.

At last I had to fetch Eliza, who lit the lamp again. When that failed to console Louisa—when soft words and lullabies had no effect—Eliza removed her from the nursery. The cot, however, remained. Expecting that they would both return within minutes, I promptly fell asleep.

I was woken some time later by the sound of Louisa screaming, and for a moment I lay in a fuddled state, collecting my thoughts. The room was dark. Louisa was not in it. She was nearby, though. In Mama's room? She sounded inconsolable, hiccoughing the way she often did when she had been crying for a long time.

'A-coo, a-coo, a-coo,' Eliza was saying, in a futile attempt to offer comfort. Then a door closed, and the sound of wailing became muffled. I wondered if I should get up, before deciding that Mama probably would not appreciate my help. And I turned over.

It is quite astonishing what a child will sleep through. I believe that I must have dozed again, briefly, despite Louisa's noise. It was not her voice but Mr Barton's that roused me.

'No!' Mr Barton said loudly, out on the landing, and my eyes sprang open. 'No you will *not*!'

A door banged. Louisa shrieked. My mother protested: 'Perhaps if I give her something . . .'

'*I'll* give her something!' Mr Barton snapped. 'I'll give her the back of my hand!'

'Shh. Please, George. Remember the others.'

'She has to *learn*!'

'I know. I know.'

Louisa was still crying. Quickly I scrambled out of bed, and tip-toed to the door. Pulling it open, I saw my mother holding a candle. She was dressed in her nightgown, and her hair was loose. Beside her stood Mr Barton, also in his night attire. His arm was wrapped around her waist in a manner that disturbed me.

Eliza was with them, carrying Louisa—who looked quite ill with distress. Her face was blotched and wet with tears. Her breathing was ragged. Her trembling was visible even from my vantage point.

'I'll not have her up here again,' Mr Barton told Eliza. 'Not tonight, or I won't answer for the consequences.'

'Aye, sir, but—'

'What? *What?*'

Eliza cast a quick, frightened glance at my mother. 'It's just—I'm worried she'll stop braything.' As Louisa began to howl, Eliza raised her voice. 'Or have a fit, Mam. She went blue in the face, earlier.'

'Oh dear,' said my mother, in obvious distress, and reached for Louisa.

But Mr Barton pulled her back.

'No,' he growled. 'She'll not die of it. She must *learn.*' Louisa's shrill and mounting scream pushed the blood to his cheeks. He thrust his face into hers and snapped: '*Stop it! Now!*'

Louisa paused for an instant, shocked into silence. She and Mr Barton regarded each other, their faces equally flushed, before she opened her mouth again and roared.

There was a sudden flurry of movement. Mr Barton began to push Eliza towards the stairs. 'Wait!' my mother exclaimed, but was disregarded. Louisa sobbed uncontrollably. Mr Barton kept saying, 'Go! Go! Get out!' Eliza turned in obedience, looking more dishevelled and distressed than I had ever seen her.

My mother tried to follow.

'Let me settle the poor child,' she offered, pitching her voice above Louisa's screams. Mr Barton immediately tightened his grip on her waist.

'No,' he said.

'But—'

'This is our *wedding night!*' he barked. 'I am your *husband!*'

'I understand that—'

'She will *have to learn!*'

I do not know how much force he employed to propel my mother back towards her room. There can be no doubt that she was torn; her resistance was not as strong as it might have been, since her guilt was pulling her in two different directions. I know that she caught at one of the banisters before releasing it again. I know that she turned a troubled face towards the sound of Louisa's fading screams, which, though loud, did not mask the clatter of Eliza's retreat down the staircase.

Finally Mama crossed the threshold of her room, clasped to Mr Barton's side. Glancing over his shoulder, his face wreathed in shadow, he must have caught sight of me in the dwindling light of my mother's candle.

'Get back to bed!' he snarled, with an astonishing degree of venom. Then the door slammed shut, and I was alone.

I cannot convey to you the shock that I felt. It was as if I had been struck across the face, or fiercely berated. Such loud, angry scenes were normally restricted to the kitchen and convict huts; the house itself had always been a peaceful place. Moreover, I was shaken by all the other changes that had occurred. I could not believe that Louisa had been sent to sleep in Eliza's room. I could not believe that my mother was sharing her bed with Mr Barton.

Withdrawing into the nursery, I crept under my own covers and lay shivering in the dark, weighed down by a strange sense of foreboding. This must have been occasioned by the domestic upheaval that I had just witnessed. The shouting! The weeping! The slamming doors! Naturally I was concerned about the future of our calm, domestic existence.

But it transpired that I was strangely prescient in at least one other way. For the following afternoon, Thomas Smith was murdered—whereupon I first became acquainted with the sinfulness of John Lynch.

Eight

I knew Thomas Smith, but only slightly.

He was one of the assigned men, and had been with us for as long as I could remember. Even so, I doubt that we ever exchanged a word. He was short, with light brown hair and a ruddy complexion. There was a raised mole on his left cheek. Though I cannot tell you how old he was, I learned after his death that he had come from Worcestershire, and that he was serving a life sentence for horse-stealing.

He was a troublemaker, too. I was vaguely aware of this, for my mother did not like him, and complained about him regularly. She called him lazy and insolent. Only six months before his murder he had been charged with neglect of duty, and sentenced to fifty lashes. (He had been dispatched to collect mail at Bong Bong, and had returned three hours late.) I had heard him speaking to my mother once or twice. I had seen him slouching against a wall, arms folded, as he addressed her. 'Do not take that tone with me, Thomas Smith!' she had exclaimed, her voice suddenly rising. 'Or you will find yourself up before the Bench!'

What else can I say about Thomas Smith? Not very much, unfortunately. I do know that he smoked, and that there was a scar on his left thumb. I also know that, on the fourth of March, 1836, his head was smashed to pieces, and he was concealed under a fallen log, on top of a small pile of tinder.

It was as if someone had tried to set his body alight, before realising that the smoke of a fire might be seen.

If, like Mrs Louise S.A. Cosh, you have read my letter to the *Evening News*, you will remember the fallen log. You will also remember my tale of one *Ned* Smith, who was given a ticket-of-leave for his outstanding service as a groom in our stables. I said that Ned Smith was murdered by John Lynch. I also said that his emancipation was regarded with suspicion by the other convicts—who believed him an informant—and that he was murdered as a result. I said that John Lynch had escaped from Cockatoo Island after he was charged with the murder.

All lies, I fear.

There *was* a groom called Ned Smith at Oldbury, but he was never murdered. In fact I am quite sure that he had left us by 1836. As for the escape from Cockatoo Island—well, what would you have had me say? That my stepfather's drunkenness aborted a trial? That with George Barton's help, Lynch was set free to kill and kill again?

I should never have mentioned John Lynch in the first place. I had a suspicion, you see, that my letter might not be published without mention of a notorious crime—that it might be ignored, like the products of so many other aged gentlewomen. So I succumbed to temptation, and raised once again the spectre of John Lynch. How was *I* to know that there were others still living who had some inkling of the truth? I had thought it buried in the crumbling back issues of the *Sydney Gazette*. There are few now who even remember John Lynch, let alone his first murder. Had he still been as notorious as he once was, no mistake would have been made in numbering his victims. For you may be sure that *I* never accused him of killing twenty-three people. That figure somehow came to replace the correct tally in my letter. Perhaps it was a mistake. Unless the Editor felt that eleven corpses would not be enough to arouse public interest, and doubled the total.

I would not put it past him. He certainly eviscerated my letter. When I read it in the *Evening News*, I was furious to discover how much had been left out. All the material about the ploughing matches that my father organised, his experiments with turnips, his 1829 pamphlet, *On the Expediency and Necessity of Encouraging Distilling and Brewing in New South Wales*—all of this (and more) had been removed. With the result that my prose had the disjointed, confusing flavour of something produced by a victim of advanced senility.

You may be sure that I shall not be writing to the *Evening News* again!

But why dwell on my own concerns? It is George Barton who interests *you*, I am sure. You must be wondering what he did. How he became involved. You must be asking yourself: why was Thomas Smith murdered, and what did George Barton do to set the murderer free?

I should tell you, first of all, that Smith's corpse was not found immediately. He simply disappeared, and his absence was remarked upon. I distinctly recall mention of it at breakfast; there was still conversation at the table, in those early days, and Mr Barton observed to my mother (as he shovelled gammon into his mouth) that Thomas Smith had 'skipped'.

'Oh dear,' said my mother. 'You mean he has run away?'

'He did not return last night,' Mr Barton replied. 'And will wear a red shirt for it when he is caught.'

'A red shirt?' James looked up, his interest aroused. 'What do you mean?'

'I mean, my lad, that he will have the hide torn off his back, stripe by stripe, until it is all gone,' said Mr Barton, with a certain lingering relish. Then he caught my eye. 'What are you staring at, Miss?'

'Nothing.' I dropped my gaze, anxious not to offend. I had been thinking about the stripes torn from Mr Barton's own back, and wondering why he showed himself so keen to condemn others to the same savage punishment.

'Should we notify the police?' my mother asked him, whereupon he nodded.

'I shall send someone to Bong Bong,' he said. 'Someone reliable. Leave it to me.'

'I should not be sorry to lose Thomas Smith,' my mother observed, dabbing marmalade onto her bread. 'He has always been troublesome, and inclined to shirk.'

'He is a damnable out-and-outer,' said Mr Barton, pushing aside his plate, 'and will come to a bad end.'

By that time, of course, Thomas Smith had already come to a bad end, though we were unaware of it. I cannot tell you exactly when news of his demise reached Oldbury. The corpse itself was discovered on the fifth of March. It was brought back to Oldbury on a dray, and subsequently buried in the graveyard at Sutton Forest. No doubt there was a lot of talk at church that week, but I was not present to hear it, for my mother was reluctant to face the congregation—what with her recent marriage, and the murder of her assigned man. Therefore I was unable to wring the facts from my cousin John, who undoubtedly would have been thoroughly acquainted with the matter.

As it was, I had to piece together details gleaned from my mother, Mr Barton, and the Oldbury staff. This was more difficult than you might expect. No doubt my mother would have preferred to keep the news from me entirely; when the shrouded remains were delivered to our doorstep, she provided me with the briefest of explanations.

'It is Thomas Smith,' she declared, as I stood gaping at the solemn procession that creaked past our house. 'He died out in the bush, yesterday.'

Then she wrapped her shawl around her and went back inside. I tried to press her further that evening, without success. She told me simply that we should pray for Smith's soul, and not dwell on such unhappy topics, especially in front of Louisa. 'Mr Barton has the matter in hand,' she said. 'There is nothing else to be done.'

Mr Barton may have had the matter in hand, but he was unwilling to discuss it with me. ('Get along with you, now,' was all that he said.) For more information I was obliged to question the servants. Bridget was very cagey. "'Twas an ill turn befell him,' she muttered, 'or so I heard.' Robert was more forthcoming. 'Aye,' he acknowledged, 'the poor lad was set upon, and his head laid open. There's folk will swing for it.' But the whole affair seemed wrapped in a kind of uneasy silence—at least on the Oldbury estate.

This I found odd, even at the time. For you have to understand that there was no lack of violent incident in the Argyle region back then, and when it occurred it formed the meat of any gossip from Campbelltown to the Five Islands. A year later, for example, Private Thomas O'Brien was cudgelled to death near the Kentish Arms, on my uncle's estate. One of our convicts, John McCaffrey, was subsequently accused of the murder, along with John Jones (my uncle's man) and a settler named John Moore. Jones hanged for his crime, and you may believe me when I tell you that there was no lack of discussion among the Oldbury servants on *that* occasion. Neither were they close-mouthed when the Reverend Vincent's family were attacked by bushrangers in their own home—a month after Thomas Smith's murder—or when William Brown, a runaway convict, was arrested for robbing a traveller on the road between Bong Bong and Sutton Forest, just a few weeks after that. I did not need to question my cousin about these events, because they were so exhaustively discussed in our kitchen, stables, and stockyard.

But the death of Thomas Smith elicited a different sort of response. I overheard no free speculation on the subject; instead there was an almost complete lack of comment. No one seemed eager to answer my questions. Eliza became even vaguer than usual. Jane dropped a handful of cutlery, and begged to be excused. Bridget tried to turn the conversation. ('Would ye be fancyin' a taste o' me batter, Miss Charlotte?')

I was puzzled, though not much concerned. Convicts killed each other all the time. Besides, I had not been intimately acquainted with Thomas Smith. So I turned my thoughts to more important concerns, at least until the police arrived.

There were three of them, and they interviewed Mr Barton at length. They also questioned some of our assigned men, formally, one by one. When I saw the line of mute convicts on our veranda, each with his hat crushed in his hands and his bleak gaze fixed on his boots, I went straight to Eliza for an explanation.

'Why are our men standing idle, out there?' I demanded.

'On account of them traps, Miss.' By 'traps', Eliza meant the mounted police. 'They bin rounding 'em up.'

'For what reason?'

Eliza shrugged.

'Is it something to do with Thomas Smith?' I pressed, and her expression became blank, as if a curtain had been pulled across it.

'So I heard,' she said cautiously.

'But I thought he was killed by a bushranger!' This had been a natural assumption to make. 'Surely they cannot blame any of *our* men?'

'That I couldn't say, Miss,' Eliza replied. She was clearing the breakfast table, and hid any confusion that she may have felt in a vigorous flapping of linen. Frowning, I turned away. It was suddenly clear to me why the murder had occasioned such little remark. For if the murderer was among us, no one would want to talk freely lest he suffer the same fate as Thomas Smith.

I ran directly to my mother, who was checking the contents of the store cupboards.

'Mama,' I said, 'the police are questioning some of our men!'

'Yes, dear, I know.'

'They're none of them *murderers*, are they?'

'Shh.' My mother put a finger to her lips. She glanced towards Louisa, who was perched on the kitchen table, eating apple peel out of Bridget's hand. 'Not too loud, if you please.'

'But—'

'The police are making inquiries. You must not fret, Charlotte. This is a matter of convict discipline. It does not concern any of *us*.'

She was wrong, as it happened. Because it was Mr Barton's statement that condemned John Lynch. I found out later that George Barton claimed to have seen Lynch in the vicinity of the corpse, around the time that the murder took place. No sooner was this fact presented to the Chief Constable than he immediately sent for Lynch, who—surprisingly enough—had not already absconded. Had I been in his shoes, I should *certainly* have taken to my heels at the first opportunity. Or perhaps he was about to do so? At any rate, though I did not see him brought in, I was to witness his departure.

And here we arrive at the infamous John Lynch, of evil memory. No doubt you will recall what I have said on another occasion: that I knew most of our assigned men by sight, though not always by name. This was the case with John Lynch. I believe that he spent a good deal of time on our stations, away from the house. Certainly he was not a man often applied to in the domestic sphere. Nevertheless, he was vaguely familiar. When I saw him that day, waiting in the sun, I recognised his crooked nose, and the hairy mole on his jaw.

He was standing near the back veranda with a constable beside him. I would hardly have spared him a second glance, had he not been chained. Though I had seen such chains before (one could hardly avoid them, during that far-off era), they were rarely worn at Oldbury. You might have seen chained men on the roads sometimes, for there were gangs based at Berrima and Bong Bong. But on private estates, chains were less freely employed. Certainly they were not used on *our* estate.

That is why I was so surprised when I caught sight of the iron shackles, and the heavy links dangling from Lynch's roughened hands. I stopped short, staring. Whereupon he caught my eye, and winked.

You may want to know what he looked like, this fiend in human form. The fact is, he was not in any way remarkable. Like most of the assigned men, he was quite short. He had freckled skin and mousy hair; I cannot recall what colour his eyes were. I do remember that he was very neatly got up for a labourer, with none of the frayed hems and missing buttons that you so often saw about the place. He was also quite neatly put together, well proportioned for his height, and neither too fat nor too thin.

Looking at him, you would have thought: domestic staff. You would have marked his jaunty, well-groomed, unthreatening appearance, and you would have imagined him cleaning shoes. This is what I find so very puzzling. Because I have seen my share of desperate characters. They were in the chain gangs, hewing rock. They were on the drays that rumbled down the old South Road. They were in the streets of Sydney, loitering near the wharves and the grog-shops. We even had one or two among our assigned men, on occasion, though not for very long; invariably they would abscond, or assault a fellow convict, or commit some other crime. They struck me as being men who had lost at least a portion of their manhood—brute beasts without regard for the trappings of civilisation. They were always noticeable. A kind of fury hung about them like a cloud of gnats. They demonstrated their disdain for authority in all kinds of ways: refusing to shave their beards, speaking only to utter a curse, flaunting their scarred backs. There was nothing to be done with men like this. They each had one foot planted firmly in the Fiery Pit, and were refusing all aid with the most obdurate vehemence. So embittered were they that life had lost its savour for them.

The sinfulness of convicts is something that I have discussed at length with various religious men over the years. While some maintain that convicts were born to sin, others claim that ill treatment can warp any conscience, no matter how tenderly reared. I am not well placed to pass judgement on this matter. As a child, I was carefully shielded from any direct observation of convict punishment. Yet I could not entirely escape its consequences. Though our assigned men were always flogged at the stockade, and were often attached to the local iron gang for long periods thereafter, it was impossible to ignore the change wrought in them when they returned.

Physically, they were often much affected. I have seen many scarified backs, some bearing only a net of thin white lines, others horribly ridged, with the skin all gouged and deformed as if by a massive burn. Such injuries can be disabling for life, especially if they are not given a proper chance to heal. But the physical effects are no more damaging than the spiritual. I do not doubt that flogging will often result in a great deal of unseen harm. Surely it cannot be a coincidence that I saw the worst scarification on the backs of men whose faces had lost all semblance of humanity? Clergymen like the Reverend Vincent might argue that the heaviest penalties are naturally inflicted upon the most degraded objects— that a severe flogging is the inevitable consequence of moral degeneracy, and not its cause. I wonder if this can be true. Sometimes I think it likely. At other times I recall certain incidents that took place at Oldbury when I was a child, and begin to question their meaning. I remember one man who hid behind the woodpile, screaming and sobbing, when Mr Throsby paid a visit; this man had apparently been sentenced to fifty lashes by the local Bench, over which Mr Throsby had presided. Then there was the man who went to his punishment with a cocky grin on his face, only to return hollow-eyed and shuffling like someone thirty years older. I heard much later that he tried to hang himself while in Captain Nicholson's employ. Memories like this do nothing to persuade me that corporal punishment has a wholly salutary effect on those who receive it. And they suggest that men who are treated like vicious dogs might become like vicious dogs.

John Lynch was certainly vicious. Whether his character was irreparably deformed by the flogging that he had received while employed by my mother is impossible to judge. Was it some cruel notion of revenge that propelled him to commit his loathsome crimes, or was he born evil? Only God can be sure. One thing I *can* say, however, is that Lynch was not among the ranks of those who no longer pretended that they were anything but beasts. There was nothing wild about John Lynch—or so it seemed to me. In later years I read that he had been transported for robbery. This is not quite true. My father, into whose care Lynch was assigned straight from his ship, once told my mother that John Lynch had been convicted of false pretences. In other words, he had been caught impersonating someone else.

Perhaps that was his special skill. Perhaps he was able, with utter conviction, to impersonate a tidy, cheerful, ordinary little man. That is what *I* saw when I looked at him.

'Who is that?' I asked my mother.

'Go inside,' was her response.

'But he is one of *our* men.'

'Obey me, Charlotte!'

As ever, she wanted her children well shielded from the more troubling spectacles that afflict a penal colony. I can understand this now, though I did not at the time. Forced inside the house, I went straight back to Eliza, who was standing at the window of the breakfast room, looking out.

'Who have they put in chains?' I asked her.

'John Lynch,' she replied.

'Did *he* kill Thomas Smith?' It seemed doubtful. 'Is that what they think?'

There was no immediate response. Instead Eliza watched for a moment, before observing: 'They have John Williamson, too.'

They did have John Williamson. And several others. Peering through the little panes of glass, I saw George Barton stride across the beaten earth towards Constable Cheater, waving his arms. He seemed to be protesting about something. They began to argue. Though unable to hear a word, I quickly understood why Mr Barton was enraged.

The police had herded most of our farm workers into a tight little group. There were so many that there were not chains enough to go around: twelve men altogether, including John Lynch.

I counted them.

'What are they doing?' I could not keep the astonishment out of my voice. 'Why are they taking our men?'

But Eliza was at a loss. She simply stood there, gaping. I daresay that the Chief Constable was being careful. He was probably hoping to find witnesses among our assigned men, and did not want to risk leaving anyone behind who might run away before being questioned. So he had decided to march the whole crew off to Bong Bong lock-up, where he could interview them at his leisure.

My stepfather did not take kindly to this decision.

'. . . whole field of maize to harvest!' he was saying, his words becoming audible to me as he raised his voice. '. . . fetch the mail . . . load of pumpkins . . .' When Cheater placed a reassuring hand on his arm, he flung it off. 'This is a damnable liberty!' he roared. 'I shall write to the Colonial Secretary, and demand compensation!'

My mother hovered beside him, trying to calm his ruffled temper. She, too, was not pleased; I could sense this from the stiffness of her back, and the set of her shoulders. She tried to reason with Cheater, but to no avail. The Chief Constable stood firm, defying my stepfather in the most public way imaginable. He simply took most of our assigned men and forced them off the estate, leaving no assurances as to when (or if) they would be returned.

After they had gone, Mr Barton vanished for a while. He must have retired to a quiet spot with a few drams of rum, because when he finally reappeared, in the late afternoon, he was well primed and staggering. He went straight to the piggery, and drove our swine into the pumpkin patch with a bullwhip. 'No bloody use to anyone now!' he yelled. 'Just pig-feed now!'

With Robert's help, my mother managed to save about half the crop. She received one stripe in the process, however; Barton accidentally caught her across the ear. I overheard him begging her pardon later that evening, when they were in her room. He was loud and maudlin, his voice breaking on a sob. I had to wrap my pillow around my head to block out the sound.

Later, I learned to shut my eyes as well. But it never worked—not any of it.

There was really nowhere to hide.

Nine

Most of our convicts returned to Oldbury within a week. Only John Lynch and John Williamson remained in custody. They were sent up to Sydney, where they were tried in the Supreme Court. This trial was set for the twelfth of August, and George Barton, as a material witness, was summoned to appear.

Do not ask me exactly when his summons arrived. In July, perhaps? Whenever it was, I could not have received more welcome news. I would lie in bed trying to calculate the length of Barton's proposed absence. The trip into town would take several days, as would the trip back. For how long, I wondered, would the trial run? A day? Two days? I made a special application to the Lord one night. 'Please God,' I prayed, 'let Mr Barton be away for more than a week.'

I was on my knees at the time.

Four months had elapsed between Lynch's arrest and his trial. During that interval, I had spared the convict hardly a thought. For one thing, there had been very little talk about him. Not once had I overheard the servants discussing his fate. Not once had anyone mused upon his guilt or innocence at the dining table. Like

George Barton's flogging, the subject of John Lynch had been stringently avoided—at least in front of me. Yet I am quite sure that this overwhelming silence did not indicate a lack of interest. Looking back, I am inclined to wonder if the cause might have been fear. Fear of my mother, perhaps, who did not want her children unnerved? Fear of Lynch's confederates? If Lynch had killed Thomas Smith for speaking out of turn about the attack on George Barton—as was later claimed in the newspapers—there can be no telling what his friends would have done in similar circumstances.

Or perhaps the fear was a kind of unease, engendered by that curious contrast between the innocent-seeming man himself and the crime that he was charged with. People are always inclined to fear what they cannot understand. The fact that a cheerful, common, jaunty little Irishman should have revealed so black a heart is almost beyond understanding. It casts such doubt on human nature that the majority of folk would prefer to turn away and ignore its implications, rather than face them squarely.

At the time, I gave no thought to the reasoning behind this curious attitude of discretion. For I was preoccupied with other matters. There was the attack on our rector's family, for instance. There was the opening of the Kentish Arms on the Mereworth estate, an event that prompted my mother to meet with my uncle for the first time in many months. (She returned from the encounter full of scorn and disgust. 'What kind of a man,' she said, 'enlists his wife to supervise the distribution of spirits to all the scaff and raff of the district? Better to live humbly, in a bark hut, than expose her to such degradation.') Finally, there was the utter collapse of that domestic harmony which had always distinguished our house, even during the last, terrible days of my father's fatal illness.

The first cracks appeared very quickly. Looking back, it is easy to plot the course of George Barton's descent into madness, though at the start we had no notion of what exactly we were witnessing.

Every outrage came as a terrible shock; only gradually did we learn to expect (and fear) the unexpected. After some consideration, I would say that Bunny was the first casualty of my stepfather's bottomless rage. Do you remember Bunny, our pet kangaroo? He would come to the stockyard of an evening to be fed, and was quite a favourite with everyone—except George Barton. George Barton warned us about Bunny. 'There's not a beanstalk nor a turnip green is safe from those beasts,' he said. 'If one sprig of sage goes missing, I'll have its hide.'

This must have been in early April, and there were still some late figs on a tree near one of our sunniest walls. When some of these figs disappeared, Barton blamed Bunny. He pointed out that only the fruit on the lowest branches, within Bunny's reach, had vanished. And he forbade us to feed the poor creature anymore. 'It must be chased off,' he ordered, with the jovial menace that characterised many of his pronouncements when he was sober. 'It must not be encouraged. Sentiment is all very well, but we cannot fill our bellies with it. Unless it learns to keep clear, it'll meet its Maker, I warn you. Just stay away from the stockyard, and it will soon understand.'

'You should stay away from the stockyard in any case,' my mother added, when I turned to her in protest. 'It is not safe when the men are working, and James has fallen off that fence often enough.'

'I will not climb it again, Mama, I promise!' James cried, but my mother just shook her head, smiling.

'That is what you always say—and you always break your word,' she replied. 'I believe that fence must exert some strange, supernatural force.'

'You obey yer mother, now,' Barton added, reaching across the table to lay his hand on Mama's. 'Yer Ma knows what is best for you.'

We children were not impressed by this argument. My mother may have known what was best for *us*, but she appeared to have lost sight of Bunny's best interests. I had my suspicions about the assigned men, who could be very cunning when it came to stealing food. What if one of them had taken the figs, and shown enough restraint to make it seem as if Bunny was at fault? Emily, for her part, was terribly concerned about the kangaroo's health. What if it should become ill and weak? What if it should starve?

'It will wait and wait for us, and we won't be there,' she fretted.

In the end, we defied George Barton. We agreed that I should leave kitchen scraps near the stockyard whenever Barton was away from the house. As the eldest sibling, I shouldered the risk myself. I reasoned that, if caught, I would have the best chance of formulating a believable excuse. For Emily had a tender conscience, and James was still too small to have completely mastered the English language.

I made my secret trips for about a week. Then one morning, when I took some fig skins and pumpkin rind to the stockyard, I found Bunny waiting for me.

He was hanging from the lowest bough of a nearby gum tree, gutted and cloaked in flies.

I brought up my breakfast then and there, before hiding in a corner of the stables. It was a while before I could speak. You have to understand the *threat* implied. I said nothing to my mother. How could I? Though I knew in my heart that she was unaware of Bunny's dreadful fate, I had nevertheless disobeyed her strict instructions. And it was Bunny who had suffered the punishment due to me.

I said nothing to George Barton, either. I simply could not find the words. We would meet on the staircase or at the table, and he would tip me a sly wink, or sit chewing slowly, watching me with a glint in his eye. The silence between us grew and grew. It was an exclusive silence, for I had told my brother and sisters nothing about poor Bunny. I had said only that the scraps were being left untouched. 'Perhaps Bunny has found a lady kangaroo, and married,' I suggested, for Emily's benefit. 'Perhaps he is too busy with his babies to spare us a thought.'

A horrifying event, you will agree. It made me very wary of my stepfather. But our lives were still not distinguished by *unrelieved* misery, for in those early days Barton was capable of self-control. I distinctly remember seeing him near the stables once, teaching James how to crack a whip. He repaired the swing near the dairy with his own hands, and dressed one of the dogs in my mother's leghorn bonnet and lace tucker. Sometimes he would sit in the sun reading a newspaper, and when we children passed would toss a coin at us, to see who could catch it. Sometimes he would open a pot of jam, and eat perhaps half of it with a spoon before passing the rest to James or me, so that we could make ourselves sick.

It was James who attracted his attention, initially. Before I rose up to challenge him, drawing his fury down upon myself as a conductor draws lightning, George Barton was chiefly interested in James. Not that he was *much* interested. But when he did pay us any mind, it was James who seemed to catch his notice. There was talk of my brother's abilities with a firearm, and on horseback. Barton would prod him at dinner about his future role as master of the estate. Would he learn how to brand his own calves? How did he propose to deal with the gully-rakers who preyed on Oldbury's stray cattle, incorporating the beasts into their own herds? What would he do about the native dogs, and the swarming parrots, and all the other creatures that would strip us naked, given half the chance?

'He will address that problem when he is ready,' my mother would say. 'He is young yet, and will make a fine master when he is grown.'

'Oh aye,' Barton would rejoin, 'if he does not stuff his head too full of nonsense about Greeks and seashells, he will do well enough.'

I am convinced that Barton nursed a deeply buried grudge against my brother for being my father's heir. Though not immediately apparent, it became more obvious as the weeks rolled by. Even as he taught James to crack a whip, and tie a sailor's knot, he also began to plague him with tormenting little challenges, proposing that he mount a frisky horse, for instance, or climb up onto the roof to 'view his domain'. My brother (not being a fool) would decline to cooperate, and ignite a slow-burning rage within my stepfather which surfaced once or twice in his complaints that my brother had no 'bottom'. James, said Barton, was altogether too ladylike.

Then followed the game of hide and seek.

It happened early one afternoon. Emily and I had looked everywhere: the dairy, the stables, the kitchen, the piggery, all the rooms in the house except my father's study, which was kept locked. We had wandered down to the creek and back again. We had even explored the area around the convict huts. But we were unable to find James.

'We surrender!' I yelled up the staircase—across the yard—into the woodpile. 'James! You win!'

There was no reply.

When he failed to join us for dinner, I became worried. My mother was also concerned. She knew that James would never miss a meal—not even to tease us. So she left her mutton cooling on her plate, and went on a tour of the house and its immediate environs, calling his name. She even enlisted Eliza's help. After about an hour, more of the staff were instructed to join the search. They did a short sweep of the bush behind their huts, and another of the land beyond the creek. Someone proposed that a message be sent to the police at Bong Bong, who had often enlisted the services of a fine black tracker known as Michael. There were no native men or women working for us at that time, though they often came and went; had there been even a gin about the place, my mother would certainly have appealed to her. By this time the shadows were long, and Mama was becoming quite frantic.

You may be asking: where was George Barton, all this time? The fact is, he had gone off into the bush to supervise the felling and splitting of timber. My mother knew this, and was half hoping, I am sure, that James had gone with him. But her husband returned without her son. 'The young rascal,' Barton said, when she broke the news, and then disappeared upstairs to wash his face and hands.

It was my mother who finally found James. She went down to the cellar for some wine to calm her nerves, and discovered him there. He was locked inside. I cannot tell you exactly what she said to James, or what he said to her. I only know that she carried him back upstairs as if he had been Louisa, and spent a long time nursing him on his bed, like an infant.

Need I point out that only two people at Oldbury possessed the keys to our cellar?

No one heard what Mama said to her husband afterwards. The discussion did not take place in their bedroom, of that I am sure. But the following day, my mother appeared with a bruise on her cheek—for which Barton was almost certainly responsible. I was not immediately aware of this. If I had any suspicions, they were banished when I saw how helpful and affectionate he was towards my mother in the wake of his offence. I was not then accustomed to the pattern of his moods.

I knew enough, however, to make my report when Mama was alone.

'Mama,' I said, 'James was locked in the cellar. Mr Barton locked him in there.'

'Mr Barton regrets that very much,' my mother replied. She was sorting through some linen, her head bent over her work. 'It was a silly accident, and will not happen again.'

'But Mr Barton said something to James,' I pointed out. 'James did not call out to us for help because of what Mr Barton said.'

My mother's hands stopped moving.

'What did Mr Barton say?' she asked, without looking up.

'I don't know, Mama. James will not repeat it.'

Nor did he ever break his silence. But he was not the same boy subsequently. I can testify to *that*. Something inside him had withered and died.

As for the rest of us, we became far more cautious. Wherever Mr Barton went, we did not. Only when he was away could we enjoy the house and its surroundings with impunity. During his visit to Sydney, in August, we were restored to a state of happy carelessness such as we had enjoyed before my mother chained herself to George Barton unto death. And because we were children, we delighted in our freedom without thought for the morrow.

The morrow came, however—as it always does. Barton returned very late one afternoon, and retired almost immediately to bed. The next morning he eschewed breakfast, but we heard him roundly abusing a convict in the dairy. My mother promptly came to a decision.

'Eliza,' she said, dabbing at her mouth with a napkin, 'please take the children to Sutton Forest today. They have been so good that they deserve a reward.'

'Aye, Mam,' said Eliza. 'Shall we take the gig?'

'No. You must walk.' As our faces all fell, my mother added: 'But I shall give you each a few pennies so that you may buy whatever you choose from Mrs Davey's shop.'

So we walked to Sutton Forest. Much has been made of my sister Louisa's indefatigable exploration of the Blue Mountains, and the walks that she took across their escarpments as an adult, through ferny gorges and over wooded ridges, sometimes riding her horse and sometimes leading it, her habit looped up to form trousers and her specially designed plant wallet slung over her shoulder. I have no reason to doubt that her excursions were as wide-ranging as she claimed. But let me tell you now that she was a *most* unenthusiastic participant in that walk to Sutton Forest. It was a damp sort of trip, because there was mist about, hanging over Gingenbullen and drifting between the lofty boughs of the eucalypts, which were as pale as if recently peeled, their bark hanging like shredded rags, or strewn across the ground in heaps. The track, consequently, was moist, and the branches that we brushed against were unpleasantly clammy. Louisa disliked this. She grew tired quickly. She dragged her feet, and whimpered, and refused to sing songs or play games or watch for birds in the trees. Thanks largely to Louisa, I cannot recall that walk with any delight.

At last, however, it ended. We came to Sutton Forest and crowded into Mrs Davey's shop, which was hardly big enough to contain us all. If you have read *Tom Hellicar's Children*, you will already be familiar with this shop. Like the one belonging to Mrs Susannah Page, it was in the front room of a wooden cottage, stacked with bottles of castor oil, tins of fish, bundles of tobacco, bags of sugar, jars of sweets. Even the open cask of treacle was there, though I never saw any letters being fished out of it. That was just Louisa's fancy. Mrs Davey was always very efficient when it came to mail; whether claimed or unclaimed. And she also took delivery of newspapers.

As you may imagine, the difficult task of selecting a treat was not accomplished with any haste. There was much on offer: lozenges, lollipops, sugarplums, marbles, almonds, currants, silk ribbons ... My own eye immediately fell on a sheaf of lavender writing paper, which ravished me; I bought it at once, before anyone else could snatch it away. I was then free to entertain myself while my siblings tried to decide between the liquorice and the lollipops. After drifting about for a few minutes, I noticed a fairly recent edition of the *Sydney Gazette*. It was dated August the thirteenth. With real interest I surveyed the advertisements on the front page, before flipping over to the second and third.

Mr Barton's name leapt out at me from the court reports.

'A gentleman named Barton,' I read, 'from the neighbourhood of Bong Bong was called as a witness yesterday in a case of murder, before Mr Justice Burton. When in the box, such was his appearance, that his Honor felt it necessary to call in the assistance of a medical practitioner in order to ascertain whether or not he was sober.'

The doctor then took Mr Barton into a private room for a long consultation, before returning to be sworn. He declared that Mr Barton had been drinking, and was not in a fit state to give evidence. 'Mr B. himself,' the report continued, 'by way of confirming his idea of sobriety, appealed to the prisoners to say how they thought he was.'

He was finally placed in the custody of the Sheriff, and ordered to stay in prison until he had paid a fifty-pound fine for contempt of court. John Lynch was not named.

You may imagine my feelings when I read all this. I was shocked and disgusted—and also alarmed. It seemed to me that George Barton would not take kindly to such public disgrace. I already had some inkling of his inflamed pride, which would brook no challenge or insult. I dreaded what we would encounter when we returned to Oldbury. Had Barton read this newspaper or not? Almost certainly he had. On the thirteenth of August, he would still have been in Sydney.

He had probably travelled back to Bong Bong in the same coach as the *Gazette*.

I said nothing to the others. But you may be sure that I did not rush home with any eagerness. How I dragged my feet on the return journey! How I lingered over every rivulet and insect that we passed! All to no avail, though; at last we arrived, and were greeted by an eerie silence.

It was still damp and misty. No one would have been inclined to linger outside, except to do a job of work. Moisture dripped from the eaves. Smoke drifted from the chimney. A dairy pan lay in the mud near the veranda, shot full of holes.

It was a promise of things to come.

Ten

You may be wondering if I asked my mother about the article that I had read. The answer is yes—and no. I *did* go to her with that express intention. I said to her: 'Mama? I saw a newspaper at Mrs Davey's, and I read something in it.'

Before I could continue, however, she looked up from her desk and interrupted. She declared firmly: 'You should not be reading newspapers at your age, Charlotte. They are very rarely accurate, and they will take away your peace of mind. I want you to ignore the newspapers. Is that clear? I want you to disregard everything in them, unless I approve the text first.'

What could I say to that? 'No, Mama'? It is a fine irony, when you consider that my sister became a newspaper correspondent. But it was ever so, with my mother.

Did she really believe that she could protect us, by keeping us shut away from the truth? Or was it her own shame that dictated her actions? Even now, I am not absolutely sure. All I can tell you is what I discovered on my own, without her assistance. She would not even tell us about the dairy pan.

It was Bridget who provided *that* information. She informed us that George Barton had 'taken against the set o' the cream', and had attacked the offending receptacle as if it had been a mortal foe. Afterwards, he became reclusive. Having retired to my father's study, he chose to spend most of the next three days there, putting my mother in a difficult position. She had to assume many of Barton's duties, directing the men and making decisions about a sick cow. Her children's education was much neglected, during this time.

But the next edition of the *Sydney Gazette* broke the uneasy calm that had settled over Oldbury. This became evident to me only because I had been watching keenly for the latest delivery of newspapers. I had some notion of examining them myself, though I was never given the opportunity. George Barton seized both publications before I even realised that they were on the premises. I saw him clutching them under his arm as he made his way through the vestibule into my father's study. I saw him drop one as he tripped while crossing the threshold.

I then braced myself for some kind of reaction, which was not long in coming.

My father had left many fine and valuable items in his study. There were oil paintings and leather-bound books behind glass. There were two magnifying glasses framed with silver, and a quill-knife inlaid with ivory. There was an embroidered cedar pole screen, and a German clock.

When I heard a crashing sound from the study, I feared very much for all these wonderful things.

'Mama! Mama!' I cried—but she was already beside me, hastening towards the study door. It was locked, alas. Though she twisted the handle, it would not yield.

'Mr Barton!' she cried. 'Mr Barton! Let me in!'

There followed another, louder crash. Without a word, my mother turned and ran towards the front door. I followed her. We hurried down the steps and around the side of the house until we reached the study window. My mother peered through it. She tapped on a pane with her little clenched fist.

'George!' she said.

All at once she flinched back. The window exploded an instant later, showering her with glass. We both screamed.

'*Mama!*'

Fortunately, she was not much hurt. Though she sustained many nicks to the left side of her face, and along one forearm, there were no bad cuts or contusions, and hardly any blood. The window itself suffered far worse. Its leadings were badly damaged and many of its panes were shattered, for it had been hit by a marble bust.

My mother quickly recovered from the shock of the broken window. George Barton was still flinging ledgers around the study when Mama told Eliza to take us (that is to say, my siblings and me) out into the bush for a 'botanical walk'. I protested, but in vain. Together with my brother and sisters, I was forced into mittens, loaded up with specimen jars, and packed off to wander the slopes of Gingenbullen with Eliza until dinner-time.

It was winter, as I have said, and very cold. There was a lowering sky and a piercing wind. In those days, the Oldbury acres were still heavily wooded. From the top of Gingenbullen the view was one of almost unrelieved olive drab, rolling hill after rolling hill, each bearing a thick, woolly green coat. Much of the cedar had already been cut, but native oaks abounded. In the more sheltered gullies, gum trees were hung with silvery lichen, which we called 'faery-tassels'. Some of these trees were of a monstrous size, the base of their trunks so broad that they could easily have accommodated a couple of bullocks. In drier spots, we sometimes came upon specimens of the grass tree, from which we plucked the long, light spears to use as shepherd's crooks and walking sticks. There were also rare examples of the Booroowang plant, which fruited in winter; I remember having to write an essay on the method by which native women prepared the nuts of this plant for ingestion, by roasting them and pounding them on flattened stones.

It was my mother who had originally pointed out to us the Booroowang, speculating that it must provide winter food for those animals which otherwise would have been sorely in want. She had examined with us many a choice example of *lepidopteron*, and had warned us against the perils of digging up fresh mounds of earth. ('For there was a little boy residing in Wingelo who did just that,' she once related, 'and found buried there the body of a poor black infant. The silly child ran home with it, saying, "Look, mother, I have found a little black baby!" Whereupon he was told to take it back *at once*.') Whenever my mother accompanied us on such an excursion, it was always replete with colour and interest. She would bring my father's magnifying glass, and tell stories of his explorations around the Shoalhaven, and discuss the habits of those natives still remaining in the area.

Eliza was different. She exhibited almost no interest in her surroundings. Rather she would nag at us about tearing our skirts, or dirtying our stockings. Indeed, she was so deficient in enthusiasm that she affected us with the same malaise, and we trudged along quite dully that winter afternoon until we were fortunate enough to encounter my cousin John.

It was not an unprecedented meeting. The two properties of Oldbury and Mereworth adjoined, and John himself was a great wanderer. Nevertheless, such a happy conjunction engendered great excitement. Even John seemed pleased, and got down from his horse to speak to us. So did the man with him, who was introduced as John Jones. For all I know, he may have been the same John Jones hanged for murder the following year, though I could not now swear to it. John Jones is a common name, after all.

'We are tracking a pair of my father's cows, which have strayed,' my cousin revealed. 'Have you come upon any trace of them on your journey? A small black heifer, and a larger brindled?'

Sadly, we had not. There was some discussion as to whether the animals might have been taken by a gully-raker, before Jones suggested that he 'bile up a cup o' tea', for it was 'mortal chilly'. This proposal was well received. We therefore gathered around as the fire was built, exchanging news and remarking on the weather, until our water was boiling away merrily in my cousin's billy.

John Jones shared his cup with Eliza, while my siblings and I drank our tea out of a water-bottle. I need hardly add that the two assigned servants became friendly at a rapid rate, laughing and talking as if they had been acquainted for years. James, for his part, was *most* taken with my cousin's fine bulldog, and Emily soon fixed her attention on the horses. Thus I was left alone with my cousin—alone, that is, save for Louisa, who had as little to say as the stump on which she sat.

I had not seen my cousin for some time. (My own family's attendance at church had lapsed terribly since my mother's marriage, and John himself was not as keen a churchgoer as he should have been.) Not wishing to waste the precious time allotted to us, I came straight to the point.

'Have you been reading any newspapers?' I inquired, in muted tones.

'The latest, you mean?' Surreptitiously, he glanced over at the two servants. 'The latest *Sydney Gazette*?'

'Any of them.'

'Of course.'

'What have they been saying? About ...' I cocked my head towards Oldbury. 'About *him*.'

John regarded me for a moment. My mother always maintained that he greatly resembled my father in his appearance, and he certainly looked at me then with a remarkably grown-up expression, both sad and sympathetic, as he sipped his tea.

'What do you want to know?' he murmured.

'Has more been printed?'

'Since when?'

'Since the thirteenth of this month.'

'The thirteenth? Oh yes.' He drained his cup, and shook the last drops of tea out onto the dirt. 'There was more last Monday, in the *Herald*. And the *Gazette* ran something on Tuesday as well. I read them last night.'

'What did they say?'

'About your stepfather?' John spoke cautiously, in a low voice. He was obviously reluctant to shock or offend. 'Well—you know that he was fined?'

'Fifty pounds. For being drunk. I know *that*.'

'He tried to appeal against the judge's decision, but the judge said that there was no appeal.'

'What does that mean? "Appeal"?'

'Oh, well . . .' My cousin shrugged. 'It means that he had to pay.'

'Did the newspapers say bad things about Mr Barton?' I pressed, puzzled as to the cause of my stepfather's all-consuming anger. 'Anything besides the fine, or the drinking?'

'The judge mentioned "gross improprieties",' said John, with a worried look at Louisa—who was drawing in the dirt. 'And Lynch was acquitted. Lynch and Williamson both.'

This *was* a surprise. My jaw dropped.

'You mean they went *free*?' I gasped.

'Not quite.' John explained that the two men, though acquitted of the murder, still had certain charges pending against them. ('The *Gazette* didn't mention what. Theft, I daresay. Items found in their possession.') As a result, they would be remanded in custody until fresh evidence was filed. 'At least that is what the newspapers *say*,' John finished. 'But journalists can be mistaken. The *Gazette* was. That flogging took place in January, yet the *Gazette* said it happened on March the first.'

'What flogging?' I was confused. 'Mr Barton's flogging?'

'Of course.'

'But what does that have to do with anything?'

'The *Gazette* said that Thomas Smith was somehow involved in the attack against Mr Barton. And that he expressed himself too freely on the subject, so his mates killed him.' John scratched his nose thoughtfully. 'It seems curious,' he went on, 'for if Smith is dead, and Lynch was acquitted, then who told this story to the police? Where did they get the notion at all? From your stepfather? From one of the other convicts? My father says that it is all very puzzling.'

'Do you mean to say that *Thomas Smith* flogged Mr Barton?' I demanded, in utter disbelief.

'Or knew who did. My father thinks . . . that is to say, he was remarking that Lynch is a suspected thief, and may well have had dealings with the bushranger gang now troubling all our sheep stations—the same gang that bailed up Mr Barton. Papa thinks that Lynch *did* kill Smith, and would have swung for it if Mr Barton had not . . . well.' A pause. 'It is all a tangled web, according to my father,' he concluded feebly.

'Thomas Smith could not have flogged Mr Barton,' I protested. 'Nor could John Lynch have done it. Mr Barton would have *known* them. He would have *reported* them after it happened. Would he not?'

'Yes. If he had any sense.'

'I don't understand.'

'Neither do I,' my cousin conceded. 'Perhaps there will be more in the next editions, and all will be explained.'

Unfortunately, this hope was soon dashed. At our next meeting, outside the Sutton Forest chapel on Sunday morning, my cousin quietly passed to me a crumpled clipping from the *Sydney Herald* of August the nineteenth. In it, I read only that the Attorney-General had questioned the propriety of returning Lynch and Williamson to my stepfather's employment—my stepfather having been fined for contempt of court. Judge Burton, however, had ruled that 'there was nothing in Mr Barton's conduct which would authorise him (the judge) to interfere with his assigned servants'.

'Mr Foster,' the report continued,'wished to read some affidavits in exculpation of Mr Barton's conduct, but Mr Justice Burton refused to hear them read. The offence had been committed in his own presence, and he had called in a medical man who confirmed his opinion. Mr Foster stated that he had certificates from medical men to show that Mr Barton's state of health was such that it might have caused the appearance complained of by His Honor, but His Honor said that there was no complaint but one that would make a man smell of rum.'

'Oh dear,' I sighed, aware of how badly George Barton would take all this.

'The Gazette said much the same thing,' my cousin remarked. 'It didn't mention Smith's murder.'

'I wish they would stop talking about it,' was my fretful response, whereupon my cousin cleared his throat and gazed off into the distance. He did not ask what I meant—perhaps because he hardly needed to. The gossip about George Barton and his explosive rages had almost certainly reached Mereworth.

There was one incident in particular that must have been widely discussed. It occurred shortly after the final newspaper report on John Lynch's trial. Mr Barton was still recovering from the shame attendant upon this public exposure; he had declared himself 'ill', and was not much seen about the place. (Whether he was truly ill I cannot say, though all the doctors' certificates that he had procured in his defence, on top of the fifty-pound fine, must have depleted our yearly income by a very considerable amount.) In his absence, my mother had struggled to manage the estate, while at the same time making determined efforts to educate her children. These efforts were greatly resented by George Barton. I had no idea how much, until he burst into the breakfast room one day when my mother was trying to teach us French.

'So,' he said, clutching a blanket around his shoulders, '*here* you are, then.'

'Here I am,' my mother replied. She spoke firmly, but I could feel her limbs tense. 'What do you want?'

'An attentive wife is what I want,' he rejoined, scowling about the table. 'What are you playing at? What is this nonsense?'

'It is French,' said my mother.

'French? *French?*' Barton snorted. 'What have the Frogs to do with us, may I ask? *French*, by God! It is as good as treasonable.' He flipped at a book with one finger, upsetting his fragile sense of balance so that he reeled slightly where he stood. I saw then that he was drunk. 'Why fill their heads with such nonsense?' he demanded. 'What good will it do them, croaking like a Frog?'

Why I spoke at that instant, I cannot understand. Perhaps my knowledge of Barton's drunken exploits had filled me with a dangerous contempt for the man. Or perhaps I felt secure that he would not recognise an insult if it was delivered in French. Whatever the reason, I turned to Emily and whispered, in scornful accents: '*Je prefererais coasser comme une grenouilles que grogner comme un cochon.*' (I'd prefer to croak like a frog than grunt like a pig.)

It is doubtful that my sister understood what I was saying. George Barton certainly did not. But he understood my intention just as well as if I had slapped him across the cheek. His face became red, his eyes seemed to bulge, and he seized a handful of my hair.

'*What did you call me?*' he bellowed.

'Mama!' I shrieked like a kettle, for I was in agony. 'Help!'

'Stop it *at once!*' my mother exclaimed, leaping to her feet. Louisa was crying, and James was yelling, and George Barton was dragging me out of my seat by the hair, tugging and shaking me much as a dog worries a rat. Tears spurted from my eyes. The pain was unbearable.

'*Mama-a-a!*' I screeched.

Had I been made of more durable stuff, I would have hung off him, a dead weight, and prevented him from moving out of the house. As it was, I felt that I *had* to stagger after him, lest he denude me of my hair altogether. He pulled me through the door of the breakfast room, across the veranda and into the yard, pursued by the rest of my family. Their cries—and my screams—attracted the servants, who spilled from doorways and rushed around corners, only to stop in their tracks when they saw what was going on.

'Stop! *Stop it!*' my mother shouted, wrapping herself around my stepfather's free arm. He shook her off, and caught her across the jaw with the back of his hand.

Before she had even hit the ground, Robert—our dairyman—started forward. But George Barton turned on him. 'Lay one finger on me,' he bawled, the blanket slipping from his shoulders, 'and you'll feel the lash for it!'

I do not blame Robert for hesitating. What Barton had said was true: any convict daring to restrain his master would have run the risk of being flogged for his pains. At the time, however, I was frantic. Why did they all hold back? 'Mama!' I wailed. '*Help me!*'

And then Barton found what he had been seeking. With a convulsive twist of his forearm, he thrust me to the ground, plunging my face into a cowpat. I was on my back again almost before I realised what had happened; he had released me at the very moment of contact, allowing me to roll away. Still, the stench made my stomach heave. I began to gag and retch.

'If you want to talk filth, you should know what it tastes like!' Barton hurled at me. After which he retrieved his blanket, wrapped himself up in it, and marched away unsteadily, leaving behind him a silence broken only by the painful noises that I was making as I brought up my breakfast.

It was a truly dreadful moment, which I have never forgotten.

Mama was the first to speak. Though much shaken by the blow that she had sustained, she had lost neither sense nor consciousness. Picking herself up, she staggered over to me.

'Charlotte,' she croaked. 'Charlotte, my darling . . .'

I am moved even now to recall how she took up a corner of her shawl, and wiped the excrement from my face with it. Meanwhile Eliza had come. Together she and my mother lifted me and guided me into the kitchen, where I was able to wash myself. Hardly anyone spoke. The servants were utterly silent, displaying their concern only by the speed with which they fetched water and towels. My mother said very little, perhaps because her jaw was aching. Even Louisa held her tongue, in a way that came to concern my mother very much. While James would bawl, and Emily whimper, Louisa—from that time on—comported herself with a troubling restraint. I remember the sudden pain I felt in my heart, when first I read Louisa's description of her heroine's earliest days in *Myra*. '*The child had an unchildlike way of showing grief,*' she wrote, '*that plaintive, silent shedding of tears which tells of long acquaintance with sorrow, long, even in three or four brief years of life.*'

This was an exact portrait of herself. It upsets me even now when I contemplate it. God knows how it affected my mother.

Yet for all that, my mother was blameworthy. Though she cleaned me, and embraced me, and tried to comfort me, nevertheless she showed herself deficient. No doubt Louisa would argue against me, had she been alive. No doubt she would contend that my mother did everything in her power to protect us. George Barton, after all, was her husband. He was her master in law. Only by resorting to the most drastic measures could my mother offer us complete protection, and even then (as we eventually discovered) such efforts could be undermined by threats from another source. How she fought, my mother! I will concede this. I cannot deny it.

But *she married George Barton*. This is the crux of the matter. She married him, and in so doing she knowingly relinquished all power over my father's estate. From co-executor, she became a humble lease-holder. It was inevitable. It became her fate the moment Barton's ring was slipped onto her finger.

She threw everything away. Everything. And she would *not say why*.

I had asked her why, before her marriage. I asked her again, after that filthy villain attempted to humiliate me like a dog in the yard. Cradled in her arms, rocked to and fro before the kitchen fire, I struggled to suppress my sobs and said: 'I hate him! I want him to go!'

'Shh. Shh,' she replied.

'You must send him away! You *must!*' Observe my hysteria: I addressed her as I would have addressed a humble skivvy. 'This is not his house! This is *our* house! I *hate* him here!'

'I cannot send him away, Charlotte.'

'Why not?'

'Because he is my husband. I cannot command him.'

'Yes you can!' I protested, drawing back to look up into her face. 'You are in charge of Papa's will!'

'No, Charlotte.' She spoke quietly, staring into the fire. 'When I married Mr Barton, I relinquished my role as executor. Mr Berry and Mr Coghill are the only executors now.'

This, I must confess, was a terrible blow. I could hardly believe my ears. Yet when I stared at her, I saw that she was telling the truth.

'Then—then why?' I stammered. '*Why? Why* did you marry him, *why?*'

'Hush.'

'*Tell me!*'

'Compose yourself, Captain.' My mother's voice was suddenly strong and harsh. She could be formidable if she chose to be. (Mr Berry once called her a 'she-dragon'.) 'These are not matters that should be discussed with little girls,' she said firmly. 'When you are older, you will understand. Meanwhile, you will kindly show

114

some restraint. If you had been more polite, this would not have happened. You should *think* before you speak. You are the eldest, and must set a good example for the others.'

It makes me laugh, to remember those words. '*When you are older, you will understand*'! How many years would pass—how many *decades*—before I would come to understand? And not through my mother's agency, I might point out. It was solely through my own efforts.

For she would never tell me. Never. She took her secret with her to the grave.

Eleven

An interlude

I was not expected at my mother's funeral.

She was buried at All Saints, Sutton Forest, and I was living in Mittagong, more than ten miles away. That was in October of 1867, about a year after the Iron Works closed. My husband had lost his job then, but we were fortunate; the railway was still being laid, and Mittagong station was being built. He had therefore secured a good labouring position, and we were able to stay in our little house—one of those humble slab cottages whose ruin my sister lamented four years later, in the *Sydney Morning Herald*. (Why did she visit Mittagong? Surely it could not have been in search of *me*? So much time had elapsed; I had been gone from the place for at least two years.)

I must confess, I have no very pleasant memories of Mittagong. Mining and smelting are never productive of great beauty, and the land around the works was arid and barren, though the peak of Gibraltar, rising up about a mile away, often looked as misty and mysterious as Gingenbullen. From our front door I was able—if given a moment's rest—to look out across a little watered valley towards the Iron Works, with its great, black chimney and its dilapidated tramway. Soot lay everywhere, on everything, until the works closed. After that, I was always cleaning away red dust, for the ore was inescapable. It could be found in the banks along the roads, as red as the flames of the smelter whose glow had once been visible from our windows at night.

As for the township, it was hardly more beautiful than the Iron Works. Most of the houses were made of bark and corrugated iron, though some more substantial buildings had recently been erected. W. Coull's store, for instance. The Wesleyan Chapel. The Roman Catholic school where I sent Ernest and Emily and even Charles to be tutored by a certain Miss Lyons—who was the most hapless soul I have ever encountered in all my wanderings. But what else could I do? Edwin was still tiny then. Eva was born in the autumn of '67. And the others . . . I will not talk about the others now.

Flora helped me at first, and would have continued to do so, had she not become a wife. Her marriage to George Garlick occurred a year before Eva's birth, in 1866. I only wish that Flora's wedding could have taken place in Mittagong, though of course there was no proper Catholic church, in those days—just the rough little weatherboard structure that also served as the school. Besides which, the Garlicks were better placed to host a wedding breakfast. My husband had just lost his job, while I had more children to feed than the Garlicks, whose brood was all grown up. So the wedding took place at St Nicholas's, in Penrith, near the house of George's parents. And I was able to contribute nothing except my daughter's trousseau, though I worried about her a good deal. I worried about her future, and wondered how she would fare.

She fared very well, as it happened. Her father always said that she would. But he was somewhat prejudiced, having introduced George Garlick into the family himself when they were both carriers together. They were very good friends. In fact I have always had a suspicion that George married Flora so that he might remain close to her family. For George worshipped my husband. He thought him the very best fellow in the whole world.

It was no coincidence that we went to Orange shortly after George and Flora went to Blayney. George would have had it no other way, I am sure. He was so lavish in his praise of the region that we would have been foolish not to try our luck here. And his advice was good. Though not the Promised Land, it was certainly fertile ground. I would not go so far as to say that we have all *flourished* in Orange (God knows, I have lost three children here) but there can be no doubt that we have met with some success.

In 1867, however, we were faltering. While my husband had quickly secured a new job with the railways, he knew that it could only be a temporary post. The line reached Mittagong in March of '67, when the station was finished. By the end of that year all the track would be laid between Mittagong and Moss Vale, and we would be faced with a choice: either follow the work to Marulan or find some other occupation. In April Eva was born, leaving me sadly worn down—for I was not young, and she did not thrive. In July, flooding rains destroyed part of our roof, ruining many of our possessions and ushering in the most terrible fevers. It was a bad year. A very bad year.

And then, in October, my mother died.

I believe Flora's wedding announcement must have alerted Louisa to my whereabouts. I had not seen my sister since 1865, nor kept her informed of my movements; she sent her letter to the post office at Mittagong, where the postmaster knew me. Though still nursing Eva, I took the first mail coach to Berrima with a hold-all as my only luggage. Then, upon arriving in Berrima, I threw myself on the mercy of the Reverend Hassall, who kindly sent me in his carriage to Sutton Forest. But it was a close-run thing. I almost missed the funeral. Perhaps there were some who would have preferred that I had.

Or am I being ungenerous? Though James looked quite stricken when I accosted him outside the new stone church, one would have expected him to look stricken; he had just lost his mother, after all. And though Louisa seemed startled, I cannot really blame her for that. I must have been a startling sight, with my hair all awry, and my eyes red-rimmed from long night watches, and my shabby shawl (sporting many a crusty stain) wrapped tight around my pale, mewling infant. I could have been a beggar, from my appearance. And indeed, I almost felt like one. Some of the Throsbys were in evidence, you see. And the Nicholsons. And the Badgerys. I have no idea why they felt constrained to come. In honour of my father, perhaps? But come they did, and in all their mourning glory. I have never seen so much black satin and jet in one place—unless it were at the Orange Town Hall on the occasion of Queen Victoria's death.

James was very sprucely dressed too. As was Louisa. *They* did not disgrace their mother's memory. *They* were not encumbered by a wailing infant who had to be removed from the church at least twice during the ceremony. I can still recall feeding Eva in the churchyard, near my mother's open grave. My mother was buried to the west of the church, under the stone vault that we had erected in my father's memory. Emily lay there also, and Emily's poor little son.

There was a family reunion, in other words. And a far more peaceable one than that which occurred above ground.

I will not lie to you: it is a terrible thing to bury one's mother, no matter how estranged from her one might have become. There had been nothing resolved. Nothing forgiven. And I was tired—so tired. Fatigue had eaten into my very bones. I almost envied my mother, because her sleep was the deepest there is.

Yet I did not break down. While Louisa silently wept, and James lifted his chin as if to hold the tears back, I stood there with a face of stone. The others had not buried children, you see. There is nothing worse than that: nothing. When you have watched your darling precious child suffer torments that you cannot ease—when you have opened your arms to release him, and laid his fragile, flaxen head to rest beneath falling clods of earth—then you can truly say to yourself: I have suffered the worst punishment that heaven and earth can inflict.

So I did not shame my blood by falling to the ground, or wailing uncontrollably. I might have *looked* like a gypsy, but I did not behave like one. Instead I kept my spine straight, as my mother herself would have done. And the other mourners, who had been well disposed to pity me as the 'black sheep' and the 'poor relation'—who no doubt would have liked to witness, for their own edification, the way in which poverty and its attendant ills can slowly destroy one's dignity and self-worth—these good people were sadly disappointed. When they approached me with their words of comfort, I turned on them an eye of flint.

They were obliged to cluster about Louisa instead, for she looked very ill. In truth, she *was* ill. I saw it at once, for I was accustomed to the signs. This was not mere grief. This was the pallor, the sluggishness, the wasted appearance of physical debility.

'Has Louisa been ill?' I asked James, in a low voice. We were making our way across the churchyard, past many familiar names.

'Of course,' he rejoined. 'Her strength has been sorely tested. She nursed Mama devotedly for two years, in the most dutiful manner. Mama's fall affected her spine, you know. She had to be lifted and guided. And being so deaf, she required a great deal of tendance. Poor Louisa tired herself out simply talking to Mama. You know how bad her lungs are. She has ruined her health for Mama's sake. She laid all other considerations aside.'

In contrast to *my* behaviour. I heard at once the implied criticism, but chose to ignore it. Bickering at funerals is not the proper occupation of anyone with a respectable background; I was not about to have the Badgerys and the Nicholsons shaking their heads primly over my lack of decent self-control. So I postponed our discussion until a more suitable time, and turned to accept Mrs Elizabeth Throsby's condolences.

You will remember Mrs Elizabeth Throsby, whose childhood adventures were always the subject of such great interest at Oldbury. In 1867 she was nearing her sixtieth year, a rather stout and placid woman still wearing her widow's weeds, which were enlivened to some degree by a very elaborate arrangement of white lace on the head and at the throat. I had always liked her as a child. As an adult, I admired her for the fortitude with which she had endured the deaths of four children.

For this reason I heard her out in a spirit of meek acceptance. Following a formal exchange of compliments, she went on to inquire after other members of my family, as if unaware that I was an unlikely source of information. (This may have been true courtesy, or it may have been absent-mindedness; I have no way of knowing.) She asked about my uncle, who had long since moved to the Tumut plains, and I was obliged to confess my ignorance as to his present state of health. She asked after my cousin John: was he married yet? I did not know. She then gave me an account of his marvellous cattle-driving feat, which I have already mentioned in this narrative.

'You know, my dear,' she added, placing a gentle hand on my arm, 'that I was always very fond of your dear mother. As was Mr Throsby. We were both deeply troubled by all the terrible reverses that she suffered.'

I said nothing to that. If I had, I might have regretted it later. But Mrs Throsby must have sensed something of my feelings, for she continued.

'I should have been a better friend to her, but there were family considerations. My sister-in-law Mary took against her to such a degree after that voyage to New South Wales. Mary was always a great friend of Harriet Macarthur, you see. And Harriet was *so* disappointed at losing your mother that she became ungenerous.'

'Losing my mother?' I was utterly confused. 'What do you mean, Mrs Throsby?'

'Why—because your mother was such an excellent governess, of course.' Mrs Throsby smiled her tranquil smile, sublimely unconscious of the tumult that had suddenly arisen in my breast. 'Mrs Macarthur was most unreasonable, I think. She persisted in viewing your mother's conduct in the very worst light, and Mary was loyal to that opinion. But *I* cannot agree with them. Your mother had every right to fall in love with your father. They were ideally suited. And she was, after all, the daughter of a gentleman.'

'But—but—' I could not help myself. I had to reveal my ignorance. 'But my mother came over with my father. He brought her here.'

'Oh no. No, Mrs *Macarthur* paid her passage. Or perhaps it was her sister, Mrs Philip Gidley King. Yes, I believe that Mrs *King* engaged your mother's services, for Mrs Macarthur's sake.' Mrs Throsby put a finger to her chin, and furrowed her brow. 'Do you know, there was so much talk at the time, but I have quite forgotten . . . it is so long ago . . .'

'Do you mean to say that my mother and father met *on board* the *Cumberland*?'

'Oh yes. Such a romantic tale. But the Kings were furious, of course. And the Macarthurs. And Mary would hear nothing good about your mother, for all that no offence had been committed against *her*.' Realising what she had just said, Mrs Throsby hastened to elaborate. 'Not that any offence was committed. Your mother had no blameworthy object, or the marriage would not have been so successful. And if there had been any impropriety, your father would certainly have felt it, for he was an honourable man. No, no—the match was perfectly acceptable, for all Mary's talk about your mother giving herself airs. And if the truth be told, my dear . . .' Mrs Throsby leaned closer. 'I believe that my sister-in-law may have been a little jealous. She was not married *herself* at that point, if you recall. And your father was such a prize. Such a wonderful man.'

'Yes. He was.'

'In this time of trial, you have that one comfort, at the very least,' Mrs Throsby concluded, with genuine feeling. 'At last your mother has gone to meet her husband again in that place where sin and sorrow and sighing are forever done away. How happy she must be, after all her long years of waiting. How joyfully he must have welcomed her.'

There was no mention of my mother's *second* husband, of course. It was as if he had never existed. All the same, I regret that I did not respond more graciously to Mrs Throsby's good wishes. I regret that I simply mumbled something incoherent, and turned from her abruptly.

No doubt she attributed my rudeness to a sudden access of grief, and freely forgave me. But it was not grief that shackled my tongue. It was shock. It was outrage. I find it hard to believe that I was able to contain myself through the walk back to the parsonage, where funeral meats were being served to a select group of mourners. How did I ever keep silent during that interminable reception, with its muted clinking of tea-cups and murmured remarks about the weather, and the state of the crops, and Sir John and Lady Young's visit to Mittagong in April? I suppose that I must have been distracted by other considerations. The ecclesiastical sobriety of the furniture, for instance. The unhealthy shade of the wallpaper. And my brother's settled air, as he helped Miss Sarah Anne Horton—the Reverend Horton's eldest daughter—to distribute cakes and sandwiches. It seemed to me that James was very much at home. He was quite obviously such a favoured guest that I no longer asked myself why the parsonage had been offered up as a venue for this genteel gathering. And I was not surprised when, years later, I learned of James's marriage to Miss Horton.

But my brother's marriage lay far into the future. At the time of which I speak, his thoughts were not fixed on that 'star of every wandering bark'. On the contrary, they were fixed on Death, and his hands shook, and his face was stiff with suppressed feeling. His knuckles looked red and raw.

Louisa was more composed. She still wore her hair in girlish ringlets to her shoulders, but the face framed by these curls was far from youthful. There were heavy pouches under her eyes, and dark lines around her mouth. She looked as tired as I felt.

When most of the mourners had departed, leaving the three bereaved in possession of Reverend Horton's front room, I said to her: 'You should rest. You don't look well.'

Louisa turned to regard me, in her quiet way.

'Neither do you,' she rejoined.

'It has been a hard winter, I suppose. For everyone.'

'How *is* your family?' Louisa asked, very much as if she wanted to know. I swallowed some obscure resentment and said: 'Depleted.'

'Depleted?'

'I was just talking to Mrs Throsby.' No longer could I restrain myself. 'She told me something very interesting. Very interesting *indeed*, all things considered.'

'And what might that be?' said James, in a dull voice—as if he found me inexpressibly wearing, with my impassioned outbursts and sudden, unlooked-for appearances. But I kept my temper. I told myself that he was in a nervous state, and had never been particularly stalwart to begin with.

'It appears that Mama was a *governess* when she married Pa. A governess engaged by Mrs Hannibal Macarthur.' Glancing from face to face, I was startled to observe no great change of expression in either of them. 'It is quite well known, apparently. Except by her own children.'

There was a brief pause. Then Louisa spoke.

'*I* knew it,' she admitted.

'*You* did?'

'She told me. And I told James.'

I could hardly believe my ears. 'She *told* you?' It was an effort to keep my voice from rising. 'When? When did she tell you?'

'Not long ago.' Louisa's small white hands began to twist about in her black silk lap. 'You have to understand, she had very little with which to occupy herself,' my sister explained gently. 'She could not hold a book for long, and she could not hear me if I read to her. So she talked. She talked about London, and our grandparents . . . she talked about the time that she spent teaching five children in Lancashire, without any assistance. Apparently, mention was made of it in the newspapers while she was fighting for us in court—which is why we were never permitted to read them, Charlotte.' Louisa smothered a cough, in which I could detect a rather ominous rattle. 'She was fifteen years old when she began to teach. It was a considerable achievement. In many ways, it is a cause for pride.'

'Then why did she not think to mention it sooner?' I was almost beside myself with rage, though I managed to bank it down. 'Why this quite *obsessive* concern with the distinctions of *rank?*'

'Charlotte—'

'Why these interminable lectures on the subject of *ill-judged unions?*'

'It is not the same thing at all, Charlotte, and you know it,' my brother declared. Whereupon I fixed him with such a look that he flinched, and lifted one hand in an involuntary gesture.

'Please—James. Both of you.' Louisa put her own hand over her eyes, and her voice cracked. 'I couldn't bear it. No. Really. I could not bear it.'

'And what else did she tell you?' I demanded, ignoring this plea for mercy. Rounding on my sister, I took full advantage of my superior strength. 'What else did she happen to reveal in these nostalgic monologues?' I spat. 'Did she tell you *why*, Louisa? Did she finally *explain*? Am I actually going to discover why we've had to endure such misery over the years?'

'Charlotte—'

'Why did she marry Barton?' I leaned forward. 'Did she tell you that? Did she tell *you* that?'

'Don't speak to your sister so roughly,' said James, but I ignored him. He saw himself as the head of the family, no doubt. He believed that the possession of Oldbury gave him precedence in any gathering of the clan. He was wrong, however. He had neither the sense nor the authority to direct *my* actions.

And that was Barton's fault. It was all Barton's fault.

'She did not mention George Barton,' my sister replied huskily, uncovering her face. 'Not once.'

'Nor Belanglo?' I pressed her.

'Oh, no.'

'She must have said something.' I could not keep my voice steady. 'Just a word of explanation . . . an apology . . .'

'Recollect her position, dear.' Louisa responded to my obvious distress by softening her tone. 'The whole world knew that she had gone with him into the forest. What could she do but marry him?'

I shook my head. 'No,' I said. 'No. You are not thinking clearly. Consider the woman. Consider her conduct. Time and again, she defied convention. Did the world's opinion affect her decision to renounce the marriage? To fight that villain tooth and nail in court? To go with him to Belanglo in the first place? Would loss of reputation have outweighed for her the loss of all her legal rights over her family, and her family's estate?'

'I—'

'Something *happened*, Louisa. Do you see? Something happened to her, and now . . . now I don't suppose I shall ever know what.'

There was a long silence. I cocked my ear for any warning cries from Eva, who had been laid down to sleep in one of the back rooms. But I heard only the distant clash of cutlery being washed in the kitchen.

'She mentioned you,' said Louisa, all at once.

I raised my head again. 'What?' I said.

'She mentioned you,' Louisa repeated. 'Towards the end.'

I swallowed. My sister was regarding me with a clear and steady gaze. Her courage had always been of the quiet sort.

'What did she say?' I asked.

'She said that you had endured too much, and that it had affected your judgement,' Louisa replied. 'She said that she was sorry for it.'

I began to cry, then. I could not help myself. And James crossed the room to give me his crumpled handkerchief.

Twelve

1838

It was the shooting that truly unhinged George Barton.

The attack took place on the twenty-third of June, 1838. Before that time, Barton's spells of unreasonable behaviour could usually be traced to a bout of drinking. Something would distress or weary him; he would ease himself with a few drams, and then another few drams, and another; finally he would commit a violent or disturbing act, and then fall into a stupor, from which he would emerge ill and unhappy, but more or less sane.

Consequently, we lived our lives as many do who are at the mercy of the sea. There were long stretches of calm sailing, in sunny waters. But always there would be a lookout posted, to watch for signs of coming squalls. And when encroaching storm-clouds were espied, there would be a hurried battening down of hatches, and a securing of gun ports. *That* is how my family lived, throughout 1837 and the early part of 1838.

As to the outside world, we saw little of it. We kept ourselves very much to ourselves, though whether this seclusion arose from choice or necessity I do not know. Certainly, we were not much feted at church, where the congregation had doubtless heard certain rumours. And my uncle and aunt grew ever more frosty as they became more and more financially embarrassed.

Our own financial affairs were not what they should have been either, though I saw nothing of this at the time. I was too young, and the signs were too subtle. My stepfather, you see, was a man distinguished neither by good sense nor industry. He made poor decisions, and when the consequences of these decisions became evident, was insufficiently energetic in his attempts to reverse them. He was intemperate, lazy, and destructive. He was also a bad farmer, and a poor master. He did not like to leave Oldbury, and gave his excuse as the 'flagellation' that he had endured. Consequently, he was taken advantage of. And where Fate and Nature failed to undermine his efforts, there were those among his assigned men who must have been delighted to play a saboteur's role. For he was not beloved. That much became clear in the winter of 1838. By then, someone had decided that George Barton would have to pay for his many offences.

It was a frigid evening, and a fire had been lit in the sitting room. All of the family were gathered there except James, who had been in bed for most of the day with a feverish cold. This cold had been contracted first by Louisa, then by my mother and James in rapid succession. I was slated to be the next victim, though at the time I was still healthy. That is why I had been asked to read aloud. My mother was tired, and hoarse from coughing. Emily was unequal to the longer words in Carlyle's *Sartor Resartus*. As for George Barton, though he *could* read, I had seen him moving his lips when consulting a newspaper. And in any event, he was not of a disposition to find any pleasure in gratifying others. He was especially inimical to books. I do not think that he ever picked up a book, voluntarily, in his whole life.

But he did like to fall asleep with the murmur of prose or poetry in his ears. It soothed his soul, for some reason. He refused to have us read novels or plays, for in novels and plays there is always a good deal of lively conversation, which caused him some disturbance when he was drifting off. He preferred essays, or volumes of history, or botanical texts. The slow rhythms of these works affected him like a species of lullaby.

He would snore away while we read, with a noise like a cross-cut saw on ironbark. (*How* I hated the man!) No one was sacred: neither Byron nor Coleridge, neither Crabbe nor Hume. I am glad now that he would not allow us any Shakespeare. Shakespeare was never spoiled for me by the snorts and gurglings of George Barton.

There we were, then, in the sitting room. My mother was sewing. I was reading. Emily was attempting a portrait of Louisa, who had a remarkable facility for sitting still.

George Barton sat collapsed in an armchair, his head thrown back, his mouth open, his breathing loud.

All at once, the room seemed to explode around us.

It was the noise that frightened me more than anything—the deafening clap of gunfire and the shattering of glass. Screams rang in my ears. I remember a smell of powder and the roaring oaths of George Barton. Suddenly I was on the floor; I do not know how. Perhaps my mother had pulled me. 'Get out!' she shrieked. 'Get away from the window!'

Confused and frightened, I began to crawl towards the door.

But my stepfather reached it first. He overtook me, bent double, and flung it open. One hand was pressed to his neck. 'My gun!' he shouted. 'Get my gun!'

He was out of sight before I had even reached the vestibule.

'Upstairs!' my mother ordered, her voice shrill and breathless. But my sisters and I clung to her, crying. We would not be separated. By this time James had appeared at the top of the stairs. He had wet himself, and his face was dead white.

'Mama!' he bleated. 'Mama!'

My mother saw then that she could not leave us. Instead she rushed us up to the nursery, where we all huddled together on one bed, while she locked the door and stationed herself at the window. There was a candle burning. It had been left alight to comfort poor James.

We could hear cries echoing in the darkness outside: cries of interrogation and excitement. It sounded as if the whole estate had been roused.

'What happened? Mama?' There was still a ringing in my ears. I could not seem to collect my thoughts. 'Was it an accident?'

'Perhaps,' she replied. Her eyes and brows looked very dark in her pale face. She was panting, as if from extreme exertion.

'It was a gun!' said James, hoarsely. 'I heard it!'

'Shh. Everything's all right, now.'

Even as my mother spoke, however, there was a rap on the door. She jumped, and Emily cried out.

"Tis only Eliza, Mam!' came a muffled, unsteady response. 'Mrs Barton? You're not hit?'

'No, Eliza.' Moving away from the window, my mother admitted our nurse. 'Where were you?' she demanded. 'Why were you not with James?'

'I went to empty the pot,' said Eliza, whose eyes were stretched wide and whose lips were shaking. 'I—I heard—it saymed like—'

'It was a shot,' said my mother. 'It came through the sitting-room window.'

'And the master?'

'What of him?'

'He was a-holding his head, Mam. When I saw him in the yard.'

My mother turned to address her children.

'You must stay here with Eliza,' she instructed. 'I shan't be long.'

'*No!*' James screamed.

'It's all *right*, James. Nothing will happen now—the men are all alerted.'

'*No! No!*'

In his weakened state, James would not be reasoned with. He sobbed, and clutched at my mother's skirts. At last she had to succumb.

'*You* must go down,' she told Eliza. 'Find out if it's safe. Find out what's happening.'

'Yes, Mam.'

'Find out about Mr Barton. He might have been shot.'

How wonderful for us all, if he had been! But alas; he had escaped unharmed. The ball of the musket—or large pistol—had passed through his collar, burning his skin slightly. He had sustained no other hurt. When Eliza reported back with this information, she also told us that the grounds were being searched, and that no intruders had yet been discovered or detained.

Even at the time, I wondered if the culprit *had* been an intruder. It seemed to me, when I considered the countless small offences committed by George Barton against his staff, that there was quite enough ill feeling among the Oldbury convicts to provide a motive for killing him. And I was angry at my stepfather for putting us in such a position. If it had not been for George Barton, we would never have been attacked at our own hearthside.

I was also very frightened. I knew well enough what could happen when a convict came into possession of a firearm.

There was little rest for anyone that night. Not knowing if we had experienced the first assault of a gang of bushrangers, my stepfather mounted guards, and distributed sharp-edged farming implements. Then, when no further incidents occurred before sunrise, he sent one of our men to notify the police—who had been transferred to Berrima from Bong Bong the previous year. This man was given strict instructions to *bring back a constable*, and look sharp about it.

While awaiting his messenger's return, Barton had my mother write out an advertisement. I overheard him dictating to her as I hovered at the study door; he was offering a reward of fifty guineas to anyone who might help to identify the perpetrator of such a dastardly assault. His advertisement was published in *The Australian* two weeks later.

It did not, as far as I know, elicit any useful information from anyone.

I have no wish to apportion blame for something that was clearly the product of a diseased mind. A person with impaired faculties can be very suggestible; he (or she) will identify almost every approach as a threat, and almost every gathering as a conspiracy. Therefore I cannot say: the police were at fault. For they were only doing their job.

Nevertheless, they planted a notion in George Barton's head. They asked him about his own staff, and searched the convict huts. And though they came away empty-handed, with no evidence or testimony of any significance, from that time on my stepfather was increasingly mistrustful of those around him.

In some measure, he had good reason to be. I have said before that he was not beloved. He had been attacked, not once, but twice. He was surrounded by men well acquainted with violence, and had not the strength of character to lead them—only to drive them. Is it any wonder that he was afraid?

At first the measures that he took did not seem unreasonable. He bought a pistol from one of the officers of the Berrima garrison, and took to carrying this pistol with him wherever he went. He insisted that all the shutters be fastened in the downstairs rooms every night. He applied to the Colonial Secretary's Office, which posted an additional reward for information relating to the attempted murder.

None of this, you will agree, could be construed as inappropriate. But as time went on, his actions became more extreme. He took to sleeping with the bedroom door locked and a candle burning beside him. He refused to leave Oldbury's immediate environs. He would bring one of the more amenable dogs to the table with him at every meal, and feed it morsels from his plate before sampling the food himself. Nothing would persuade him to go anywhere near the itinerant labourers who were employed at certain seasons to shear and harvest; indeed, he came to regard all visitors with acute suspicion, no matter how respectable they might be. And his attitude towards the resident staff was just as deplorable. Increasingly he was to be found hiding about the place—behind doors, in cupboards and under beds—not because he was frightened of any immediate danger, but because he distrusted the servants and was spying on them.

He seemed not in the least put out to be discovered in such undignified circumstances. On the contrary, he would simply smile a chilling smile, as if to say: 'You see? I am Omnipresent.' We all endured this without complaint until one day Jane, surprised to stumble on him lurking in the dairy, dropped and broke a jug of milk. When my mother was informed of the accident, she took it upon herself to remonstrate with her husband. In fact, she lost her temper.

I remember how alarmed I was. We had long ago learned that it was foolhardy—even dangerous—to take George Barton to task about anything. He could not control himself when challenged: he was quite capable of throwing a hot cup of tea in one's eyes. Moreover, he had begun to secrete weapons about the house in preparation for an attack. So he always had ready access to clasp-knives, sickles and other sharp instruments.

Imagine my feelings when I saw my mother storming off to confront her husband. Looking back, I realise that she must have been driven to the edge of endurance by fear and fatigue, having shouldered many of the burdens that rightly belonged in George Barton's domain. More and more, as the months passed, she had been forced to ride out to our far-flung properties at Wollondilly and Budgong. More and more, she had found herself admonishing sullen farmhands and poring over accounts, while at the same time trying to shield the whole establishment from my stepfather's fearsome intemperance. Is it any wonder that she suddenly snapped?

As her shrill voice was raised in the study, the entire household held its collective breath. There was no knowing what Barton would do. Had I been older, or less inured to shouting, I might have felt ashamed of my mother at that point—for she sounded like a common publican's wife upbraiding a drunken housemaid. As it was, I just stood in the kitchen doorway praying to the Lord, my arms wrapped firmly around Louisa.

For a long time we waited, but heard no answering shouts from George Barton. When my mother's raging ceased, and silence ensued, I was suddenly sure that he had killed her. He seemed perfectly capable of killing. And in that instant it occurred to me: had Barton killed Thomas Smith as well? Had he *lied* about seeing John Lynch near the body? Was that why Lynch and Williamson had been acquitted of the crime?

Was that why my stepfather had become so frightened of John Lynch? Could a troubled conscience have led Barton to fear reprisal from a man who had been falsely accused?

Surely not.

'Mama!' I shouted, and broke away from my sister. I ran from the kitchen into the vestibule, not thinking even to snatch up a fish-knife or fire-iron before I did. The study door was standing open; through it, I could see my mother. She was stooping over her husband, who was slumped in my father's chair.

They were locked in earnest conversation.

'You are over-anxious,' she was saying. 'These are loyal servants. They can be trusted. I trust my children with them—would I do *that*, if I had any doubts?'

He shook his head, and mumbled something into his neckerchief that I could not hear. He seemed very subdued; I guessed that he was still suffering from the after-effects of a long night's tippling.

'How is such a thing possible?' my mother pressed him. 'The huts were searched. The men were questioned. They were all accounted for within minutes of the shooting. How could any of them have hidden a musket, in such a short time?'

'Easily. If they were all involved.'

'Oh, George.' I sensed that my mother was struggling to remain patient. 'Would they *all* be conspiring, without exception? When the Colonial Secretary is offering a conditional pardon to any assigned man who comes forward? It makes no *sense*, George.'

'They are afraid of John Lynch. John Lynch has friends everywhere.'

Barton was wearing one of my mother's shawls, and pulled it tightly around his hunched shoulders. His complexion was pasty, his gaze skittish. 'Lynch sent one of his confederates to kill me,' Barton growled. 'He can send others to kill anyone who peaches on him.'

My mother's expression changed. She pressed her lips together, and straightened.

'John Lynch is at the Newcastle stockade,' she said, clearly bemused. 'How can he possibly dictate anything that happens at Oldbury?'

'Perhaps he has escaped. Perhaps he has returned here, to seek me out.'

'Nonsense.'

'He has killed once. What's to stop him from killing again?'

'The stockade!' exclaimed my mother. 'He is *imprisoned*, George!'

Barton looked up at her, narrowing his eyes. But he said nothing.

'It was a bushranger,' my mother continued. 'Who else could have secured a firearm? Look at what happened to the poor Vincents. It was a failed robbery, George.'

'Lynch has many cronies among the bushranger gangs hereabouts,' Barton mumbled. 'Him and Smith and the others—they were all conspiring together.'

He lapsed into a morose silence, which made me acutely uncomfortable. My mother was also affected. She shifted nervously from foot to foot. Then she glanced around, and caught sight of me.

'Charlotte!' she exclaimed. 'What are you doing?'

'Spying,' said Barton, under his breath.

'It is *wrong* to eavesdrop on other people's conversations,' my mother continued, ignoring him. Before I could protest, she added: 'Go and look after your sisters, please. *Now.*'

'Are you all right, Mama?'

'Of course I am. Now go—and close the door behind you.'

Perhaps she was trying to protect me, as I had been trying to protect her. Or perhaps she was simply directing at me the anger and impatience that should more justifiably have been directed at George Barton. I have no way of knowing.

All I do know is that, in defending our staff, my mother made a fatal mistake. For instead of calming my stepfather's fears, she simply inflamed them.

From that day on, he began to regard *her* with suspicion.

Thirteen

Budgong was our cattle station on Budgong Creek, near the Shoalhaven River. It was a long way from Oldbury, across very rugged terrain; a week was hardly sufficient for the return journey to Budgong. Yet my mother was obliged to make that journey, owing to George Barton's reclusive behaviour. She had no choice.

She went there twice: once in 1838, and again a year later. On both occasions she took with her certain convicts in whose competence and goodwill she placed enormous trust. James Barnett was the best of them. She came to rely a good deal on James Barnett, who had been a farmhand of some description back in the Old Country. I remember him well—he was quite tall for an assigned man, with heavy eyebrows and a serious, taciturn demeanour. If he had any reservations about my mother or her husband, he never displayed them. He was always calm and usually quite courteous, even when being berated by George Barton.

Barton disliked him intensely, the more so as my mother came to depend on him. There were arguments about James Barnett. No doubt my stepfather was jealous; three years later, he would formally accuse my mother, in a sworn statement, of having 'improper and criminal intercourse' with the convict. I know this because I read Barton's statement after secretly unlocking my mother's desk. That was in about 1844; we were still in Sydney, and I was perhaps fifteen. At the time, I was very anxious to uncover the secret of Belanglo. So I surreptitiously consulted my mother's papers, wherein I discovered a copy of my stepfather's accusation against her.

It was the usual rubbish. I had heard him scream such things at her on more than one occasion in the past. James Barnett was the only co-respondent actually named, but Barton did mention 'convict men and various other persons'. He also mentioned 'the illegitimate children of Jews and convicts'; it was a moment before I realised that he was referring to *us*. (That is to say, myself and my siblings).

Other young maidens, more gently and carefully reared, may have been dreadfully affected by such vicious slander. Certain of my school-fellows may have been catapulted into hysterical fits when confronted by the sure and certain knowledge that they had been identified, to the Equity Court, as half-Jewish bastards bearing an inherited Stain. But I was made of sterner stuff. Though the blood rushed to my head, and my heart began to pound, I swallowed my passion and laid the monstrous document to one side. For it was not germane to my inquiry.

In the same statement, Barton described how he refused to admit my mother into his bed after she returned from her first trip with James Barnett. This was a lie. Though my stepfather did stop sleeping beside his wife in the latter part of 1838, it was not on account of jealousy or disgust. It was on account of his own madness. Having decided that my mother could not be trusted, he took to locking himself in the back bedroom at night, where neither she nor anyone else could reach him. No doubt he slept with his pistol cocked. Certainly he kept his candle burning, for the light could be seen through his window.

This happened soon after he had stolen my mother's keys.

You must understand the context of their disappearance, for it was all related to James Barnett, and the proposed trip to Budgong. My mother did not want to leave her children, you see. Not in the care of Eliza and George Barton, at any rate. She was concerned about our education—and our safety too. So she proposed that we hire a governess.

'It is not my preferred choice,' she said one day, with obvious bitterness, as we sat around the dinner table. 'You know my feelings on the subject. But I have been left with no alternative.'

George Barton chewed for a while, moving his jaws heavily. By this time he rarely joined the family for dinner, preferring to eat alone. When he *did* appear, it was to cast a deadly pall over the entire meal, during which no one dared speak. Even a belch could expose one to the most violent imprecations. My stepfather once threw a cake-stand at James because he sneezed when his mouth was full.

Barton took care to swallow the contents of his own mouth before replying, 'There will be no governess in *my* house.'

My mother laid down her fork. Seeing this, I shrank back—as did James and Emily and Louisa. We knew enough by then to recognise the first warning shot of an all-out battle.

'I cannot neglect the children's education,' my mother said, her nostrils flaring dangerously. 'If I *must* go on tours of inspection, then someone else has to teach them.'

To my surprise, George Barton did not respond by throwing his glass or slamming his fist on the table. Instead he began to drum his fingers on the cloth, very slowly, as he bared his teeth in a kind of ghastly rictus.

'What is it?' said my mother, a little wildly. Small spots of colour were appearing on her cheeks. 'What are you grinning at?'

'Do you think me a fool?'

'What?'

'I've dropped down what o'clock it is, never fear. *I* know yer bounce.'

'What on earth are you talking about?'

'You and Barnett both. And some bunter crony.'

'You are making no sense whatsoever.'

'Gammon. If you did it once, why not again? You've a taste for Dungaree-settlers, so why not for Norfolk Dumpling?'

While my stepfather's jargon was incomprehensible, his tone could not be misconstrued. My mother folded her lips, and picked up her fork again.

'There is no point discussing this now,' she said.

'There's no point discussing it *ever*,' Barton rasped. 'I'll not have a governess in my house, not while I'm master here. And I *am* the master. Don't you forget it. I am still the master.'

It is impossible for me to know exactly what was going on inside Barton's head. I am convinced, however, that he perceived a grave threat in my mother's association with James Barnett. Whether or not he regarded them as lovers, he certainly came to see them as co-conspirators. Perhaps he believed that James Barnett was planning to replace him. Either that, or he regarded Barnett as a tool of John Lynch, who from his dank cell in Newcastle had ordered the convict to seduce my mother, and thereby gain access to George Barton.

You may be asking, at this point, what John Lynch had to do with *us*. He had disappeared from Oldbury long before, and had been acquitted of murder in any case. Why was my stepfather so preoccupied with Lynch? In Barton's eyes, the absent convict seemed to constitute a growing and terrible threat, for no logical reason that I could identify. Was it a symptom of his burgeoning madness? Sometimes I thought so. At other times, I wondered if he knew more about Lynch than he had chosen to reveal.

I still wonder about this even now. It is not a question to which I am likely to find an answer. But in hindsight, I would say that long before the extent of Lynch's depravity became known to the world, he had assumed a formidably intimidating aspect at Oldbury—purely on account of my stepfather's unreasonable fear of the man. Thanks to George Barton, John Lynch never really left Oldbury. (Indeed, it was perhaps inevitable that he should have returned to the region shortly before he was banished from this world altogether.) With Barton perpetually fretting about Lynch, one could hardly fail to become conscious of a brooding sense of menace hovering above our farm, which dark cloud comprised all of its inhabitants' worst fears about Lynch and Barton both.

Years later, when Lynch's name had become a byword for wickedness, it seemed almost as if Barton's perverse imagination had *created* this fiend—as if, by insisting that Lynch constituted an unparalleled danger, my stepfather had poisoned reality itself with his violent delusions. For John Lynch was never a true threat to my family. What affected us far more profoundly was Barton's fear of him, which tainted the very air we breathed. Though John Lynch did, indeed, eventually expose himself as something less than human, his true nature was not revealed until long after he had become the embodiment of evil to those of us at Oldbury. My stepfather, you see, needed an enemy to blame for his irrational sense of dread. And whenever he began to fret about John Lynch—whenever the topic of Lynch was raised in his presence—my family had to brace itself for yet another bout of senseless and erratic behaviour.

It is quite possible, for instance, that my stepfather viewed the proposed governess as part of Lynch's plot against him. Nothing would have struck him as far-fetched, or too incredible. Not in *his* state of mind. Only a man with a very fragile grasp of actual events would have felt constrained to steal my mother's keys.

Let me give you an account of my mother's keys. My mother's keys were sacrosanct. They seemed almost a part of her, since she jingled and jangled wherever she went. She had mislaid them once or twice, but never for very long, since she normally carried them at her waist; at night she left them on a washstand beside her bed. Only in exceptional circumstances would she lay them aside, or surrender them to another's keeping.

Yet they had vanished. This, at least, was her account: she had left them on her washstand and they had disappeared. The whole house was in an uproar. Even the huts were searched, much to the staff's disgruntlement. '*She* fails to attend, and *we* are blamed for it,' I heard someone mutter, in the ensuing commotion. It must be confessed here that my mother was not wholeheartedly admired by her assigned staff. She lost her temper too readily, and was too quick to condemn. She had not my father's easy, confident way with inferiors.

Perhaps she had been too long in an inferior position herself.

After scouring her bedroom and questioning the servants—to no avail—my mother began to think more clearly. She began to wonder how the theft had been accomplished. If the keys had been filched from a table or a window sill, that was one thing. But how could they have been taken from her washstand, now that George Barton made a point of locking all the doors and securing all the shutters every night?

So she turned on him a measuring stare.

'I cannot account for it,' he said with a shrug. 'Unless you are mistaken. Are you *sure* that you left them on the washstand? Have you checked the cellar door?'

It is curious how reluctant my mother was to believe the worst. She actually hurried off to check the cellar door, when all of her children had long ago come to the correct conclusion. We were in the habit of watching our stepfather very closely, you see. We plotted his moods and observed his movements. We were therefore expecting the mottled complexion, nervous eyes and quick breathing of a man under siege. His most terrible fears had come true, after all; at night, while he was asleep, a mysterious stranger (perhaps

one employed by the iniquitous John Lynch) had invaded the house
and made off with its keys, for some nefarious purpose that might
very well have been connected to his eventual assassination.

Yet he seemed quite unmoved. While my mother rushed about
the place, snapping and scolding, he sat on the veranda in the sun,
nursing a newspaper and puffing at his pipe. I remember watching
him through the window of the breakfast room, with Emily and
James beside me.

'He did it, didn't he, Charlotte?' Emily whispered.

'Of course,' I replied.

'Where could he have put them?' asked James. 'In his pocket?'

'Maybe.'

'Oh, poor Mama!' Emily's voice cracked. 'You must tell her,
Charlotte!'

But I had been thinking. I had been considering what *I* would
have done, had I been George Barton. It was easier than you might
believe to put myself in his shoes. For his malice had a childish
cast to it; he was constrained by no sense of his own dignity, nor
by the reasoned opinions of others.

I thought to myself: 'George Barton has the only set of keys
now'. And I went to my mother with a question.

'Mama,' I said, 'why do you not ask Mr Barton for *his* keys? You
might have left your own in the tea-chest. Or in Papa's desk. Or
in your jewel-case. And he might have locked them inside.'

My mother straightened. She had been poking around the
campaign chest, where she often sat to do her accounts. But
the drawers in the campaign chest were never locked, because
someone had long ago lost the key.

We looked at each other for a moment, my mother and I.
Though I was only ten years old at the time, we looked at each
other like two grown women. Then something changed deep in
her eyes. She turned abruptly, with a swish of blue merino, and
marched from the sitting room.

'Stay here,' she said to me, over her shoulder.

It was a cruel command, in the circumstances. Yet I obeyed it. I stood in the doorway straining my ears, certain that my mother had gone to wrest her keys from George Barton's clutches. And I was right. For James and Emily were still in the breakfast room, and they saw everything.

They later informed me that my mother accosted her husband on the veranda, asking him for *his* keys. 'I have searched everywhere,' she said, 'and now I must check the tea-chest and the jewel-case.'

'Not if they are locked,' he replied, without lifting his gaze from the newspaper spread across his knees. 'If they are locked, then you cannot have left the keys inside. And if you did leave the keys inside, then how can they be locked?'

'Give me your keys,' my mother insisted, stretching out her hand to receive them.

At this, my stepfather languidly raised his eyes to her face.

'Didn't you hear what I said?' he rejoined.

'Give me the keys, and I shall set my mind at rest.'

But he simply shook out his newspaper, and turned a page. 'When I have finished my pipe,' he declared, 'I'll check the tea-chest myself. *And* the jewel-case. At present I am occupied.'

My mother dropped all pretence, then. She put her hands on her hips and said: 'Give me my keys.'

'I don't know where they are. You lost 'em.'

'You *took* them.'

Poor James and Emily ducked beneath the window sill at this point. They felt sure that George Barton would lash out at my mother in his usual fashion. Great was their astonishment when he simply drawled: 'Nonsense.'

'Give them to me *now!*'

'I would if I could,' Barton assured her, with as much kindly patience as he was capable of mustering. 'But I cannot.'

'Empty your pockets!'

Very slowly, Barton set aside his newspaper. Then he stretched his arms until his joints cracked, pushed himself out of his chair at a leisurely pace, and turned out his pockets one by one.

There was nothing in any of them, except Barton's own set of keys.

My mother was at a complete loss. What could she do, after all? The Oldbury estate was vast; it contained an infinite number of hiding places. And she was reluctant to break open every locked vessel to be found within its borders, for how could they ever be repaired afterwards? As for my stepfather, he refused to be goaded. Indeed, he was strangely tranquil for the next two days, seeming to take an enormous delight in playing the attentive and sympathetic husband. 'Hush, children,' he would say. 'Yer poor mother's nerves are sadly frayed since she lost her keys.' He would pat her on the shoulder, or offer her his footstool. It must have driven my mother half mad with fury.

Certainly her distress began to show. I had never before seen her so short-tempered, or so careless in her grooming. Her ruffled hair and hectic impatience must have stemmed from her almost ceaseless search for the hidden keys, which she sought out in the oddest places: in flour bags, behind wardrobes, under the kitchen dresser. Or perhaps she was simply shaken to her core by the loss of control to which her keyless state had condemned her.

Without her keys, she was deprived of all independence. Without her keys, she could not effectively command her staff, nor feed her children. Every visit to the cellar, every cup of tea, every attempt to leave the house of a morning depended entirely on George Barton's goodwill. Because he refused to hand over his own keys, my mother had to apply to him fifty times a day, or risk supplies being taken from unlocked storerooms.

You can imagine how much my stepfather enjoyed his position of absolute power. Naturally, he abused it with gusto. He would disappear for hours when ingredients were required, thereby spoiling jam tarts and suet puddings. Or he would refuse to get out of bed in the morning, so that my mother would be unable to leave the house.

But he had a fatal weakness. Knowing this, my mother did not fly into a grand passion. She had the sense to realise that, if she bided her time, he would finally drop his guard. And he did, of course. After a couple of days he began to drink, until he was so drunk that she was able to approach him without risk. Slumped at my father's desk, he did no more than grunt when she removed his keys from his person.

I heard this grunt because I was hovering in the vestibule, waiting for her to leave the study.

'You found them!' I exclaimed, when I saw her emerge.

'Shh!' She put a finger to her lips. 'No,' she said, 'but I *shall* find them.'

As she tripped away, I followed her, with many a backward glance. 'Mama,' I suggested, 'perhaps you should lock up the study, first?'

'Nonsense,' my mother rejoined. 'Why don't you take the others to watch the shearing, Charlotte? You can finish your essay tomorrow,' she said.

I obeyed her, but not out of cowardice. I knew that it would be a long time before my stepfather was clear-headed enough to realise how deceitfully he had been used. And I was correct in my assumption. Though he began to stir in the late afternoon, and was able to move about by early evening, it was not until we were all preparing to retire for the night that he reached in vain for his keys. Had he been in a less befuddled and liverish state, he might already have been alerted by my mother's demeanour. For she was quite transformed, despite the fact that she had been unable to find her own keys. Her step was light, and her eyes glittered. There was a dangerous brightness in her tone. When I heard it, I was filled with dread. My heart was positively in my mouth as she helped with my hair-rags and commenced the bedtime story. It seemed to me that she was preparing herself for a very particular fight, and that George Barton, when he finally confronted her, would be throwing gunpowder on hot coals.

Sure enough, when he kicked open the nursery door, she whirled to face him like a fighting dog trapped in a corner.

Fourteen

How wearying it is to revisit these old scenes! How unrelieved was the distress and uncertainty! My natural inclination is to turn away. I should like to summarise all the screams and blows and tears in just a few well-chosen words.

But I have begun now, and must continue to the end.

Picture George Barton, framed in the nursery doorway. Picture his heaving chest and red face. He was dressed in his nightshirt, and his feet were bare. But he looked no less dangerous, for all that.

'Where are they?' he demanded, through clenched teeth.

'Where are what?' said my mother.

'*You know damn well!*'

'Don't speak like that in front of the children.'

He lunged for her, and we screamed. Luckily, she was able to dodge him—for his sense of balance was still affected by the copious amounts of rum that he had been ladling down his throat.

Our screams drew Eliza, who could be heard running up the stairs.

'Give them to me,' he said hoarsely, 'or I'll *break yer neck!*'

'Break my neck,' Mama spat, 'and you'll never find them!'

This time, when he lunged, she was unfortunate. The rocking horse blocked her way, and he seized a handful of her thick, dark hair. My mother's cry was drowned out by the shrieks of her offspring.

'*Give me my keys!*' he bawled, shaking her. At which point I sprang from my bed, and grabbed my brother's home-made cricket bat. It was small but solid—and it made a satisfying *crack!* upon hitting Barton's knee.

He dropped my mother with a furious oath.

'You'll get your keys when I get mine!' she panted, snatching the cricket bat from my grip. Wielding it like a club, she edged towards the door while my stepfather hopped about clutching his injured knee. 'Out! All of you!' she cried. 'Eliza! Take them! *Now!*'

Everything happened so quickly that I can scarcely remember the exact sequence of events. But all at once we were on the landing—my mother, my siblings, Eliza and I—while Barton was yelling on the other side of the nursery door.

My mother had locked him in.

'*You bitch!*' he screeched, and the whole house shook as he slammed against the door-panels. '*Let me out, you bloody mott!*'

'Go downstairs,' my mother told me.

'Mama—'

'*Do what I say!*'

'Come,' said Eliza. 'Come, children.'

We went downstairs, but only as far as the bottom step. From there we could see very little, since the only light was coming from the back bedroom, where Barton must have left a candle burning. But we could hear my stepfather's thunderous roars, and feel the impact of his mighty blows. It was fortunate that my father had built the house so well; all the joinery was made of thick cedar, impervious to most forms of assault.

As Barton ranted and raved, I thought to myself: where shall we sleep tonight? In Mama's room? In the guest room? I had no wish to occupy Barton's chamber. Not while it still smelled of his pipe-smoke and hair-oil.

Finally he became tired. There was a lull in the noise. My mother immediately took advantage of it.

'Will you listen to me now?' she said.

'You'll pay for this,' was his hoarse reply.

'Will you listen to me, or do you wish to spend the whole night in the nursery?'

'If I do, there'll be no nursery left by morning. Do you hear?'

Louisa clutched my hand. No doubt she felt exactly as I did. Our toys were being held hostage up there. Our dolls. Our rocking horse. Our miniature tea set.

'Tell me where my keys are,' Mama continued, 'and I shall return yours.'

'You damned *whore!*'

'I shall not let you out until you agree to see reason.'

There was no immediate response. My mother waited. We waited. Then we heard the sound of a window opening—followed by a terrible *crash!*

It was not the sound of Barton's body striking the portico. Instead, he had decided to throw all of our most precious possessions onto the front lawn, beginning with the rocking horse.

Its pale and shattered remains were just visible in the twilight when we stumbled outside.

'*No!*' Louisa screamed. James burst into tears. Emily hid her face.

But my mother would not be persuaded. While her children stood weeping, she set her lips and refused to buckle. Though slates and books and wooden animals fell like snow, she simply folded her arms and waited. And waited. Gradually, the shower of beloved possessions ceased—perhaps because my stepfather could find no more toys to throw.

At last, after a very long silence, he called out.

'Hello?' he shouted. 'Are you there?'

'I am,' my mother replied.

'Free me, and I'll tell you where yer keys are.'

'Tell me where my keys are,' Mama rejoined, 'and *then* I shall free you.'

Another silence. Shorter, this time.

'They are in the dung-heap,' George Barton announced, from the nursery window.

My mother sighed. 'I don't believe you,' she said.

'It's the truth.'

'Do you truly think that I would look there myself?' (There was so much contempt in her tone!) 'I will have the men search for me. They will be at it all night. And where will that leave you? Exactly where you are now.'

'Very well.' Suddenly, my stepfather surrendered. Perhaps his head was troubling him. 'They are in the old ironbark near the stockyard,' he revealed. 'There's a hollow halfway up.'

My mother absorbed this information. Then she turned to Eliza.

'Go and look,' she said. 'Use a lamp, and take James Barnett with you.'

It was a victory, of sorts. But my siblings and I were not well positioned to appreciate the fact. As we followed my mother into the house, Louisa was praying, her eyes screwed tightly shut. James was shaking uncontrollably. Emily was sobbing as if her heart would break, because the rocking horse had been her favourite toy.

'Stay here,' said my mother, at the foot of the stairs. Then she proceeded to climb them.

'Mama!' I cried.

'One moment, Charlotte.'

She vanished from our sight; then the boards creaked above us. We heard her moving across the floor towards the back bedroom. After a few minutes, she retraced her steps.

'Mama!'

This time she leaned over the balustrade. 'What is it?' she said.

But I could not risk being overheard by George Barton. Instead I beckoned to her, anxiously.

'Very well,' she murmured, and within seconds she was at the top of the stairs, a dark silhouette.

Glinting in her hand was the barrel of Barton's pistol.

We were fortunate, in many ways. My stepfather had appeared at the nursery door in his nightgown. Clearly, he had been preparing for bed when it became apparent that his keys were missing; perhaps he had been at the point of locking himself in. So he had left his clothes and his boots and his pistol beside his bed, and had gone looking for my mother.

Now he was trapped in the nursery, and my mother was armed with his pistol.

'What is it?' she said, descending the stairs. She was trying to conceal the weapon beneath her shawl. 'Quickly, now.'

'You—you shouldn't let him out, Mama,' I whispered. 'He will be so angry.'

'He cannot stay in there, Charlotte. He must come out at some point.'

'But—'

'Have no fear.' My mother's eyes looked huge in her white face. Her neck seemed as taut and fleshless as a bow-string. 'He will not hurt you.'

Louisa began to wail. 'Mam-a-a!' she howled. My mother stooped to stroke her cheek with one hand, while nursing the gun with her other.

'Don't cry, my love,' she said. 'Charlotte, take them out to the kitchen.'

'No!'

'It will be better away from the house, dear.'

'Oh no.' I shook my head violently. 'No! We have to stay with you.'

'Charlotte—'

'We have to stay!' I was not about to yield, and my mother must have seen it. I suppose, in some ways, we were not dissimilar.

In *some* ways.

'Very well.' She straightened. 'Go and get into my bed. All of you—go with Charlotte. You may sleep in my bed tonight.'

We all stared at her, our jaws dropping.

'Go,' she instructed. 'You'll be safe in my bed.'

You can imagine how I felt about mounting the stairs again. With Mama directly behind me, however, I managed to reach the landing without stopping once. For a moment I stood mesmerised by the nursery door, which had assumed a truly awful aspect in my mind. Then my mother gave me a little push, and I was in her bedroom.

It had never been a very welcoming chamber. The dark oak hanging cupboard, the liver-coloured marble on the washstand, the massive carved pillars of the high, white bed in which my father had perished—all of these things affected me with a wary, uncomfortable feeling at the best of times. Now, in the evening dimness, they seemed especially formidable.

Louisa must have been filled with a sense of unease similar to mine, for she clutched at my mother's skirts.

'Don't go, Mama!' she squeaked.

'I shall be directly outside,' she said. '*Directly outside*, Louisa.'

'Please don't close the door, Mama,' I begged, in a trembling voice. Whereupon my mother agreed to leave the bedroom door open.

'But you must get under the covers,' she insisted. 'At *once*, Louisa. I don't want you catching a cold.'

So we climbed into her bed, and sat there shaking. Barton had been ominously silent for a good while. My mother began to pace up and down, sometimes pausing to examine the pistol, sometimes listening at the nursery door. I was able to see this because her bed was positioned directly opposite the entrance to her bedroom, from which there was a very good view of the nursery landing.

I do not know how long we waited. Louisa was actually beginning to fall asleep when at last we heard the sound of heavy footsteps from the floor below.

'Mam?' said a voice.

It belonged to James Barnett.

My mother darted back towards the stairs, so that I could no longer see her. There was a long, low, murmured exchange somewhere nearby, followed by more heavy footsteps. My mother appeared again just as I was preparing to get out of bed and set off in pursuit. Behind her hovered James Barnett, carrying a colza lamp.

Mama approached the nursery door, jingling. I noticed that her keys were in her hand. I also saw that her other hand was wrapped around the butt of Barton's pistol.

'Mr Barton!' she said loudly. 'Do you hear me, sir?'

No reply.

'My keys have been returned to me, Mr Barton,' she continued. 'You have kept your word, and I shall keep mine. I shall unlock the door now. But before you make any rash decisions, be aware that I am armed. Mr Barnett is here, and he has shown me how to load and prime your pistol.'

Still no reply.

'Mr Barton?' My mother frowned. 'Do you understand me? I am willing to defend myself, though it is my earnest desire that we come to a mutual agreement concerning the welfare of this—hello?'

Some noise from within must have alarmed her, for she stepped back suddenly, raising her weapon. Then she jerked her head at James Barnett.

'Unlock it,' she ordered. 'Quickly.'

On reflection, I can only assume that my mother, upon taking possession of her own keys, must have surrendered her husband's set to James Barnett. At any rate, he advanced to obey her. Before the door-knob had even been turned, however, there was a terrible scream from outside, accompanied by a sickening thud.

Bang! With one sharp push, James Barnett flung back the nursery door. He and my mother stood for a moment, transfixed. Then my mother whirled, and ran for the stairs.

'Ahh! Ahh!' The distant scream had become a high-pitched groan, less audible but equally disturbing. I could hear other voices, too. James Barnett hesitated a moment, before following my mother.

He left the nursery door standing open behind him.

'What happened?' said Emily, in a dazed fashion. 'Charlotte?'

'He has fallen from the window,' I replied, with absolute conviction, pushing back the covers and sliding to the floor.

'Mr Barton?'

'Who else?'

'Where are you going?' James demanded shrilly, but I was already out of the room. In the nursery I paused only for an instant to survey the damage, which was considerable. My mother's watercolours had been torn or knocked from the wall, and some of the bed-curtains had felt the full force of Barton's temper. Barton, however, was gone.

I saw why, when I reached the window. It had been shoved open to its fullest extent. My stepfather's plan, evidently, had been to drop onto the portico—which was directly beneath the window-ledge—and from there slide down one of the two wooden pillars holding up the little roof over the front door. There had been nothing unreasonable about this plan. The drop to the portico was no more than a couple of feet in length, and the slide down the pillar, though tricky, could have been accomplished quite easily by someone tall and nimble.

But it was dark, and my stepfather's sense of balance was impaired. Though he had reached the portico roof without mishap, he had somehow lost his grip while swinging himself over its edge—and had landed on top of a rose bush.

I could hear him groaning. Moreover, by scrambling onto the sill, I was able to look down and see him. He was rolling about in the light of James Barnett's lamp, swearing and clutching his ankle.

The fall had not been long enough to kill him. Nevertheless, he must have fallen on one foot, which was either broken or badly sprained. The rose bush, too, had inflicted a good many minor injuries. I could see bloody scratches even from my vantage point.

Only a complete madman, I decided, would have attempted such a climb in bare feet and a nightshirt.

'What were you *doing?*' my mother exclaimed, as if she had read my thoughts. She stood directly beneath me, the pistol still in her hand. 'Eliza, take these keys. Go to my medicine chest. Bring back the little blue bottle of laudanum powder, do you hear?'

I realised, then, that there were servants gathered about on the lawn, many of them half-dressed. Their pale shirts glimmered in the shadows.

'What happened?' James was pushing me from behind, trying to squeeze onto the sill. 'Is he dead?'

'No. I don't think so. Ouch! Stop *shoving!*'

Below me, my mother surrendered her weapon to James Barnett. It startled me to see this, but I suppose that she must have weighed her options; better to arm a convict, after all, than to risk having her husband snatch the pistol from her when she approached him.

For she *did* approach him. Her courage was incredible. Though her pale, outstretched hand shook so violently that its tremor was clearly visible from the nursery window, she nonetheless went over to her husband and crouched beside his cowering form.

'What have you done?' she said. 'George? Where does it hurt?'

He tried to crawl away. The immediate agony must have abated a little—from which circumstance it would have been obvious to my mother that no bones were broken. Certainly, Barton was still able to move his injured leg. He even began to pull himself up, using the stone wall of the house. But his nightclothes had been shredded by the rose bush, and the pain in his ankle was still disabling. He cried out when he attempted to put any weight on his right foot.

'Oh, George . . .' My mother also rose, and reached for him. Whereupon he flung out an arm to protect himself.

'No!' he croaked. He seemed terrified. 'Don't touch me!'

My mother hesitated. She looked towards James Barnett, as if seeking an explanation.

'If you shoot me here, they'll all see! All of them!' Barton cried, making a sweeping gesture that encompassed the entire front lawn and every one of its occupants.

My mother stepped back, as if struck by a blow. There was a brief pause. Then she addressed James Barnett.

'Take the pistol inside,' she ordered. 'Leave the lamp.'

'Aye, Mam.'

'Ahh. Ahh.' My stepfather was almost crying with pain as he tried to limp away from her. He kept falling to his knees. With every clumsy step that he took, the shadowy arc of watching servants retreated slightly.

Not one of them made a move to assist him.

'George? Do you hear? We want to help you, not hurt you. Look—here is Eliza, with some laudanum. It will ease the pain. George?'

I shall never forget that scene. I viewed it as God must have viewed it, from high above, and perhaps for that reason it remains engraved on my memory. At the centre of it all was the colza lamp, shedding a golden ring of light. To one side of the lamp, my mother stood with both hands spread, her hair tumbling across her shoulders. Not far from her, a bleeding, white-clad figure was crawling across the grass, between the broken remains of the rocking horse. And on the very edge of the ring of light, silent figures remained as motionless as the black shapes of the eucalypts that reared up behind them.

I remember every detail. I also remember the way I felt, looking down at George Barton. Do you know, I nursed not a single shred of pity in my heart?

If he had been within my reach, I probably would have spat on him.

Fifteen

In *Tom Hellicar's Children*, there is a certain Mrs Heland who spends most of her day sitting in an arm-chair under a greasy chintz, with her feet encased in slippers run down at one side. Fancying herself an invalid, she doses herself at eleven o'clock every morning with a glass of porter, and at night with a glass of hot gin.

When first I read this description, I recognised it as an almost perfect portrait of my stepfather after his accident. My stepfather was very much subdued by the fall. Though his injury was not serious, it required several drops of laudanum for three days running, and the laudanum worked on him in two ways. At first, it made him sleepy. Then, after it was withdrawn, he became costive. Being now well acquainted with opium in its various guises, I must say that its effects on the bowels should always be taken into account. At the time, however, these symptoms were less well known. There was some concern that damage might have been inflicted on my stepfather's internal organs. Certainly he was in a great deal of pain; I even wonder, now, if the problem was partly a nervous one, for I have known nervous tension to aggravate the bowels and stomach to an enormous degree in some people.

At any rate, George Barton became ill. My mother fed him soda water, beef tea and arrowroot, which he immediately brought up. She then tried croton oil, and would have given him calomel if he had accepted it. But by this time his physical discomfort was affecting his mind. He refused to be treated by my mother. I heard him crying out in the back bedroom, accusing her of trying to poison him.

In the circumstances, I would have shut the door on his agony and gone about my business.

My mother, however, had already applied to the Throsbys for help. You will recall my mentioning Mr Charles Throsby's sister, Mary, who had disapproved of my parents' romance aboard the *Cumberland*. She had married Dr Patrick Hill, the Superintendent of Liverpool Hospital, and the couple were visiting Throsby Park at the time of Barton's illness. My mother, in desperation, sought Dr Hill's advice—for she had very little faith in the local doctors. Dr Allen, who treated the prisoners at Berrima Gaol, was a renowned drunkard, and Dr Montgomery was an emancipated convict who had no formal medical training at all, though he was said to be a gifted herbalist.

Perhaps, too, my mother preferred that her domestic troubles not be aired in front of someone with a local practice.

In any event, Dr Hill rode straight out to Oldbury, where he proceeded to bleed, dose and poultice my stepfather into better health. It was his opinion that Barton's complaint proceeded from a deranged stomach and an enlarged colon, which had almost the same effect as a stricture. Dr Hill warned my mother against the use of calomel pills, and advised unlimited doses of castor oil, with rhubarb and magnesium by way of a change.

He was a man of enormous authority, very tall and businesslike. Even my stepfather obeyed him without protest. Only Dr Hill could have persuaded my stepfather to endure a colocynth purgative. Indeed, Dr Hill inspired such trust that he was able to dispel some of George Barton's fears concerning my mother's intentions. I do not know exactly what passed between the two men. But I did overhear part of Dr Hill's advice to my mother before he left Oldbury.

'You must not blame yourself,' he remarked. 'I see no evidence that your husband ingested anything harmful. If he had, there would have far more vomiting, and perhaps a fever. I have told him this, and I believe that I may have convinced him. Even so, he remains in a peculiarly agitated state, Mrs Barton.'

'Yes,' my mother murmured.

'I cannot pretend that I am ignorant of his predilection for strong drink,' Dr Hill continued, very dryly. 'I have told him that such intemperance will invariably result in poor health—and in grossly impaired mental faculties. Your husband is displaying early symptoms of melancholia, Mrs Barton, and will only grow more unhinged if he continues to indulge himself.'

My mother remained silent. What, after all, was there to say? She had married George Barton for better or worse; she had made her bed, and should expect to lie in it. The Reverend Vincent must have advised as much when she appealed to him for counsel.

This appeal was made within days of Barton's accident. While my stepfather lay sleeping in his room, heavily dosed with laudanum, my mother took it upon herself to visit the parsonage at Sutton Forest. She must have been greatly shaken by the events leading up to Barton's 'accident', or she would not have exposed herself to such a humbling experience. My mother, in effect, was forced to swallow her pride. For not one of our neighbours had supported her decision to wed, and the Reverend Vincent had been reluctant to perform the ceremony. As a result, she had held herself aloof for two long years.

But when at last she was driven to seek help, she was sadly disappointed. I know this, despite the fact that she never discussed with me the outcome (or even the purpose) of her consultation with John Vincent. I know it because she brought her children with her to the parsonage, fearful of what might happen if she left us at home. And though we were not invited into the Reverend's study, I saw my mother's face when she emerged from it. I also witnessed the curt manner in which she took her leave.

Looking back, I wonder if she asked him for his views on Divorce. Though the subject was not as widely discussed then as it is now, it was certainly not unheard of—even in the colonies. For Mary Wollstonecraft Godwin, author of *A Vindication of the Rights of Women*, was the aunt of Mr Alexander Berry's particular friend Edward Wollstonecraft. And Edward Wollstonecraft lived in Sydney with his sister Elizabeth.

Be that as it may, I have no reason to believe that our Reverend was in any way sympathetic to the cause of women seeking release from demented husbands. I doubt that *anyone* was, among our neighbours. There may even have been some secret delight that my mother, whose forthright and froward manner had not met with universal acceptance, should have been so suitably punished for her improper conduct. The incident at Belanglo had not been forgotten, you see. And when it became apparent that my mother was still riding out to visit her stations, unaccompanied save for two or three *male convicts* . . . well, you can imagine the talk.

Yes, it is true; my mother rode out to Budgong. She was able to do this because of my stepfather's weakened state. It gave her the upper hand. For although his ankle had healed quickly, and Dr Hill had cured his costive attack, he spent some weeks recovering from both afflictions, hunched in a chair under a greasy chintz, alternatively dozing and reading newspapers. (While his energies might have been very much depleted in all other facets of life, his interest in the newspapers remained keen. Even at the time, I wondered if he was watching for news of John Lynch's release from the Newcastle stockade.)

Taking advantage of his slow recovery, my mother went and hired a governess. Her name was Miss Rudd. Governesses of high calibre were not widely available in New South Wales then. The Throsbys, on losing Miss McRae in 1840, paid for the passage of her replacement, whom they hired in England. My mother had not the resources for *that*. So she was obliged to advertise in Sydney, and to take what she could get. The result was Miss Rudd.

Miss Rudd was not young. She was between thirty and forty, and had come to New South Wales with the intention of establishing her own Ladies' Academy. Alas; there was already an overabundance of such private institutions in town. They would open and shut like so many daisies, each struggling to attract the small number of respectable girls then living in New South Wales. Faced with such heavy competition, only the strongest survived—and Miss Rudd was not strong. Perhaps her years of hard work as a governess had undermined an already fragile constitution.

She was tall and thin, with a soft little voice and a refined manner. Though not particularly handsome, she had an inoffensive, colourless sort of face, set off by a small but beautifully selected wardrobe. Miss Rudd took great care of her clothes, which were all of the best quality. She was a needlewoman of superb skill. She also spoke French, and could play, and draw, and manage a set of household accounts.

All this was mentioned in her application, which happened to be the only acceptable one that my mother received. *Not* mentioned, however, were Miss Rudd's various peculiarities. She had a delicate appetite, and a nervous disposition. Her demeanour was immensely retiring and timid. Yet for all that, I would not have called her humble. It only gradually became apparent that she nursed an unassailable self-regard, predicated on the fact of her own refinement. She viewed herself as a genuine *lady*. Few others, in her opinion, could even begin to appreciate the extent of her good breeding.

Certainly there were few who could emulate it. Miss Rudd believed that true refinement was the loftiest goal of a good education.

In this, as in many other things, she and my mother were at odds.

My mother had a low opinion of Ladies' Academies. She particularly disliked those in which the acquisition of 'accomplishments' overrode all other considerations. In her view, too many governesses shared the same fault; I must admit that I laughed when I first read *Myra*, for it could have been my mother speaking through my sister's pen: '*By the aid of the governess . . . she had learnt to strum horribly on the piano and do wool work, and crochet, and to dance, and know the fashions, and a great many other wonderful things, which made her, at least in some eyes, quite a lady.*'

I would not accuse Miss Rudd of being *this* deficient, but it is true that she saw no great advantage in studying botany, geography or astronomy. Instead, she placed enormous emphasis on posture—the placement of the arms, the carriage of the head—and on 'correct pronunciation', for she was horrified by colonial vowels. To her way of thinking, exercise should always be taken in a sedate manner, and occupations should reflect a delicacy of mind.

What she made of my mother's habits, I cannot imagine. My mother often had to raise her voice. Her walks were not dignified perambulations along well-worn avenues but scrambles across rocky outcrops and plunges into dense, pristine tangles of brush. The rides that she took were energetic. Her constant companions were coarse, low-born men, whose turns of phrase she occasionally echoed. And she did not put a great deal of thought or effort into her mode of dress. Owing to the demands of her busy life, which took her into piggeries and stockyards, she favoured old, loose clothes, and sometimes forgot to change from morning to afternoon gowns.

All this was very alarming to Miss Rudd. Even in Sydney, she had not met with such behaviour. And my mother did not improve matters by grilling the poor woman about her teaching methods, and the content of her lessons. I have no doubt that this was generally done in private, but its effects could sometimes be witnessed at the dining table.

'So you are got to the Spanish Armada?' my mother might say. 'Excellent. And can you tell me where Spain is to be found, James?'

'It is to be found in Europe, Mama.'

'Yes, but *where* in Europe?'

'Uh . . .' A wild plunge. 'In France, Mama?'

'I think it is time to consult our Atlas, do not you, Miss Rudd?'

Whereupon Miss Rudd would smile thinly, and pick at her coddled egg, while my mother explained that if James ever joined the Royal Navy (as was his stated intention, back then) he would have to learn exactly where Spain was, lest he run his ship aground on it.

Poor Miss Rudd. Even at the time, I thought her a feeble specimen. And I obeyed her only when I chose to, setting a very bad example to my brother and sisters. It annoyed me, you see, that Miss Rudd should denigrate so many of the skills that I had mastered in my years on a working farm. 'Oh, my dear,' she would say, when informed that a good dairy cow can be identified by prominent milk veins on its udder, 'this is hardly a suitable topic for young ladies wishing to shine in the drawing rooms of Sydney.'

In my defence, I should add that I never teased Miss Rudd, nor intruded upon her privacy, nor reported any of her little errors to Mama. I positively *admired* her beautiful embroidery, which I strove (in vain) to imitate. And I did my best to protect her from George Barton.

Not that Barton perceived Miss Rudd as dangerous. No one could, upon observing her in person; she was such a very diffident soul. When she first arrived, he was still an invalid, confined to a couple of rooms and disinclined to communicate with anyone—let alone the governess whose appointment he had opposed so vehemently. No doubt he viewed her presence as a direct challenge to his authority, and was black-humoured in consequence, scowling and brooding for days. Then he began to gain strength. And though he could not yet, in his weakness, directly attack my mother, he *could* discomfort Miss Rudd, using methods that had long ago ceased to alarm Mama.

He began by offending Miss Rudd's overwrought sensibilities. Having dined in his room for some weeks, he suddenly started to appear at the table, where he would discourse on manure, or his recent costiveness, or the castration of male pigs. When my mother was present, she was usually able to turn the conversation. But thanks to her countless duties, she was not always present for an entire meal. And when that occurred, my stepfather was given free rein to torment Miss Rudd with all kinds of distasteful remarks. His appearance also seemed designed to offend her, for he dressed himself without regard for the time of day or the dictates of common decency. He would shuffle about with the skirts of his dressing-gown flapping around his white, hairy legs, or his shirt hanging open to expose a wide expanse of wiry pelt across his chest.

If poor Miss Rudd ever protested about this to my mother, she may have been received with impatience. My mother had endured much worse from George Barton. She may have seen his behaviour towards Miss Rudd as generally harmless, and advised her governess to ignore him. I do not know. All I know is that my mother finally felt secure enough to make her long-anticipated trip to Budgong.

She would be gone for a week, she told us. In her absence, we (her children) were to mind Miss Rudd, while George Barton was to manage any emergencies that might arise on the farm. Privately, she may have had a quiet word with Bridget or Robert. She may have instructed one of them to communicate with Benjamin Carter—Captain Nicholson's overseer—in the event of a crisis. Certainly she said something of the sort to *me*. 'Remember that

Mr Carter is within easy reach,' she advised. 'I would not have him troubled for any minor concern, because he is a busy man with many dependants. But he is also a reliable, upright farmer, who will know exactly what must be done.'

Having delivered her instructions, my mother left. I shall pass over the misery attendant upon her departure; you may imagine how reluctant I was to see her go. She promised that she would return in about a week, and that she would bring back an interesting array of specimens for us. Then she rode off into the sunrise, with many a lingering backward glance. Perhaps she was worried that Miss Rudd would be unequal to the task set her.

It was a justifiable concern.

Poor Miss Rudd! She had been given custody of my mother's keys, and the responsibility weighed far too heavily. I doubt not that she dreamed about those keys. They figured always in her consciousness, even when she was taking a lesson; her hand would wander down to them repeatedly, as if she were afraid that they might be lost. Her manner became even more nervous, and her dealings with the servants even more fraught with difficulty. For the servants, though they did not always like my mother, afforded her some deference—if only because she had a temper. Miss Rudd they simply despised. This was evident to me in the way they drawled when addressing her, and in the way that Bridget would need yet another pinch of saffron or cup of rice from the storeroom at least ten times a day.

Eliza was the only servant who offered Miss Rudd even a modicum of respect. It was partly, I think, because Eliza was in a position to appreciate our governess's skill with a needle, and partly because she admired Miss Rudd's clothes, and air of gentility. To Eliza, Miss Rudd was a *true* lady. I am sure that our nurse envisioned English drawing rooms as the natural setting for innumerable young women whose occupations were restricted to reading tracts, playing the piano, embroidering antimacassars, and painting screens. In such an environment, Miss Rudd would have been perfectly at home.

'There now,' Eliza would say with satisfaction, on observing the state of Miss Rudd's room, 'you'd hardly know that the bed had been slept in.'

I wish I could record that my siblings and I offered Miss Rudd the same degree of reverence, but we did not. Neither did George Barton. Watching my mother ride off with James Barnett seemed to sour his mood. Whereas it *had* been sullen and lethargic, only lightly irrigated by drink, it swiftly turned more dark and troublous. The morning porter and bedtime gin became the start and finish of a daily journey through our cellar, which yielded up dram after dram of rum, glass after glass of wine. When not sousing himself in his room, my stepfather would emerge for brief tours of inspection which invariably finished in a torrent of abuse, since the work at that time was not being done with any degree of thoroughness. How could it have been otherwise? Our servants were being left practically to their own devices, and many of them had little knowledge of husbandry.

Though the decline of Oldbury had already begun, it first became obvious towards the end of 1838.

I remember how swiftly the empty bottles accumulated during this memorable week. Louisa described the scene well enough in *Debatable Ground*: the bottles *'ranged in the fire-places, beneath the side tables, in every accessible spot, labelled hollands, cognac, stout and trebble X'.* I believe that they might have been left about in such a shameless manner to discompose Miss Rudd, who was certainly very shocked to see them. She was no less shocked by George Barton's language when he berated the servants. More than once, I witnessed tears welling in her eyes at the sound of his raised voice, because he was always very free with his 'lags' and 'buggers' and 'croppies'. Such crude epithets seemed to cause Miss Rudd an almost physical pain.

I was more accustomed to them, but still I did not like what I heard. Moreover, I was beginning to recognise that Miss Rudd was the object of my stepfather's concentrated ire. He would take exception to the meals she ordered. If she asked that a fire be lit, he would immediately countermand the request. Wherever she sat, he would soon begin to smoke nearby. Sometimes he would invade our lessons, causing all of us to lose concentration and fumble at our tasks. Then he would take pleasure in accusing Miss Rudd of failing to earn her keep. 'Not that there's a deal of wit to sharpen, in this brood,' he once remarked. 'For they're all of 'em fools, and the victims of mismanagement.'

As the week slowly passed, he devised ever more vicious torments for Miss Rudd. Her workbox disappeared; he blamed the 'damnable thieves in our employ'. He caused her to be moved from one bedroom to another, for no other reason than to inflict upon her a great deal of fuss and trouble. Of an evening, he would tell her to read aloud, not sermons or essays or histories, but the newspaper accounts of murder trials. While so engaged, she would be forced to endure some kind of childish harassment; he might knock out a ceaseless tattoo on her chair leg with his boot, for instance, or blow clouds of smoke into her face. It was as if he wanted to see how far he could push her. Would she, or would she not, lash out?

As it happened, she did not. Once or twice she asked him, in a trembling voice, to please desist. (God knows what it must have cost her.) Whereupon he simply smiled and did something else repellent, such as spitting or breaking wind. Under treatment such as this, Miss Rudd soon began to crumble. She had no defences whatsoever. I wonder if she was *physically capable* of raising her voice; certainly she could no more have challenged him than she could have cut off his head. I quickly noticed the change in her. She kept more to her own room. Her conversation became less coherent, as if her thoughts were always somewhere else. Even her grooming suffered. She would lose her gloves, or forget to fasten her buttons.

I pitied her, naturally. Nevertheless, I was also shamefully relieved. For with Miss Rudd about the place, drawing fire, I was able to dodge my stepfather's evil humours more effectively.

I could not shun his attention for long, however. Because as the seventh day drew to a close, I began to grow uneasy. And at the end of the eighth day, with my mother still absent, I asked myself a truly terrible question.

Would she ever return at all?

Sixteen

O n the morning of the ninth day of my mother's absence, I resolved that Miss Rudd should be informed of the facts.

My fears had kept me awake for most of the previous night. I had passed many black hours reflecting on Thomas Smith, and John Lynch, and the curious sense of persecution that Lynch seemed to arouse in my stepfather. Was this a symptom of the diseased state of Barton's mind? Was it fear of reprisal, for having agreed to testify against Lynch at all? Or was it the sign of a guilty conscience? Had Barton killed Thomas Smith himself, because Smith was involved in the flogging—or because he had jeered at Barton on account of it? Had Barton falsely accused Lynch, who might have spotted him near the corpse, before Lynch could effectively accuse *him*? Alternatively, had Barton *hired* Lynch to kill Smith, and reneged on their agreement? Was that why Barton seemed to live in perpetual alarm at the prospect of Lynch's re-appearance? Was that why he had been drunk in court?

I was only ten years old, but such thoughts were not new to me. They had crossed my mind more than once in the past, owing to George Barton's influence and my own familiarity with certain common colonial events: fraud, murder, assault, pillage, highway robbery—even the wholesale slaughter of settlers by bloodthirsty natives. The reasoned logic of a mature intellect was as yet beyond my powers; I nursed only a mass of confused suspicions and desperate fears. All the same, they were compelling. They were *convincing*. And though I knew nothing of John Lynch, I did know a great deal about my stepfather. I could easily imagine George Barton killing a man.

If he had killed Thomas Smith, what was to stop him from killing my mother?

Young though I was, I realised that he could not have committed such an act directly, with his own hand. But I was frantically worried that he might have engineered it somehow. He might have poisoned my mother's supply of flour. He might have sent men ahead of my mother, to arrange an ambush. Or perhaps the trap had been sprung when she was on her way *back* from Budgong.

Alternatively, she might have suffered a stroke of misfortune unrelated to her husband. She might have met with an accident or a gang of bushrangers. Even the notion that John Lynch had escaped and returned to our neighbourhood did not seem utterly irrational to me; my stepfather had discussed the possibility so often that I naturally wondered if, by a dreadful coincidence, Lynch's path might have crossed my mother's.

You will observe that my fears were all predicated upon the belief that some violent fate had overtaken her. It never once occurred to me that she might have fallen ill. Yet this was Miss Rudd's immediate suggestion upon being approached. By way of preamble, I said to our governess: 'Mama should be back by now.' Whereupon Miss Rudd replied: 'She might have been taken ill, Charlotte. She might have found her way impeded. You must not begin to worry yet.'

'We should send someone. We should send a party out to find her.'

Miss Rudd's expression changed. She shifted uneasily. 'Well—that is hardly in my province,' she replied, with an unconvincing little smile. 'You must consult Mr Barton on that subject.'

'*He* will not do it.' I could scarcely believe that she needed to be informed of such an obvious fact. 'He wouldn't even *want* her found.'

'Now, Charlotte—'

'He would like to see her dead. He said so. I heard him.'

'Oh, but he—he was not himself, I daresay.' This was Miss Rudd's way of referring to my stepfather's drunkenness. 'He did not really *mean* it, I am quite sure.'

'Yes, he did.' I proceeded to tell Miss Rudd about Thomas Smith's murder, and George Barton's drunken appearance in court, and John Lynch's subsequent acquittal. I was trying to explain that Smith's murder might not have been committed by John Lynch, in which case Barton himself was an obvious suspect. Miss Rudd, however, preferred not to be enlightened.

'My dear, these are not fit subjects for a gently reared young lady,' she interrupted. 'Rather than indulge in such morbid reflections, you should direct your thoughts towards our Heavenly Father, and pray for your mother's safe return.'

'But—'

'We shall say a little prayer together, shall we? I always find prayer such a comfort, at times like this.'

It became apparent to me, then, that Miss Rudd was a broken reed. So I approached Robert the dairyman. I asked him to arrange a search party, comprising a handful of reliable men who could be trusted to return. His response was a look of complete incredulity.

'Ye'll have to ask the Master about *that*, Miss,' he said. And when I appealed to some of the other servants, they shared Robert's opinion.

I could not condemn them for it. Most of them were as afraid of George Barton as I was. However, the life of my mother was at stake—or so I thought. My fear for her outweighed my fear of him.

I went to his bedroom and knocked on the door.

'*Get out of't!*' was his response.

I knocked again. 'Mr Barton?' I said—and flinched away as something solid (a boot, perhaps?) hit the panel on the other side.

'*Go away!*'

'Mr Barton, you must send out men!' I spoke very loudly, conscious that Louisa and Emily were listening at the foot of the stairs. 'My mother should be back by now!'

There was no reply.

'Mr Barton?'

Still he said nothing. But it was an ominous silence. Emily began to beckon to me, in a frantic fashion. 'Come away!' she whispered. 'Stop it, Charlotte, leave him alone!'

My instinct told me that to press any farther would only elicit a storm of indignation. Yet what else could I do? Abandon my mother to whatever perils awaited her? 'Mr Barton,' I repeated, whereat the door was flung open.

There he stood, in his nightshirt. I caught a glimpse of Emily and Louisa ducking out of sight to my left as he thrust his mottled, unshaven, contorted countenance into mine.

'*Are you bloody deaf?*' he bawled. '*I told you to get out of't!*'

'But my mother—'

'*Yer whore of a mother can rot in hell!*'

SLAM! I was lucky. Rather than box my ears or throw me downstairs, my stepfather chose merely to shut his door in my face—nearly bruising my nose in the process. Perhaps he was feeling unequal to any kind of physical exertion.

'I told you,' Emily muttered, when I joined her in the vestibule. 'He will never allow it.'

'Perhaps we should go and look for Mama ourselves,' Louisa suggested. She had a way of saying the most absurd things with the most tranquil self-assurance.

'Oh, don't be ridiculous, Louisa!' Emily snapped. I said nothing. Having already resolved to communicate with Mr Benjamin Carter, I did not want anyone to know what my intentions were. If my sisters were inclined to believe that I approved of Louisa's proposal, well and good. For then, upon being questioned, they might allude to my sympathetic attitude. And the search party would set off in the wrong direction—towards Budgong, instead of Newbury.

I had no doubt that a party *would* be organised. Though Miss Rudd was reluctant to institute a search for my mother, she could not, in good conscience, allow one of her charges to wander off into the bush alone. Even if George Barton opposed her, she would undoubtedly make some effort. She might even send to Newbury or Sutton Forest for help. That would be the ideal solution. If my stepfather would not cooperate, and Miss Rudd went to Newbury herself, then it would hardly matter whether I completed my journey or not. For Mr Carter would learn of my mother's extended absence through Miss Rudd, and would act accordingly.

On the other hand, Barton *might* cooperate. A search party might be organised. In which case I would have to avoid the dogs. Though not afraid of the convicts, I was concerned about the dogs. We had some very good tracking dogs at Oldbury. And I feared that they might trail humans as well as they trailed cattle.

Still, I had to try.

Leaving the house was no great challenge. Every morning Miss Rudd would take a lesson in the sitting room. All I had to do was ask permission to leave, feigning stomach cramps; someone suffering from diarrhoea could not be expected to return from the pot very quickly. Mr Barton was still upstairs. Few of the servants were about, and those I passed were intent on their various allotted duties. Only the convict huts presented a problem. I did not want to be seen from the huts, since it would then be known that I was heading for Gingenbullen.

I therefore went out of my way a little, skirting the rear meadow and entering the forest of stringybark that lay to the north-west of the house, before swerving east again.

You must understand that I was avoiding the roads. On the roads I would have been picked up in no time. I reasoned that by cutting through the bush, around and over Gingenbullen, I would have a better chance of reaching Newbury unhindered. In those days, there was a great deal of uncleared land on both the Oldbury and Newbury estates—and the heights were more heavily wooded than the flatter country to the south of Gingenbullen. Furthermore, I knew Gingenbullen quite well. My family had explored it many a time on long, rambling rides, which had also taken us into the more rugged terrain towards Berrima. So I was familiar with the endless stretches of woolly gum, the hidden groves of tree fern and sassafras, the lavish yields of topaz that could be gathered from White's Creek and the Medway Rivulet. I had collected mimosa blossom and the curious banksia pods. I had sheltered from the rain in gibber-gunyahs, and heard cockatoos quarrelling in the high branches of a red cedar.

Consequently, I was not much afraid to penetrate the woods on my own. After all, it was broad daylight, and perfectly dry, with a cloudless sky that gave me all the navigational assistance I needed. On such a day, the menace of John Lynch (who might have escaped from Newcastle, and come back to wreak his revenge on George Barton) seemed far less palpable than it did in the evenings, when mist concealed the rocky heights of Gingenbullen. I thought it unlikely that John Lynch would jump out at me. At night, in bed, my siblings and I might frighten each other with the threat of John Lynch. We might discuss the possibility that a troll-like Lynch was living in a wombat hole near the native burial mounds, or hiding in our wine cellar. During the day, however, this prospect felt altogether less likely.

My only real worry was the threat of snakes. We supported a rich crop of snakes at Oldbury. My mother had been long ago informed by a native of the area that snakes were best avoided by making a great deal of noise. But it had occurred to me that if I *was* noisy, I would be heard by anyone within earshot. So I tried to tread softly, though I was also very careful.

As a result, I made rather slow progress.

My path did not take me directly over the spine of Gingenbullen. Instead I struggled along its northern flank for a while. It being early December, the day was already warm, with not a breath of wind. Dry grass crunched beneath my feet. Lizards skittered out of my way. As the hillside grew steeper and stonier—as its basalt ribs began to show through the earth—its covering also grew sparser; I became nervous that someone might spot me up amongst the blackbutts, and dropped down a little until I found a shallow gully to follow. Here I was pleased to discover a specimen of terrestrial orchid. But I left it where it was, having no time for botanical pursuits.

From the eastern slopes of Gingenbullen, the Nicholsons' residence at Newbury lay to the south. There was nothing much in between, save for clumps of forest, and some patches of cleared land. You might wonder at my courage, faced with such a rough trek. But recall that I was not heading west, into the wildness of Belanglo and the Wollondilly. To me, this was simply a stretch of land that intervened between Gingenbullen and Sutton Forest. Such a journey was not beyond my powers. Even if I veered off to the east a little, I would eventually hit the Argyle Road, and could follow it back down to Newbury. I was not in the least afraid of getting lost.

I was, however, concerned about getting caught—and for good reason. Because as I passed to the east of Swanton, I could hear the distant sound of barking. This was not the steady, repetitious barking of a bored and lonely sentinel but a volley of yelps from a group of excited dogs. I knew at once that they were looking for me. Nothing else seemed as probable. I could not, however, identify their exact position. Were they heading straight for me, or were they rounding Gingenbullen's western tip? It was difficult to tell.

For a while I crouched motionless behind a grevillea bush, listening. At last I concluded that I was not at any immediate risk, though this decision was perhaps prompted less by my own reasoned judgement than by the fact that I was positively beset by flies. When the flies are as bad as they were then, one's only real defence is to keep moving. So I went on, down to the flats, leaving the slopes behind me.

It was at this point that I lost my bearings. The horizon was masked by a screen of treetops, and the sun was high overhead. It became more difficult to judge direction. Consequently, I strayed a little further south-west than was my original intention. Indeed, my discomfort was such that I almost lost interest in navigating. I was conscious of very little save the heat, the flies, and my own thirst. I also had a blister on my heel, which was quite painful. Once my cocked ear picked up the faintest sound of a distant 'Coo-ee!' Once I came upon the skeletal remains of a sheep, and wondered whose flock it might have strayed from. I encountered no snakes or bushrangers. Nothing attacked me except the ants and the flies.

Still, it was a dangerous expedition to have made. Without food or drink, I had left myself little margin for error. And back then the bush was fraught with peril. Why, my own father had once presided over a case in the local magistrate's court, involving two natives who had murdered two sawyers in the cedar country beyond Fitzroy Falls. This sort of thing was by no means an everyday occurrence—any more than was the assault on George Barton, or the murder of Thomas Smith. But recall the many attacks by bushrangers on isolated farms. Recall the high incidence of robbery on the roads. Even where 'nature never did betray the heart that loved her', the work of Man was often less benign. While a lone female child adrift in the bush would more often have met with hospitable tendance than brutal handling, her safety was by no means assured.

Even so, I probably felt safer on my own, in the woods, than I did at Oldbury.

I walked on unmolested, as the sun traced a path into the western sky. And suddenly I came to a post-and-rail fence, which I followed southwards. It did not lead me to the Nicholsons', however. I found myself in the paddocks to the west of Sutton Forest, with a view of the church through the trees, and a faint smell of kitchen smoke on the air. Newbury lay some distance to my left.

I might have veered off in its direction, had I not been so thirsty. I was also very footsore, and it seemed to me that I might just as well approach Mrs Wright, or Mrs Davey, or even Mrs Vincent, as Mr Benjamin Carter. *Any* responsible adult must see that my mother was long overdue. So I slipped under the fence and crossed the well-watered pastures that perhaps belonged to Mr Wright, past motionless dairy cows and an overgrown potato field, through the Medway Rivulet and around the edge of an associated lagoon. Skirting the cemetery, I finally reached the Argyle Road, coming up to it between Mrs Davey's shop and the Talbot Hotel.

There were horses outside the Talbot.

It was a moment before I recognised one of them as Angel, my mother's filly. The poor beast was dusty and sweating and laden with bags; I have never seen an animal so manifestly disillusioned with the role allotted her. Trapped in a cloud of flies, she twitched and stamped and flicked her tail. She seemed ready to bite someone.

My mother stood some distance away, looking almost as weary as her mount. She was talking to a small clutch of interested young men, most of whom I recognised. James Barnett was holding the horses.

'Mama!' I screamed.

My mother turned. So did everyone else; even the horses swung their heads. I stumbled down the rutted dirt road towards Mama, limping a little on my blistered foot.

'Charlotte!' my mother exclaimed, and glanced around, as if in expectation of spying the rest of her children partly concealed by fence-pickets and tree-trunks. 'What are you doing here? Where is Miss Rudd?'

'You're safe!' I cried, flinging myself at her. She returned my embrace absent-mindedly.

'Where are the others? Charlotte?' she said.

'I thought you were lost!' My voice was muffled by layers of muslin. 'You didn't come back!'

'What? What are you saying?' She pushed me away, so that she could look into my face. 'Charlotte, *where are the others?*'

'At home.'

'At Oldbury?'

I nodded, wiping my eyes. My mother's expression hardened.

'Surely you did not come here *alone?*' she said.

'I had to! You told me! We thought something had happened!'

'You are not making sense, Charlotte.'

'I was going to Mr Carter! You should have been back!'

My mother took a deep breath. All around us, the men had retired politely to a discreet distance. The flies, however, had not extended us the same courtesy. My mother flapped them away with an irritable gesture.

'It has been barely ten days, Charlotte,' she pointed out. 'There was no cause for alarm.'

'You said a week!'

'I said that I would *try* to be back in a week. Did you tell Miss Rudd where you were going? Does she know where you are?'

I hesitated.

'*Really*, Charlotte!' My mother sounded frankly cross. 'I would not have believed it of you! Running away in such a foolish, irresponsible manner! Have you *no* consideration for Miss Rudd's feelings? I am disappointed in you. These are the actions of an hysterical child, not a sensible young lady.'

'But *anything* could have happened!' I wailed. 'You could have been *dead*!'

'Nonsense,' said my mother.

And that was all the thanks I received for my pains. Mama scolded me on the way home, and punished me when we arrived. Perhaps she did it as much out of fear as anything else—fear of my wayward habits, and where they might lead me—but I must also attribute her unsympathetic stance to a fatal lack of imagination. Had she *really* no notion of how afraid I had been? Did she not realise how hard it would be to forgive her, after such a betrayal?

I never did—not entirely. Although I might have been foolish, my intentions had been good. My mother did not seem to recognise this. She preferred to believe that my actions had been dictated, not by an overwhelming sense of dread (which, God knows, was a common enough affliction at Oldbury), but by my own perverse and wilful character.

Consequently, for the first time, a rift opened up between us: a rift that was to become wider and wider as the years passed. It was never the same again between my mother and me.

In one sense, the battle lines were drawn that day in the summer of '38.

Seventeen

An interlude

I last spoke to my mother in the winter of 1854. We exchanged harsh words. I regret them now, but the fault was not entirely mine. There were many factors contributing to our quarrel, not least of them the distressing event that brought us together.

It was the occasion of Emily's funeral, you see.

Emily was buried at All Saints, Sutton Forest, by the Reverend William Stone. There was hardly room enough to accommodate all the mourners. Among them were her husband of less than one year, Mr James Warren, and her newborn son Henry. I was also present, as were my own husband and children. We were living at Cutaway Hill, to the north of Berrima, where we had bought a small property just three months before—so the trip to Sutton Forest had not been very taxing.

The funeral, however, was a perfectly dreadful affair. Except where I have buried my own children, no other internment has so shaken me. The afflictions of poor Warren were terrible to behold. My mother, though she presented an expressionless face to the world, could hardly stand. She had to be helped to her feet by my brother, who kept breaking into sobs throughout the service. It must be remembered that my mother had never before lost even one of her offspring. I know now that the age of the child in these cases is immaterial, for I have laid to rest as many grown children as I have little ones, and language refuses to utter the pain experienced at every loss. At the time, however, I looked at my mother with a dull and wicked resentment. I thought to myself: 'At least you had Emily for twenty-four years.'

It was wrong of me, I admit. But consider the circumstances. I was still in mourning when Emily's death had inflicted a fresh wound on my already savaged heart; though my darling little Thomas had been dead for more than a year, I had not yet recovered. I was also stricken with guilt, owing to the estrangement that followed close on Emily's marriage. I felt that I had wronged her, although I was not solely culpable. My mother's overwhelming delight at the match, her eager desire to welcome so respectable a man as James Warren into our family, contrasted far too cruelly with her behaviour to *my* husband. *My* husband was not the son of an officer of the Royal Navy. *My* husband was not the new master of Mereworth. Therefore my husband did not elicit anywhere near the same degree of flattering attention as James Warren, who was as much feted and praised as my own husband was ignored and condemned.

In the circumstances, is it any wonder that I did not attend my sister's wedding? I had a perfectly valid excuse—for I was seven months' gone at the time, and perpetually tired—but my mother was not impressed. To her, it was irrelevant that I was hardly fit for decent company; that I would be stared at and whispered about and patronised as the bedraggled, ne'er-do-well sister of the radiant bride. To my mother, I was being rude and selfish. And as a consequence, she did not visit me when I was confined in December of '53. Nor did she send me a gift for Charles James, or acknowledge his existence.

You may imagine how I felt about *that*. It is one thing to punish your daughter for her perceived failings—it is quite another to deprive your innocent grandchild. My mother did not even attend Charles's christening in March, for all that it was an Anglican service. (Flora's, being Catholic, had displeased her very much.) And although my sisters were kind enough to dispatch to me a small bundle of hand-worked garments when my time came, neither Emily nor Louisa made the journey to our humble abode. No doubt they were unwell. Louisa's heart had always been weak, and Emily, who would have been expecting by then, may have suffered greatly in her first few months.

Nevertheless, I was in no condition to be reasonable. It seemed to me that I was being snubbed, and therefore I behaved accordingly. None of my siblings received any birthday greetings from me, that year. I sent my mother no news of my family's various little triumphs. When Louisa's first published writing appeared in the *Illustrated Sydney News* (her 'Notes on the months: October'), I had written her a short letter of congratulation. By early 1854, however, I was disinclined to trouble myself. I was busy enough without the additional inconvenience of family correspondence. Had Louisa been half so busy, I thought, she would never have had the *time* to discourse at such length on the native arts, or the habits of magpies.

As for Emily, I had once encountered her in Berrima, where we were both provisioning ourselves. But she was with her husband, and I had felt constrained by his presence. While she chattered happily, her face all aglow and her adoring gaze for the most part fixed on his benign countenance, I had remained stubbornly reserved. It must be confessed that I begrudged her some of that overflowing joy. Shamefully, I found comfort in the thought that disillusionment was inevitable—after the baby was born, perhaps?

Poor Emily. My poor sister. There was no time for disillusionment; she died so soon after the birth of her son that I wonder if she was given the chance to suckle him. What a terrible shock it was to all of us. I remember weeping over the little cambric muslin frock that I had made for my nephew, because his mother would never see what pains I had taken with the scallop embroidery. She would never know how deeply I regretted my own stupid pride and cruel intransigence, which contrasted so sharply with her own sweet, modest, amiable nature. In many ways, she was the best of us all. Though she never raised a strapping family, nor achieved general recognition as a writer or a naturalist, she deserved all the praise that was lavished upon her at the funeral. For she was good, and kind, and gentle, and clever. She had the prettiest face you have ever seen, so pale and delicate, with soft eyes that were a mixture of grey and hazel, like the mist when it lay across Gingenbullen. And she had such a *graceful* way about her, too; no wonder James Warren had fallen in love. It must have been immediately apparent to him that she would make a perfect wife. As she did, I am sure—for the little time that she was given.

How I mourned her. How we all mourned her. Yet after the funeral, when we made our way back to Oldbury, there was a dreadful scene. I regret it exceedingly, even now, though nothing could have prevented it. Our nerves were in shreds. Everyone was exhausted. The babies had been crying lustily throughout the entire morning, and the weather was miserable: wet, frigid, blowy. At one point on the trip from Sutton Forest we had to endure a quick shower of sleet, which made me fear for the children. Charles, after all, was barely six months old. As for poor Henry, it seemed to me that he should never have been exposed to such weather in the first place. *Most* unwise, in my opinion. And his father wanted to take him straight home from Oldbury!

'Oh no!' was the general response. 'No, it will be the death of him!' My mother insisted that there would be room enough for all the children, and the Warrens' nurse too, but James Warren was adamant. 'We cannot be sure that there will be any improvement tomorrow,' he declared, and set off for Mereworth after the most modest refreshment imaginable: a cup of tea and a slice of bread and butter. I think it quite probable that he could not endure company—*any* company—and one can only sympathise. Nevertheless, it was a dangerous decision. The fact that poor little Henry's life was so short indicates to me that he was never a robust infant, and children like that should not be forced to breathe chilling winter air.

After James Warren and his son had departed, the other children were taken upstairs to rest. I did this myself, with Louisa's assistance. Not having set foot in the place for a couple of years, I was mildly curious to see what changes had been effected on the first floor—and was surprised at how few there were. My mother still occupied her old bedroom. Louisa was still sleeping in the nursery. James was now in possession of a back bedroom, though not the one formerly damaged by fire.

That chamber, Louisa told me, would be put at my disposal for the night.

'And you?' I queried. 'Where will you sleep, now that the children are in the nursery?'

'I shall sleep in Emily's old room,' Louisa replied, before pausing on the stairs to place a hand over her mouth. Tears pricked my own eyes as I watched her struggle for composure; having shut the door on my fretful children, we were once again left to contemplate our awful loss. Louisa, I should acknowledge, was always very good with my children. Though hesitant around babies, she had won Flora's heart by gravely attending to everything my daughter cared to say about chickens, mud-forts and puddings. It was Louisa, as well, who had unearthed some old illustrated books for Flora's amusement, and who had generously allowed Flora to use her colour-box and paint-brushes.

I was too busy with the baby to worry about Flora.

'Has James done much, since coming into possession?' I asked, in an attempt to direct our thoughts away from Emily. 'I see there has not been any painting or papering done.'

'It has been difficult, with so few funds to draw on,' Louisa responded, much to my sour amusement. So few funds! My own family was living in a slab hut, glazed but not shingled, its whitewash already stained with damp and its floor uncovered even by Indian matting. We shared one hairbrush between us, and ate treacle on our bread instead of butter. Yet Louisa was lamenting my *brother's* want of money!

'Oh yes,' I drawled. 'What a trial it is, when one cannot afford to have the carpets replaced!'

Almost immediately, I regretted these words. While *they* were not unkind, my tone certainly was: it implied that my brother was dreadfully spoilt. And Louisa responded as she often did, withdrawing into herself as she detached her thoughts from the unpleasant bickering of our family circle and fixed them on Nature, or Art, or perhaps the Life Beyond. You could see the shift in her gaze, which suddenly lost its bright intensity, becoming distant and abstracted.

I felt thoroughly ashamed of myself as I followed her small, slight figure downstairs. In fact I was about to apologise. But upon reaching the vestibule, I overheard my mother talking in the sitting room. She was addressing my husband, who could expect nothing from my mother but an attitude of the most extreme condescension. 'Indeed, Mr McNeilly,' she was saying, 'I think it a very good thing that Flora should be learning her alphabet. To be thoroughly literate is the proper desire of every respectable person, and a good grounding in literature is far more important than the acquisition of so-called "accomplishments" that enable a girl to do little more than thump on a piano at Christmastide, and perhaps crochet a few antimacassars. I could not be more proud of dear Louisa, who as you know has distinguished herself in *several* well-regarded journals. There are some who might regard such work as demeaning to a lady, but I say: Nonsense! What can be demeaning about literature? Did not Thomas Carlyle say "of the things which man can do or make here below, by far the most momentous, wonderful and worthy are the things that we call Books"? My greatest achievement (aside from my children) has been the publication of that modest little work you see on yonder shelf. For civilisation has been built on the written word, and there is no greater human endeavour than its mastery.'

Need I add that my husband could do little more than spell out the sign over a hotel door? He was virtually illiterate.

My mother knew this quite well, of course.

'Speaking of newspapers,' I snapped, upon entering the room, 'did you read the *Sydney Morning Herald* in March?'

My mother looked up. She had aged a good deal; her hair was almost entirely grey, and her face was haggard. 'Why, Charlotte . . .' she murmured, and trailed off. Sitting before the fire, in a low chair, she was at something of a disadvantage.

I crossed to the hearthside, and stood over her.

'Did you read about George Barton's trial in Bathurst?' I went on, causing James to wince.

'Please,' he said. 'Not now.'

'If not now, when?' I rejoined, before once again addressing my mother. 'Are you *aware* that he was convicted of manslaughter?'

My mother turned her face away. 'Yes,' she replied. 'I read of it.'

'And sentenced to two years' hard labour at Parramatta gaol,' I continued. 'Quite a paltry sentence, in my opinion. But then, I always considered him a murderous fiend.'

'Hardly that,' Louisa interjected quietly. 'Hardly *murderous*, Charlotte.'

'No? But he shot a man in cold blood, did he not?'

'Yes, but—'

'*I* should call that murder.'

Before continuing, I must perhaps explain—for it is unlikely that you are familiar with the case. It occurred at the Yarrows, on Winburndale Rivulet near Bathurst, early in 1854. Having been summoned to the Yarrows one evening at about eleven o'clock, District Constable Waller of Kelso discovered William Rogers—a reaper employed by George Barton—with a large hole torn through the lower portion of his belly. Barton himself was in bed, 'evidently suffering from the effects of overindulgence'. According to evidence given by Barton later at the trial, Rogers had entered his bedroom with an axe in his hand, threatening to cut him down. Rogers's version of the affair was very different, however; it conveyed 'the irresistible impression that the deed was committed either under strongly excited feelings or temporary delirium or both'. According to the *Bathurst Free Press*, every witness save one had been drunk at the time of the shooting.

You may imagine what my feelings were, upon encountering this report. It was the sheerest accident, I assure you. At the time, we did not have the funds to subscribe to the *Bathurst Free Press*, and I might have remained wholly ignorant had I not one day accompanied my husband into the Crown Inn at Berrima, which was then the change house for coaching teams on the Camden–Berrima–Goulburn run. It was the day of Charles's christening, and we had just come from the church at Bong Bong. My husband, in his customary style, had decided to celebrate the event with a few festive drams, while at the same time arranging some kind of delivery. So I had consented to stop at the Crown. Though not a particularly respectable hostelry, there were far worse in the vicinity of Berrima. And the proprietor's wife, if rather coarse in her speech, was at least not a former convict.

As I recall, everyone at the Crown was talking of poor Isabella Osborne's suicide, which had occurred that very morning—the morning of her wedding day—at nearby Eling Forest. It was on account of her proposed wedding, in fact, that we had been unable to secure the Reverend Hassall for Charles's baptism. But there you are: 'who thinks that fortune cannot change her mind/prepares a dreadful jest for all mankind'. Though Charles was christened, the wedding was never performed. Instead James Hassall conducted Miss Osborne's funeral the very next day.

I often find myself dwelling on what Miss Osborne's final thoughts might have been, as she tied the rope with which she hanged herself. What was it about the marriage that had caused her such fatal distress? I wish that I could have spoken to her. While my own marriage was in many ways a terrible mistake, it was not without its redeeming features. And if that were true in my case, how much more so would it have been in hers? For she was engaged to a man of good birth and ample property.

However, this is irrelevant. The fact is, I was at the Crown Inn on the twenty-first of March, and it was here, while nursing Charles in a dark corner, that I found myself glancing through a pile of discarded newspapers. An inn like the Crown was always a repository of newsprint from all over the colony, since there were carriers perpetually passing through on their way from one town to another. I remember flicking through the *Goulburn Herald* and the *Illustrated Sydney News*, as well as the *Bathurst Free Press*. But it was the *Bathurst Free Press* that held my attention. In the January 14th edition, I read of Barton's crime: at the time of publication, his victim was still living, and Barton had been 'remanded for further evidence'.

I tore out the article, and have it with me still.

It need hardly be said that I cast around frantically for more copies of the *Bathurst Free Press*. But the only other reference to Barton that I could locate at the Crown was in a *Sydney Morning Herald* of the previous week. It stated that Barton had been sentenced for the crime of manslaughter in Bathurst. The presiding judge, Mr Justice Therry, had referred to 'the monster Lynch' in doing so. With increasing consternation, I read an account of

Therry's moralising on the effects of strong liquor. He had used the occasion of Barton's sentencing to remind the court of another trial, at which Barton had been an important witness and he, Therry, had been the assistant Crown Prosecutor. At that trial, John Lynch had been accused of his first murder, but had been acquitted owing to the fact that Barton was 'grossly intoxicated'. Now Barton's career of intemperance had put him in the dock, and would have earned him a far more severe sentence had he not been of such advanced age and infirm health.

That, at least, was good news. George Barton was in poor health. As for the rest, I hardly knew how to take it. On the one hand, Barton had at last been clapped in irons. On the other, he and Lynch and the bloody years at Oldbury had once again been dug up and thrust into the public's face, no doubt to engender all kinds of whispered remarks around the neighbourhood.

I wondered if my mother had seen the item. She was still married to Barton, after all. And now her husband was gaoled at Parramatta. How, I thought, would the respectable Mr Warren take this?

It was something about which I questioned her after Emily's funeral, back at Oldbury.

'Louisa was telling me that you and she are planning to move,' I remarked, gazing down at my mother's bent, grey head. 'I assumed it was because there must have been a lot of talk hereabouts. On account of the newspaper reports concerning Mr Barton's trial.'

My mother then lifted her chin, and fixed me with a quelling look.

'We are moving,' she said coldly, 'to aid Louisa in her work. It is better that she should be closer to town, if she is to publish more widely and profitably.'

'Ah.'

'The people with whom we associate,' my mother added, 'are generally charitable, and do not concern themselves with squalid details. As do some.'

And in this remark, I must assert, lay my mother's mistake. She should not have spoken thus. Having insulted my husband, she deserved a set-down, and should have taken her punishment. Striking back was inadvisable.

For I was younger and stronger, and had more to forgive.

'So Mr Warren is not concerned that he has a felon for a father-in-law?' I asked, seating myself on the battered sofa. 'That *does* surprise me, in the circumstances.'

'Ah, Charlotte.' For the first time, my husband interjected. 'Leave't alone, lass—there's no luck'll attend such talk. Not now.'

'Oh, but I naturally thought that Mr Warren's sensibilities were easily offended, there having been such a concerted effort to keep *us* away from him.' I saw James cover his face with his hand. 'Indeed, I was most surprised that Henry was to be permitted to sleep in the same room as *my* children.'

This, perhaps, was a little strong. I must concede it. James gasped, and Louisa was moved to protest.

'Charlotte,' she said, her voice breaking. 'How could you? Today of all days . . .'

'Indeed, Charlotte, it is ill breeding that arouses the deepest disgust in anyone of a refined nature,' my mother interrupted, narrowing her eyes. 'And I am very grateful that Mr Warren was not exposed to yours.'

'Yes, I fear that my manners have rather coarsened, over the years. What with my prolonged exposure to ceaseless domestic strife of the *very worst description* in my youth.'

'Oh, what nonsense!' My mother sat up straight, her nostrils flaring. 'I do not see that your brother and sister have become bereft of their finer feelings, as you have!'

'Which is to say, I suppose, that they have not had the temerity to ask for an explanation?'

'*George Barton went mad!*' my mother exclaimed, her voice quivering. 'You know that perfectly well, and yet you persist in tormenting me with these cruel questions—'

'Insanity does not enter into it.' I folded my arms. 'George Barton was vicious *long* before he went mad, but you married him anyway. And I want to know why.'

'I refuse to discuss this.'

'*What happened at Belanglo?*'

'Your lack of consideration is utterly repugnant.' My mother rose. 'If you wish to remain here tonight, Charlotte, I suggest you confine yourself to your room. Or *I* shall.'

'Mama, please . . .' Louisa began, but was not permitted to finish.

'I no longer wonder that you married as you did, Charlotte,' my mother continued, a patch of bright colour flaring on each cheek. 'Indeed, I would have to say that Mr McNeilly, despite his humble birth, sets an example of gentility that you would do well to emulate, if such a thing is within your powers *at all*. I am ashamed of you.'

'Is that why you're moving? Because you're ashamed of me?'

There was no reply. My mother turned on her heel, making for the door.

'You've a deal to be ashamed of, have you not?' I called after her. 'More than you'll admit to, perhaps?' At which point James stepped forward.

'Stop it, Charlotte,' he said. 'I will not allow this kind of talk in my house.'

'I used to wonder why you never accused anyone—since some of our men *must* have been involved in the flogging,' I continued, ignoring James as I addressed my mother. 'Had they not been, Thomas Smith would never have been murdered—or so it's been assumed. I used to wonder if you might have had something to hide. Something that Thomas or his cronies might have seen, when they came across you and Mr Barton. Something that they might have revealed in court!'

The words (much regretted, I have to admit) were barely out of my mouth before my mother attacked me. She positively *flew* across the room, heavy as she was, and slapped me hard across the cheek. I might have returned the compliment had my husband not intervened. James, too, was quick to join the fray. He grabbed my mother while my husband grabbed me.

'How *dare* you!' my mother shrieked. '*Get out! Get out of this house!*'

'You can't order me out of this house!' I spat. 'Remember? You threw this house away when you married a drunken peasant!'

'Speak for yourself, Charlotte McNeilly!' my mother cried—and I swear to you, I saw red. I could have killed her. My husband knew it, too; he picked me up bodily, his arms clamped tight around my breast, and swung me into a corner. There he bent his head to murmur in my ear.

'Enough,' he said. 'D'ye hear? I'll not have this, Charlotte, shamin' us in front o' the family.'

Louisa was sobbing. My mother was whimpering, her hands to her cheeks, while James tried to soothe her. 'The ingratitude!' she gasped. 'The effrontery!'

'Shh,' James begged. 'I know, but—'

'The sheer *gall* of it!'

'Mama, please recall, we are none of us ourselves. Not today.'

'What have I done to deserve such treatment?' My mother was in tears. 'Do you all hate me so much? All of you?'

'Of course not!'

'I have lost two daughters! Not one, but two!'

She was right, as it happened. For I would not stay, preferring to avoid a discordant evening and perhaps more fractious breakfast. I roused my children, packed them onto the dray, and departed.

I never spoke to my mother again.

Eighteen

1839

Oldbury's decline gained momentum in the beginning of 1839.

It was a very bad year. Summer was marred by drought. The crops were an almost total failure. From fifty acres we reaped only about thirty bushels, and were obliged to purchase our flour. We lost many of our sheep too, and those left were in a parlous state. Then, when the rain *did* come, it came in such great force that there was some flooding, with the usual accompanying diseases. And while our neighbours suffered equivalent setbacks, ours were aggravated by George Barton's complete inability to deal with them.

Slowly, item by item, we were deprived of every luxury. First went Miss Rudd, then our annual delivery of new books, then our hock and sherry and soda water. The selection of spices in our kitchen was much reduced, though there was no shortage of meat; feed being in such short supply, we were obliged to kill off many failing animals who would have flourished on a better diet. The men did not want for anything (there being laws governing the exact content of their rations, and the distribution of their slops), but they did begin to grumble at the disappearance of those little luxuries that my father and mother had once been moved to bestow on them: extra tobacco at Christmas and Easter, for instance, and plum duff on the Sabbath. George Barton could see no merit in such 'coddling', especially in view of the fact that he himself was being deprived.

Though not of his newspapers, I might add.

While he agreed to stop buying some of the English journals, we continued to subscribe to the *Sydney Herald* and the *Sydney Gazette*—since their perusal had become almost his main occupation. Whenever my mother tried to suggest that we did not in all prudence require *both* Sydney journals, he would lash out at her. I once saw him flailing at her head and neck with a rolled-up *Herald*. On another occasion, he hurled a pot of hot tea across the room. He was fond of throwing hot tea. I myself was once scalded on the left arm when I put it up to shield myself from a flying tea-cup. The scar is there still. It is one of many, both visible and invisible.

And the reason for this assault? I seem to recall that I had given my stepfather a sullen look on being informed that, if I once more talked to any of the male convicts in my usual 'shameless fashion', I would be 'flogged like a bullock' and locked in the cellar for a week. My 'sullen looks' were something that George Barton found increasingly hard to stomach. As I approached my eleventh birthday, I became more and more the target of his rage. This may have been on account of Oldbury's rapid decline, which undoubtedly aggravated my stepfather's uncertain temper. Or it may have been the effect of my own growing sense of outrage and contempt, which I sometimes found hard to disguise. Although I do not wish to suggest that I was anywhere near the age at which one could expect to 'come out', I *was* on the point of developing, with all the concomitant changes—both physical and emotional—which that implies. Girls can become very fastidious as they approach womanhood, and George Barton revolted me. His foul breath and bloated face made me shudder. When he addressed me, I could hardly forbear to wince. My dislike of him became less a silent, seething resentment than a wild and open hatred, which must have flashed in my eyes a dozen times a day. Is it any wonder that he began to turn on me with increasing anger?

Not that I was his main target. My mother occupied that unenviable position. As our circumstances deteriorated, she was frequently obliged to present her husband with bad news, which he never received in a tranquil spirit. I remember an incident early in the winter of 1839, when Barton was being particularly reclusive. He disliked the cold weather, and would sometimes not emerge from his room all day. I cannot pretend that such conduct was viewed with disfavour among the children, but for my mother it could be exceedingly awkward, especially when there was business to address. The business arising in this instance was a letter from one of my father's executors, Mr Alexander Berry. It had made my mother very anxious, and she was keen to discuss it with her husband. But he refused to oblige her.

Though she knocked and entreated, he would not unlock his bedroom door. When she offered to push the letter *under* the door, he threatened to set it alight if she did so. That, at least, is what I assume he said—for I could not hear his responses from my concealed vantage point down in the vestibule.

I could only hear my mother's voice.

'Burning the letter will not solve our problem!' she said sharply. 'This is a *serious matter*, George, it will *not go away* . . . what? No, of course not! It is to your own advantage—much more so than mine! He has taken against you thoroughly! He intends to terminate your lease, and sell all the livestock! Listen: only hear what he has to say . . .'

And she began to read the missive aloud, through the panels of the closed bedroom door. I do not remember every word. Much of it, however, remained with me, no doubt because the insults were so numerous and cutting. Mr Berry declared in his letter that he feared for the property of myself and my siblings, purely on account of Mr Barton, whose intemperance was known to the whole world. He described Barton as 'a useless idler who neglects his own concerns', complaining of my stepfather's refusal to set foot outside of Oldbury. In the circumstances, he said, there was reason to fear that everything would be squandered.

'"Therefore the step I intend to take is to put the remainder of the property beyond his control,"' my mother read. 'Do you hear, George? "You and Mr Barton have often attributed the anxiety of myself and Captain Coghill to get the property out of Mr Barton's hands to sinister motives . . ." (That is true, at least!) "This step, however, will convince you that we are disinterested, as the property will then be entirely beyond our control . . ." George, are you listening? We will be thrown out of our own home! George!' She hammered once again on the door. 'Is this what you want? To see us paupered and homeless? Are you going to lie there drinking while your livelihood is sold from under you? George! Answer me!'

He would not, however. And soon I heard the muted sound of sobbing, which brought me to the bottom of the staircase.

My mother was sitting on the top stair, her face in her hands.

'Mama!' cried Emily, who was with me. 'Don't cry, Mama!'

'Oh!' My mother uncovered her face. She searched in her sleeves for a handkerchief, and finding none, dabbed at her cheeks with her apron instead. 'What are you doing here?' she demanded hoarsely. 'Can you find no other employment? I thought you had darning to complete.'

'Mama,' I said, with a trembling lip, 'will we have to leave Oldbury?'

'Were you eavesdropping?' My mother's voice was crisp. 'You should not be so ill-mannered, Charlotte!'

'We could hardly help but overhear,' was my equally crisp response, 'since you made no attempt to speak softly!'

'We will not have to sell our sheep, Mama?' Emily interrupted, shrill with distress. 'All our lovely sheep and cows?'

'Certainly not,' my mother snapped. She rose, sniffing, and tucked the letter into her pocket. 'I shall write some letters of my own. Mr Berry is wholly misguided, and will be made to see sense. You may be sure of *that*.'

Her protests, however, fell on deaf ears. Mr Berry's plans continued apace, without regard for my mother's wishes. And as she fended off his attempts to sell our livestock, George Barton's behaviour became increasingly erratic.

He seemed to think himself the victim of a huge and complicated conspiracy. Though my mother was at her wits' end, and complained ceaselessly of being persecuted, Barton preferred to see her as a party to the executors' attempts to throw him off the estate. Once or twice, in his cups, he even raised the possibility that my mother and Mr Berry had together *hired* the would-be assassin whose gunshot had shattered our sitting-room window, the previous year. (I have no doubt at all that, during his more delusional periods, Barton actually believed that Mr Alexander Berry was colluding with John Lynch, as well.) And when my mother fretted over the cost of a lawyer's advice, Barton would simply growl, '*You* have no need to be concerned. *Your* situation will not be affected.'

For a while she disregarded him, but some remarks cannot be ignored. On the morning of my eleventh birthday, matters came to a head.

My anniversary was celebrated in a very modest fashion that year. My gifts were few and inexpensive: from my family I received some coloured ink, a sheaf of writing paper, a knot of yellow ribbon and a bouquet of unusual wildflowers, as well as a length of cotton stuff (for new chemises) which my mother would have ordered in any case, since our wardrobes were sadly dilapidated. The servants gave me a jar of dessert apricots, on the understanding that I would return the jar. George Barton gave me nothing but some ill-timed advice. He told me that I should behave myself, for I was altogether too froward for my age. 'If you had any looks to speak of,' he said, 'I'd be worrying about yer reputation.' Then he complained about the cost of celebrating my birthday.

'All I ever hear is talk of retrenching and economising,' he rumbled, 'yet here is a roll of cloth at four pounds nine shillings, and there must be half a pound of currants in that cake. Is this sheer, unjustified extravagance, or are you keeping something from me?'

My mother sighed.

'You know perfectly well,' she said, 'that the expense of this celebration was defrayed by the sale of the epergne. You *know* this.'

'I know only what I am told. It seems to me that you are making yourself very comfortable for a woman on the verge of ruin.'

'Comfortable?' My mother's mouth twisted. 'Is that what you call it?'

'If you were truly worried, you would not be throwing your money away on trinkets and titbits. *I* know your game, Madam. You think yerself a deep 'un, but I can read you well enough.'

'What is the point of reading *me* when you will not read Berry's letters?' my mother rejoined, flushing. 'Can you not understand that he *loathes* me? That he would rather see me a pauper than grant me the slightest condescension? Would he be looking for a tenant if he intended that I should stay? He is *advertising*—you must have seen it! Do you actually *read* the newspapers, or is it all a pretence?'

I believe that I was not alone in flinching at this last remark. It was of the type guaranteed to annoy Barton, whose face suddenly turned red under a lowering brow.

'I read as well as any man in England,' he spat.

'Then read Berry's letters! Satisfy yourself as to the urgency of our situation!' My mother's voice began to rise, as her harried nerves failed her. 'I have told you that he intends to sell our flour mill to Charles Throsby, yet you persist in doing *nothing*! And how much can *I* do, without your help? You hold the lease, not I! Under the law I have no claim whatsoever, and must stand helpless while my own dear husband's legacy is broken up—while the sleek cows that he was so proud of are driven from the pastures—his favourite riding horse is disposed of . . .'

As my mother faltered, close to tears, Barton scowled horribly. His eyes narrowed and his nostrils flared. He slammed his open palm onto the breakfast table.

'*I* am your husband now! *I* am!' he barked. 'God damn you to hell, with your arrogance—you think you can get rid of me like this?'

'Run away, children,' my mother croaked. 'Go and play.'

'He is no longer the master here, *I* am!' Barton roared. 'And you will not force me off, by damn, or you will suffer for it! D'you hear?'

'*This is not my doing!*' Mama cried, rising to confront Barton across the table. She had forgotten, I think, that her children were still in the room; we had not obeyed her, partly out of concern and partly out of fear. (To move would have been to attract our stepfather's notice.) '*They blame me as much as they blame you!*' she screeched. '*Look! Look at the letters! Read them!*' Drawing a crumpled sheet of paper from her pocket, she threw it at him. '*They threaten me! In the name of my own children, they would have me cast onto the street!*' Another paper missile followed the first. '*And you accuse me of conspiring with* them? *How can you say that when I work and toil and beg and you do* nothing *to help us*, nothing! You *are the villain here, you have deprived us, Berry is right to accuse you—*'

At this point the storm broke. Barton had caught both sheets of paper and crushed them in his fist. He brandished that same fist as he leapt towards my mother, shouting. But the table intervened. Forced to skirt its edge, he was slower than he might have been, and my mother was granted a few extra seconds. She used them to pick up a chair, which she used as a shield, jabbing at him with its legs.

'No! Mama!'

James was screaming. Emily and Louisa were wrapped in each other's arms. Seeing Barton wrench the chair from my mother's grip, I cast around me. There were butter knives on the table, but I could not reach them. Barton was in the way.

'*Whore! Filthy whore!*' he yelled, pitching the chair aside like a dishcloth. When my mother turned to run, he grabbed the back of her neck with one hand, forcing her to her knees. Then he tried to stuff the letters into her mouth. I saw her clawing at his face and arms. I saw him thrusting the ball of paper into her throat, choking her.

'*You can eat your words now!*' he bellowed.

Bent double, Barton presented me with a wide expanse of buff-coloured corduroys stretched tight across his nether regions—which protruded between the split skirt of his coat. His pistol, I saw, was shoved deep into the pocket of this coat.

I plucked it from its place of concealment almost without thinking.

'*Let her go!*' I shrieked. '*Let her go or I'll shoot you!*'

Everyone froze. For several seconds, the only movement was the heaving of my mother's shoulders as she coughed. Slowly, Barton turned his head to look at me.

Any reasonable man would have raised his hands in alarm. There can be nothing, surely, more likely to cause terror than the sight of an eleven-year-old girl wielding a pistol. Of course, I had no notion of how to shoot the thing. In those days, before the coming of revolvers, the firing of a pistol was not easily accomplished. Nevertheless, when primed and loaded, even a heavy, old-fashioned weapon like my stepfather's constituted an awful threat.

And the gun *was* primed. I knew that quite well, having listened to Barton proudly boasting about his good eye, his quick hand,

and the fact that his pistol was always ready for use. 'There's none will get the drop on me,' he would say, polishing the handsome wooden butt and long, gleaming barrel.

Now that same barrel was pointed directly at him, wobbling in my unsteady hands.

'Let—let her go,' I stammered, hardly able to breathe.

And Barton obeyed, though not for the right reason. He dropped my mother only to spring at me, bawling incoherently, his eyes wild and his teeth gnashing. Out of sheer fright I pulled the trigger. I made no conscious decision. My finger simply moved.

But the gun was not cocked.

Nothing happened.

'*Devil!*' howled Barton, and struck me across the face. I lost my grip on the weapon, which he snatched away from me. Though *I* hit the floor, his pistol did not.

The blow left me momentarily deaf. I could not hear what foul imprecations Barton was jabbering as he raised the gun and cocked it. For an instant that seemed as long as an aeon, I looked down its dark barrel. Then it jerked away and exploded.

My mother had thrown herself bodily against him, spoiling his aim. He had staggered and dropped to one knee; the pistol-ball had buried itself harmlessly in a door-jamb.

Nothing was hurt but a fine piece of cedar.

In the confusion that followed, I took no part. My mother and stepfather were locked together in a flurry of combat, but I made no move to interfere. Servants spilled into the room, but I did not try to explain what had happened. I saw my siblings cowering under the table. I heard a dog barking frantically. I tasted blood, and smelled gunpowder.

When my mother shrieked for help, James Barnett helped her. He had been standing on the threshold, hesitant and appalled. Given a direct command, however, he obeyed it, stepping forward with a flustered air to seize hold of Barton's wrist. His aim must

have been to disarm my stepfather. 'Please, sir—please!' he exclaimed.
'If you kill your wife, you will hang for't!'

Barton panted up at him, eyes glaring. Gripped firmly around
his right wrist, my stepfather was prevented from pounding my
mother's head to mush with the butt-end of his pistol. For his
other hand was fully occupied, plunged into a great hank of her
dark hair.

'Let go!' he gasped.

'Please, sir—'

'*Let go!*'

Barnett glanced helplessly back at the other servants who were
ranged around the walls. Following Barnett's gaze, my stepfather
must have come to his senses. He must have realised that James
Barnett was right. If he killed his wife in front of so many witnesses,
he would hang for it.

So he dropped my mother and lurched to his feet. He dropped
his pistol too; it hit the floor with a *clunk*. Seeing this, James
Barnett released him, reaching for the weapon just as Barton did.
They both paused, eyeing each other and breathing heavily.

'Will *you* take it, Mam?' said Barnett.

'No!' cried Barton, but his wife was too quick for him. She grabbed
the weapon and whisked it away, scrambling under the table.

Whereupon my stepfather suddenly bolted.

I am not certain to this day what was in his mind. Nothing,
perhaps; I doubt that he was thinking clearly. He simply pushed
Barnett aside and ran, hurling himself out the door into the dining
room, his heavy soles echoing on bare boards. We heard him dash
into the vestibule and clatter up the stairs.

'Gone to guard 'is shot and powder, I'll warrant,' Henry speculated
in a dry voice. 'Locked 'isself in, and to hell wid t'lot of us.'

Sure enough, a door slammed overhead. After which we heard
the faint sound of keys jangling.

'Shot and powder don't fret me,' Barnett murmured, 'so long as he's got nowt to put 'em in. Mam? Is it safe to leave him? There's no musket upstairs? No paired pistol?'

'No, I—no.' My mother could hardly speak. 'Ch-Charlotte,' she whispered. 'Charlotte, my darling . . .'

She crawled towards me, the dreadful weapon still in her hand. When I saw it, I winced. So she pushed it across the floor to James Barnett.

'Are you hurt? Charlotte? Did he hurt you?' she croaked, and wrapped me in her arms, rocking me like a baby.

I shook my head.

'Show me.'

But I could not. How could I? The bruise on my jaw was nothing—nothing compared to the terrible wound inside. I had pulled the trigger, you see.

I had pulled the trigger, and stared Death in the face.

Nineteen

I t was a long, dark tunnel that we entered in the winter of
1839.

I doubt that I can explain to you the nature of the shadow
cast over us. I felt myself perpetually under siege. We lost many
of our assigned men, for we could no longer keep and feed them.
Eliza, who received her ticket-of-leave, left us to marry. My uncle
John abandoned Mereworth for Goulburn, taking my seven cousins
with him. As for Barton's temper, it became worse and worse.

You should know, by the by, that the incident on my birthday
was never mentioned. It being far too horrible to contemplate,
there was a concerted attempt to ignore what had actually occurred:
namely, the fact that I had tried to shoot Barton, and the fact that
Barton had tried to shoot me. Having shut himself in his room
after that unspeakable act, my stepfather had proceeded to drink
himself into a two-day oblivion, from which he emerged with an
impaired memory—or so it appeared. For he never again referred
to his murderous impulse, rather as if it had vanished from his
entire consciousness.

He did, however, inquire as to the whereabouts of his pistol.
Therefore I am convinced that it was all a pretence: that he

remembered everything, but chose to 'forget'. As did everyone else in the house. We ignored or put aside unpleasant thoughts and feelings in order to concentrate on more favourable ones.

My siblings and I were particularly adept at such stratagems. We lost ourselves in books, for example. We created our own epic stories, and acted them out. We also acquired a pet—a native bear—called Maugie, to whom Louisa, in particular, became utterly devoted. Attending to Maugie's needs kept us thoroughly occupied, and therefore reasonably cheerful, for he was a dear little thing, as good as gold, though we did have to mind his claws. The claws of a *Phascolarctus fuscus* should not be trifled with, I assure you.

It was partly on Maugie's account, and partly owing to Barton's baleful presence, that we began to spend more and more time in the bush. With Eliza gone, this was easily accomplished; my mother was so busy that she was not always available to supervise our movements. At eleven, I had also grown very bold, and would happily lead my small band of siblings out into the wilds of the stringybark forest in search of adventure. It was a species of recklessness that cannot be wholly attributed to my advancing age. Something in me changed after my birthday, and not for the better. I became more subject to sudden, hot moods, and flurries of furious excitement that propelled me to do rash and ill-considered things.

Upon stumbling across a clutch of snake eggs, for instance, I brought them home. My intention was to keep them as pets, and perhaps frighten my stepfather with them. Since they had to be kept warm, however, I placed the eggs under one of our hens—where they were discovered, and destroyed, by a horrified servant.

On another occasion, I decided to excavate the tumulus that stood on the slopes of Gingenbullen. My mother had informed me that this large hillock, about one hundred feet long by fifty high, was the resting place of numerous natives, though the last burial had occurred long before I was born. The importance of the site could be deduced from the carved trees that stood about it, and the signs of excavation that lay in front of it. Having been exposed to Gibbon and his tales of the Roman Empire, I was determined to discover any treasures that might have been interred with the old bones. So I put my brother and sisters to work, and we hacked away at the side of the mound until my gang of workers refused to pretend anymore that they were Roman slaves, assigned men, or tomb-robbers. 'I don't want to see any bones,' Emily declared. 'And if you bring some home, I'll tell Mama, and you shall have to bury them again.'

She was rather a squeamish soul—unlike her elder sister. One of my dearest wishes, at that age, was to happen upon the remains of an escaped convict. My cousin John claimed to have done just that; some distance from Mereworth he had found a weathered corpse, all bones and leather, wearing a few tattered shreds of prison garb and chains around its ankles. Whether this was true or not, *I* certainly believed him. And I strove to emulate him also, searching hidden gullies and rocky fissures for skeletons, disappointed when my efforts turned up nothing. I cannot emphasise too strongly my strange preoccupation with mortality, at this time.

Perhaps my nerves had been somewhat overthrown by illness in the family. Winter had brought its usual budget of colds, and Louisa was very sick with congested lungs. I remember many long, dismal days, when the rain fell ceaselessly, and the dark clouds brooded low over Gingenbullen, and damp patches began to show on some of the walls. For Oldbury was already sinking into a state of disrepair. It is always the fences that go first, followed by the roof-shingles. Our fences were not in good condition. Moreover, some of the huts were beginning to subside, and several of our windows were kept shuttered because we could not find money to mend the glass.

Needless to say, George Barton was to blame for the cracked windows. Because his drinking was by this time almost constant, he was unable to contain his anger, no matter how minor the offence. He was drinking his way through my father's cellar, which, though greatly depleted, had not been entirely drained; our want of funds was therefore no impediment to his headlong descent into madness. Had he been forced to buy his grog, we may have suffered less.

He was drunk on the day that we received tidings of John Lynch, whose very name seemed inseparable from dark and troublous times.

It was a chilly August afternoon. Owing to our reduced staff, there was far less wood to burn, and fewer fires lit as a consequence. So we were pretty much confined to the sitting room, where—as we awaited dinner—my sisters and I tried to coax Maugie down from his high perch on top of the book cupboard. James was struggling with a French translation, and my mother with our latest delivery of mail, which was full of unwelcome missives: reminders of debts to be paid; waspish correspondence from Mr Alexander Berry; notices from various dealers in Sydney, whose goods we could no longer afford. The newspapers, too, were depressing. They seemed concerned with a busy, prosperous, alluring world full of recently docked ships and performances at the new theatre. How dreary our own lives looked, compared to the eventful bustle of Sydney!

My mother was entertaining us with a few choice excerpts from the latest *Sydney Herald* when she suddenly fell silent. I looked across at her, and saw that her jaw was set and her brow creased as she pored over the newsprint. Something in it had struck her like a blow.

'What's wrong, Mama?' I inquired.

There was no response.

'Mama? What is it?' I crossed the room, and my approach seemed to startle her. She straightened suddenly, and shook out the flimsy, black-and-white pages.

'Nothing,' she said. 'Nothing at all.'

Immediately, however, she fell into a brown study, knitting her brows and chewing at her bottom lip. I sidled around the back of her chair, and peered over her shoulder. The *Herald* was open at the Supreme Court news. Buried among its murders and armed robberies was a paragraph that began with the words: *'Thomas Barry was indicted for stabbing John Lynch, at Newcastle, with intent to murder him, and Charles Wilson and Thomas Bolson were indicted for being present, aiding and assisting.'*

'Oh!' I said. But my mother did not even hear me.

The item went on to explain that both victim and accused were members of the 'ironed gang' at Newcastle, where Lynch had apparently given offence by informing on his attackers. Since they all slept in the same room, revenge had come swiftly. Lynch reported being stabbed in the chest one night by Barry, as he was held down and gagged by Bolson.

The verdict, I saw, was 'guilty'. And the punishment was to be Death.

'If only they *had* killed him,' I muttered. 'It would have put Mr Barton's mind at rest, perhaps.'

'What?' said my mother. She turned her head, and frowned. 'Charlotte, are you prying?'

'Killed who?' asked James. 'What are you talking about?'

'No one has been killed,' my mother declared. Then she rose, still clasping the newspaper, and looked about her in a nervous, troubled fashion, as if searching for a place of concealment.

My own thoughts were keeping pace with hers.

'He will miss it,' I pointed out. 'He will ask where it is.'

'Shh. Let me think.'

'The servants will not lie, Mama. They'll be afraid to.'

'*Will* you be quiet, please?'

I shrugged, and subsided. As my mother moved towards the blazing hearth, Emily leaned close to me, whispering in my ear. 'What has happened?' she asked. 'What is in the newspaper?'

'John Lynch,' I replied. 'Someone has tried to kill him.'

'But he is not at large,' my mother added, in a firm voice. She was feeding the *Herald*, sheet by sheet, into the fire. 'There is nothing to fear, I assure you.'

Except, of course, from George Barton. No one queried my mother's decision to burn the newspaper. We all of us understood that any mention of John Lynch would be detrimental to my stepfather's peace of mind (such as it was).

Unfortunately, the disappearance of the *Herald* left him equally disturbed. Though it had seemed to me that this might be the case, I was not prepared for the violence of his reaction. It began with a worrying restlessness, which commenced during dinner. We heard his heavy tread move up and down the stairs several times, into the study and out again, across the back veranda. We also heard hinges creak, and doors slam. When he entered the dining room, we could see at once that the signs were not good. Though well primed with liquor, he was not by any means incapacitated. He could still make a fist, and employ it accurately.

'Where is the latest *Herald*?' he demanded of my mother.

'The latest *Herald*?' she repeated, with a kind of bland sprightliness that I found utterly unconvincing. 'Why, it did not come.'

'It did not *come*?' he echoed. 'What do you mean, it did not come?'

'It was not included among the rest. If you refer to the edition of the nineteenth of August, then yes, it did not come.' My mother swallowed. 'I shall write to complain, of course.'

Barton scowled. I held my breath. He was a truly awful object, with his wild, untended bush of greying hair, and his scrubby chin, and his bloodshot eyes. It was incredible to see him in the same room as my mother, whose pale, refined face and upright posture were clear evidence of her superior intellect and breeding. I recall how in *Myra*, Louisa described the union between her villain, Guy Kershaw, and his unfortunate spouse: '*There is nothing more melancholy,*' she wrote, '*than the binding together of the dove and the vulture. Coarse, sinful, without one spark of nobleness about him, how could even his kindness not be revolting?*'

Of course, we rarely had to endure George Barton's kindness, revolting or otherwise.

'Are you not hungry?' my mother continued, trying to turn the conversation. 'Will you not be eating?'

Barton's reply was a snort. He turned on his heel and left the room, shoulders hunched, slippers flapping. I hoped with all my heart that he was satisfied. But my hopes were dashed, for soon there were more noises: the rattle of papers being shaken and tossed; the scrape of drawers being pulled in and out; the low mutter of a man unhinged by anger and suspicion. He shuffled out of the house and shuffled back in again. He jangled his keys and cursed under his breath.

At last, as we were finishing our stewed apple, he strode across the vestibule from the sitting room and kicked open the dining-room door. He was carrying a small iron shovel full of ashes.

Some of the ashes, I saw with horror, were not properly consumed. There were a few yellowed fragments of newsprint, scorched around the edges.

'You burned it!' Barton spat, wide-eyed and panting.

'No.' My mother rose. 'No, those were old pages. We lit the fire with them.'

'*You burned it!*' Barton raised the shovel, scattering clouds of grey and white ash. '*What are you hiding from me?*'

Wielding the tool like a two-handed sword, he ran at my mother. But it was an awkward weapon, heavy and ill-balanced. His first blow glanced off the edge of the mantle, leaving a splintered scar. By the time he had swung the shovel back up over his head, staggering slightly, we had all of us escaped through the great double doors into the breakfast room—and James was already on the veranda.

I cannoned into him there. My sisters joined me moments later, and Mama dodged the second blow just in time. She yanked the rear door shut an instant before Barton's shovel smashed against it.

'Lock it! Charlotte! Quickly!' she cried, clutching the knob with both hands. She hung her entire weight off that sturdy brass fitting, bracing herself against the doorstep and leaning back. I fumbled with the bunch of keys that dangled from her waist; fear was making me clumsy. Perhaps, if Barton had had his wits about him, he would have broken through to us at that point. He would have stopped hammering on the door with his shovel and tried to turn the knob instead.

Fortunately, however, he did not. He kept pounding on the door until I turned the key in the lock. Then, at the sound of that crisp little *snick!*, he seemed to come to his senses. I heard him thudding out of the breakfast room.

He was heading for the study, I knew. The study also opened onto the veranda.

'Run!' gasped my mother. 'Quick!'

We ran. We followed her straight to the kitchen, where Bridget stood, open-mouthed. My mother snatched up a huge carving knife on her way to the larder.

'In here!' she snapped. 'Quick!' And she unlocked the larder door with her free hand.

'Mama—'

'*Get in!*'

Hearing Barton's shouts, my siblings and I tumbled through the open door. My mother slammed and locked it, just as Bridget began to speak.

'Please, Mam,' she quavered, her voice muffled by the intervening walls, 'is it the Master comin'?'

'If he runs at me, you must strike him with that saucepan.'

Beside me, Emily squeaked, '*Oh no! Oh no!*' The four of us were huddled in a corner, amidst bags of flour and half-empty jars of rice. The shelves of the larder were miserably depleted. Even the serried ranks of bottled preserves had thinned out.

'Shh!' I whispered, straining my ears. Was Barton's raised voice getting louder? Yes, it was.

'*You'll not escape me! I want to know!*' A terrible crash made us jump. Later I discovered that Barton had swept a litter of dirty plates off the kitchen table with one swing of his fire-shovel. '*What are you hiding, damn you?*'

'John Lynch,' my mother informed him.

There was a brief silence.

'John Lynch has been stabbed, and the men who did it condemned to death.' My mother's voice was surprisingly steady. 'There was a report in the *Herald*.'

'Is—is he—?'

'He is alive. He was in court. At Newcastle.' Another pause. 'I knew it would discompose you,' my mother went on (more firmly now), 'and sought to spare your feelings. Next time I shall know better. Of course, you have every right to read even unpleasant news.'

There was a clatter, as if something heavy had dropped onto the stone flags. A long silence followed. I could hear only the loud, anxious breathing of my sisters; Louisa looked quite ill with shock, her eyes shadowed, her lips slightly blue.

After a time, footsteps approached the larder. A key scraped in the lock. 'You may come out now, children,' my mother said hoarsely. 'All is well.'

When she opened the door, I saw that she was no longer carrying her knife.

'Where is he?' I blurted out.

'Gone back upstairs.'

'Why? What happened?'

'Yeer Ma knacked the wind right out of 'im,' Bridget opined, in shaky tones of awe and congratulation. ''Twas Lynch's name did it.'

'That's enough, Bridget,' my mother snapped. 'Attend to this mess, if you please.'

Had she not been deeply upset, she would not, perhaps, have been so short with Bridget—who became quite sullen as a consequence. The broom was fetched in a grudging manner, while Louisa and Emily clung to my mother's skirts. 'Mama! Mama!' they sobbed.

'Shh.' My mother smoothed their hair. 'Don't cry. You are big girls, now—you must learn to be brave.'

'He tried to kill you,' I pointed out sharply. 'You should send for the police.'

She said nothing.

'Mama? Did you hear?'

'Calm yourself, Captain. Things are never that simple.'

'What do you mean? He tried to kill you!'

'No crime was committed. These are matters beyond your understanding. You should be patient, and pray to God, and He will protect us.'

Even now, I find these words difficult to stomach. There can be no doubt that the Law, in those days, did not favour a wife's situation in cases of ill usage. It had long been accepted that a man might administer moderate correction to his spouse (since he had to answer for her misconduct), and that he might restrain her liberty if she gave him cause. I will acknowledge that to interfere in a domestic dispute was not something that the authorities felt very often justified in doing. After all, a wife back then had virtually no claim to her property or her children, let alone her own person or peace of mind. Nevertheless, I do believe that *something* might have been done. Surely a visit from the police might have worked on Barton's conscience? At least it might have stayed his hand.

But my mother appealed to no one, as far as I can see. And I am convinced that this was partly on account of her own shame. She would never concede that the bruises on her body were her husband's handiwork, not even to her children—who were well placed to know the truth. Her pride rebelled against it. So she must have been even more determined that the sordid secrets of her marriage should not be publicly exposed. Perhaps she thought that the results would hardly be worth the unpleasantness. What man in the colony was ever arrested for beating his wife, after all? None that *I* have heard of.

Still, she might have tried—for her children, if for no one else. It seems to me unconscionable that a misplaced pride should have held her back.

In this, I think, she failed us. And it was something that I came increasingly to feel during the spring of 1839.

Twenty

I n early October, my father's prized flock of Saxon merinos was put up for auction. These sheep were descended from thirty fine ewes and rams that my father had acquired in Germany. They had been transported to Australia in a specially designed pen, from which they were unloaded into a dray boarded around the sides. One ewe was lame from the voyage, and when the dray camped in the Cowpastures on its way to Oldbury, old John Macarthur came to look at the sheep and bought the lame ewe.

Yet this notable flock, with its unimpeachable ancestry, received not a single bid when first it went under the hammer. Opinion seemed general across the colony that our sheep could no longer be good, after having been managed for some years by George Barton. That, at least, was the view expressed by Mr Alexander Berry, who wrote repeatedly to my mother warning her against any plans that she might have to oppose the sale. To do so, he said, would be to deprive her children of their rightful property.

I know this because my mother could not contain her indignation. On the edge of hysteria, she would relate with scorn certain assurances that were repeatedly made in Mr Berry's correspondence. 'He claims to have the welfare of my children at heart,' she scoffed, 'yet he proposes to sell their inheritance! And then he has the gall to claim that my *husband* would deprive them of their last morsel! When he himself is the despoiler! What hypocrisy! What treachery!'

I shared her dismay. It seemed to me disastrous that we should be forced from our home, to live modestly on those sums raised from leasing out Oldbury and disposing of our livestock. On the other hand, I was sometimes moved to sympathise with Mr Berry. Though I was only a child, I could see with my own eyes that if Berry did not sell off a good portion of the estate, then Barton certainly would. He was doing it already. He had sold cattle, and flour, and several old hand-mills—none of which were legally his to sell. All these things belonged not to Mr Barton or to my mother, but to myself, James, Louisa and Emily. *We* were to inherit them. Yet what would be left for us to inherit, if George Barton drank all the proceeds?

I see this clearly now, though it was very confusing to me at the time. I found it hard to understand why my mother should not be permitted to remain at Oldbury if Barton was forced to go. (Perhaps I still did not truly regard George Barton as her husband, and therefore her master in all things.) I would lie in bed at night, turning matters over in my head, trying to make sense of them. I would escape to the heights of Gingenbullen, where I would sit all alone, perched on a favourite rock, mindlessly swatting at ants and flowers with a dry stick while I stared out at the unsullied, enigmatic landscape and pondered our situation.

It seemed to me very bad. As Barton became increasingly unstable, we were losing more of our servants. Bridget left in the spring, as did Jane, her daughter. Louisa's health was not good. Neither was Barton's; a man who drinks so unceasingly becomes prey to all manner of ills, both mental and physical, and Barton would have cut a pitiable figure had he not also behaved in such a frightening fashion. He was now subject to fainting spells, and his appetite was completely spoiled. His colour was bad, his headaches were appalling, and his hands trembled so that he could hardly light his pipe. Yet for all that, he could not be disregarded. When the mood was upon him, he had still strength enough to punch a hole in a wall.

Even more alarming were his delusional episodes. The first of these occurred in November. My mother was taking a French lesson in the sitting room one morning when her husband rattled the knob on the door. He could not freely walk in, however; she had recently begun to lock any doors that might separate her from my stepfather, because it afforded her some protection. (He frequently lost his keys, you see—and even when they were in his custody, he was often too drunk to insert anything as small as a key into a keyhole.)

'Who is it?' asked my mother, raising her head. But to everyone's surprise, Barton did not kick or shout.

'Let me in!' he whispered hoarsely. 'Quick—quick!'

'Why? What is the matter?'

'*Quick!*' His voice caught on a shrill note. 'It's him! He's here!'

'Who is?'

'*Lynch!* He's come!'

My mother's jaw dropped. We all stared at each other.

'For pity's sake, will you *open the door?*' Barton pleaded.

I have never heard such genuine fear in anyone's voice. Responding to it, my mother got up and opened the door, while my siblings and I glanced nervously at the windows. Though the day outside was as perfect an example as God ever made, all warm spring sunshine and gentle zephyrs, I was suddenly struck down by cold fear. Was John Lynch lurking nearby? Had he escaped from the Newcastle chain gang at last? By now, of course, he was invested with quite monstrous capabilities in our eyes. Nothing seemed beyond him, if only because he filled George Barton with such unalloyed terror. It is always hard to believe that fear of this sort is *utterly* unfounded, no matter how demented the unfortunate soul who displays it. And I suppose that, if John Lynch had indeed killed Thomas Smith, it was reasonable enough to dread the reappearance of the murderer.

Though I myself had never seen Smith's remains, my stepfather had; possibly their condition had been enough to leave anyone permanently affected, let alone a man as troubled as George Barton.

'Why—why, what do you mean?' my mother stammered, as Barton entered, throwing his whole body against the door to close it behind him. He was white, breathless, and shaking with fear. 'How could John Lynch be here?' my mother pressed him. 'Lynch is in Newcastle, surely?'

'No, no.' Barton laid his forehead against the panel of the door, sagging under the weight of a truly debilitating terror. 'No, he is here! I saw him!'

'Where? In the woods?'

'Upstairs!'

'*Upstairs?*'

'On the landing.'

My mother lifted her gaze in a kind of reflex. As it returned to her husband, an expression of alarm flitted across her face, quickly dissolving into one of doubt and dismay.

'On the landing?' she repeated. 'How could that be?'

'I saw him! He was there! He has come for me!'

My mother knew better than to take issue with this. Had she done so, she would only have been condemned by my stepfather as a traitor, a liar, and a bloodthirsty villain. Besides, she could not be absolutely sure that Barton was delusional.

So she summoned James Barnett, and ordered him to conduct a search of the house and its grounds. Nothing was discovered, however. There were no strangers in the vicinity. Nor were there any signs that a stranger had ever been present: no latches were forced nor valuables stolen.

Nevertheless, Barton was not reassured. He kept his bedroom window shuttered and bolted, day and night, from then on. And he became obsessed with ensuring that every dark corner was well lit, distributing lamps and candles around the stairs, landing and vestibule. We children appreciated this, for we were none of us fond of the dark, but my mother abhorred the practice. Not only was it ruinously expensive; it was also dangerous. She therefore made a point of staying awake until she heard her husband's snores. Then she would go about extinguishing every flame, claiming in the morning that they had guttered, or consumed all their oil.

I was very much afraid that Barton would begin to suspect her. Though his faculties were dulled by drink, he was not a *complete* fool. It happened, however, that Mr Ash arrived towards the end of the month. And his appearance so enraged my stepfather that the matter of the mysteriously draughty landing was forgotten.

I never knew Mr Ash's first name. He never used it, and we never required it—for he was as pale and dry and bloodless as his namesake. He was sent by Mr Alexander Berry for the express purpose of keeping an eye on George Barton, though he also carried letters for my mother. In these letters, Mr Berry informed her that the Oldbury sheep had at last been sold. He also urged my mother to prevent George Barton from selling off our furniture. I do not know where Mr Berry's information came from, but he roundly condemned George Barton as a thief, instructing my mother to tell anyone who might buy our furniture that, for every shilling paid to Barton, another would have to be paid to my father's executors in recompense. Mr Berry also announced that he intended to take legal action against my stepfather to recover money collected for flour milled at Oldbury—money that rightfully belonged to James Atkinson's heirs. And he informed my mother that Mr Ash had been engaged to supervise the farm.

Stationed under the sitting-room window, in a patch of sweetbriar, I heard much of what my mother said in response to these proposals. For she made no effort to moderate her tone as she discussed them with Mr Ash. She thought it outrageous that her children's estate be encumbered with the cost of an overseer. How could such a thing be justified, she demanded, when we were being forced to sell off our sheep? Mr Ash replied calmly that the decision had not been his. He was simply acting under instructions, and would do his best to prevent George Barton from selling any property henceforth. In the meantime, he suggested that my mother make her own preparations. If she herself sent various fitments or furnishings to Sydney for safekeeping, then they would not be accessible to her husband once he decided to dispose of them.

'You'll forgive me for saying,' he declared in his quiet, level voice, 'that yer inability to reason with Mr Barton in the past does not bode well for the future. Mr Berry is determined that measures should be taken to preserve yer children's birthright. He feels that, if I am here, Mr Barton's excesses must be curbed.'

'On the contrary, Mr Ash—your presence will only anger him, and drive him to even wilder acts,' my mother replied. 'You cannot know—it is quite impossible—oh, this is *absurd*! What *right* has your master to dictate to us like this? And I suppose you expect to inhabit Swanton, now you are here?'

'It being empty,' said Mr Ash, 'I would have no objection.'

'You cannot live in *this* house, not even for a night.' My mother was adamant. 'Mr Barton would not allow it. He will be angry enough, without a stranger occupying the next room. Oh dear, this is such a very bad notion. This will end in disaster, I know it will. And *I* shall be blamed, as usual.'

There was a brief pause. 'Perhaps, if I were to explain to Mr Barton that I am acting under Mr Berry's orders—' Mr Ash began, but was prevented from finishing.

'Oh, he will not listen to *you*,' my mother said fretfully. 'By all means, though—talk to him! See what success *you* have in persuading him to see reason! He is asleep upstairs at present, but no doubt when he hears your voice he will come down to demand an explanation. I only hope that the one you give him does not condemn us all to the most dreadful scene.'

Another pause. When Mr Ash spoke again, his tone was more desiccated than ever.

'Is Mr Barton armed, Ma'am?' he inquired.

'No. At least—I think not.'

'Then you must set yer mind at rest,' said Mr Ash. 'For I am.'

Hearing this, I immediately scrambled away to inform my siblings that Mr Ash had a firearm. And there was a good chance that he might shoot George Barton with it.

'I hope so,' James remarked. 'I would do it myself, if I wasn't afraid to hang.'

'You should not say so, James,' Emily reproved him. 'Murder is a sin.'

Sullenly, James kicked at a stone. We were behind the dairy, where the grass had been let go. Clumps of it stood as high as our knees.

'You might not hang if you were defending yourself,' I speculated. 'But you would still go to prison, I daresay.'

'Well, I don't want to go to prison either,' said James. 'And neither does Mr Ash, I expect. Has *He* come down yet?' (We always referred to Barton as 'He' or 'Him', when we were talking among ourselves.) 'Does *He* know about Mr Ash?'

'Not yet,' I replied. 'But He will soon.'

'I wish we could go away,' Louisa suddenly observed. 'Into the bush. I don't want to be here when *He* comes down.'

'There's no need to fret, Louisa. I told you—Mr Ash is armed.'

Luckily, Mr Ash was not required to use his weapon. I myself was a witness to the first confrontation between the new overseer and the old one, and I can testify that Mr Ash handled it with quite astonishing poise. It occurred near the stockyard, late that afternoon. Though Mr Ash was newly arrived, and must have been very tired, he did not immediately repair to Swanton after interviewing my mother. Instead he commenced an inspection of the estate, beginning in the kitchen and proceeding through the dairy, the piggery, the huts and the gardens. My mother refused to accompany him. That, at least, is what I assume, for she remained in the house. Her children were of a different mind. We preferred to avoid the house when Barton was in it—and besides, we were curious. We thought Mr Ash rather small and thin to be defying our stepfather. Had he the strength of character to oppose such a violent and tempestuous man?

We soon found out. While Mr Ash carefully examined every inch of the stockyard fence, kicking it here and shaking it there, we stationed ourselves near the old ironbark, watching him. He paid us no heed, though I am convinced that he saw us. How could he have failed to? But we said nothing, and he said nothing. He simply continued to prod at the fence-posts, as if searching for evidence of ant damage.

He did not even react to the sound of distant shouting when it occurred, but proceeded with his inspection, while my siblings and I concealed ourselves behind a larger tree. We knew that Barton must be coming.

'Mr Ash,' I said, 'can you hear that shouting, sir?'

'I'd be deaf if I could not,' he replied, without looking up from the fence-rail that occupied him.

'It is my stepfather shouting, Mr Ash. It sounds as if he must be awake.'

'It does indeed,' said Mr Ash in a grave voice.

'He can get monstrous angry, Mr Ash,' Louisa piped up. 'You must be very, very careful.'

At this, Mr Ash turned to regard us all. He was wearing a slouch hat pulled low over his forehead, and gave it a tug as he studied us with a pair of small, dark eyes like chips of shale. He did not seem to sweat like other men.

'You must be the heirs of Mr James Atkinson, esquire,' he said, and we nodded. 'Are you afraid of Mr George Barton?' he wanted to know.

Again we all nodded. More vigorously.

'Well, I am not,' he declared. Whereupon—to our astonishment— he returned to his work, moving along the fence in a meditative fashion, sometimes throwing his weight against it, sometimes standing back to squint at it, his thin lips pursed to cover his small, sparse teeth.

After a while, we heard my stepfather draw near. '*Ash?*' he yelled. '*Ash? Where the devil are you? Show yourself, damn your eyes, or I'll hunt you down like a dog!*'

Mr Ash straightened. Adopting a casual stance, he slowly unbuttoned his dusty blue coat—revealing the butt of a pistol protruding from his waistband. Barton must have spotted this from some distance away. For after approaching noisily, shouting and stamping, he suddenly came to a halt, and seemed to hesitate.

'Mr Barton, is it?' asked Mr Ash.

'And what the devil is your bounce?' Barton had turned pale. His eyes were fixed on the pistol butt. 'Who sent you?'

'Mr Alexander Berry, sir.'

'To shoot me where I stand?'

Mr Ash blinked. 'No,' he replied. 'Not at all.'

'Don't lie to me! You want me off this place, *I* know! You would do anything, God damn you to hell! You would leave me under a fallen log, like a dead convict!'

Mr Ash said nothing.

'You think you can lure me out here to kill me?' Barton raved. 'Is that what you think, you murderous bugger?'

'Not at all,' Mr Ash repeated politely, and jerked his head in my direction. 'Not in front of witnesses, at any rate.'

My stepfather had failed to notice the four pairs of eyes peering out at him from behind a tree. He turned, and started, and swore under his breath. Then he threw an empty gin bottle at Mr Ash before taking to his heels.

The bottle smashed harmlessly against a fence-post.

'Hmmm,' said Mr Ash. He regarded the shattered glass as he re-buttoned his coat, his expression unreadable. I have to confess, I felt hugely reassured. It seemed to me that, with Mr Ash about, we would all now be safe.

I was wrong, of course. In fact I discovered *how* wrong when George Barton nearly burned our house down.

Twenty-one

I t was Louisa who woke me.

'Charlotte!' she coughed. 'Charlotte, wake up!'

'What . . . ?' I threw off her hand, peering into the gloom as I lifted my head. 'Go 'way . . .'

'There's smoke, Charlotte! Can't you smell it?'

I could. At once. And I knew instantly that something was wrong.

'Where's Mama?' I swung my legs out of bed, pushing back covers and curtains. There was smoke in the room, and a frightful stench. It set me coughing. 'James! Emily! Get up!' (How hard it was to breathe!) 'Wake them, Louisa!'

When I opened the door, I saw only smoke. It was illuminated faintly by an orange glow, which seemed stronger to my right than to my left. 'Mama!' I cried, before the vapours caught in my throat. But someone else was yelling too. I could identify George Barton's voice, though it was hoarse and high. 'Fire! Fire!' he shouted.

There was swirl of movement through the smoke. I heard thudding footsteps and the crackle of burning wood. My mother coughed a few feet away. 'Charlotte!' she choked. 'Downstairs!' She was beside me suddenly, hacking her lungs out.

I cannot convey to you how frightened I was. To be wrenched from a deep sleep and thrown directly into a scene of utter confusion—of raised voices and deep shadows and suffocating fumes—is a truly dreadful experience. I had very little understanding of what was going on. I recollect that Emily clutched me at one point, sobbing and retching. We must have been dragged or pushed downstairs, past the seat of the conflagration. My mother was with us. She screamed for help, though not with much force. The atmosphere was too thick; it strangled her cry.

We were fortunate that no nightshirts caught alight. There were cinders in the air, but they did not hurt us. The vestibule was full of smoke. The front door stood open and we stumbled through it, heaving and spluttering, our eyes awash. The air outside seemed immeasurably fresh and cool.

'Mrs Barton!' someone yelled. A dark figure approached us, faintly visible in the meagre moonlight. It was one of the servants; my mother grabbed his arm.

'Water!' she croaked. 'Fetch water!'

He vanished into the shadows as more servants came running. Some of them must have brought full buckets, because they plunged into the house. Raucous shouts were answered by further shouts. My mother turned to me.

'Stay here,' she gasped. 'All of you. Do not move from this spot.'

'No! Mama!'

'*Stay here!* I'll be back directly.'

And she hurried off, though not through the front door. Instead her dim white shape disappeared around the side of the house, heading for the kitchen. A lantern appeared then, swinging from the hand of James Barnett. But he took it inside with him.

'Where is Louisa?' Emily whimpered.

I reached out, groping, and found only two other bodies pressed against mine. Both were shivering violently. Here and there a tearful eye glinted, or a glossy lock gleamed—but none belonged to Louisa.

'Louisa?' I exclaimed, peering into the night. '*Louisa!*'

'She came out!' James said. 'I know she did!'

'Are you sure?'

'*Louisa!*' Emily shrieked. 'Oh no! Oh no!'

'Shh. It's all right . . .'

'She came out!' James sounded shrill. 'I saw her! She's not in there!'

'*MAMA!*' I bellowed at the top of my voice. No one seemed to notice. There was too much activity. 'Stay here,' I ordered. 'Don't move.'

'No!' Emily grabbed my sleeve. 'No! Charlotte! She told us not to!'

'Louisa is missing! She has to know!'

'You mustn't go, Charlotte,' said James, clinging to my other arm.

'*MAMA!*' I put the full force of my lungs into this cry, and it attracted some attention. Charley, our native servant, seemed to materialise out of the shadows.

'What, Miss?' he said.

'Louisa!' I wailed. 'Where is Louisa?'

He stared for a moment. 'With the Missus?' he suggested.

'No! No, we don't know *where* she is, Charley, you must tell her! You must tell the Missus! Quickly!'

He bolted, but in the wrong direction. We saw him go into the house.

'No! No, Charley!' I screamed. 'She's in the kitchen! *In the kitchen!*'

'Perhaps he went to see . . .' Emily sobbed. 'If—if Louisa—'

'*Louisa is not in the house!*' James stamped his foot. 'I *told* you!'

'Shh!'

You cannot conceive of our fear and despair. Where was Louisa? I tried to comfort the others. I assured them that she must have become separated from us in all the fuss and flurry. Perhaps she had gone to the kitchen. Perhaps she was with Mama. More lanterns had appeared on the scene, borne by half-dressed convicts who must have run down from the huts. I saw my mother amongst these people. She had returned from the kitchen with a brimming bucket, which she handed to one of the men.

'*Mama!*'

But she was occupied. Streams of hurrying figures were moving in and out of the house, forming a kind of irrigation chain. My mother stopped at one knot to consult Robert.

'*MAMA!*' I bawled.

This time she heard me, and abruptly broke off her conversation. She strode across the lawn towards us, her white robe flapping.

'Where is Louisa?' were the first words out of her mouth.

'Mama, we don't know!' Seeing her expression, I began to cry. 'Is she not with you?'

My mother caught her breath. She whirled around to face the house, while James insisted: 'She came out! I saw her! She came out, Mama, she did!'

'*Robert!*' my mother called, beginning to run. We followed her. 'Miss Louisa is missing! Oh God . . .'

'Nay, Mam.' Someone's soft Irish voice wafted across the smoky air. 'Nay, there's not a soul up there.'

'Are you sure? Did you check? *Louisa!*'

'She bail inside, Missus.' This was Charley, who had suddenly reappeared, coughing. 'I look.'

'Then where is she?'

No one knew. And no one could help, not with a fire to extinguish. It seemed at first as if our beloved home might burn to the ground, though we soon realised that the flames were not as voracious as we had feared. Even as we stood there, I noticed a certain easing of the frantic, scurrying activity that had been so apparent only minutes before. There was still a great deal of smoke, but blankets and buckets had been brought to bear on what was, essentially, a rather small fire. James Barnett said as much when he staggered out the front door, coughing.

'We broke its back,' he wheezed. 'It'll not be going further, God be praised.'

'Did you see Louisa?' Mama demanded. 'Is my daughter up there?'

'No, Mam.'

'Are you sure?'

'Sure and certain. We cleared the beds, Mam.'

'Then where is Louisa? *Louisa!*' All at once Mama spotted George Barton, and hurled herself at him like an avenging fury. '*What have you done?*' she screeched. '*Where is my daughter?*'

Barton had not burned to death in his bed. I must have been expecting something of the sort, for my heart sank when I saw him; subconsciously, I must have assumed that he had gone to sleep with a pipe in his mouth, dead drunk (as was his habit), and set his own bedclothes alight. Unhappily, though, he was safe. A later inspection revealed that the source of the fire must have been one of the many candles that he had placed on the upstairs landing. My mother, in trying to snuff them all out, may have inadvertently knocked down a single wax taper, or simply failed to extinguish it. Whatever the cause, it had ignited a portion of the Indian mat, which in turn had set fire to the finish on the skirting. A portion of wall, the door frame and some floorboards suffered badly, but the damage was contained. In general terms, the house remained sound.

Unfortunately, my mother was ignorant of all this at the time of the fire. Perhaps she believed, in her overwrought state, that George Barton had set it deliberately so as to kill us without fear of reprisal. Whatever the cause of her fury, it utterly transformed her. She rushed at her dishevelled husband and began to slap him around the head.

'*You cur, you sot, God damn you to hell!*' she raged. '*What have you done, you—murderer! Assassin!*'

It was an immensely stupid thing to do. Barton hit back; he punched her in the face, and she dropped like a stone. People rushed at them from all sides. I reviled him at the top of my voice as I threw myself onto my mother's collapsed form. Barton tried to kick us both, but lost his balance instead, staggering sideways. James Barnett finished the job with a discreetly timed push.

Barton fell on one knee.

'*Who did that?*' he yammered. '*Who was it? I'll have you flogged!*'

Some of the men immediately melted away into the shadows. James Barnett, however, stood his ground. His fists were clenched and he was breathing heavily.

My mother sat up. 'You're insane!' she lisped, through a stream of blood. 'Your mind is gone! How could you *do* such a thing?'

'*I? I?*'

'You would kill us all!'

'You're trying to kill *me*!'

'You are mad! You're a madman!'

'*Shut your bloody mouth!*' Barton roared. He went for her, and I went for him. When I tried to push him back, he knocked me aside as if I had been a curtain. 'Ah, the bairns . . .' someone muttered in protest. Still, however, nobody intervened. Nobody except my brother, that is; he picked up a heavy rock from one of the borders and hurled it against Barton's ribs.

Then he ran. He simply ran. Without waiting for Barton to recover from the blow, he shot away into the night.

'No! James! Wait!' cried my mother. 'Don't you touch him!'

'I'll break his bloody neck!' Barton howled, and fetched me such a box on the ear that I fell to the ground, stunned. He hit out again and again as we tried to restrain him. I remember curling up to ward off his flailing foot, which (to my eternal gratitude) was bare. Had he been shod, I might have suffered irreversible injury.

He lost his mind, I think. He became irrational at that moment, no doubt viewing his attack as self-defence. I have never seen such terrifying, unrestrained, inexplicable violence. At one point, reeling back, he encountered a small bush and trampled it underfoot, with deliberate yet uncontrolled venom, as if it had been his worst enemy.

Shielding Emily, my mother sobbed and screamed. I could hear James Barnett's hoarse voice pleading: 'Jesus, sir—you'll hang for it if you kill 'em—ah Christ, Henry, what'll we do?'

'Where's the gun?' Henry drawled, from out of the darkness.

The word 'gun' had an effect like a pistol-shot. Barton froze. Then he bolted. One moment he was there, on the lamp-lit front lawn. The next moment he was gone.

James Barnett went at once to my mother's side.

'God have mercy,' he protested. 'Just look at you . . .'

'Where is my son?' Mama struggled to her feet, pushing Barnett away from her. 'Charlotte? What has he done to you? Can you hear me, Charlotte?'

I nodded, unable to speak. The nod made my head pound like a drum.

'Go and find my son!' Mama ordered shrilly, addressing the convicts who stood motionless, watching us. 'Find James! Find Louisa! You must find them before he does!'

'Find the gun first,' Henry suggested, and I knew that he was right. James Barnett instantly got up and disappeared. Emily was weeping without restraint. I turned to my mother.

'Perhaps Louisa is hiding!' I said brokenly, my hand clamped to my throbbing ear. 'Perhaps she is scared to come out, Mama.'

'Perhaps.' My mother's voice trembled. Pressing Emily to her, she looked around in a helpless fashion, her face a mess of blood and tears. 'Yes, you may be right. Perhaps she *is* hiding.'

But we were wrong. And I will tell you what did become of Louisa, because the matter was soon enough resolved. It may not surprise you to learn that, when my siblings and I emerged from the house, Louisa kept running. She must have been so frightened that her feet refused to stop, carrying her across the front lawn, through the gate and into the bush. You will recall that it was Louisa who woke me with news of the fire. Before doing so, being a good and obedient child, she had put on her slippers. Consequently she was able to run without hurting herself on stones and thorns, though she was very lucky not to have rammed her head into a tree, or fallen down a slope—for despite the gibbous moon it was very dark.

Poor Louisa ran and ran. Eventually she must have looked around for sisters, and realised that she was alone. I cannot tell you the exact sequence of events, because Louisa never described them. She never once spoke of her wanderings that night. Her family were left to piece them together as best we could.

I do not know if she turned back or went on. But with so many large trees and dense thickets separating her from the house, she could not have seen her way back with any certainty. Instead, she would have been forced to rely on distant noises to plot her path—and such noises can be very misleading. They can bounce off hillsides, and bury themselves in scrub. Furthermore, they can be unhelpfully intermittent.

At any rate, Louisa got lost. I am certain of this, though she would not admit to it. Mr Ash heard her sobbing and moaning as he rode towards our house. And he stopped and called out, and finally told the servant who was lighting his way to follow the sound of Louisa's voice.

They came upon my sister halfway between Oldbury and Swanton.

We were very, very fortunate that Mr Ash was so alert. He had heard faint but suspicious cries in the distance, carrying through the still, dark night from the direction of our house. Perhaps they had awakened him, though I have my doubts; it seems more probable that he had been lying sleepless in bed, pondering the difficulties that lay ahead of him. Whatever the case, on being thus disturbed, he had quickly risen, dressed, and saddled his horse. He had then set off to discover the cause of the commotion—and had encountered my sister along the way.

It was some time before he reached us. Riding even the most placid horse through bush at night is not something that should be attempted with any haste or impatience. At last, however, he arrived, and was accompanied to the kitchen by some of the men who had been sent to scour the estate with dogs and lanterns.

News of Mr Ash was conveyed to my mother before her youngest daughter was. Mama had found refuge in the kitchen with myself and Emily and James. (My brother had been discovered hiding under the kitchen table, carving knife in hand.) While her children sat huddled around the hearth, my mother tried to dress her own wounds, quite frantic with worry. My own head was aching, and my ribs as well, but Mama was in a far worse state. Her split lip continued to bleed. Her eye was swollen. She hissed in pain whenever she was obliged to stoop. Yet she would not rest, constantly pacing and fidgeting, fussing with lint and vinegar, moving to the window and back again.

She had barred the door against her husband, and jumped when she heard Charley's knock.

'What is it?' she said. 'Who is it?'

'Miss Louisa come, Missus,' Charley replied.

'What?' My mother ran to the door, unbarred it, and hurried into the dimness. 'What? Charley? What do you say?'

But no explanation was required. Even as she spoke, Mr Ash rode out of the shadows, exhausted convicts illuminating his path. Louisa was perched on the saddle in front of him.

My mother shrieked.

'Louisa!' she cried. With a foolish disregard for the feelings of his horse, she rushed straight at Mr Ash, her arms outstretched—and received Louisa into them.

Mr Ash dismounted carefully.

'She was wandering in the woods,' he said, adjusting his reins. 'I heard her crying.'

'Oh, Mr Ash . . . oh, thank you,' my mother sobbed.

'There was a fire, I am told?'

'Yes, but it was put out. Louisa? Do you hear?' Mama and my sister were by now tightly entwined. 'The fire is out. We are safe, my love, you must not be afraid.'

'Where is yer husband?' Mr Ash inquired, and my mother looked around nervously.

'I—I am not entirely sure . . .' she stammered.

'Was he responsible for yer face, Mrs Barton?'

This was more direct an inquiry than I would have expected. It certainly affected my mother, who was struck dumb—whether from shock or shame I have no way of knowing.

As she struggled to reply, Mr Ash surveyed the scene in front of him. Though his eyes were engulfed in shadow, I could feel his gaze travelling over me before it moved on to Emily, and James, and the dark, smoky shape of the house.

'Mrs Barton,' he said, in reflective tones, 'this state of affairs cannot continue.'

'No, I—no.'

'If I were you, Mrs Barton, I should take my children and go. As soon as possible.' Mr Ash was standing with one hand wrapped around his horse's reins. The other he placed on his hip, pushing back his coat to reveal, once again, the butt of his pistol. 'It will then be my responsibility to deal with Mr Barton.'

'But this is our home! It is our *home*, Mr Ash!'

'Is it?' Having thoroughly examined every aspect of his surroundings, Mr Ash brought his wandering regard back to my

mother's face. 'I do not know how you would define a "home",
Ma'am, but this looks nothing like one to me. This looks like a
battlefield, in my opinion. And I'm a-wondering if the battlefield
is worth the cost of the battle. All things considered.'

In response, my mother opened her mouth. But no sound
emerged. She simply stared at Mr Ash with her one good eye (the
other having practically swollen shut) as Mr Ash returned her
stare blandly. Around us, the assigned men shuffled wearily from
task to task. A dog barked somewhere nearby. The air was heavy
with foul-smelling fumes.

Suddenly, my mother sighed.

Two weeks later we packed up our dray and left Oldbury.

Twenty-two

An interlude

Louisa wrote in great detail about my family's escape to Budgong. She wrote of how we packed our tents and earthenware, and my mother's writing desk, and made the long trek over Meryla mountain into the Shoalhaven. She described how Maugie, our pet bear, dug his claws into the side of a bullock and caused it to run amok, scattering its fellows, breaking crockery and releasing the bear. (Maugie immediately climbed up a tree, which had to be felled before his retrieval could be effected.) She mentioned Charley, and our three bullock drivers, and the young gentleman who, upon arriving at the Throsbys' shortly before our departure, had applied to accompany us—since he was heading for a station near Budgong. He was newly out from England, and for the life of me I cannot remember his name. Edwards? Edison? Something of the sort. All I remember about him is that, when we were confronted by a mysterious speck of light at one of the campsites, he was not paralysed by fear, as were his companions. Indeed, he had the presence of mind to throw more dead branches onto the almost expiring fire. The resulting blaze revealed, instead of a bushranger's smouldering pipe, a small, brown beetle with a glowing spot on its belly.

I recall *that* incident very well. So did Louisa, apparently—for she gave an account of it in the *Sydney Morning Herald*. I cannot tell you the exact date of publication, but I do know that the year was 1861. It was after my husband and I had left Cutaway Hill, you see. We were in Goulburn, and my daughter Emily was just a few months old. Though our financial condition was dire, we were still buying the *Herald* and selling it on afterwards; I could not seem to give it up, though Louisa's writing seldom afforded me much pleasure. (She had a regular column by that time, which usually concerned itself with the natural world.) I was especially displeased in 1860, when I read her observations about the month of August, for they seemed to mock all my troubles and futile attempts to forestall disaster. '*The incessant rain which has fallen during the present winter*,' she wrote, '*has not been without its effects on vegetable and even animal life. It is probably owing to this cause that many things are earlier in budding and blooming, and the birds in building*.' She made no mention of the hardship that had resulted from so much rain. She ignored the fact that it had continued through summer as well as winter, destroying the livelihoods of countless struggling settlers like my husband. The Hawkesbury flooded. The bridge at Berrima was washed away. Our cattle contracted black leg, and rust appeared in our district's wheat for the very first time. It was a disastrous year. We lost our small but precious farm, which my husband and I had worked so diligently. We were obliged to sell almost everything. We were declared bankrupt.

And what help were we afforded, in this most difficult time? None. None whatsoever. Granted that my mother and sister were by then living up at Kurrajong, miles and miles away, in the foothills of the Blue Mountains; they were consequently not within easy reach. James, however, was still at Oldbury. He himself suffered reverses on account of the rain. But they were not so bad as to prevent him from contributing more than thirty-three pounds to the construction of the new stone church at Sutton Forest. Nor from investing heavily in the Fitzroy Iron Works a couple of years later. He did eventually incur serious losses from the Iron Works, but that was not for at least another decade. In 1860, he would certainly have been in a position to lend us money, had he been so inclined.

Of course, I did not ask him. I could not bring myself to make the request, in light of our strained relations. Nevertheless, I do think that he might have offered. *I* certainly would have, had our positions been reversed. But James took his orders from my mother, and my mother seemed determined to forget my very existence. Having ignored poor little Ernest's birth in 1858, she proceeded to ignore Emily Louisa's as well. And though my sister was permitted to correspond, my mother never set pen to paper herself. Evidently, she was reluctant to communicate with me until I had apologised for my behaviour at that ill-fated funeral in 1854. Never mind that *she* had committed certain offences—oh, no. There could be no question of a shared culpability. For my mother was rarely disposed to acknowledge her own faults.

Through Louisa, she went as far as conveying to me her best wishes. But she would unbend no further.

Do not mistake me—I will freely acknowledge my own guilt in this sorry state of affairs. The fact is, I made no great effort to mend bridges. Certain dire events having occurred just a couple of years previously, I had become quite desperate to banish from my thoughts all trace of my early life, as well as the people associated with it. Louisa's correspondence prevented me from doing this. Though her letters rarely referred to anything but domestic pursuits, they would set me thinking about my mother, and from there my reflections would inevitably lead me down black paths towards Oldbury, and George Barton. Without fail, I would find myself once again confronting George Barton.

So I did not encourage Louisa to write. And when we moved to Goulburn, she lost track of me. I did not lose track of *her*. No literate colonial could have avoided her in those days, even if her identity was not always clear. 'An Australian Lady' is what she called herself—or 'L.A.', or 'L.A. Fernhurst' (Fernhurst being the name of my mother's house in Kurrajong). Louisa was publishing all over the place: in the *Sydney Morning Herald*, the *Sydney Mail*, the *Illustrated Sydney News*, the *Band of Hope Journal*. And there were her novels, too. Her second, *Cowanda*, was published approximately a year before I left Cutaway Hill. It angered me no end, though I scoured it for news of the family almost against my own inclinations. There was one particular scene that I thought directed at me. Captain Dell, the gruff old grandfather of Rachel (*Cowanda*'s heroine), was fond of engravings. Among the many that he owned was a picture of Christ and the Magdalene: according to my sister, it portrayed perfectly the Saviour's power and will to forgive. '*Even in that hour of bitterness,*' Louisa narrated, '*Rachel's eye wandered up to the place suspended on the wall above her, and the lesson it conveyed smote heavily upon her soul: the noble qualities of that old man who had just left her were blotted by a want of mercy, and in his sense of untarnished honour he judged harshly, and in opposition to Him who in His perfect purity yet said, "Neither do I condemn thee".*'

I pondered over this extract from time to time, puzzled as to how much I should read into it. Was it addressed to me or to my mother? To both or to neither of us? I could not decide. I did, however, instantly recognise the character 'Elice', whose nature, like her 'fair, refined countenance', grew in beauty with familiarity, and 'unfolded a peculiar sweetness, which at first was entirely overlooked'.

This, I need hardly say, was a perfect portrait of Emily. I wept when I read it. And I honour Louisa for her tender memorial, though it was no more than Emily deserved. My own memorial died long ago. She lived exactly as many years as did her aunt, and might have been her aunt resurrected, they were so alike. The death of both my Emilys has quite turned me off the name, I must confess—though my children will not be warned, and continue to use it regardless. Flora has her own Emily now. And Edwin has his. Even the wretched Eva has employed it, in an attempt to curry favour. She named her fourth illegitimate child Charlotte Emily, no doubt because I had welcomed the child's prodigal mother back to Orange. After Eva's first transgression, I could not abide to have her anywhere near me—to contemplate the ruin of her prospects and character, which had been so promising. But by the time Charlotte Emily was born, I could not afford to be so profligate with my children. I did not have many left, by then. So Eva returned from Sydney, dragging her bastard brood with her, and delivered herself of Charlotte Emily here in Orange.

Whether the child will survive with such an ill-fated name is questionable, though at twelve she seems quite hardy, not to say foolhardy. A chip off the old block, in fact.

But I digress. My concern is not with the future; it is with the past. Specifically, with the year 1860, when my husband and I were forced off our land. I shall not dwell on all the painful stratagems to which we were reduced, nor on the details of our rapid decline. I shall only say that my visits to Berrima became more frequent as we undertook various measures to stave off ruin. I found myself often at the Post Office, and on the premises of a certain stock and station agent, and in those shops whose proprietors were willing to extend us credit. I also entered negotiations with Mr James Powell, Berrima's first banker. How I disliked that man! He gave himself *such* airs, though he was really nothing more than a successful storekeeper. But some people perceive money as an ennobling force, and think themselves superior because they are in possession of it.

I have never shared this view.

In desperately pursuing every avenue open to us, I was asked to provide a letter testifying to my good character, and to that of my husband. It was an insolent request, and never did us any good at all that I could see. Nevertheless, I secured just such a letter from the Reverend Hassall. He was always a loyal friend to me, and to the rest of the town also. Never have I encountered such a noble and generous man of the cloth. As Chaplain of Berrima Gaol, he attended those prisoners sentenced to solitary confinement, and taught many to read, even supplying them with books. He fought for the wrongly convicted, and visited the poor. When the National Board school closed in 1862, he opened a school in his own stables and coach house. I therefore decided to approach him, despite the fact that I was not the most faithful member of his congregation. Cutaway Hill is quite a distance from Berrima, you see, and my husband, being Roman Catholic, was not always eager to spare me on a Sunday morning.

At that time, the Hassalls were living in Berrima's new rectory. It was a handsome stone house of Gothic design which overlooked the Wingecarribee River; though slightly out of town, it attracted a steady stream of visitors, even at odd hours of the day and night. I myself was careful to call when Mrs Hassall was receiving her morning guests. I did not bring my children, either—partly out of politeness and partly because I wished to shield them from our woes. Flora was twelve, then, and old enough to mind her brothers.

I remember that I wore my Sunday gown, which was of dark blue silk, with stripes. I also donned my best shawl and bonnet. And I was glad that I had made the effort, because when I arrived, Mrs Hassall was already entertaining a handful of other guests, all of them tricked out in their most respectable garments. Mr Harper was dressed in a black coat, a waistcoat and a white spotted silk necktie. Someone (Mr Halls, perhaps?) had divested himself of a black chimney *chapeau*. And Dr Salter was clutching the most dandified pair of lavender kid gloves that I have ever seen.

I knew these men, naturally. Mr Halls was the local schoolteacher. He went often to the rectory, no doubt in search of Mrs Hassall's delicious cakes and sandwiches—for he was a bachelor, poor fellow, and looked perpetually underfed. Mr Harper was the licensee of the Surveyor-General Inn, and may have been consulting the Hassalls about a baptism. Dr Salter was a good friend of the Reverend Hassall. They had worked together frequently, sometimes at the gaol, sometimes in the town or surrounding parish. Wherever Dr Salter pronounced a death, the Reverend Hassall—as often as not—would have been the one who had called him in.

All three men rose when I entered the parlour. To my disappointment, I saw at once that the Reverend was not himself present. Mrs Hassall, however, made me very welcome, inquiring at once into the health of my family. I mumbled something inane about colds and wet weather, whereupon Dr Salter took pity on me. He immediately raised the subject of croup, clearly touching a chord with the schoolmaster. They began to discuss the prevalence of croup among Mr Halls's students, and whether the appalling condition of the school (which was practically without a roof, and had to be closed during heavy rains) could perhaps be contributing to the number of sick children. As they talked, Mrs Hassall came close to me.

'May I ask, Mrs McNeilly, if all is well with you?' she said in a low voice. 'Or were you wishing to consult my husband on any *particular* matter? For if that is the case, he will be returning in an hour or so, and you are welcome to take your ease at our fireside.'

'Thank you. I should like that very much.'

'Tea, perhaps? It's a fresh pot.'

'Yes, please.'

'Milk or lemon?'

I allowed her to press on me all kinds of dainties, some of which I secretly pocketed for the children—it having been many months since they had enjoyed orange cake or almond biscuits. Meanwhile, talk had turned to Berrima Gaol. Dr Salter was then the visiting surgeon, and he was concerned at the number of prisoners who had recently contracted inflammation of the lungs. 'Conditions are not what they should be,' he opined, dipping an almond biscuit into his tea. 'The solitary confinement cells are very damp, and there is no circulation of air whatsoever, since the only opening is a small grate in each door.'

'Ah, but you can't be too careful,' Mr Harper pointed out. 'There's some hard men among 'em would use any little hole to break free. I recall those two bushrangers who escaped through the sewer. Now *there* was a desperate couple.'

'Indeed?' said Mr Halls. 'And when did that occur?'

'Oh—a while since.' Mr Harper glanced at Dr Salter. 'I cannot recall—my father spoke of it, God rest him. My father had his regulars among the Berrima police, so he knew all the stories of all the great cases: John Lynch, Lucretia Dunkley—'

'Ah!' said Mr Halls. 'Now, I have heard mention of these people, but never a full account. The children refer to John Lynch as a kind of ogre, whose ghost haunts the gaol, axe in hand. And Lucretia Dunkley—she was hanged, was she not?'

'For murder,' Mr Harper confirmed. 'And Lynch too. My father was there. He told me it's true what they say—that Lynch danced a jig on the scaffold before the trap was dropped.'

Mrs Hassall opened her mouth at this point, perhaps to change the subject. But the doctor was too quick.

'Lynch is much admired for that, you know,' he said. 'They still talk about him in the gaol, even twenty years after the fact. I gather that he had a sharp wit about him, and defended himself with aplomb: to most of the prisoners, this seems of much greater moment than his devilish crimes. Though I am convinced that much of what I hear about Lynch is fabricated. He has become larger than life, over time.'

Mr Harper, however, was shaking his head.

'Not Lynch,' he said firmly. 'My old Dad swore blind that man was the Devil Incarnate. There's things that never came out in the papers, things which George Bowen told him. Bowen was Police Magistrate; he took down Lynch's confession the day before he was hanged. Dad used to say, when Bowen finished, he headed straight for the bar at the Surveyor-General, as white as snow and shaking like a newborn lamb. It turned old Bowen off his job, Dad said, and he was back in England within the year.'

'But what did he say?' Mr Halls asked curiously. I was glad that this question had been put to Mr Harper, for I could not speak myself. Yet I desperately needed an answer.

'About Lynch?' Mr Harper replied. 'Oh, well, there was all those other killings. The ones at Bargo Brush, and so forth, that would never have been laid at his door save that he confessed to 'em. But there were more, too, and they happened *long* before he escaped from Hyde Park barracks. Bowen told my dad, when Lynch was in the chain gang at Newcastle, he blamed three other lags for stabbing him in the chest, and they were hanged for it. Well— according to Lynch, it was all a lie. He stabbed himself, so as to bring down punishment on the others. And very pleased he was that the ruse had carried.'

'Oh, Mr Harper,' said Mrs Hassall, turning pale, 'what dreadful wickedness!'

'We'll never see his like again, Mrs Hassall, God be praised. Why, he boasted of his tally. There was another killing he confessed to which he was never convicted of, though they charged him with it—a fellow convict down this way . . .'

All at once, Mr Harper stopped. I believe that his memory may have caught up with his tongue, and he had suddenly recalled the circumstances of Lynch's first trial, and the name of the man whose drunkenness had caused Lynch to be acquitted. At any rate, his gaze veered towards me, and he coloured, and fell silent. For although our acquaintance was slight, he knew whose daughter I was.

Both publicans and rectors are generally well versed in local affairs, I have found.

'There will always be incorrigibles among us,' Mrs Hassall remarked smoothly, after an awkward silence, 'for all that we might work with tireless hope to rescue them. More tea, Mr Harper? I see that your cup needs filling.'

What was said thereafter can be of no great interest. The conversation moved on to other topics: the wet winter, the dreadful condition of the roads, the survey of the proposed village of Wingecarribee (later known as Bowral). I played almost no part in it, being far too shaken. All at once I was cast back to that day at Oldbury, when John Lynch had winked at me across the yard.

Upon Mr Harper's rising to leave, I rose with him.

'Oh, but Mrs McNeilly—will you not stay until my husband returns?' Mrs Hassall protested, very much surprised. 'He is coming directly, I assure you.'

'No, I—I had best return later,' was my inadequate response. 'Forgive me. I must be getting home.'

'Yes, of course,' said Mrs Hassall. But she *would* follow me to the door, and load my arms with fruit, and delay me with her good wishes until I was forced to run after Mr Harper, lest he escape before I could question him. He was almost at the Great South Road when I caught up—and seemed greatly surprised at my suddenly addressing him in a most urgent and breathless manner.

'Mr Harper! Mr Harper!' I panted.

'Why, Mrs McNeilly,' he said, turning with a start. 'Is something wrong?'

'Nothing. I merely—I wished to ask you—excuse me.' I placed a hand to my breast and strove to recover myself, my lungs labouring pitifully. 'You were speaking of John Lynch,' I gasped at last. 'Of the murder at Oldbury. It happened when I was a little girl.'

Mr Harper's expression immediately became hunted. His gaze slid sideways, and he cleared his throat.

'Yes,' he said.

'I know that Lynch confessed to it—the newspapers said so—but there was no suggestion as to why he might have committed the murder. Indeed, no one seems to have *asked* him. Can you shed any light on this, Mr Harper? Did Mr Bowen ever tell your father why Thomas Smith had to die? Was it because Smith had decided to report certain information about an attack on my stepfather?'

'Mrs McNeilly . . .' Nervously, Mr Harper adjusted his necktie. 'I never even knew that his name *was* Smith. My father died when I was very young. He told me some things, and my Ma told me others. The rest came to me later, in the public bar—people told me what my father had told *them*. I'm not what you would call a witness, Mrs McNeilly. All I know is that some around here blamed Barton for Lynch's killing spree, because Barton was drunk, and couldn't testify at the first trial.'

'But John Lynch mentioned Smith's murder to Mr Bowen.'

'So they say.'

'And revealed nothing about his motive in committing it?'

Mr Harper spread his hands.

'It was a long time ago, Mrs McNeilly,' he said. 'I doubt there's anyone left to remember, even if they *were* informed. Least said, soonest mended, in my opinion.'

'The newspaper reports were wrong,' I insisted, determined to wring him dry. 'They stated that the murder took place in 1835, yet it happened in 1836. Do you know if that was Lynch's mistake, or their own? Did your father ever remark on it?'

'Mrs McNeilly . . .' The publican retreated a step, shaking his head in a rueful yet determined manner. 'I cannot help you, Ma'am. Indeed, I cannot help you.'

And he went off to tend his grandfather's hotel, which did not merit such faithful service. It seems to me quite frightful that generation after generation should be shackled to the same licence, shouldering a heavy burden of guilt for the corruption of countless men and the ruin of their families.

I have heard tell that the Harpers are still to be found at the Surveyor-General even today. And it saddens me to think that they none of them saw the light in all those long, regrettable years.

For every inordinate cup is unbless'd, and its ingredient is a devil.

Twenty-three

1842

I was in Sydney when John Lynch finally met his Maker.

By that time it was 1842, and my family was somewhat acclimatised to life in town. Not that we were ever denizens of Liverpool Street, or any other bustling metropolitan address. From Oldbury and Budgong we moved first to Rose Bay and then to Darlinghurst, which in those days was a little outpost on the ridge above a bushy, uninhabited Woolloomooloo. My mother paid ninety pounds a year for a house not far from the residence of Bishop Broughton and his wife. Our neighbours included the Griffiths, the Macleays and the O'Connells, so we were very respectably placed. Our home was not a large one. Nor was it lavishly furnished. But it was in a high and healthy position, with grounds enough to keep hens and a cow.

I regret to say that our native bear had died before reaching Sydney.

City life being notoriously busy and distracted, and not at all conducive to peace, we found ourselves much fretted and troubled during this time. For all its primitive comforts, Budgong had supplied us with many a long, drowsy day by the river, and many a quiet, cosy night around the hearth. At Budgong we were not continually pestered by lawyers, nor beset by ceaseless tumult, nor tormented by the slovenly, unreliable servants who seem to populate any metropolis. The noise of the city was particularly trying. We had no objection to the church bells, but the distant thunder of artillery practice in the Domain, and the 'clip-clop' of horses' hooves, and the cries of peddlars and knife-grinders, were very grating to the ear of those accustomed to birdsong and cattle lowing. So was the drunken singing of our servants, who were all of them partial to a 'drop of the creature' at any time of the day or night. And while a drunken servant is bearable on the spacious grounds of a country estate, he or she is not so easily endured within the confines of a very small town house. All I can say in favour of our various housemaids, with their fatal weakness for strong liquor and maudlin shanties, is that they were not George Barton. Though we endured much, we no longer had to endure George Barton. We made a concerted effort to expunge him from our lives—something that is evident from my mother's book.

It is a curious thing to be the stuff of literature. Believe me when I say that, while aware of my mother's undertaking, I had no idea that I was to figure so prominently in the work entitled *A Mother's Offering to Her Children*. Not that I appear under my *own name*, of course. Since Mama published the book anonymously, she could hardly have used real names. But when at last *A Mother's Offering* appeared—delivered to our house in a brown-paper parcel—and we all crowded about, snatching at the modest pile of volumes that was scarcely large enough to furnish each member of the family with his or her own copy, I saw at once what my mother had done. She had taken scenes from our childhood, and had set them down as moral or botanical lessons. 'Emma', obviously, was Emily. 'Julius' was James. 'Lucy' was Louisa, and I was 'Clara'. On one page I read what was practically an extract from my essay on the Booroowang. On another was the description of an incident at Bondi Bay, when I had tried to catch a cuttlefish. All of our favourite shipwreck stories were there: the wreck of the *Charles Easton*, the loss of the *Stirling Castle*, the sad affair of the *Joseph Forbes*. There was even an account of one of our black servants, Jenny, whose three infants apparently perished in the bush, and who was herself later killed by another native.

I remember exclaiming over all this, and being more pleased than offended. I was also impressed by the attention received by *A Mother's Offering* in the newspapers. Glancing through the yellowed clippings that I placed inside the back cover of my own copy, I see that mention was made of it in *The Australian* and the *Sydney Morning Herald*. There was even a full-length review in the *Sydney Gazette*, which began with the words: *'In these dull monotonous days, when we hear of nothing but Jeremiads on the state of the times, long-winded yarns on the Debenture Bill, scarcity of cash, failures, scrip, Loan Companies, Coolies, Banks, and impending ruin to every man, woman and child throughout the length and breadth of the Colony—we say, in these cut-throat days it is a relief to forget, for a moment, the harassing details of everyday life. We venture to say that this unpretending little volume before us will assuredly have that effect . . .'*

Not the most elegant of recommendations, but heartfelt. It even concluded with the hope that *A Mother's Offering* would obtain a 'cordial welcome in the house of every colonist in New South Wales' and remarked that my mother, through her commendable work, was entitled to the 'best wishes and patronage' of the public. By actually naming my mother, the review simultaneously ensured that she would in all likelihood *lose* the best wishes of half the public, since there were many persons in the colony who deplored the fact that a lady should lower herself to the point of pursuing a literary career. This slip of the pen, however, was not deliberate. The review was kindly meant. For the book itself was printed at the office of the *Sydney Gazette*, whose editors would have had no compelling reason to ruin its prospects. And in case you might be questioning the degree to which such a notice could be entirely disinterested, in light of its provenance, let me assure you that the book's publisher, Mr Evans, had nothing much to do with the paper otherwise. He was a bookseller on George Street; we used to frequent his bookstall, which lay south of the new marketplace not far from the emporium of Mr David Jones. Despite the fact that we rarely had enough money to make a purchase, Mr Evans and my mother were in the way of being friends. And when my mother mentioned to him her idea for a children's book of amusement and instruction, Mr Evans promised to 'consider it'.

At first, as I said, the book pleased me. It won my mother some small fame, which proved more useful that otherwise when I began to attend school. It was also a source of extra funds, which were badly needed, since the ladies of Sydney dressed so very well. I myself was becoming quite conscious of the deficiencies of my wardrobe, and was anxious to present a stylish figure.

But as my relations with Mama became more strained, *A Mother's Offering* began to irritate me. I noticed certain aspects of the book that I had previously ignored—for example, the fact that 'Clara' is portrayed as such an *overbearing* child. ('*Julius,*' she scolds, '*let Mamma tell it without interrupting her so often: we shall understand it much better.*') It is 'little Lucy', moreover, who seems to express most frequently the wisest and prettiest opinions. She will not laugh at 'naughty, bad people' as Julius does. She commends kindness, and longs to rescue people in distress from their terrible condition. She is the only child shown kissing her mother—whereupon 'Mrs S.' warmly returns her fond embrace.

No one else in the narrative exchanges so much as a lingering glance. Indeed, the impression I receive from the work even now is that no one is as favoured as 'Lucy', nor as worthy of regard. Perhaps I am prejudiced. No doubt I am overly sensitive. But I gradually came to reject the book, and was embarrassed when any acquaintance chanced to read it. For I felt that, however subtly, it portrayed me in a poor light. And I resented my mother for using me in such a fashion.

Nevertheless, I do acknowledge that she had good reason to publish it. Firstly, as I said, it brought us a little income. Secondly, it demonstrated beyond all doubt that Mama was an excellent mother. The children in the book are happy and well informed. There is no suggestion that 'Mrs S.' is in any way neglectful, immodest or unfit. My mother, in recreating many of our happier family moments (with George Barton noticeably absent from every single one of them), intended to make a point. She was proving to Messrs Berry and Coghill that she did not deserve to be parted from her children.

For this is the exact task that they had set themselves: to deprive my mother of her offspring. After she left Oldbury for Budgong, relations between Mama and my father's executors deteriorated rapidly. The result was a drawn-out legal contest that I will not describe in great detail, it being so very tedious and deplorable. Besides, I was never permitted to read about it in the newspapers, and therefore do not have a full and proper understanding of the case.

Suffice it to say that *Atkinson Versus Barton and Others* continued for six years, absorbing in the process nearly two thousand pounds of my father's money. It began in 1840, when my mother petitioned the Chief Justice. She blamed Berry and Coghill for her own impoverished state, because they had mismanaged Oldbury, letting it first to George Barton and then to an insolvent, Thomas Humphery, who from July of the following year stopped paying rent at all. She declared that she was in desperate need of funds. From the date of her departure from Oldbury she had received no allowance, and had been forced to sell furniture and obtain loans to support her family. I can testify to the truth of all this. There were times when we could not afford to buy tea, nor to keep the candles lit at nightfall. And Mr Berry was *most* unsympathetic when my mother appealed to him for assistance. I believe he felt that she had brought down her woes upon her own head. (And who is to say that he was entirely wrong?)

The Master in Equity was also unhelpful. Rather than proving himself a friend to all destitute widows and orphans, he was the exact opposite, and held an inquiry into whether my mother was a fit guardian. Messrs Berry and Coghill thought not. In a statement to the court, they accused her of imprudent conduct 'since her intermarriage with George Bruce Barton'. According to the executors, my mother was an improper guardian because she lived apart from her husband, and because she had been obstructive in her dealings with them. George Barton's vicious attack on her morals was presented to the court at this point.

I recall weeks of anguish, as it was decided who should best be appointed guardian to myself and my siblings. My uncle refused. So did various solicitors. For a short time, James was placed in the custody of the Reverend George Turner, of Hunters Hill parish. But he did not remain there long, for my mother fought back, denying all the claims made by Messrs Berry, Coghill and Barton. Another of her petitions came before the Supreme Court in July of '41; it was described as 'impertinent and scandalous', and she was ordered to pay costs for that reason. Nevertheless, in an interim judgement, she was appointed guardian of her own children.

Do not assume that I was fully aware of all these events as they unfolded, though I could not be entirely ignorant. On one occasion, for instance, my siblings and I were brought before the Master in Equity, in order that we might demonstrate the full extent of our education. (He found that we had been very well instructed, to a degree not generally found in public schools.) There was also talk of my being enrolled at a boarding academy in Liverpool. And my mother was constantly having to take the omnibus to town so that she might consult her solicitors, leaving us to fill many an empty day as best we could.

Nevertheless, she preferred that we not be exposed to much of what went on. I daresay that she did not want us upset. Her pride, moreover, would have revolted against our becoming acquainted with some of the particulars that might have appeared in the press: her past as a governess, for example, or the fact that she did, for a while, pursue an unsubstantiated claim of bigamy against her husband. I discovered this last circumstance a couple of years later, when I broke into her desk; Louisa further enlightened me at my mother's funeral. Yet during the early '40s I was for the most part uninformed. I knew only that Mr Berry was a fiend, that there was never enough money, and that lawyers were a breed of men with nothing to recommend them.

When the interim judgement was made in our favour, I also learned that my mother was to have a fixed allowance of 350 pounds per annum. And as a consequence, she told me, I would be permitted to attend school.

'School?' I echoed, more astonished than I can convey. 'But—'

'Yes, yes.' She laughed and nodded. 'I know that I have made my feelings plain on the subject of Ladies' Academies. But this school, I am persuaded, will be very different.'

She went on to explain that she had been corresponding with Mr James Rennie and his daughter Christina. Mr Rennie had opened his College High School for boys in the middle of 1841. His daughter had most recently worked as a governess to the Throsbys. 'She is still very young,' my mother admitted, 'but I have every faith in Mrs Throsby's judgement. And since Miss Rennie has studied in France and Prussia, as well as England, there can be no question of narrow or stunted perceptions.' Upon discovering that Miss Rennie intended to open a 'ladies' department' at her father's high school, my mother had written to her for a prospectus.

'Mr Rennie has very sound ideas on education,' my mother continued. 'He believes, not in flogging, but in the discipline of kindness and diligence. He tells me that he is earnest in his desire to have girls receive the same education as boys. In his view, moreover, education does not mean the acquisition of knowledge or accomplishments. It means the formation of habits of attention, the exercise of the reflective faculties, and the love of truth'. My mother could have been describing her own philosophy; her eyes were bright as she lavished praise upon Mr James Rennie's lofty goals. 'It will mean that you and your brother may attend the same school as day pupils,' she said. 'Three guineas a quarter for you and two for James. Very reasonable, I think, considering the range of branches offered. Reading with Grammar and Dictionary, Writing, Accounts, Botany, French—'

'But what about me, Mama?' Emily interjected, looking rather lost. 'Am *I* not to go as well?'

'Oh, my darling.' Mama pulled her close. 'This is by way of an *exploratory* manoeuvre. You know that James and the Captain are my little soldiers. You and Louisa are my little flowers. If all goes well, and my two soldiers are happy, then I shall consider placing my two flowers in Miss Rennie's care.'

My mother's plan was reasonable. We none of us were familiar with the ways of an academy, and Louisa, in particular, was very delicate. It made sense that James and I should test the waters, so to speak. Therefore, in January 1842, at the ages of nine and thirteen respectively, he and I were enrolled at College High School as day scholars.

An important event in our lives, I assure you.

At that time, Mr Rennie's establishment was to be found on Elizabeth Street. It stood opposite the northern end of Hyde Park, and backed onto Castlereagh, not far from the large, brick building that housed the Catholic and Anglican parish schools. My memory is no longer what it should be, but I seem to recall that Mr Rennie's premises were quite elderly, and in need of repair—or at the very least, of a little whitewash—with two storeys and four chimneys.

Though made of brick, the building had a stone trim, and stone flags on the ground floor. It was therefore a very *solid* structure, of the sort most required by an educator of young boys. Though the joinery was scarred by innumerable boots, and the door-knobs were wrung like cow-teats, and the windows were banged down with a savagery that set them rattling, I witnessed no really dreadful mutilation of the sort that you so often saw in flimsier houses of bark and weatherboard. In other words, it was a suitable address. It was conveniently placed, adequately furnished, and of exactly the right size and construction.

Most of the building was occupied by the male student body, which seemed to spend a lot of time thundering up and down the staircase and scraping chair-legs across the floor. I was most dreadfully shocked when first I heard the sound of boys unleashed, for the noise was extraordinary—like a load of barrels tumbling from a loft. Soon, however, I grew accustomed to the conditions, and hardly noticed them. Even the shouting of the masters ceased to make me flinch in my seat. I did not have to endure such loud reproof myself, because no voice was ever raised in the ladies' department. Nevertheless, until I became used to it, I was always reminded of George Barton, and my pulse would quicken accordingly.

But the teachers at College High School could not have been more *unlike* George Barton. They were without exception cultured and genteel. Most displayed exactly the kind of curiosity and excitement that Mr Rennie saw as necessary to the pursuit and acquisition of knowledge. Mr Dodd, who taught mathematics, tried to convey to us the *beauty* of numbers. Mr Chambers was one of Sydney's best teachers of music. As for the Rennies, I must confess that I adored all three of them.

Miss Rennie was young and energetic, with clear-cut features and masses of wavy hair. She looked very much like her father, whose own hair, though greying, was still thick. They shared the same dark brows, chiselled noses and piercing grey eyes. Mr Edward Rennie had not quite such striking looks, though his appearance was perfectly inoffensive, and his manner reassuringly quiet. Indeed, when he later became the Auditor-General for New South Wales, it did not surprise me in the least. For I can still recall the extraordinary quickness of his intellect, and the way he would subdue a gang of rowdy boys simply by fixing them with his steely and level gaze.

It was his father, however, who became the object of my most fervid devotion. Mr James Rennie was a man of *character*. Though not by any means young, he was immensely energetic, with a fresh and vigorous mind of the type that you will rarely encounter outside the Groves of Academe. His qualifications were impeccable, for he possessed an M.A., was the author of a respected series of works entitled *Scientific Alphabets*, and had formerly held the position of Professor of Natural History at the University of London. This alone would have recommended him to my mother, even if he had not already earned her approval with his educational theories. For Mr Rennie made no secret of his beliefs. Several months before I enrolled at his academy, my mother took the entire family to the Sydney School of Arts, where we witnessed a debate on the topic: 'Would it be expedient to give to ladies the same education as is given to gentlemen?' Mr James Rennie was then secretary of the Debating Society, and I remember how impressed we all were at the figure that he cut as he defended the 'affirmative' side of the debate. He had a strong, clear, musical voice, and employed many a poetical turn of phrase. Moreover, he seemed to believe very strongly in the position for which he was arguing.

'I do think,' said my mother, at the conclusion of the event, 'that Mr Rennie would be one of the few schoolmasters to whom I would willingly entrust my daughters. For there is no side to him, and his ideas are very sound.'

He was also quite canny, I think. Certainly it was clever to stage such a debate shortly before his daughter opened her 'ladies' department'. I am sure that my mother was not the only parent inspired by his performance to make inquiries about the school. His series of public lectures on 'Beauty', which occurred in the early part of 1842, must have had a similar result. For his 'ladies' department' grew steadily throughout the same period, forcing Miss Rennie to engage another pair of governesses. Even those who did not attend the lectures must have had their interest piqued by newspaper reports.

I attended the lectures, naturally. So did my mother, who was sceptical at first—though not after Mr Rennie had plainly described the injurious effects that can be expected from the wearing of corsets. Mr Rennie, you see, was an opponent of Unnatural Beauty. He was adamant that Beauty could not be separated from Health. According to Mr Rennie, good penmanship depended on good posture. He himself, at his school, adhered to a set of rules concerning posture that resulted in penmanship of the highest order—as could be seen by the specimens that he had brought along by way of illustration.

I remember quite well that a sample of my own handwriting was among these specimens. Seeing it, I sat very straight in my chair, almost bursting with pride. For I revered Mr Rennie. I believed every word that he uttered. And I was happy at his school, where I excelled to an extraordinary degree. It is very gratifying, when I look back, to reflect on how well I performed there. In the middle of the year my results were as follows: first in drawing and geography, second in Italian and ornamental needlework, third in history and journal-writing.

Not that I can take sole credit for my performance. Without my mother's meticulous grounding, I should not have achieved such success. But I must admit that I was insufficiently grateful. Though sometimes moved to boast about her literary achievements,

I was, for the most part, discreetly silent about my mother. Partly this was on account of her irregular marital status. Chiefly, it was because I wished to turn my back entirely on the past—especially where George Barton was concerned.

My ambitions, at this time, were simple. I wished to be accepted as a young lady of the metropolis. I wished to be admired, and praised, and invited to adorn as many drawing rooms as Sydney had to offer. I wished to throw off all traces of my somewhat dubious background, and shine with what Mr Rennie called 'woman's peculiar glory'—that is, the ability to elevate the tone of every social circle that she might adorn.

So you may imagine my feelings when, on the morning of March the sixteenth, 1842, Miss Jessie Knight asked me (in her inimitable, wide-eyed way) if I had ever *personally* known the murderer John Lynch.

Twenty-four

J essie Knight was not my friend. I had thought her so once, for her demeanour was very sweet and insinuating, so that I was initially deceived. She had mastered the kind of subtle malice so freely employed in certain metropolitan drawing rooms, where ladies are brought up never to speak their minds, but to smile on their enemies, and use their tongues as double-edged swords.

I myself was not acquainted with the technique. My mother was always frank—even blunt—in conveying her impressions, and I had inherited this trait. It was therefore some time before I realised that Jessie Knight's intentions were purely spiteful when she let drop her careless little remarks, for all that she did it so innocently. In opening her eyes very wide, and seeming quite astonished that offence had been taken, she was merely attempting to disguise her true nature—which was wholly ill disposed towards everyone and everything.

She was vicious, but did not appear so. With her golden ringlets and bird-like voice, she seemed more angelic than otherwise. Indeed, she was much admired by the younger girls, who would often compete for her attention. And she in turn was a capricious friend to them, sometimes offering and sometimes withdrawing her favours. I can only assume that she was practising upon these hapless creatures the various stratagems with which she would have preferred to ensnare young men. It surprised me that she did not exert herself more to captivate some of Mr Rennie's male scholars. But I am persuaded now that she thought them poor things, callow and lumpish compared to the gentlemen who seemed to move through her mother's drawing room in waves.

She was the daughter of a merchant. Yet she gave herself *such* airs, and seemed to think herself better than anyone, if only because she lived in a fine house, wore beautiful clothes, and was connected in some remote way with Sir Thomas Mitchell—whose property at Darling Point she had visited on one occasion. No doubt she was jealous of my own, more respectable ancestry. At any rate, she did everything possible to denigrate it. I remember her once asking if Mrs Atkinson, who conducted a Ladies' Academy on the premises of the old Australian College, was perhaps an aunt of mine? And why, in that case, was I not enrolled *there*? ('For the poor soul must be desperate for business.') On another occasion, she questioned me about *A Mother's Offering to Her Children*. Why, she asked, had it been dedicated to the Governor's son, Master Reginald Gipps? Was my mother perhaps *acquainted* with His Excellency?

No, I had to admit. She was not.

Then she must have written to him, seeking permission to dedicate the book to his son?

I believed so.

'Ah,' said Jessie Knight. 'How *enterprising*. And does Mrs Barton receive a portion of the six shillings charged for every copy? Or was the money paid to her in one sum, before publication?'

I confessed that I did not know.

'No, of course not,' Jessie said sweetly. 'Who wants to bother with all the dull details of a mercantile transaction?' Thereby implying that my mother, in earning her money, was no better than a common woman with a grog-shop licence.

My only defence against this sort of thing was rudeness. Not being able to reply in kind, I would ignore Jessie, or tell her to shut her mouth. My true revenge was to outdo her in almost every branch of learning offered to us. It irked her horribly when I received the first medal for general superiority at the end of the year. I know this because of the clumsy way she tried to insult me after the presentations, when Mr Rennie announced that a prize would be given, at the commencement of the next school term, to any pupil who spent a portion of the holidays writing a set of books by double entry, consisting of a Day Book, Cash and Bill book, journal and ledger, accurately balanced.

'I suppose you and your brother will be entering *that* competition,' my foe declared meanly, 'now that Mrs Barton has started to earn a good wage.'

It was a stupid remark, which did not endear her to Miss Rennie. Our teacher promptly declared that if Jessie had a mind to be unpleasant, she could go straight home and miss all the dancing. This was in December, long after the death of John Lynch—whose trial took place in March of the same year. Jessie and I were still on speaking terms in March. We had little choice, since Mr Rennie favoured the modern system of 'pairing' pupils. If the system does not seem so modern now, back then it was the latest thing: senior girls, or 'monitors', would correct the production of those who were younger and less able. Jessie and I were both monitors, along with Mary Mullen, and a handful of others whose names I forget. Therefore we were thrown very much together. Often we would sit beside each other at the front of the room. Sometimes we were asked to check each other's work.

It therefore required no great ingenuity on Jessie's part to address me in a low voice one fine March morning as we prepared for class.

'Tell me,' she murmured, 'did you ever *personally* know the murderer John Lynch?'

I dropped my books. The noise of it resounded throughout the high-ceilinged chamber, making everyone turn with a start.

Everyone, that is, except Jessie. She just stood there smiling.

'Papa was reading from the *Gazette*,' she continued, 'and it said that John Lynch, who is being tried for murder in Berrima, was tried once before. Back in 1835, for killing a man called Smith at Oldbury. Oldbury *is* the name of your father's estate, is it not?'

I gaped at her, unable to speak. Then Miss Rennie came to my rescue.

'No gossiping, if you please,' she warned. 'Attend to your work, Miss Knight. If you wish to discuss vulgar subjects, kindly do so outside the school premises.'

As you may imagine, I could scarcely concentrate on the task at hand. There was a little girl—Isabella—whose stilted reading I was required to correct, and I am quite sure that many a gross error slipped by me unperceived, since I barely heard her. As a result, I was unprepared for the exercise that followed. Our textbook contained a series of questions relating to every extract included therein; I found myself asking 'Why was not Jane happy while taking care of the baby?' and 'What kind of persons are not happy?' without having the least idea whether Isabella's answers were correct or not!

Jessie did not approach me again, that day. Yet she watched me closely, delighting (no doubt) in every mistake that I made as a result of my preoccupation. It was a dreadful experience. The strain was immense. And at the close of the final lesson I hurried out to meet my mother in a state of extreme anxiety, hardly able to contain myself.

My mother, I should tell you, unfailingly caught the omnibus to town so as to escort her children home from school. At least that was her *professed* motive. I sometimes wonder if she did it partly in order to exchange a few words with Mr Rennie, who was always very polite to the parents of his pupils. But if she did, I cannot blame her. I would probably have done the same myself.

He was an extremely personable man.

'Mama,' I said, without sparing a thought for James or Emily. (Louisa had been left at home, on account of her poor health.) 'Mama, John Lynch is being tried at Berrima! For *murder*, Mama!'

We were walking south, towards Market Street. My mother stopped in her tracks.

'Who told you so?' my mother demanded.

'It was in the *Gazette*. Surely the *Gazette* could not be wrong?'

'Is it true, Mama?' James blinked up at my mother in alarm. 'Is it the same John Lynch?'

'It must be,' I interjected. 'For the newspaper said that he was tried years ago for the murder of a man named Smith at Oldbury—'

'Hush.' My mother made an abrupt movement. 'Not here, if you please.'

'But—'

'*Hush*. There is no need for concern. John Lynch is in custody at Berrima. He will not trouble us here.'

'But Mama . . .' I could not believe her obtuseness. John Lynch was the least of our worries. 'Mama, where is Mr Barton? He will not be testifying, will he?'

My mother took a deep breath. She looked about her quickly, her lips pressed tightly together.

'Mr Barton is in Berrima also,' she replied. 'He is undertaking an action against Mr Humphery before the local court. Now stop fretting, and show a little self-respect. We are on a public thoroughfare, Charlotte. This is neither the time nor the place to discuss such matters.'

I should perhaps explain why we were so nervous. You must already be aware that any mention of John Lynch had a bad effect on George Barton. You will not be aware, however, that the state of George Barton's temper was still of some interest to us. Having been forced to surrender Oldbury to the new tenant, my stepfather was often in Sydney, making legal claims against Messrs Humphery and Berry with equal vehemence. He felt himself so ill used that he would drink himself into a frenzy, and would sometimes appear on my mother's doorstep, crying out for vengeance. It had happened thrice since our removal to Sydney. Indeed, his conduct was such that in early 1841, my mother had applied to the magistrates at the local Police Office for protection.

That was after he had smashed a window and vomited onto our only surviving rug.

It was partly on account of George Barton that we had vacated our house in Rose Bay. With her husband about, my mother felt safer at an address that was closer to town. And her instincts were good, because we had so far received no unexpected visits from my stepfather in Darlinghurst.

Nevertheless, we could not hide from him indefinitely. And we all of us knew that, if anything was bound to inflame Barton's drunken temper, it would be public mention of Thomas Smith's death. *Especially* in connection with a new murder. As the days rolled by, and the details of Lynch's crimes became generally known, we grew more and more alarmed. For we could easily imagine what was being said in Berrima. Years later, Mr Roger Therry said the very same thing: he declared that, had Barton not been drunk at Lynch's first trial—thereby aborting it—the carnage that followed might never have happened.

And what carnage was this? Here I had better break off to describe John Lynch's terrible career of slaughter, for there are not many nowadays who remember it. You will recollect that in 1836 Lynch went to Newcastle, where he subsequently concocted a false accusation against certain fellow convicts. Shortly afterwards, he was sent to the barracks in Sydney, from which he escaped in

November 1840. (This event was not widely reported at the time.) From Sydney he headed straight back to his old haunts, around Berrima and Sutton Forest. According to his confession—which was published in newspapers and broadsheets after his death—his intention was to approach one John Mulligan of Wombat Brush, who owed him money. You may well ask: how is it possible that an assigned convict should be owed money, when he could have possessed nothing to sell? The answer is that he simply made off with the possessions of others. Lynch himself admitted that Mulligan had served him as a 'fence', disposing of property purloined by Lynch.

Upon learning this, it occurred to me that the property in question had almost certainly belonged to the Oldbury estate. In fact the oft-blamed bushranger gang may not have been responsible for all the flour and sugar and sheep that went missing from our stations, back in 1836. I said as much to my mother, who was poring over the dreadful details of the confession. Whereat she looked up, almost despairingly, and said: 'It is worse than I ever imagined.'

It was very bad, in all truth. For Mulligan, when applied to, would not pay John Lynch for the articles left with him. So Lynch stole eight of our tenant's bullocks. His intention was to sell them in Sydney, where they would not be known or recognised. But on Mount Razorback he encountered a certain Mr Ireland, who was also heading for Sydney. Mr Ireland was in charge of a dray belonging to Mr Thomas Cowper. It contained a large quantity of bacon and other produce destined for the Sydney market. Lynch decided to abandon his bullocks in favour of the dray and its contents. He therefore killed Mr Ireland, and the black boy who accompanied him, with an axe. He then concealed the corpses under a pile of stones, and proceeded on his way to Sydney, taking Mr Ireland's dog with him. But here, I adjure, is the remarkable thing: he was not far from Sydney when he *encountered Mr Cowper, the owner of the dray.*

Did he kill Mr Cowper? He did not. Rather, he calmly and genially explained that Mr Ireland, having fallen ill, had asked Lynch to take charge of Cowper's load. Inexplicably, Mr Cowper believed this. Instead of summoning the police, Cowper arranged to meet up with Lynch in Sydney. And thereafter the dray's owner went happily on his way, very fortunate indeed that his head was still on his shoulders.

It has been mentioned that Lynch was transported for the crime of 'false pretence'. I believe that this incident, as much as any other, displays his peculiar genius. The man was utterly convincing. Whatever he did, and whatever he claimed, he never failed to impress his interlocutors as amiable, intelligent, and thoroughly good-hearted. Why, even Mr Ireland's faithful *dog* was won over! At Lynch's trial, moreover, the defendant never faltered once. I myself read in the *Examiner*—an English journal which concerned itself with the case—that '*the man's appearance and manner on his last trial is described to have been . . . not of a forbidding, but of a mild and prepossessing character; and, though undefended by counsel, he conducted his own defence with self-possession and coolness, as well as with remarkable ingenuity*'. Yet beneath this pleasant veneer lay a soul bereft of any human spark—a great, black hole wherein dwelt some kind of monster which hardly resembled a man at all. It is this that I found most frightening. For it begs the question: whom *may* we trust, if God allows such creatures to roam the earth? How are we to find our way, if we cannot rely on our own instincts?

It need hardly be said that Lynch disposed of his goods and was gone from Sydney long before Mr Cowper ever returned there. Even so, Mr Cowper moved quickly. By the time Lynch regained the Bargo Brush, its constabulary had been alerted to his theft of Cowper's dray. They were actively spreading word of it—to the eternal misfortune of Lynch's next victims. These unfortunates were Mr William Fraser and his nineteen-year-old son, also called William, who were heading down the Old South Road.

The Frasers had been entrusted with a horse-team, and a dray loaded with valuable goods. Yet they were unaccustomed to such work, and were making a pretty mess of it. Upon meeting up with Lynch near the Stonequarry, they must have congratulated themselves on their good fortune—since John Lynch, in his own words, was 'clever in the management of draft cattle'. He professed to have wished them no harm, at first, though confessing to have 'managed to get from them an account of the whole of their and their master's concerns'. Together the three men had travelled on to Bargo Brush, where they were joined on the second night by another party. All save Lynch were asleep by the fire when a stranger rode up and proceeded to make inquiries about Mr Cowper's dray. In the darkness he cannot have seen Lynch, who lay very still; Mr Fraser the elder, as he conversed with the mounted man, was 'between asleep and awake', and only answered 'something at random'. Yet after the rider had departed, Lynch said to himself: 'This is sharp work—this will never do—I must get rid of this dray, and obtain another somehow'.

Thus was poor William Fraser's fate sealed.

Now—observe the ice-cold intellect of John Lynch. He knew that Mr Fraser might at any moment connect him with Mr Cowper's dray. He also knew that both Frasers were keen to stay in his company. So at daybreak he went off, pretending to search for his bullocks but in reality driving them deep into the bush. He then strangled Mr Ireland's dog, and stayed away so long that the companion party—two men and one woman—had left before he returned. The tale he told the Frasers was, as usual, completely convincing. He claimed that the bullocks were nowhere to be found, and had probably returned to their home beyond Berrima. It was agreed, therefore, that he should leave his empty dray at Bargo Brush, and accompany the Frasers to Cordeaux's Hill.

It was here that he killed them, the following morning. Though Mr Ireland had been dispatched while he slept, the Frasers received no such mercy. Lynch first accompanied young William 'over the ridge', ostensibly to help fetch the horses. Instead, he struck the poor boy on his head with an axe. ('If people knew how easy it is to take away life,' Lynch here commented to Mr George Bowen, 'things of this kind would happen oftener.') The unfortunate father was dealt with in a similar fashion soon afterwards, whereupon John Lynch buried the bodies.

The following day, he arrived at Mulligan's farm.

It must be clear by now that John Lynch felt defrauded by Mulligan. I myself believe that he always intended to kill the man, though he never said as much. He merely remarked that he spun his old friend a tale about being hired to deliver a dray, before sending to Gray's hotel for rum. By the evening he and his hosts had 'got very sociable', though he himself took care not to over-indulge. I should tell you, at this point, that Mr Mulligan lived with a woman, Bridget Macnamara, who was not his lawful wife. She had one son, a boy of eighteen, and a daughter four years younger. These are the people whom Lynch resolved to murder that cold, windy night in August of 1841.

Here is the account he gave of himself.

'I looked up at the bright moon and I prayed to the Almighty God to direct me. I said to myself, I am an injured man, and the Mulligans have defrauded me of what I perilled life and liberty to obtain. That fellow, when I was starving in the Berrima Iron Gang, has often passed me by without as much as giving me a shilling, when he had many pounds that were justly mine in his hands. And now, wouldn't it be right that they should lose all they possess as a judgement upon them for withholding his own from the poor prisoner? Heaven guide me and point out to me what to do.'

I can hardly bear to contemplate what happened next. After taking up an axe, he offered to go and chop some wood if the boy, John, would help him. Lynch claims that, as soon as they were alone together, John spoke roughly of Mulligan, saying that God would soon take the man away and if He didn't, John would 'give him maybe a helping hand'. Whether this is true or not, only God Himself can judge. But Lynch made it his excuse for smashing the boy's head with the axe. 'Ah, John,' he remarked, 'you shouldn't speak that way; you don't know what may be in store for yourself.'

Lynch then returned to the hut. He told Bridget that her son was busy with the wheelbarrow, and they shared another glass of rum. This I find more terrible than I can properly convey: to kill a mother's only son before drinking with her, calmly, knowing what he knew . . . it is past belief. Lynch told Bridget that John had gone into the bush to check the horses, but the woman soon became restless. She spoke of a dream she'd had the night before, in which she had been holding an infant child, horribly mangled and covered with blood. 'I hated this old woman,' Lynch observed, 'for she used to toss cups and balls, and could foretell things.'

Not her own death, however. If that had been so, she would have seized Mulligan's gun. Instead she went to the door, and 'coo-eed' for her son—without result—until Mr Mulligan finally rose, and took up his gun, and said: 'Perhaps the lad is lost in the bush.' He was about to fire, so that young John might hear the sound and find his way back in the dark, but Lynch prevented him. 'You'd better not fire,' Lynch said. 'People will come—perhaps the police; and if we're to deal, it won't answer that the dray should be seen here.'

I do not know why Mulligan should have agreed. Lynch had told him that the dray was not stolen. Yet the fool obeyed Lynch, folding his arms as he stood outside in the moonlight. Though Lynch was with him, the murderous fiend still had his eye on Bridget, inside the house. He saw her take out a large knife and conceal it in her clothes, before changing her mind and passing it to her daughter. I wish that she had run at him with it. I wish that she had trusted her Second Sight, and killed him then and there.

But she did not. She waited. So Lynch pretended that he had to tie a troublesome dog to the wheel of his dray. While occupied thus, he concealed his axe beneath his thick coat. Meanwhile, Bridget had taken matters into her own hands. She had left the house, and was moving like one bewitched towards the very spot where her son's body lay, concealed beneath a pile of wood. 'Now or never,' thought Lynch. He saw Mulligan's head turn, and struck the man down. Then he proceeded to meet up with Bridget, who had found her son's body and was returning with all haste to the house. 'Lord!' she exclaimed in desperation. 'What brings the police here? There are three of them getting over the fence!'

Alas, however, she had met her match in cunning. Lynch killed her there, in the dark, with his axe—after which foul act he returned to the house, where Bridget's daughter was waiting. 'Now, my little girl,' he said to her, 'I will do for you what I would not for the others, for you're a good girl; you shall have ten minutes to say your prayers.'

It is many years since I first read of this abomination, but still I have to wipe away tears. Lynch, it seems, was similarly affected. According to Mr Bowen: *'Lynch paused, as if he had a difficulty in going on. I suppose it might be a feeling of remorse, and I could easily imagine that the scene of the child begging for her life must have been a most pitiable one.'*

I shall pass over this event. It is far too awful. I shall say only that Lynch decided against burying the bodies in such a well-frequented neighbourhood. Instead he burned them. It troubled him to do so, he said, but he concluded that it mattered not to the deceased whether they were burned or buried. He also confessed himself surprised at the way they were consumed, flaring up 'as if they were so many bags filled with fat'. By the morning there was nothing left but a heap, 'like of slacked lime', which he buried in another part of the paddock.

He then proceeded to dispose of the family's clothes, and pass himself off as the lawful owner of Mr Mulligan's farm.

It was done very cleverly. First he read through Mulligan's papers, and gained a complete understanding of the man's affairs. After that, he went to Gray's hotel, where he asked the proprietor what kind of a man Mulligan was. When inquiries were made of him in return, he replied that he had come from Sydney, and had concluded a bargain with Mulligan, who had failed to deliver his side of it. To others he acknowledged that Mulligan had borrowed a valuable mare from him, and pretended to be shocked when told that he might never see the animal again. 'Some of them seemed to look down on me as a kind of flat,' he remarked in his confession—and I can almost see the glint in his eye as he spoke.

Lynch subsequently returned to Sydney, where he called at the offices of the *Gazette*, pretending to be Mulligan. He paid for an advertisement in Mulligan's name, declaring that, Bridget having absconded from his home, he would not be answerable to her debts. Furthermore, he wrote to several persons in the neighbourhood of Wombat Brush about Mulligan's affairs, signing Mulligan's name instead of his own, before returning there in the guise of Mulligan's victim. He even wrote a letter to himself, which was purportedly from Mulligan. By these means he secured the dead man's property. And he proceeded to farm it, with great efficiency and expertise, for all of six months.

He called himself Dunleavy, and employed an immigrant couple to work for him. (*'I told them that Mulligan and his wife had had a row,'* Lynch related, *'and that he had turned her out, and that he had been obliged to go to the Five Islands and hide, on account of a horse found in his possession which was all wrong—that is, stolen.'*) Such was the respect felt for him by his neighbours that one of them pressed Lynch to marry his daughter. The landlord of Mulligan's farm was not so easily gulled. But Lynch was 'as deep as he', and managed to arrange matters to the satisfaction of both. I can easily imagine the scene at that farm of an evening, after Lynch had bidden his servants a pleasant and cheerful goodnight. I can envision the way he must have sat at the table, listening to the wind, his pale eyes reflecting the firelight as he planned and schemed, and tried to keep the ghosts at bay.

Had he been a man in truth—a human being, with a human being's heart—he would still be living. For what had he to do but work diligently, and enjoy his ill-gotten gains? The Devil, however, is not easily quelled. One day in February, he was returning from a trip to Sydney when he camped on the north side of Razorback. Here a man named Kearns Landregan accosted him. Kearns said that he wanted to head off, without anyone knowing it. 'Why?' asked Lynch. 'You do not look like a bushranger.' No, Kearns replied, he was not; but he had quarrelled with his wife, and never wanted to see her again.

Lynch needed a man to do some fencing. So he agreed to hire Kearns for six months, and together they travelled towards Berrima. During the journey, Kearns told Lynch that he and his wife had earned a large sum during the last harvest, which he had kept for himself. 'And can you,' replied Lynch, 'defraud your own lawful wife of the money she has hardly earned by the sweat of her brow? I would myself take a musket and rob upon the highway sooner than be guilty of such cruelty.' He argued with Kearns about this (or so he said), and turned against him as a 'selfish and hardhearted man'. But I do not myself believe that Lynch killed Kearns Landregan out of disgust. I believe that he changed his mind when Kearns began to show himself far more cunning than he had initially appeared. 'On getting better acquainted with him, I found he was by no means simple, as I at first supposed,' Lynch admitted. 'If I took this fellow with his law to the farm with me, it would certainly be my ruin; for, after using his wife as he had done, he would not stop at informing against me.' Even if Lynch told Kearns to be off, the sly fellow would take him to Court for breach of agreement, and questions would be asked. Or at least that was Lynch's perception.

Therefore he killed Kearns Landregan. He did it with an axe, while they were breaking camp near the Nattai Bridge. Then he stripped the body and hid it under some bushes, where it was discovered the next day. A series of clues led the police to Lynch's farm; Landregan's belt, which they found there, was all the proof required. And so, at last, the monstrous career of John Lynch came to an end.

It seems to me odd that Lynch had kept the belt. He told Mr Bowen that he had at first thrown it into a waterhole, which was not deep enough. Seeing that it protruded from the water, he had retrieved it, tossed it into the back of his dray, and 'never thought of it' afterwards. Yet he was generally so careful and so clever. Why this stupid mistake?

Perhaps, as he said, his time had come. 'I can see the hand of God in my detection' was how he put it. Or perhaps he simply no longer cared. There was something lacking in him; he seemed not to accord life any more importance than a good dinner, or a well-trained dog. The newspapers reported that he had met his fate 'with the same reckless indifference about his own life as that shown to his defenceless and unsuspecting victims'.

Knowing all that I know about John Lynch, this does not surprise me in the least.

Twenty-five

You must not believe that we learned the whole truth about John Lynch all at once. On the contrary, his story was revealed little by little, in the newspaper reports that slowly trickled out of Berrima. I recall how, before Lynch was tried for Landregan's murder, he requested that a portion of his property be sold to defray the cost of his defence. (The Attorney-General, Mr Roger Therry, refused on the grounds that this property was 'supposed to belong to some of the deceased persons whom he—the prisoner—was accused of having murdered'.) In the *Herald*'s account of the trial, published four days later, I read that Lynch only reddened once during the proceedings, and questioned the witnesses with a degree of ability 'far beyond the expectations of those who saw them'.

The following day, another report appeared in the same journal regarding Lynch's punishment. It described how Sir James Dowling, having placed a black cap upon his head, addressed the prisoner before pronouncing sentence. '*It is now credibly believed, if not actually ascertained, that no less than nine individuals have fallen by your murderous hands,*' he said. '*How many more have been violently ushered into another world remains unrecorded, save in the dark pages of your own memory. By your own confession it is admitted that as late as 1835 justice was involved on your head for a frightful murder, committed in this immediate neighbourhood. Your unlucky escape on that occasion has, it would seem, whetted your tigrine relish for human gore . . .'*

'I do wish they would stop going *on* about that wretched Thomas Smith,' my mother complained, when she read this extract. 'I cannot see what purpose it serves to keep talking about past events in such a fashion!'

I shared her feelings. It was a very difficult time for my family, and the repeated references to Thomas Smith were only making matters worse. No sooner had Lynch's trial concluded than our own legal battles recommenced. *Atkinson Versus Barton and Others* was before the court again, with the Chief Justice ordering a complete examination of the financial management of the Oldbury estate since my father's death. Then, just a few days after the hearing, John Lynch was hanged—though not before making a full confession. His foul deeds became the chief topic of conversation throughout the colony, much to our distress. I was disagreeably pestered at school; prurient curiosity drove many a well-bred miss to sidle up to me and ask, in a whisper: 'Did John Lynch indeed work on your father's estate, Miss Atkinson? Was he truly as terrible as they say?'

Now, you must understand the strain that I was under. For an entire month, my nights had been haunted by savage and bloody dreams. I had dreamed of a dark mountain—Gingenbullen— looming closer and closer. I had dreamed of something squirming beneath a pile of dead wood. Again and again, it was as if John Lynch had silently entered my room, a dripping axe in his hand; I would wake with a cry, my heart racing and my face wet. I could not erase my memory of his wink, which seemed to me like a kind of brand. For the first time, I found myself sympathising with

George Barton, whose obsessive fear of John Lynch now seemed justified.

My new life in Sydney had driven away many of the Oldbury shadows for a time, but suddenly they returned in force. I began to dwell once more on the incident at Belanglo, wondering whether or not John Lynch had been personally involved. John Lynch had killed Thomas Smith—ostensibly because Smith had spoken too freely about the flogging of George Barton. But if Lynch had been implicated in the flogging, why had Barton not accused him later? Was it, as my cousin John had once speculated, because Lynch's only involvement had been with the bushrangers actually responsible for the attack? Had they formed an alliance with Lynch so as to buy from him those items that he had filched from the Oldbury stores?

It was certainly possible. On the other hand, it was also possible that Lynch had indeed been present at the flogging, and had witnessed something that Barton desired to conceal at all costs— something shameful or disgusting, which my stepfather had no wish to see aired in court. What that mysterious 'something' could possibly be, I had no idea. And I could not bring myself to question Mama about it, because she was in such a nervous state already. Thanks to Lynch's trial, and her own court hearing, and our problems with a drunken housemaid, my mother was inclined to lash out at the slightest little thing. Why, she had flown into an absolute *rage* one day because I had left a window open during a Brickfielder, and the howling westerly had coated our drawing room with dust. She had shaken me like a mop in consequence, and though she had apologised for it afterwards, her ire had made me wary. I feared to raise the subject of Belanglo. I was worried that it might send my mother into one of her black moods.

So I shared my concerns with no one. *Certainly* not with my sisters, nor yet with James—for Louisa was still unwell, and Emily was sensitive, and James was at a stage of development wherein he refused to speak of Oldbury at all. If the subject was even raised, he would stick his fingers in his ears and hum. He had thrown himself heart and soul into the world of Mr Rennie's school, and would fix his attention on nothing outside it. His every waking hour was filled with marbles, mathematics, cricket, treasure maps, pocket-knives and naval jargon.

As for me, I would have warmly welcomed a complete immersion in school affairs. But even at school I was not safe from John Lynch. Jessie Knight's influence meant that I had to endure an endless stream of questions with each new story in the newspapers—until one day, to my eternal regret, the strain of it overthrew me.

We were sitting together, she and I, at work on our daily journals. It must have been a Thursday afternoon. Mr Dodd had lately finished his lesson, and Miss Rennie had accompanied him out of the room for a moment.

Jessie put her mouth to my ear.

'Will you write about John Lynch?' she whispered. 'For he was in all the papers yesterday.'

I ignored her. Around me, the room was filled with the *scritch-scritch* of sharpened pens on paper.

'I wish that I had something half so thrilling to write about,' Jessie continued, under her breath. 'What have *I* to say, except that my sister suffers from a toothache? *You* may talk about your memories of John Lynch, and how you never would have thought that he was so *very* wicked. I suppose he was as charming as everyone would have him? Perhaps he made himself quite useful about the place, chopping wood and so on.'

Still I said nothing, though the blood was mounting in my cheek. She must have seen this. But it did not deter her.

'I have asked and asked, and no one recalls anything about the first murder,' she hissed. 'The one on your father's estate, Miss Atkinson. It was too long ago, though I am persuaded that *you* must remember the details. Was an axe used, do you know? Can you tell me why Lynch was acquitted? I have heard tell that a drunkard called Barton was involved, and I thought to myself—why, Miss Atkinson's *mother* goes by that name—'

My hand moved, then. It seemed to shoot out almost of its own volition, driving the point of my nib deep into Jessie Knight's plump wrist.

Her scream brought Miss Rennie rushing through the door.

'What is it?' our teacher gasped. 'What happened?'

'Oh! Oh!' sobbed Jessie Knight. 'She stabbed me! She hurt me!'

'Who? Who did?'

'*She!*'

'Miss Atkinson?'

The sight of Miss Rennie's face filled me with a deep, roiling shame. She looked at me in perplexity and disbelief, for I was quite a favourite with her, and had never before caused any trouble. Yet I could not defend myself; I was unable to form the words, which must inevitably have touched on tender subjects. So I stood there, mum, as Jessie displayed her wound.

'Look! She has drawn blood!' Jessie cried. 'She pricked me with her pen!'

'Is this true, Miss Atkinson?'

The pen was still in my hand. I threw it down and ran from the room. Down the stairs I ran, with Miss Rennie calling after me, until I reached the front door. Had it not been so heavy, I might have escaped my pursuer. But by the time I had dragged it open, and stumbled onto the street, Miss Rennie was directly behind me. She caught my arm before I could cross the road.

'Stop! Charlotte!'

She was panting. I was panting. We stared at each other, while a passing labourer eyed us curiously.

'Come inside, if you please,' said Miss Rennie. 'You know that you're not permitted to leave the school premises.'

'I want to go home,' was all that I could choke out.

'Why? What happened?' she asked.

I shook my head. I could not speak.

'Come inside,' Miss Rennie repeated. 'You must account for yourself, Charlotte. This is not the kind of behaviour that I would expect from you.'

So we returned inside, where I was left to sit in Mr Rennie's study for the rest of the afternoon. At one point he came in with his daughter, and they pressed me for an explanation. What had inspired my sudden assault? Why had I been so angry? Having composed myself somewhat, I was able to reply. I said that Jessie had been cruel, and that I did not want to sit by her anymore.

'Miss Knight *can* be naughty,' Miss Rennie agreed. 'But no words, however unkind, can merit such violence, Miss Atkinson. You know that.'

'Physical reproof is almost always counter-productive,' Mr Rennie agreed, gazing at me in a troubled fashion. 'Beating is prohibited here for that very reason. A well-trained mind has no cause to employ such measures.'

'I am *very* disappointed in you, Charlotte,' Miss Rennie concluded. 'And I shall have to consider what punishment you deserve.'

My eyes filled with tears. It seemed so unfair! Yet I was ashamed of my anger, which had alarmed me almost as much as it had alarmed Miss Rennie. The black tide had burst forth unheralded. It had swept me away, throwing down all my defences. I could not account for it.

When my mother arrived to escort me home, she was invited into Mr Rennie's study. James and I were told to wait on the stairs while the school emptied and my behaviour was discussed. I do not know what Mama said in that room. Not the whole truth, by any means. But some excuse must have been offered, for the punishment that I eventually received was by no means onerous. It was simply a little extra work, and a day's segregation from the rest of the class.

All in all, I was treated justly. And I was never again obliged to sit beside Jessie Knight, nor to share a book with her. Yet I had lost some small portion of Miss Rennie's high regard; her estimation of my character shifted, and she took to watching me carefully. As for my mother, her approach—as usual—was more direct. On our way home from school, she said to me: 'You appear to have learned some very bad habits from Mr Barton. It is something we must break you of, if you do not want to be hauled before the Police Courts one day.'

'She kept talking about John Lynch,' I mumbled. 'She was *trying* to make me angry.'

'And she succeeded, did she not? It was her victory. If you had merely knocked your ink-well onto her dress, you could have called it an accident and been no worse off. You should *think* before you act, Charlotte. You should follow Miss Rennie's advice, and eschew violence. It will not benefit you.'

This sounded very handsome coming from my mother, whose own impulsive conduct had left us shackled to George Bruce Barton, and who had spent a large part of the previous four years throwing things at him.

I knew better than to say so, however.

'If Mr Barton comes back,' I remarked sulkily, 'a few cutting words will not deter him. Maybe we shall be *forced* to use pen-nibs. Or fire-irons.'

'Nonsense,' said my mother. 'We shall simply summon the police.'

Unfortunately, my mother was over-confident. The police were not summoned on the occasion of Barton's next appearance. For the circumstances were too awkward, and Mama was too proud. As far as I am able, I shall attempt to describe what happened.

And you will excuse me if I am indelicate. I shall try not to be. Let me only remind you, to begin with, that my mother was still married to George Barton. Though separated from her, he retained certain rights over her property and person.

By law, she was unable to exclude him totally from her life.

To proceed, then: the meeting between them took place after the School of Industry Bazaar, which was held every year at the end of April. You may not be acquainted with the old Female School of Industry. It was one of the Macleays' pet schemes: a school for girls who were either orphaned or badly neglected, and whose situation might otherwise have forced them into lives of immorality. Some twenty boarders were housed at the school, ranging in age from seven to fourteen. They were often to be seen walking about Sydney in two straight lines, all dressed alike in white bonnets and blue frocks. Under the supervision of a respectable matron, they learned how to knit, sew, spin, cook, and master all those other household accomplishments necessary to a competent domestic. As a charitable institution the school was very popular with Sydney's most elegant ladies, many of whom taught at and managed the place. They also took out subscriptions, but cannot have raised all the funds required by this means. So every autumn, the school held a fancywork bazaar—which my mother never failed to visit.

My sisters and I generally went with her. The 1842 sale saw James in attendance as well, though I cannot remember why; perhaps he was hoping to watch some cricket being played in Hyde Park. If so, he was disappointed. We saw nothing of interest in Hyde Park, and therefore headed straight down Macquarie Street towards the School of Industry, which was accommodated in a large, two-storeyed building beside the old hospital.

My own fancywork was never of a high order. For this reason, I had not contributed anything to the bazaar—as several of my school-fellows had done. All across Sydney, for many weeks, ladies young and old had been working away at pincushions, antimacassars, handkerchiefs, collars, purses and slippers, in anticipation of the great event. I must confess, I never *quite* understood why it should be so popular. Granted that the cause was a good one. But if so many ladies were so adept with the needle, why did they all rush to buy items which they could so easily have manufactured themselves?

Perhaps it was in order to mix with other ladies of a higher station. The remaining Macleay sisters were always in evidence at the bazaar, as were the Governor's wife, and the Bishop's wife, and Mrs Mitchell, and Mrs Mitchell's eldest daughter, and a host of lesser satellites. Even the Macarthurs could be seen there, if they happened to be in town. My mother, I am sure, attended purely for the company. Where else could she—an impoverished widow with an irregular reputation—have exchanged polite chit-chat with some of the colony's leading female citizens? For the ladies of the Management Committee had no choice but to be friendly and encouraging. They were required to watch the stalls and praise the work, and if such employments put them at the mercy of eager, ill-bred women, then they could do very little to repel unwanted overtures. I distinctly recollect how, at the 1842 bazaar, my mother cornered Mrs Margaret Innes (nee Macleay), and for the price of a pincushion-cover of imitation Brussels lace was able to converse with her for a quarter of an hour about the exotic specimens planted in Mr Macleay's garden at Elizabeth Bay House.

I myself found nothing equally useful to do. With my sisters and brother I wandered about the big, airy classrooms, squeezing through clusters of gossiping women and admiring the delicate handiwork festooned everywhere: the beaded purses, the embroidered bolster-covers, the crocheted tablecloths. After a while, I took my siblings out into the garden, which was quite large, and bounded by a picket fence. Here we collected grass for the cow, and stared into the grounds of the hospital until it was time to go.

The shadows were growing long, by then. We were all very hungry. Though we passed a man selling fresh prawns, my mother would not stop; she was always nervous of being left by the omnibus and having to traverse the wilderness of the Woolloomooloo valley on foot, exposed to every cutpurse lurking therein. By the time we reached home, it was all of five o'clock. We had missed our usual dinner hour, and were keen to partake of some tea. Our cottage, I should tell you, was set in a garden full of flowers, enclosed by a hedge of china rose and a picket fence. Its front door opened directly into the drawing room, which in turn led into a kind of library through double doors. From there a back hall ran past the dining room and various sleeping chambers; at the rear a flight of stone steps led down to the kitchen, laundry and servants' room, with a well-room and larder on the other side. There was also one small room that could be reached off the front veranda, and we used this as a study.

Not luxurious accommodation, by any means. The wallpapers were execrable, the servants' quarters were damp, and the chimney in the library smoked with every hard northerly that blew. Nevertheless, it was not a bad little house. And we were happy enough to reach it that day after the bazaar, for a chill breeze had sprung up, and we were none of us dressed for the cold.

Imagine our horror when Mama pushed open the front door, and we found ourselves looking at my stepfather.

He had cast himself onto the only upholstered chair in our possession. There was dried mud all over his boots, and he wore no waistcoat. He was smoking a pipe, and nursing an old issue of *The Mirror*.

We froze on the threshold.

'Aye, stop there and let the cold in,' he snapped. 'Here is the meanest fire I ever saw, and you must fill the room with frosty winds!'

'What—what is the meaning of this?' my mother stammered, without moving.

'Come in and I'll make it plain,' George Barton replied.

We could do nothing else, though we were reluctant. As my mother divested herself of bonnet and gloves, she instructed us to 'go and fetch Mary'—causing Barton to utter a terse guffaw.

'You must drag her if you do,' he said. 'The dirty wench is in Lushington, and was already on her spree when I arrived. It was as much as she could do to admit me—I believe she all but broke her neck on the stairs. Had I been a low sort of creature, Ma'am, you'd have no property left by now. She would have let in a stray pig, or an armed bushranger, with just as little ceremony.'

My mother hesitated. Clearly, she was uncertain as to whether she should leave her children alone with such a man as George Barton, or send us off to witness a scene of squalid debauchery somewhere down the back of the house.

At last she decided in favour of the known quantity.

'Wait here,' she instructed, and vanished.

It was a truly awful moment. My siblings and I stood together against a wall, as Barton surveyed us contemptuously through his pipe-smoke. I must have been scowling, for he remarked, '*You* do not improve any', before fixing his gaze on my brother. 'And what have you been about today, in yer fine brass buttons?' he sneered. 'Paying afternoon calls, I'll warrant.'

James said nothing. It was Emily who replied, having taken to heart my mother's strictures on politeness in company.

'We have been to the fancywork bazaar,' she squeaked.

'Hah!' Barton threw back his head in a snort of derision. 'I'd have expected nothing less. Fancywork, i'faith! And did you purchase for yerself a pretty set of satin slops, my fine little man?'

'We have no money for such things, as well you know,' I interjected, pressing my brother's arm. 'You will find no money in this house, nor one single treasure.'

'Aye, just scraps and rubbish,' Barton declared, his eyes sweeping across our tense forms. He meant to imply, by this action, that we ourselves were of little value. And I took exception to his tone.

'Why are you here?' I demanded. 'I told you—we have no money!'

'And what makes you think I need it?' he rejoined, just as my mother re-entered the room. She looked flustered, but adopted a commanding manner nonetheless.

'Off you go, children,' she instructed. 'Go to your rooms and stay there.'

'What about Mary?' I wanted to know. 'Is she drunk again?'

'That is not your concern!' said my mother sharply. 'Obey me at once, if you please! I want you each to write an account of the bazaar in your daily journal. And do not come out until I give you leave.'

'But—'

'*Now*, Charlotte!'

I could hardly object. Yet I withdrew as if my feet were weighted with lead, throwing many a backward glance over my shoulder. As I shut myself in my bedroom, I heard Barton inquiring about my mother's one-thousand-pound legacy.

Behind me, Emily said: 'I am so hungry, Charlotte.'

'So am I,' was my brusque retort.

'What about tea? Will Mary bring it?'

'Mary is drunk,' remarked Louisa, settling herself onto the window-seat. I shared a single bedroom with both my sisters. My mother occupied another, while James had been given the smallest for his own.

But he had chosen to join his sisters, and sat huddled by the empty grate.

'My journal is in the library,' Emily observed. 'Where is yours, James? In your room?' She looked around nervously. 'Who will fetch them?'

'No one,' I replied. 'Do something else.'

So they did. James picked at the Indian matting on the floor, while Emily rearranged the shells on the mantle. Louisa, for her part, occupied herself with a description of the School of Industry Bazaar.

As for me, I gave an account of the bazaar that reflected my state of distraction. *'Went to the Female School of Industry,'* I wrote. *'Bought pincushion cover. Mr Barton was at home on our return. He must have bullied Mary to admit him—perhaps in exchange for rum. Mama has sent us away.'*

All the while, I was listening hard. Every so often a raised voice would make us sit up straight, ears cocked. But there would follow another low murmur, or measured footsteps, and we would know not what to think.

The minutes dragged by. I heard a door shut somewhere close. I heard the jingling of keys, and the squeak of a window shutter.

'Is He gone?' Louisa finally asked.

I shrugged in reply.

'It's getting dark,' Emily pointed out. 'How can we write, if we have no candles?'

'Maybe we should go and see,' Louisa suggested, but James shook his head.

'No!' he gasped. 'No, she told us to stay!'

'But something might have happened—'

'Nothing has happened,' I said quickly. 'We would have heard. There would have been fighting. *You* know what they are.'

'Please, Charlotte.' Louisa gazed across the room. She was only eight years old, yet already her eyes differed from the eyes of most children her age. Perhaps it was on account of the things that she had witnessed—or perhaps it was because of her bodily suffering. Whatever the cause, there was a resigned sort of wisdom in her steady regard. 'Please, will you go and look? Or I shall. But you are much quicker at running away. You can say that I'm feeling ill.'

'But are you?' asked Emily, in troubled tones. 'You're not lying, Louisa?'

'No. Oh no. I feel as if I might faint at any moment.'

'Very well.' I stood, and went to the door. 'But you must back me up, all of you. No peaching. Is that clear?'

There were nods all round.

'Word of honour?'

'Word of honour,' they chorused.

Satisfied, I took a deep breath, and let myself out of the room.

It was late. Dust motes drifted about in the last, orange rays of the setting sun, which penetrated one of our western windows and illumined a shabby patch of carpet in the hall. Everything was quiet. There seemed to be no one about. I checked the drawing room and the library, and was hovering outside the closed door of my mother's bedroom when I heard a noise from within.

There can be no explaining certain connections that take place in a girl's head, upon her abandonment of childhood. Childhood, I feel, is almost a state of mind; there are some who remain children up to the very point of marriage, or even beyond it, while others—the offspring of debauched and impoverished unions, for example—are never children at all.

You must remember that I was raised on a farm. It was a farm, moreover, staffed for the most part by coarse men of blunt manners. Yet only after spending four months at a ladies' academy were my senses attuned to a particular consciousness that infected almost every conversation. Even talk about the School of Industry's stated purpose, or the conduct of housemaids, made elusive reference to a form of union that I need not examine closely here, but which (I am afraid) very much occupied and perplexed all those young women whose stated destiny in life was a good marriage.

As I stood outside my mother's bedroom door, listening to the sounds from within, I suddenly understood something that many girls never come to understand at all until their wedding night. From stray remarks gleaned among the convict huts at Oldbury, and the conduct of fowls in the yard, and the drunken ramblings of our housemaids, and the odd, sly titter at school, I pieced together an image (not absolutely incorrect) of the kind of congress in which my mother and stepfather were engaged at that moment.

It was not a pleasant picture. I reeled, and gasped, and was horrified. I knew not what to think. Such matters are very ugly for children even where domestic harmony prevails. Where it does not, and there is a possibility of enforced submission, even the strongest and most well-developed mind recoils.

My own mind, being only half-formed, could not begin to address the subject. I fled from it. Physically, I fled from it. I hurried back to my bedroom, and slammed the door. 'They are busy,' was all that I said. 'They will call us.' I do not know if my flushed cheek and breathless voice awoke any speculation in Emily or Louisa. I only know that, when they saw my face, something about it forestalled their questions.

It was getting on to half past six when my mother finally came to our door. She was dishevelled, and moved awkwardly. Her voice sounded rough as she told us that we might come out now and eat supper.

'Mr Barton is gone,' she said, and cleared her throat. 'You have nothing to fear.'

As far as I am aware, it was the last time she ever laid eyes on him.

Twenty-six

An interlude

I am an old woman now, with a good understanding of the world. I know what happened after the School of Industry Bazaar. That is to say, I understand the act that was perpetrated. Perhaps it was an assault, in which case my mother could have done nothing to prevent it—for Mary had been rendered incapable by drink, and there were no close neighbours whom my mother might have alerted without, in the process, alerting her children. Besides which, the Law was on Barton's side. What man can be gaoled for enjoying connubial relations within his own marriage?

In this case, moreover, the Law may have been right. Perhaps it was *not* an assault. For I have learned over the years that hatred does not necessarily preclude desire. There can be no way of knowing what happened between my mother and stepfather, behind closed doors. Anger and passion are too closely related for my taste; looking back, I remember all too well evidence of the fervent reconciliations that took place between Mama and Mr Barton early in their marriage, after one or two raging rows. Of course, my mother was quickly disillusioned. There can be no doubt that she grew to loathe her husband with a poisonous loathing.

Even so, I am not about to pass judgement on an event that I failed to witness personally. Not now. Perhaps my mother suffered in silence so as to shield her children from Barton's foulness. Perhaps she remained mute because she had no need of anyone's help. At my advanced age, it is easy enough to believe either proposition.

As a young girl, however, I had not such a wide experience of humanity. I could not have reconciled blows and caresses; I was barely enlightened as to the nature of the central act itself. Floundering in the half-dark, I was prey to all the excesses of a lively imagination. How I suffered! And in the flurry of comment that followed Lynch's hanging, I suffered still more. For the *Sydney Gazette* reported something quite new, once Lynch was dead. Upon describing the tragic end of Bridget Macnamara's daughter, it made mention of an incident that occurred after the poor girl was permitted to say her prayers.

'*After this time had elapsed,*' it declared, '*and violating her person, he dispatched her soul also.*'

Consider the effect that such a remark would inevitably have on me. I brooded upon it. It inflamed my sensitivities still further. I asked myself endless questions: had George Barton 'violated' my mother after the bazaar? Had the bushrangers done so in the Belanglo forest? Could this be the secret that had prevented Barton from naming or even testifying against Lynch, lest the truth be revealed in court?

The proposition was never quite so clearly formulated in my head—not for many years, at least. I came to it piecemeal, rejecting the most painful possibilities almost as soon as I envisaged them. I was muddled and angry. On the one hand, it seemed to me that my mother might perhaps have been the victim of a monstrous crime. On the other, that she might have damaged her reputation through the careless indulgence of her own coarse appetites. What *had* she been about, riding off into the forest with her overseer?

Surely Oldbury could have spared a few men? Had their party been larger, they might not have been stopped at all.

I brooded over these points for many years. But I had no one to whom I could open my heart, for by the time my sisters were of an age to discuss such matters freely, we had parted. I wish that it had not been so. I wish that I had found the sense and courage to consult Louisa, at least. Louisa would have displayed much insight, despite her long maidenhood; she had far more penetration than was ever bestowed on me, and the leisure in which to indulge it.

Back then, however, I was ignorant. For a long time I discounted my youngest sister because she remained unmarried. How could she offer any enlightenment when she had no understanding of those dark currents which drive men towards women? It was a stupid opinion, though not entirely the result of blind arrogance. On the contrary, I was ashamed. Our positions in life were very different, and my own did not strike me as superior. While Louisa had retained a purity of mind and person, I had soiled myself with blood, sweat and tears, immersing my thoughts in a kind of sludge comprising all the impotent and purposeless emotions of an ill-considered existence.

So I said to myself: 'She will know nothing useful. And it's better that she should *not* know. Why spoil her peaceful nights and cloud her clear eye with sordid speculations? Let her be, Charlotte. Do not withdraw your protection now.'

I held to this view for many years, mostly from utter weariness. The demands on my time and energy were such that I could not re-examine those ideas upon which my general conduct was based. All my thoughts were bent on the petty business of getting through each day: the chores, the debts, the demands, the endless decisions. I gave the whole matter very little attention until 1871, when *Tom Hellicar's Children* was published.

I was in Orange, then, struggling to establish my school. This was long before Mr Richards opened Weymouth House; in those days, the building occupied by *his* school—on the corner of Byng and Sale Streets—was a police lock-up, and stood directly opposite my own little academy. Not the most salubrious position for a girls' school, I know. Far too many obstreperous drunkards were hauled in and out of that lock-up, fully visible from my classroom windows. But what choice did I have? Orange was still in its infancy, with few solid and respectable buildings available for rent. None of the really *fine* homes had yet been constructed, though Summer Street was taking on a certain solidity, with brick stores and banks sprouting up like corn, and many new settlers arriving in a steady stream, some crushed and despairing from the goldfields at Ophir, some well supplied with money and inspiration.

Nevertheless, there was not the variety of business that exists now. One could not simply stroll into Mr Norwood's shop for the latest edition of the *Sydney Morning Herald*. While the local newspaper was always in good supply, it was safer to subscribe to any other. Therefore I used to send Ernest down to the Post Office every morning to collect my own subscriptions, wherein Louisa's work could often be found. I would read about her trips to the Fitzroy Falls and Mittagong, and wonder if she might be living around Berrima again. It certainly appeared so. She had begun to offer up 'a few sketches of some of the principal sights of the districts of Berrima, Nattai, Sutton Forest, and the Sassafras', which had led me to conclude that a removal had taken place. However, I did *not* realise that this removal had followed close upon her marriage.

For she had married, you see. Some two years after my mother's death, she married Mr James Calvert. I learned this long after the event, thanks to our peculiar estrangement—which was perhaps more a product of diffidence and delicacy than any kind of mutual antagonism. If an invitation had been sent, I did not receive it. If a notice had appeared, I must have missed it. From my careful study of the newspapers, I gleaned only that my sister had moved

from Oldbury to Yass, and then back to Berrima. I also noted
something peculiar about her circumstances. In the *Sydney Mail*,
towards the end of 1871, she published a short series entitled 'The
New Bush Home'. Though the author was given as 'a Country
House Mother', I recognised Louisa's style easily enough; who else,
while on the subject of raising fowls, would have paused to discuss
tiger snakes and their prevalence? But what puzzled me was the
professed 'newness' of her home—not to mention the word 'mother'.
Louisa was not a mother, surely? And if she had indeed returned
to Oldbury (to keep house for my brother, perhaps) then why all
this talk of establishing a 'new' home?

The answer was very simple. My sister was expecting. And she
was living, not with my brother James, but with her husband at
Swanton. Had I known this, I may have been moved to write.
Relieved of any concern for her unsullied maiden state, I may have
broached the topic that was never quite banished from my
thoughts.

I did not, however. I remained in the dark. Everything that I
knew about Louisa's circumstances was derived from her journalism,
and from her latest novel. *Tom Hellicar's Children* was serialised in
the *Sydney Mail* during the early part of 1871. Of all her books,
it disturbed me the most. You will know why when I tell you that
it concerned a woman—Mrs Hellicar—who had married above
her station, and who, when widowed, was deprived of her children
by the executors of her late husband's will.

It cannot be hard to picture my emotions, when I first read the
following exchange. It takes place between Mrs Hellicar and one
of the executors, her brother-in-law, who despises her as a jumped-
up needlewoman. '*Your opinion is not required*,' he says to her. '*You
have no power*.' When she retorts that she is his brother's wife, he
retorts: '*More the pity, madam*.'

Oh, but it was a shocking thing! I read with my heart in my
throat, groaning when I reached the end of each instalment.

I simply *knew* that there were messages here for me: messages concerning my mother's conduct, for instance. Mrs Hellicar is portrayed as a feeble and timid woman. As a consequence, her property and her children are taken from her. '*You have proved utterly unworthy of the trust reposed in you,*' her brother-in-law informs her. '*I shall feel it necessary to consider you no longer, and so study only the good of my brother's children.*' Mrs Hellicar slinks away brokenly, only to return towards the end of the book, humbly caring for her adult son in the guise of an old servant. She has neither the spirit nor the intellect to stand fast and fight. '*The woman was so helpless, and friendless, and simple; had been treated as a child, and petted and fondled, and kept ignorant of business, that from very habit she deferred . . .*'

I felt the reproof in this story. I understood perfectly that it was written in defence of my late mother, as a kind of memorial, and that it was directed at me. My initial response was to communicate with Louisa at once. Then I thought that I should wait until the full tale was told. Then, about halfway through the serial, I came upon a new set of characters who annoyed me intensely. If you have read the book, you must know the family I mean. They are the Thorells of Gindion parsonage, and I found the eldest daughter (Caroline) extremely offensive. She is nicknamed 'the Captain', and takes charge of the other children in a very overbearing way. Moreover, having objected to the marriage of her sweet younger sister Esther, on the grounds that Essie's suitor is too poor, she herself goes and marries a penniless clergyman. How I ground my teeth when I read such passages as this: '*We have seen that when Richie proposed that Esther should share life with him, Caroline had pronounced it impossible, and that the rest of the family, being used to consider her opinion as the ultimate in all matters, had echoed "impossible".*'

Caroline's wedding receives a great deal of attention, none of it complimentary. Louisa speaks of 'necessary privations' and 'trifles invested with immense importance'. She describes how 'the bride-elect becomes a person whose words carry weight; who is consulted, and looked upon as an authority'. There is also much discussion about Essie's role. How is she to continue her duties as governess, and attend to the school and the sick, unaided? Happily a *third* sister, newly grown, steps in to fill the breach. (The name of this sister is not provided, but we can safely assume that it would have started with an 'L'.)

Need I add that Caroline, for all her kindness during these marriage preparations, exhibits a certain consciousness in her manner which implies 'that she was successful in her woman's affairs, and her sister unsuccessful'? Or that Esther is an absolute paragon? Much is made of her many shining qualities: 'the simplicity of a guileless nature' and the 'dignity of a highly cultured mind'. *'It's like sunlight coming in at the door,'* is how one impoverished parishioner describes Essie. Whereas Caroline finds herself in *'that position of interest, not unmingled with power, so very pleasant to some dispositions'.*

I cannot tell you how enraged I became, on reading about the Thorells. The account of Caroline's wedding, in particular, I considered utterly unfair. Why, my own marriage had been anything *but* an occasion for swaggering conceit; Louisa must have known that I had been an object of pity and contempt, rather than respect and admiration. How could she have said such things? Understand that I was not deceived for a moment. 'Caroline' and 'Esther' were not so different from Mama's 'Clara' and 'Emma', after all.

I was so deeply offended that I abandoned all thought of communicating with Louisa. Towards the end of the book, moreover, there was an episode that made me positively fearful of doing so. In it, Mrs Hellicar's daughter Ruth is approached by one Max Ibotsen for her hand in marriage. Max is a corpulent and bloated spirit merchant, with a red pimply face and dim little blue eyes; he is fifty years old when he kisses Ruth's brow in 'an attempt at youthful gallantry'. This lecherous conduct revolts her. She runs away from her uncle's house to that of her brother, hot with shame and ranting that she hates Max Ibotsen with all her heart. Whereupon her brother replies: '*Hush, dear, hatred brings sad things upon people. You know when people curse others, the curse falls back on themselves, because God will not have us take vengeance into our own hands.*'

On reading this, I was terrified. I thought: 'How much has she found out?' And I put the serial to one side for a long period, reluctant to take it up again. For if she had meant something specific by her homily, I did not want to know.

Months afterwards, I stumbled upon 'The New Bush Home'. Only then did I find myself pondering the curiously potent quality of Max Ibotsen's lascivious conduct. There was something so disgusting about it. So *deeply repellent*. It made me wonder if Louisa was as uninformed as I had previously supposed. Could some personal experience have coloured this imagined scene? Or was she writing about George Barton and my mother? Had Louisa understood their relations more thoroughly than I had ever assumed?

And if that were so, could she shed light on other aspects of Mama's conduct?

The question stayed with me. Though I busied myself with all the minutiae of daily life, I could not seem to shake it off. Occasionally I considered writing to Louisa. Then I would ask myself: when shall I find the time? At last, early in the autumn of 1872, something occurred that propelled me to act.

I was looking to engage a servant. For many years I had practically done without, but the school was consuming much of my energy, my husband was still a carrier (thus often from home), and Eva was only five years old. Good female servants were not so easily acquired in Orange, back then. I was forced to interview many a hapless and slovenly soul in my search for a suitable candidate, and one of these women was Catherine Byrnes. She was not young. Nor did she inspire me with confidence. She must have been between sixty and seventy years of age, with straggling grey hair, a heavy midriff, and feeble, stick-like limbs. Though she had made some attempt to groom herself, I noticed that the darning on her clothes was clumsily worked, and that her cuffs and hems were frayed. Her complexion, moreover, made me suspicious. It was much mottled around the cheeks, and her nose was red. A red nose may make reference to cold weather, but it was not a particularly chilly morning. Nor was my kitchen fire a poor thing; on the contrary, it sported a bright blaze strong enough to boil a kettle.

I thought to myself, 'This woman has been intemperate, at some stage', and wondered if she was still drinking. It seemed unlikely, for her hands did not tremble. They were not unsteady like the hands of an habitual drunkard.

'Have you any references, Mrs Byrnes?' I inquired, whereupon she gave me a piece of paper, very soiled and crumpled, and almost coming apart at the folds. It was a letter of recommendation, dated 1851.

I told her that a twenty-year-old reference was useless to me. Did she not have letters from more recent employers? She replied that her latest mistress had 'died afore she could be asked', and that the one preceding had been illiterate. There had also been a five-year interruption occasioned by a failed marriage, as well as one master whose recommendation would not have impressed me, since he was gaoled for manslaughter.

'Indeed?' said I, as it occurred to me that some past tragedy might account for her former intemperance. 'The victim was not closely connected to you, I hope?'

'Oh no, Ma'am. No connection, for all I liked him well enough. He were a reaper on the farm. Name of Rogers. Shot in his belly—a sorry accident. T'were the rum that did it, is what the judge said.'

'Rogers?' I echoed, my hand rising to my breast. The name was horribly familiar. 'Where—where did this event take place, exactly?'

Mrs Byrnes eyed me with something like suspicion. 'Out near Bathurst,' was her reply.

'You wouldn't be referring to the case of George Bruce Barton, by any chance?'

The woman seemed to shrink, hunching her shoulders and pulling her shawl close about her. With pursed lips and a corrugated brow, she shifted uneasily on her stool.

'What if I was?' she muttered.

'You were employed by George Barton?' I said, trying to keep my voice calm. 'You were at the Yarrows when he shot William Rogers?'

She turned bright red. Her lips began to tremble; tears sprang to her eyes. At last she blurted out: 'Aye, 'twere me! And if you want to know, then yes, I *were* the one in his bed! But I never passed him no shotgun! I never did!'

We sat for a moment, staring at each other. I was too shocked to speak. Perhaps Mrs Byrnes thought me offended, for at last she got up, and made as if to go.

'You'll not be wanting me, then,' she muttered. '*I* know. I'll allus be judged hard by them as saw the papers. But I don't partake of liquor no more, Ma'am. Not since that day, I swear. It taught me the best lesson I ever could learn—the noise, and the smell, and all that blood . . .' The colour ebbed from her face, leaving it deathly white. ''Twere the rum that did it. We was all of us drunk, master *and* servants. I swore I'd never touch the stuff again, and never have.'

'Wait!' I half rose as she reached for the door. 'Stay! Please, I—I must speak to you.' Glancing around, I saw Eva playing with a sieve, and sent her immediately into the garden. 'Please, Mrs Byrnes,' I continued, when my daughter had gone, 'believe me when I say that I would not condemn you out of hand for past excesses. But I knew George Barton. He was my stepfather, and I want to hear what he did. It's important to me . . .'

The old woman opened her eyes very wide. 'Your stepfather?' she gasped.

'I fear so.'

'Lawks.'

'I never saw a full account of the affair. Whatever your part in it may have been—'

'I were not at fault!' Mrs Byrnes exclaimed. 'I were trying to catch me rest, is all! And them boys kept comin' in, all awash with gin, trying to pull me out of his bed—and George too drunk to stop 'em—'

'So he shot one of them to protect you?' I inquired.

'Who can tell? We none of us had our wits about us. Later he told Waller that poor old Brandy were saying as how he'd "knock the old bugger's head off", but *I* never heard it. George was full of strange stories. He allus thought the men were making plans against him, and he lost all sense when he drank.'

'Yes. I know.'

'Begging your pardon, Ma'am, but he were no damn good,' the woman declared, blood mounting once again in her cheeks. 'Too free with his fists, for one thing. I were right *glad* when he got taken. He'd have killed me, else—he said he would if I ever tried to go.'

'Did he talk about his wife? About the lady who left him?'

Mrs Byrnes hesitated. She looked shifty, and scratched her chin.

'Please,' I urged. 'Don't spare my feelings, I know what he was. Just tell me what he said.'

'He said that *he* left *her*,' the old woman replied. 'On account of she was a whore that begged for his attentions afore they married and bedded other men afterwards. Begging your pardon.' Seeing me flush, she quickly added: 'I never paid him no heed, not where women was concerned. He were allus a liar when it came to women.'

'Did he—did he ever mention Belanglo?' I could hardly force the name out. 'He was flogged once—you must have seen the scars—and it happened in the forest at Belanglo—'

'Oh, aye.'

'He talked about it?'

'Said he was flogged by John Lynch, as murdered all of them poor folk at Razorback.'

'He *said* that?'

'Aye, but ... Ma'am, he'd say anything. Knowing as how we'd all gasp and gather about him.'

'What else did he say? Did he say that my mother was there?' Seeing her look away, I strengthened my resolve—and my tone, as well. 'He told me something once that I cannot believe, and I want to know if he told you the same. That is all. As you remarked, he was a liar.'

'He said as how John Lynch had flogged him, and took advantage of his wife,' the old woman announced abruptly. 'Only Lynch was never punished for it, on account of his wife's shame.'

'I see.'

'He called me a whore, and I never strayed,' she insisted. 'I were faithful to him, though he used me cruel.'

'He was a liar,' I said. 'It is nonsense. He was not even married when they flogged him. It is all a parcel of lies.'

'Aye. I've no doubt of *that*,' said Mrs Byrnes. She watched me for a moment as I brooded, adjusting the folds of her shawl. 'I never heard no more of him, after he was hauled off to gaol,' she added. 'Two years, they gave him. Do *you* know how he fared, Ma'am?'

'Oh, no!' I replied—far too quickly. 'Not at all.'

'No. Well. He weren't too spry, even then,' she mused. 'Perchance he died on the chain gang—and good riddance, I say. I never could find a good position after he dragged me name through the mud.'

She certainly did not find a position in *my* house. I was unable to employ her; the sight of her in my kitchen every morning would have been too much to bear. So I gave her some money, and bade her good luck. She understood my feelings, I believe. She may even have shared them.

After she had gone, I sat thinking for a while. And one night later in the week, I wrote to Louisa.

I wrote about Mrs Byrnes, and Belanglo, and *Tom Hellicar's Children*. I even mentioned certain things revealed to me by George Barton, though not in great detail. I could not yet feel safe enough to tell anyone about our final meeting. Then I addressed the letter care of James Atkinson, at Oldbury, and sent it off.

What was I expecting in return? I hardly know. Even now, I am uncertain as to how Louisa might have responded, given the chance. She was always so oblique. So quiet. Though expressive enough in her normal domestic exchanges, there was something kept well hidden, which no one ever saw—except perhaps her husband, Mr James Calvert.

At any rate, my curiosity will forever remain unassuaged. Because three days after the letter was posted, I opened the *Sydney Morning Herald*, and my eye fell on her obituary.

She had died on the twenty-eighth of April, leaving a husband and newborn daughter.

At first I did not grieve. I was too shocked, perhaps, and hardly had the time. Preoccupied with business and family matters, I struggled to decide on the best course of action. Should I write? Should I set off for Oldbury? But I had missed the funeral, so what was the point? Then my brother's letter arrived, and removed every inclination to visit my old home. He was not gracious. Evidently, he had forwarded my own letter, which had been discovered on Louisa's writing desk. She must have opened it minutes before her husband's riderless horse came galloping into the yard at Swanton. Seeing the empty saddle—imagining the worst—Louisa's tender heart had failed her. So that when James Calvert arrived back at Swanton soon afterwards, thrown but essentially unharmed, he had found his wife dead of a heart attack.

This was the news related to me by my brother. In the process, he all but accused me of hastening my sister's end. He was furious that I should have written, after so long a time, simply to revive a lot of distasteful rumours and unhappy memories. Had I *no* regard for Louisa's frail state? Though possibly uninformed of her recent confinement, I could not have forgotten, surely, that she had for much of her life suffered from pulmonary consumption and a bad heart? Had it not *occurred* to me that my long-awaited letter, with its disturbing contents, might make my sister ill? It would certainly have made his own wife ill, had she read it. Happily, my brother had been the first to recover it from Louisa's desk, and had burned it soon afterwards.

I was probably not aware (James added) that he had recently married Sarah Horton, daughter of the previous incumbent of Sutton Forest church. They now had two bonny sons. Louisa's infant child, Louise, would remain with her father at Swanton. And if it should ever occur to me to visit, he would be grateful if I did not conduct myself as I usually did, rampaging about, insulting my dearly departed mother and bewailing my own fate, which—if he might be so bold as to express his opinion—was not nearly as miserable as poor Louisa's, and which I had largely brought upon myself.

He concluded by hoping that I was in good health, and declared himself to be, sincerely mine, James John Oldbury Atkinson, Esquire.

There were no words of comfort. No bequests from Louisa. There was not even a final message, for she had died without saying goodbye to anyone.

I could not imagine how James Calvert must have felt.

You may ask what I did, after I had finished reading. To begin with, I burned the letter. Since James had burned mine, I extended him the same courtesy. Then I sat by the fire, and covered my face with my apron, and howled until I was wrung dry of tears.

I was weeping because I had lost the last of my family. Louisa was dead, and I never spoke to James again. For I could not forgive him. Perhaps I should have blamed his prudish wife, or the influence of George Barton, but I was far too overwrought. Instead I condemned him for his weakness, and banished him from my heart.

As for Louisa, her absence pains me still. She was a great loss, not only to me but to Australia. I do not believe that she has been sufficiently commemorated for her work, though the genus *Atkinsonia*, of the mistletoe family, was named after her. Six years ago, it was suggested in the *Sydney Morning Herald* that a memorial to my sister be erected in the Botanical Gardens—but nothing came of it. I have the clipping here. I have kept everything ever published by and about Louisa. It is all that I can do for her now.

She was cut down like a flower in the midst of her days. Yet her soul resides where there is no more loss, and she lives always, a bright and cherished ghost, in the dark corners of my memory.

Twenty-seven

1844

I was fifteen years old when I first met William Cummings.

It was high summer, and I was feeling ill-used. One always does at that age. Nevertheless, I had more cause than many to lament my circumstances, which were hardly ideal. Not that they were unbearable. I was not starved, nor imprisoned, nor otherwise mistreated. But I had been raised in a certain fashion, and was now expected to pursue an entirely different style of existence.

To begin with, I was cramped. We were all cramped. Having once enjoyed unlimited space amidst the wide rooms and airy meadows of Oldbury, we had never truly become accustomed to the narrow confines of our little house, nor to the crowded shops and omnibus rides that were our experience of town life. As we grew older, the constraints imposed on us grew even more irksome. Had we been rich, with a mansion like Rockwall or Elizabeth Bay House, we would not have suffered so much. Had we been permitted to roam freely around the harbour, we might have resigned ourselves to other limitations. But thanks to my mother's wishes—and to the demands of polite society—we were perpetually circumscribed, and baulked at every turn.

Our funds were low. In 1843, my mother's income was reduced from 350 to 215 pounds per annum, as a consequence of the ailing condition of my father's estate. So we could not afford the kind of amusements available to others. There were no music or language lessons; no lavish dinners; no visits to the theatre or to Manchester warehouses. Our clothes were made at home: my sisters and I seemed to spend most of our time hemming and frocking. Nor had we the money to buy books. Instead we borrowed them. But my mother's one-pound subscription to the Commercial Reading Rooms was hardly adequate to supply the entire family with new titles, especially since the range of works on offer was limited. Unfortunately, our choice of libraries was also limited. The Australian Subscription Library and Reading Room, which charged *three* pounds a year for a wider selection of volumes, was quite beyond our reach.

We went to a great many sermons. When good, they were always unbearably crowded. When bad, they were tedious. We went to free lectures at the School of Arts, the Commercial Reading Rooms, and the Colonial Depositary of the Bible and Religious Tract Society. In all these places we sat crushed together, under a pall of heat, listening to endless disquisitions on the evils of drink or slavery. Sometimes we were fortunate: once we heard Mr Michie lecture on phrenology, and on another occasion Mr Marsh gave us his views on music. But for the most part we were not much enlightened, and frequently bored.

There were picnics, of course, as well as the odd boat trip. Sydney Harbour was a cornucopia of natural wonders in those days; we often enjoyed exploring tidal pools, nesting sites and heavily wooded bays. After a time, however, even these delights began to pall—largely because we had no one with whom to share them. We were so very *isolated*, you see. Our modest style of living, my mother's notoriety, and the strain brought about by our endless legal problems combined to prevent us from enjoying much in the way of social intercourse. Where once we might have moved in the most superior circles, my father's death—and my mother's remarriage—had put paid to any ambitions of that kind. And though I, personally, would not have objected to visiting a few of the more humble drawing rooms scattered around Sydney, my mother would not allow it.

She turned up her nose at the types of acquaintance available to us in town. Perhaps it was the result of her own pride, since the rich tradesmen of Sydney (unlike the poor convicts of Oldbury) would have felt themselves superior to us—and shown it, too. Or perhaps she objected not so much to the low origins of the newly rich, but to their defiant lack of education. She deplored them in the way she deplored traditional Ladies' Academies. Because in each case a kind of shallow and frivolous façade was preferred over sound, solid learning.

'There is so little true education hereabouts,' Mama would complain, after yet another insipid tea-time discussion about imported lace, or the price of beef. 'These people are so trivial in their interests! They will spend hours talking about the position of the pulpit at St James, and never once make reference to the content of a sermon preached there.'

She also condemned the 'coarse mode of expression' adopted by so many metropolitan ladies. I do think, however, that their speech irritated her less than the way they employed it, for they were very much given to bantering with the opposite sex—and not on elevated subjects, either. Sydney drawing rooms were awash with jokes about regattas, and horse-racing, and which country-bred gentleman had been seen at the Pulteney Hotel with an actress from the Theatre Royal. This kind of talk repelled my mother. For all her frankness, she had never been fond of prurient or vacuous discussion. She spoke her mind on subjects that were either far more lofty or far more simple; in her opinion, it was ill-bred to converse at length about a young lady whose shoes had been washed out to sea during a rockpool ramble, and who had been forced to parade her naked feet past any number of gentleman in consequence.

'Male and female created He them,' she would say. 'And if He created them differently, that is no reason to spend half an hour twitting some poor fellow about the growth of his beard, or his sister about the re-arrangement of her hair. It is not only ill-mannered—it is *boring*.'

That was my mother's opinion. But I did not share it. On the contrary, I was very much excited by the vibrant exchanges that I sometimes witnessed. They would occur in the street, or in a public park, or perhaps even in a shop; a group of ladies would encounter a group of gentlemen, and there would be a flurry of teasing remarks, and the air would seem to glitter all about them. This was particularly the case where military gentlemen were concerned, for they were always the boldest. I once heard a red-coated officer remark to a lady in spotted muslin: 'Shall I tell the mess table tomorrow that you want to be a soldier's bride?'

How it thrilled me!

You may wonder why it did not thrill Mama. After all, she was a spirited woman, careless of her appearance and—it seemed to me—of her reputation. Had she not been, we would not have been so impoverished, nor so widely shunned by our peers. Yet she would sniff, then turn away. She would mutter disapprovingly about 'colonial manners', when her own had turned most of the Sutton Forest gentry against her. I suppose, looking back, that her manners were of another era, for all that they had caused such offence in her youth. By 1844 she was almost fifty years old, though she did not look it. She was accustomed to a far more restrained demeanour. Furthermore, her outspokenness had never been of a flirtatious or mischievous cast. She abhorred frivolity, superficiality, and domestic incompetence, believing that ladies should be strong-minded, efficient, knowledgeable and devout.

'These girls who fritter away their valuable time dancing, and shopping, and making love to officers, are of no use whatsoever, in heaven or on earth,' she once declared, as we marched down George Street. 'I have no patience with such creatures, and can only comfort myself with the certainty that they will not attract good, respectable men, but trivial and capricious rogues who will make unreliable husbands.'

You can imagine my own thoughts as I listened to this. Unreliable husbands! I sneered and said: 'One need not be a giddy girl to marry an unreliable husband, Mama. One can be the mistress of a large estate, and the mother of four children.'

We had just passed a jolly cluster of currency youth, both male and female; my mother, greatly annoyed at having been forced off the footpath onto the road, had announced her opinion of them in a voice that was not quite low enough. Yet she flashed me a furious glance when *I* spoke frankly.

'Really, Charlotte!' she hissed. 'We are on a public thoroughfare! Have you *no* sense of decorum?'

I wanted to ask: 'Have you?' For I was growing tired of my mother. On the one hand, she had undermined my prospects with her foolish marriage. On the other hand, she would not allow me to explore those ranks of society now open to us. More and more, I viewed her as hypocritical. More and more, I found the courage to speak my mind.

'A sense of decorum must be learned from example,' I rejoined tartly. 'You have said so yourself.' It was a veiled insult, but not too oblique for my mother. She caught her breath, and her face went red.

When we turned into the Post Office, she was trembling with anger.

'Oh, Charlotte,' Emily whispered, as the postmaster attended to my mother's wishes. 'She will take away your books again. You will not be able to finish Bewick's *Book of Birds*.'

'I don't care. What good is that book to me? We see no European birds here.'

'And she will not buy you a lollipop,' James added, at which I gave a most unladylike snort. Lollipops were practically the reason for his existence, at that time, but I had passed beyond the concerns of childhood. And as if to demonstrate this fact, I was suddenly hailed by a familiar female voice.

It belonged to one of my school-friends, Fanny Rickards.

'Why, Charlotte! How are you?' she exclaimed.

Fanny was the daughter of a well-off auctioneer. Having recently turned sixteen, she had left Mr Rennie's school; I had no idea how she was occupying herself, though she had always been partial to male company. I liked her, I must confess. She was so friendly that one could hardly *dis*like her, for all that she was somewhat dull-witted. Her pretty face, cheerful manner and generous nature appealed to me. So did the fact that she regarded me with a kind of awe.

Not being a scholar herself, she thought me quite brilliant. Truth to tell, she viewed my whole family as staggeringly accomplished, and did not make the mistake (common to Sydney society) of valuing wealth above good breeding. It did not matter to Fanny that I wore the same clothes year after year, and trimmed my own hats. She would sing my praises regardless, wishing that she were half so talented. Upon leaving Mr Rennie's school, she had presented me with an exquisite silver pencil-case, instead of the modest articles of clothing that she had distributed among her other class-mates. 'Because you are so clever,' she explained, 'and have a mind above kid gloves.'

I was obliged to relinquish that pencil-case in later years. But I remember it still, just as I remember the way her face lit up in the Post Office.

'It is so long since we met!' she trilled, and introduced me to her companions: her mother (the faded daughter of a provincial

English clergyman), her elder brother Thomas, her younger sister Blanche, and her brother's good friend Mr William Cummings, who was visiting from Liverpool. Mr Cummings was a fair young man of about twenty-five, very neatly and fashionably dressed in a velvet coat and Bedford cords. I was immediately struck by his sunny smile. And I wished that I had been wearing something other than my chocolate muslin, which was a hideous shade, though my mother considered it 'practical'.

'Where is Mrs Barton? Oh! There she is,' said Fanny, who had met my mother before. 'Thomas, these are the Miss Atkinsons, who are so prodigious clever, and their brother James, who takes out all the prizes at College High School year after year. Mama, you remember Miss Atkinson, do you not?'

Various pleasantries were exchanged, none of them particularly memorable. Out of the corner of my eye I saw my mother hurrying to complete her business. She kept glancing over to our group, her brow furrowed with concern.

Though acknowledging Fanny's charm, she had never thought much of the Rickards family. In her view, they were a commonplace breed of dolts, with absolutely nothing to offer.

'You must join us tomorrow!' Fanny insisted. 'For we are taking a picnic to Bondi Bay, with the Cartwrights and the Kellys and—oh! Lots of amusing people. You must come, Charlotte, for we can pick you up on the way. There will be at least two dogcarts, and the Dettmans' carriage.'

'And the men will be riding,' her brother added.

'Yes, indeed—plenty of room! And Mama will be present to supervise, will you not, Mama? With Mrs Cartwright. *Please* come, it will be so much fun, and you can tell us all about the marine life! For Miss Atkinson is a very learned naturalist,' Fanny remarked to Mr Cummings, 'and knows everything there is to know about native fauna.'

'I should be happy to join you,' was my bold response, to Emily's evident alarm. 'When are you planning to set off?'

This was too practical a question for Fanny to answer. She turned to her brother, who suggested that the picnic party would pass through Darlinghurst at approximately ten o'clock, on its way to Bondi Bay. I was reciting my address to him when my mother joined us, busily stuffing something into her reticule. She greeted Fanny with a very guarded smile.

'Yes, of course. Miss Rickards. I have not forgot you,' she murmured, a distinct lack of warmth in her tone. 'How do you do, Mrs Rickards? You will forgive me, but we must fly. There are one or two things that have to be done, and I do not want to miss the omnibus. Good afternoon. So nice to have met.'

As she hustled me away, I glanced back over my shoulder to smile an apology. I was concerned that Fanny's feelings should not be ruffled, but she was already chatting excitedly to her younger sister. It was Mr Cummings who caught my eye.

Whereupon he wagged his index finger in mock severity, and grinned.

'Anyone would think they were attending a ball,' my mother remarked, on our way to Market Street. 'All that white silk and lace—so *very* unsuitable. Mrs Rickards should know better than to overdress her daughters in such a fashion. They look as if they have no background at all . . .'

I let her ramble on unheeded, too startled to defend the Rickards against her sour sniping. With one broad grin, Mr Cummings had created a forceful and lasting impression. He had sympathised. That much was clear. By some means he had grasped my situation, and clearly conveyed the depth of his insight.

I pondered his intentions all the way home, blind to Emily's nervous glances, deaf to my mother's complaints. At last we arrived at our front gate, more hot and dusty and tired than you would have thought possible. My mother's first instinct was to lie down in her room with the curtains drawn. My own was to prepare some lemonade. As I served it up to my siblings, Emily blurted out: 'Will you not tell her, Charlotte? About tomorrow?'

'Of course I shall,' was my response. 'When I'm ready to do so.'

'She will never allow it,' my brother opined, and I turned on him fiercely.

'Yes, she will!' I retorted. 'As long as you all keep your mouths shut, I'll manage it somehow.'

'You're not going to *sneak* out, are you?' Louisa wanted to know. She was a canny soul, and I have to admit that the thought had crossed my mind. Sneaking out seemed to be my only chance of success. But it could hardly be done if my mother was at home, for the arrival of two laden dogcarts and a carriage on our doorstep would surely attract her attention. If she went shopping, or visiting, the thing could easily be managed. I could plead a headache and stay behind. Unfortunately, however, we had no firm engagements planned for the next day.

I decided that I would pin my faith on any chance excursion that might take Mama from our house the following morning. And if she decided to stay in, then I would inform her of my plans at the last possible moment. By this means, I would prevent her from sending a note to the Rickards, excusing me from the expedition.

And what else could she do, after all? Grapple me to the ground in front of all those strangers? Embroil herself in a screaming public argument? For she could not expect me to submit quietly. I would fight her tooth and claw.

I had learned how, thanks to her own example.

'You must not say a word about this,' I instructed my siblings. 'Not *one word*, do you hear? Or I'll scratch your eyes out.' As I fixed each of them with a baleful glare, I added: 'It will be better for you all if you stay mum. You can pretend that you knew nothing about it.'

'Oh, but Charlotte,' Emily whimpered, 'you know how I hate to lie . . .'

'You won't *be* lying!' I snapped. 'You won't have to open your mouth!'

'She will ask us, though,' Louisa pointed out. 'After you have gone, she will ask us if we knew. And she will punish us, Charlotte.'

Louisa was right. Unless we all went, someone would bear the brunt of my mother's fury. And I did not want to be unfair.

'Very well,' I said slowly, after a moment's careful thought. 'I shan't go.'

'What?' said James.

'I shan't go. If they come for me, I'll tell them that I feel unwell, and cannot go with them.'

'Truly?' said Louisa.

'Truly,' I declared. 'But they probably won't come. Why should they? I hope they stay away, in fact, or Mama will be cross with me. You won't say anything, will you? For if they do *not* come, Mama need never know a thing, and we can all be comfortable.' I looked around the table. 'What do you think? Is that a good plan?'

Emily thought so, as did James. Louisa nodded, but there was a speculative glint in her eye. I am quite convinced that she had her suspicions—though she did not express them. Even at the age of ten, she missed very little.

I do not believe that she was much surprised when I joined Fanny's picnic party the following day.

Twenty-eight

The picnic party arrived at half past ten. I had placed myself in the study, which (as you may recall) was reached from the front veranda. Therefore I had a better view of Macleay Street than anyone else in the house.

When it was time to go I simply laid down my pen, put on my bonnet, and went out to meet the first dogcart.

I had planned everything carefully. Upon discovering that my mother was too exhausted by the previous afternoon's excursion to attempt anything similar that morning, I took possession of the study at a quarter to ten. My excuse was my journal. I told Mama that Louisa's coughs were a terrible distraction—that I found it difficult to concentrate, what with the heat, and the coughs, and Betsy's warbling. Though not a bad soul in many ways, our housemaid Betsy was an incorrigible singer, with a very poor voice. When occupied, she would frequently burst into song. And though we might remonstrate, nothing came of our efforts. She continued to crow and howl from a sheer vacancy of mind. One might as well have asked her to stop breathing.

At any rate, she was enough to distract even the most dedicated scholar. So my mother believed me when I complained about the

319

din, and allowed me to use the study. She did not even notice that I was wearing my second-best morning dress, because I had disguised it quite cleverly under a long, white shawl. And the reason that I gave for wearing my shawl, in such hot weather?

'My nose is troubling me,' I fretted, hiding behind a large cotton handkerchief. 'I do hope that I haven't caught a cold.'

'Oh, Charlotte. At this time of year? How like you.' My mother noticed nothing suspicious, probably because her mind was on the legal correspondence spread across her desk. 'If it gets any worse, you must have Betsy make up a linseed poultice, with a few grains of mustard in it. And do *not* sit in any draughts.'

A more Christian spirit might have felt ashamed at this evidence of my mother's concern, in light of the trick being played on her. But my character has never been that good. Perhaps it was warped by my upbringing. Whatever the cause, I felt no pangs of guilt as I sat waiting for Fanny Rickards. Though anxious, and torn between hope and fear, I was not nursing a bad conscience.

When the merry band finally came to a halt at our front gate, I went out to meet it with a light tread and a joyful smile.

'We are late, Charlotte, I am *so* sorry!' Fanny exclaimed, leaning out of the Dettmans' carriage. It was a battered-looking barouche, with the hood pulled back. 'Can you squeeze in here beside me? Thomas will help you—Thomas, help Miss Atkinson!'

'With all my heart,' her brother replied. As he swung down from his fine bay hack, I heard my mother's voice behind me.

'Charlotte?' she said. 'What is the meaning of this?'

She was standing at the door of our house, her pen still in her hand, her slippers on her feet. I was glad to see the slippers. For the roads were so bad that no one wearing list slippers could possibly have run after the Rickards' cavalcade, even if he (or she) had been so inclined.

'We are off to Bondi Bay for a picnic,' I replied, as coolly as possible.

My mother blinked and moved forward. 'Indeed, I think not,' she said.

'Oh, but my cold is much better, you see. I was quite mistaken to worry about it.' Knowing that my mother was unlikely to risk embarrassing herself in front of so many unknown and ill-bred people, I neither flinched nor fell back. 'I shall be quite all right, Mama. You know the sea air always agrees with me.'

'We will take good care of her, Mrs Barton, never fear!' Fanny added. 'Mama is ever so strict, and will not let us anywhere near the rocks, I assure you!'

My mother had almost reached the gate at this point, but I was too quick for her. Since the stairs of the barouche had already been let down, I braced my foot against one of them and, with Fanny's assistance, launched myself into the midst of all the rustling petticoats and bobbing parasols awaiting me. With four ladies already sharing the carriage, there was hardly room for another. But Mrs Dettman being rather thin, I managed to wriggle in somehow.

'It is not my daughter's health that concerns me, Mrs Rickards,' my mother was saying. Though her face was flushed, her voice remained steady. 'She has work to complete. Work that is far more important than a day on the beach, however pleasant.'

'Oh no, Mama.' From high in the barouche, I felt quite safe—and perhaps my manner was a little cocky. 'I have finished all my work. I took care to finish it. There will be nothing for me to do at home. I shall be quite lost for an occupation.'

We gazed at each other, fiery words burning on our tongues. But they could not be expressed. Not even by my mother.

It was a matter of pride, you see. She would not have wanted it known, especially by such a very *low* set, that her daughter had defied her. Nor was she inclined to squabble in public, lest damaging remarks be made on the subject of George Barton.

And she realised that they would be made. One glance at my face must have told her that.

'Very well,' she suddenly announced, with the sweetest of smiles. 'But what are you taking with you to eat, Charlotte? You are not joining the party empty-handed, surely?'

'Oh, we are well supplied, Mrs Barton,' Fanny's mother observed, and I saw at once that she disliked Mama. Though rather bloodless and frayed-looking, Mrs Rickards clearly nursed an abiding resentment against all those ladies who, over the years, had cast aspersions on her choice of allegiance. (No doubt her own family had turned up its collective nose at her marriage, too.) Moreover, my mother fooled her not at all. Coming from much the same background, I believe that they understood each other perfectly. 'You must not think that we are meanly provisioned or ill prepared,' the pallid lady said in her tired, slightly querulous voice. 'We have quite enough for your daughter's wants, I assure you.'

'I have no doubt of it,' my mother replied. Her mildly contemptuous tone seemed to suggest that that Rickards, being intimate with many rich grocers, would naturally be prone to excessive display and over-indulgence when it came to eating and drinking. 'But I cannot think it polite to bring nothing at all. Let me just fetch you some rhubarb tart. I shan't be long.'

She was back inside the house before I could formulate an objection; her thinking had been quicker than mine. I realised, sitting there between Fanny and Maud Dettman, that I had been out-manoeuvred. As the minutes ticked by, my mother's intention became clear to me. She would stay inside the house until the Rickards and their friends became impatient. At which point I would be sent to inquire about the tart, and all would be lost. My mother would lock me in my bedroom. Or smear hot treacle all over my gown. Or otherwise delay me to the point where the picnic party could afford to wait no longer.

I wondered what would happen if I threw myself on the mercy of Mrs Rickards. If I was frank with her, would she express her regrets, and return me to the bosom of my family? Or would she take some delight in disobliging my mother?

'Perhaps you should go and fetch the tart, Charlotte,' Fanny suggested, as I had known that she would. The poor girl was frantic to proceed. 'It need not be cut or wrapped, you know. We can put it in the basket.'

I opened my mouth. I searched my mind vainly for an excuse. Before I could speak, however, I was interrupted.

'Let me go,' said Mr Cummings. 'I could do with a little walk.'

My astonishment was indescribable. Mr Cummings had come to my rescue! It would be incorrect to say that I had not noticed him, for I had. But he had figured very little in my reflections as I grappled with my mother. I had expected to fight this particular battle alone.

My surprise was such that I did not even thank him for his kindness. Instead I sat open-mouthed as he let himself through our front gate and sauntered up the path.

He was wearing his velvet coat again, and a dashing slouch hat.

'Mr Cummings is such a dear,' said Fanny. 'We like him very much, do we not, Mama? He is far and away the nicest of Tom's friends.'

'And he is from Liverpool?' I inquired awkwardly, conscious of the hot blood in my cheeks.

'His business is at Liverpool,' said Fanny. 'Wine and spirits. He comes up to Sydney for the shipments. Jamaican rum, I think he said.'

A wine and spirit merchant! Had I not been so appalled, I might have laughed out loud.

If there was one activity that my mother deplored even more than hotel-keeping, it was the wholesale distribution of wine and spirits.

'His father owns that hotel in Macquarie Street,' Fanny continued. 'I cannot recall its name. He is wearing the most beautiful coral studs, Charlotte, just a few shades darker than your muslin.'

'Do stop *fidgeting*, Fanny,' Mrs Rickards complained. 'You will tear my gown.'

I was watching the house intently—watching and waiting, my palms sweaty and my throat dry. Would my mother's temper snap? Would she push Mr Cummings down the front steps and drag me out of the carriage by my hair? Having witnessed her fights with George Barton, I did not relish the prospect of weathering an attack myself.

Fortunately, I was not required to. It was Mr Cummings who emerged from the front door, carrying a small, wrapped bundle. He brought it to the carriage and surrendered it to me, tipping his hat.

'There *was* no rhubarb tart,' he explained, with a mischievous smile. 'Only this round of cheese, Miss Atkinson.'

'Th-thank you,' I stammered.

'No trouble at all. A pleasure, in fact.'

'Come on, Cummings, stir your stumps!' Thomas exclaimed, and we were soon bowling along the narrow white ribbon of Darling Point Road—which was so rocky and precipitous that our journey was marked by many little squeals of dismay, as we lurched and bumped and juddered. Conversation proved almost impossible. Remaining seated kept us busy enough; for the rest of the time I watched the thick woods roll past, and relished every glimpse of the glittering harbour.

It being early December, the bush was not as bleached and dusty as it would later become. There was still some richness in the colour of the foliage; Darling Point was already trimmed with flowering Christmas bush, and great thatches of glowing fig-marigold adorned the sandy banks along the roadside. White sails flecked the choppy water. Gulls wheeled in the distance. A touch of Spring in the air lent some intensity to the blue of the sky, and to the green shadows of well-watered clefts that tumbled down into virgin bays.

How beautiful the harbour was, in those early years. It seemed so free and fresh, defying the grubby wharves and warehouses that huddled around Sydney proper. Though there *were* a few houses scattered about the hinterland, they were fine, big, beautiful mansions that served to ornament the bush, rather than despoil it. As for Bondi Bay, I defy anyone to name a more glorious location. With its golden sweep of sand, its gentle rivulets, its mighty headlands and sheltering trees, it was a veritable Arcadia. An earthly Paradise.

Of course, the road to the Bay was anything *but* paradisiacal. At one point I thought that we should certainly overturn. (The carriage should never have been brought so far, in my opinion.) Though our dogcarts were nimble enough to make their way over that jagged surface, which was more a track than a road, the carriage was far too unwieldy. In the end we left it some distance from the Bay, under the guardianship of an ostler. Two seats were then vacated in the dogcarts for the older ladies, and the rest of us (Fanny, Maud and myself) were offered horses.

Fanny, who could not ride, was appalled. Even with her brother leading her, she squeaked and yelped all the way to the beach, rocking about as if blown by a gale-force wind. Not that I blame her. The women were not properly dressed for riding astride, and the men had brought no side-saddles with them. Poor Fanny was therefore obliged to sit most precariously. She would have been far better walking, had she not been hobbled by a pair of satin boots.

On being called to inspect these articles, I was amazed. Why on earth wear satin boots to a beach picnic? It made no sense to me.

Maud was more sensibly attired. Nevertheless, she too preferred not to walk. I do not know why, since she cannot have been comfortable. Though she made no complaint, I saw the rigid set of her face and the white patches on her knuckles, as she strove to present a ladylike appearance while holding on for dear life.

I myself refused Mr Cummings's gelding. I valued my safety and my dignity far too much to risk either of them by riding astride in the wrong sort of clothes. When I said as much to Mr Cummings, he asked me if I actually possessed the *right* sort of clothes. I replied that I did, and we were still discussing horses when we arrived at the beach. It must be confessed that my pink tarlatan had suffered many pricks and tears during our scramble, and was never quite the same afterwards. My boots, too, were somewhat scarred. Nevertheless, that walk remains one of my happiest memories.

When we arrived at our destination, my heart turned over. Bursting through a screen of prickly branches, we passed from clustering shadows into sparkling sunlight—from the spicy scent of eucalypts into a brisk, salt wind.

'*How* I have missed the sea!' exclaimed Mr Cummings. 'If I didn't have an excuse to return here now and then, I should have to manufacture one. For my own good health.'

'The air *is* very bracing,' I agreed.

'If I could bottle it, Miss Atkinson, I would make my fortune. "Cummings's Inhalational Tonic".' As I laughed, he added: 'There must be folk in England who would willingly pay good money for fresh air. People who live beside smelting works, perhaps. Or beneath factory chimneys.'

'Except that such people would not *have* any money,' I pointed out. 'Why live beneath a factory chimney unless you are obliged to?'

'Quite so. And why live in England unless you are obliged to? When there are places such as this in New South Wales?'

He made an expansive gesture with one hand, as he held onto his hat with the other. I suppose that I should describe him, at this point, though my memories are not as clear as they should be. When I think of William Cummings, I think of his smile, and everything else fades away. He was immensely fortunate in his smile. I do not know if its charm lay in the dimples that accompanied it, or the slightly crooked eye-tooth that distinguished it, or whether there was another cause altogether: the glint in his eye, for instance. Whatever the root of its appeal, however, it was hard to resist.

For the rest, he was slim, fair, and of medium height, with sandy hair and no beard. I judged him to be older than Thomas Rickards, though I only later discovered that he was twenty-six. While he might have been described as a gay blade, there was nothing vicious or intemperate about him. For despite the fact that we all grew rather noisy and hilarious that day, there was never an instant when the proceedings could have been considered unsafe, or the jokes offensive.

At least, they did not seem so to *me*.

Lunch came first, and was much enlivened by several bottles of champagne. There followed an expedition over the rocks, during which Mr Cummings made us all laugh by striking absurdly heroic poses, and pretending to fight off a crab, and generally impersonating a man who fancied himself as a bold and gallant explorer. After that, we ran races. Poor Fanny took a tumble, and I tore my petticoat, so that a piece of it trailed along behind me in the most embarrassing manner. No sooner had this mishap occurred than I had three gentlemen pursuing me with drawn pen-knives, crying: 'Let *me* cut it off, Miss Akinson!' Whereupon I was forced to hide behind Mrs Rickards, almost sick with laughter.

By this time it was the middle of the afternoon, and very hot. Some melons were cut, and we ate them in the shade of a cliff, with the breakers rolling in only a few feet away. I explained to Mr Cummings about cuttlefish, and described some stones that I had found years before at Swan Lake, which had floated in water. ('They were pumice stones,' I explained, 'and you have never seen a more curious thing.') Mr Cummings, in turn, told me the funniest story about a talking pig at Castlereagh—or at least, a pig that was *supposed* to have possessed the power of speech. ('I said to the man, "Does it perhaps have a *Scottish accent*, Mr Larch? I have always had *great difficulty* understanding a thick Scottish accent.") I laughed until I cried, and then some of us climbed the cliff, and I tore my petticoat again. I was better off than Maud, however, who lost her hat, poor thing. It blew off her head into the sea. And though I leapt up onto a high rock, waving my arms and calling down to the others, they were too late to retrieve it. The unfortunate hat had already been sucked down in a tidal rip.

Maud was quite upset by her loss. We tried to comfort her as best we could; I lent her my own hat, and Fanny promised her some silk ribbon. But the spell was broken, and the shadows were lengthening. Mrs Rickards decided that it was time to go.

I need hardly say that we left reluctantly. The sun-dazzled joy of that wonderful day lives with me still. I do not know if I was ever so happy, so *truly* happy, as I was then. I remember standing on the edge of a cliff, with my arms outstretched and my skirts flapping, almost convinced that, if I launched myself into the air, I would be able to fly.

I also remember the sensation of being grabbed around the waist and pulled back. It was Mr Cummings who did this. 'You are making me *very* anxious,' he confessed, as the warmth of his hands invaded my entire body. 'I should hate to see you meet the same fate as your friend's hat, Miss Atkinson. What a tragic loss that would be!'

I believe that I must have fallen in love with him at this very instant. Certainly, I was filled with a wild sense of elation. Suddenly my prospects seemed bright with promise; I felt strong and pretty and immensely free. But during the bone-shaking journey back to Darlinghurst, my mood became less sanguine. Though I faced a truly awful homecoming, it was not the thought of my mother's imminent retribution that chilled me. It was the knowledge that I would soon have to part from William Cummings.

How was I to ensure that we should meet again?

'It was a very great pleasure, Miss Atkinson,' he said, upon helping me down from the barouche. 'I am not often in town, but I hope to see you at St James on Christmas Day. Or perhaps at the Anniversary Regatta in January?'

'Oh yes,' I replied. 'Yes, I hope so.'

And I determined that I should see him at both events, or die trying.

Twenty-nine

When I walked through the front door, my mother was waiting for me. She sat alone in the drawing room, straight-backed, a volume of sermons lying open before her.

'Your supper is in the study,' she declared, without raising her head. 'You will be sleeping there also, until you apologise for your conduct and undertake to improve it. I fear for your sisters' morals, otherwise.'

This was slightly better than I had anticipated. My fear had been that she would box my ears as soon as I had crossed the threshold.

'Why should I apologise?' was my defiant retort. 'I have done nothing wrong. If you hadn't been so unreasonable, I would not have been forced to lie.'

'This is my house.' Mama closed her book with a snap. She looked up, her eyes hard. 'If you do not abide by its rules, then you are not welcome in it.'

'*Your* house!' The bitter words bubbled out of me like mud from a hot spring. 'This is not *your* house! You *have* no house!

You would have nothing at all if it weren't for me and the others! You are living on *our* money, Mama!'

Her nostrils flared. She turned pale with anger.

'How dare you!' she spat. 'How *dare* you speak to me like that, you wicked, *brazen* girl!'

'Brazen? You call *me* brazen?'

'You go off on the most improper excursion, with men to whom you haven't even been introduced—'

'At least there were ladies present! At least I was *chaperoned*! Which is more than I can say for you, when you rode off *alone* with your *overseer*—'

I was interrupted, dodging her book as it sailed through the air.

'Get out!' she yelled. 'Shameless, unnatural girl!'

'*You* are the shameless one! Would we be here today, if it weren't for you?'

'Get out!'

'You can't tell me what to do!' As she rushed towards me, I shrieked: 'If you touch me, I shall tell the Master in Equity! And he will take me away! He will take us *all* away, and you will have *no money to live on*!'

What an obnoxious child I was, to be sure. And yet I was quite correct. At that particular time, my siblings and I were effectively wards of the Court, since our inheritance was still under its control. This meant that my mother was obliged to tread with great care.

Knowing this, I could defy her almost with impunity—once I had a mind to. Once I had a *reason* to. And in William Cummings, I found that reason.

After I met William Cummings, Mama could do absolutely nothing with me.

She tried, of course. She refused to take me on various excursions into town, and was terribly stingy with her Christmas presents. Whenever James, Emily or Louisa spoke to me, they incurred my mother's grave disapproval. I was no longer requested to read aloud, nor to join in the merry parlour games with which we occasionally occupied ourselves.

In return, I was rude and disagreeable. I wrote screeds of abuse in my daily journal, which I left about quite openly in the hope that she might read it. I broke into her writing desk, and examined many of the documents hidden there. I ignored her stated wishes at every opportunity, especially where Fanny Rickards was concerned. In fact, I began to spend more time at Fanny's house than I did at home.

You will understand why, I am sure. It was not for Fanny's sake but for William's. I was keen to hear news of him; even keener to see him. At first I was reluctant to confide in Fanny, thinking her far too stupid to be trusted with a confidence. I simply angled for information as best I could. As the days passed, however, I found that I could no longer restrain myself. It was nearing Christmas, and I had to know: would Mr Cummings be attending the Christmas service at St James or not?

Though Fanny was generally stupid, she could be very quick when it came to matters of the heart. One glancing, all-too-casual reference to Mr William Cummings was enough to alert her. From that moment on, we talked of almost nothing else—except her own unrequited passion for a military officer by the name of Wren. It was Fanny who pressed her brother Thomas for tidings of his friend at Liverpool, and subsequently conveyed them to me. It was Fanny who arranged that Mr Cummings and his family should join her own clan at the Christmas service. It was Fanny who, by means of much shrill manoeuvring, managed to effect an introduction between Mr Cummings and my mother on the steps of St James. Trapped by the crowds, my mother was unable to avoid this unwelcome meeting. And having been properly introduced to him, she found it difficult to justify her unfriendliness towards Mr Cummings thereafter.

Difficult, but not impossible.

'If he decides to call,' she announced, 'I shall not receive him. You may do as you wish, Charlotte—you always have—but he will receive no such condescension from *me*, I warn you. For he deals in liquor, and I regard that as a disgraceful occupation.'

'Even though you freely chose to marry a drunkard?'

My mother stood up, and made as if to leave the drawing room. Conscious that she could not afford to lose her temper with me, she had taken to removing herself from my vicinity whenever I attacked her.

'Would marrying a wine merchant be more disgraceful than marrying a notorious drunkard?' I asked. 'Why *did* you marry a notorious drunkard, Mama?'

'Oh, for—' James, who was also in the room, rose abruptly, throwing down his pen. '*Must* you do this?' he snapped at me. 'Must you ruin everything, always?'

'*I?*'

'There's never any peace for anyone, thanks to you!'

'Thanks to *me?* When was there ever any peace since *she* married George Barton?'

'Do not speak to her, James,' my mother said. 'She is unreasonable. She chooses to torment us—it gives her pleasure. Do not indulge her by paying any attention.'

'Why did you marry George Barton, Mama?'

For perhaps the twentieth time, I put this question to her. And for perhaps the twentieth time, she refused to answer it. Instead, she walked out of the room, with James at her heels.

I daresay that you could have called me the victor, though it was an empty victory. In truth, I derived little satisfaction from my role as Black Sheep, which left me bereft and isolated. Yet I could not control myself. Something bitter in my heart drove me to snap and growl at my mother like an untrained dog. And the more I did so, the more I had to complain of. For she still possessed some resources, despite her advanced age. She still had it in her to make my life miserable, though her choices were limited by her fear of the Master in Equity. Only consider the estrangement that slowly opened up between me and my siblings. *That* was largely my mother's doing—and it happened around this time.

My only comfort lay in William Cummings. After paying a brief call after Christmas, he returned to Liverpool, where he took to writing me letters. Though they were brief and ill-composed, I treasured these scraps of paper. I used to carry them with me everywhere, tucked into my bodice. There were five of them all told, and one was an invitation to view the regatta that was held every January, on Sydney Harbour, to commemorate the colony's birth. Mr Cummings had never missed a regatta in his life. And he would be honoured, he wrote, if he could perchance watch this one in my company.

You may be wondering why I was permitted to receive such correspondence. Why, you might ask, had my mother not hidden it from me? The answer is that she knew nothing of it. Mr William Cummings, being well aware of her opinions, sent all his letters to me via Fanny Rickards. You may regard this as an underhanded ploy, and you would be right. It was. But I had no reservations—not with Fanny there, urging me to indulge my wayward nature. And the more recklessly I behaved, the more William Cummings seemed to appreciate my worth.

He had his own reckless streak, though not (as you will see) to the detriment of his comfort.

I find it hard to describe him more fully after so many years. At the time, I thought him a ray of sunlight. And I was not far wrong, because he was a merry soul, with no taste for introspection, for heavy reading, or for company of a melancholic bent. He was a good rider with a pleasant singing voice. He mixed with a great many sailors and shipping agents, and though he himself had never 'turned a blue jacket' (that is, gone to sea), he was knowledgeable on the subject of lading, customs, tonnage, and all kinds of associated business. In Liverpool he must have lived the rackety existence of a single man pursuing a trade that, while not exactly disreputable, would have caused him to mix with some disreputable characters. But he was always well groomed, and had never fallen foul of the police. Indeed, he seemed to be generally respected among the mercantile fraternity—though whether this was on account of his own talents, or whether it was owing to his father's good reputation, I have no way of knowing.

I think that he must have had a canny side to him, for all that it was not immediately evident. To deal in spirits is to run the perpetual risk of becoming a sot, yet William Cummings never made that error. Though apparently insouciant by nature, and much given to attending horse races and card games, he was neither a gambler nor an habitual drunkard. I wonder now if his social activities were not somehow connected with his business—for a dealer in spirits must perforce make himself generally agreeable if he is to move his wares. Not that his happy demeanour was in any way contrived. I am quite sure of *that*. There can be no doubt, however, that commercial imperatives combined very profitably with his natural inclinations to make his life as cheerful and prosperous as one could reasonably expect, at such a young age.

If I met him now, I should probably think him just a fraction too pleased with himself. His breeziness might appear a little bumptious, his perpetual good humour a sign of emotional vacuity. But at the time I thought him so wonderful that his self-confidence seemed entirely well founded. He was my sun, moon and stars. To me, he was invested with a kind of glow, as if he carried in his hair and on his skin the vestiges of that golden afternoon at Bondi Bay, when I had glimpsed a form of existence utterly removed from my own: a life unconcerned with fear, or doubt, or mistakes of the past; a life in which the intricacies of natural existence came a poor second to the simple enjoyment of a race on the beach.

What William Cummings saw in *me* I cannot begin to comprehend. A pretty young girl, I suppose, in quite the fashionable style: dark-eyed, dark-haired and well-rounded, though rather too tall and brown. But there were many pretty young girls about, so I was hardly unique in that. Perhaps my attraction lay in the ambiguity of my status. Though well bred, I was not, on closer acquaintance, quite as well bred as I at first appeared to be. And though my origins were respectable, my nature was a little wild. The combination might have struck William Cummings as piquant and exotic.

So we arranged to meet at the regatta. I would lose myself in the crowds, and meet him in front of the Commissariat Buildings. He would then return home with me in the guise of my preserver. It would not be the most convincing story, but it could hardly be disproved. And by what other means could we possibly come together? Our mutual admiration was such that we were determined to take any risk, regardless of the consequences. Therefore, on the twenty-seventh of January, I set out to make my rendezvous.

At first, my mother had been disinclined to take me with her to watch the regatta. She remarked that I deserved no such indulgence, and should rightly remain at home, mending my worsted stockings. But when I replied that I would go alone if need be, she relented. Perhaps she was concerned about my safety. Or perhaps she was afraid that, if I was discovered wandering around the dockyards unattended, her reputation might suffer even further.

She therefore allowed me to join the family party.

Respectable people used to watch the anniversary regatta from certain specific locations. Many of the highest rank were afforded a first-rate view from aboard the flagship—in this instance, the *General Hewitt*. Others positioned themselves on private landings, or atop balustraded roof-walks. My mother's choice had always been a spot on the slope near Government House. It was a high, breezy, uncluttered vantage point, far from the noise and hilarity

336

of the dockyards, and I knew that, once there, I would have no chance at all of slipping away. I would have to make my escape either before or after the event, as we squirmed through the milling crowds. My choice was therefore a difficult one. If accomplished before the races, my retreat would ruin Mama's enjoyment of them. But if I had to wait until afterwards, I would forsake my own pleasure, and perhaps annoy Mr Cummings. How could I be sure that he would wait for me at the Commissariat Stores for the entire length of the festivities? No—the plan had to be carried out as soon as practicable. When I was passing through Macquarie Place, perhaps.

As it happened, my withdrawal was effected quite easily. There was such a mob of people pouring down Bridge Street that I had only to duck behind the high fence of the Colonial Secretary's House, and I was free and clear. Then I used an overloaded dray as a kind of screen or shield, walking close beside it until I had crossed the Tank Stream. From there, it was a sharp right at George Street, and due north to the Commissariat Stores.

I can still remember my heightened state of fear and elation. On the one hand, I felt guilty, for I knew that my mother would be terribly concerned. On the other hand, I saw my entire escapade as a huge adventure. Never before had I walked the streets of Sydney alone and unaccompanied. Never before had I explored this particular part of the city, which my mother regarded as unsuitable territory for a well-bred girl. In the locality known as the Rocks, it was not unusual to encounter vice in all its forms—or so I had been told. The proximity of the gaol and the Naval Yards meant that the Rocks attracted many hotel-keepers, loose women, and dubious characters of every type. So you can imagine my nervousness as I struggled past the dilapidated brick edifice known as Underwood's, being buffeted on all sides by loud-voiced people smelling of drink.

Though not especially beautiful, the north end of George Street was interesting. Lanes sloped down to the water, pinched between the high walls of dusty-looking warehouses. Bristling masts were visible above the sagging roofs of shipping offices and marine dealers' stores, and oily water could sometimes be glimpsed lapping at barnacled piers. The streets smelled of tar and coal, rope and rusty iron, salt and slops. They rang with the rattle of dray wheels and the whistle of draymen, many of whom were that day carrying human loads, all wedged together in hilarious confusion. Sailors bawled their shanties from pub doors as dirty children scurried about like rats among the scraps of rotten onion and orange peel. The mood at the docks was ferociously cheerful, with a pipe being played somewhere, and men chanting for victory.

I enjoyed it all, make no mistake. I could hardly do otherwise, since it was a rare spectacle. But I was relieved when I came upon Mr Cummings outside the Commissariat Stores. And I clung to him in a manner that he must have found gratifying.

He had donned a navy-blue coat, in honour of the occasion. He also wore ribbons in his hat. They had been placed there in support of a crew manning one of the third-class sailing boats, whose owner was a friend of his. If it won its race, he would feel obliged to donate a bottle of rum to each of the crew members. 'So while I *pretend* to wish them well, in my heart I hope that they run their boat into Pinchgut,' he confessed with a laugh. 'I tell you, Anniversary Day may be good for business, with everyone toasting the Queen, but I lose almost all my profit because I am such a faithful friend to so many of the competitors!'

This was no idle boast. As the day progressed, I witnessed innumerable encounters between Mr Cummings and various watermen who demanded that he wish them luck on account of some upcoming race. We viewed the course from various angles, and there was always some skiff manned by a friend or acquaintance of Mr Cummings. This fact alone made the occasion more enjoyable for me, since I had never before felt any proprietary interest in the vessels competing. But had the entire event been a complete disaster, with the *General Hewitt* sinking and every small craft being dashed against the overburdened wharves, I would still have been delighted. Because in the company of Mr William Cummings, the whole world seemed gay and gorgeous.

I shall not describe our activities at any length. We went from wharf to wharf, and cheered lustily, and ate prawns and peaches, and drank ginger beer, and waved handkerchiefs, and giggled over mishaps (such as a capsized rowboat), and gave ourselves over entirely to feverish enjoyment. There were moments when I forgot my name, my family, my very self. I seemed to be engulfed by the crowd; I laughed when it laughed, groaned when it groaned. Invested with its overbearing confidence, I became bold, screaming like a common rag-tacker and disregarding every lesson that I had ever learned on the deportment of a lady. Why, I even kissed a sailor! At least, I allowed him to kiss *me*. For he had just won his heat, and was in a perfect delirium of joy, bussing me on the cheek before I could protest.

During all these proceedings, my swain stayed close to my side. He kept up a running commentary that amused me no end, joking about the prizes, the officials, the Army Band and the poor foreign sailors who had been roped into competing without the least idea, I am quite sure, of what was going on. Yet for all his careless good humour, he made sure that I was neither jostled nor over-heated; that I always had a seat when I needed one; that I was never thirsty nor hungry. Moreover, he insisted that we leave before the final race. 'Because it is getting late,' he said, 'and I do not want you caught in the crush, when everyone *else* decides to depart.' He was—I still contest—a perfect gentleman. And by the time he handed me into the Darlinghurst omnibus, I was utterly enraptured.

'I wonder if Mama is home yet?' I mused, as we sat together, blind to the people around us. 'She will be *very* angry with me.'

'You need not be afraid,' was Mr Cummings's doting reply. 'I shall be there to protect you. With my pocket-knife, if necessary.'

'If she casts me out of the house, what shall I do? My uncle will not take me in—why, I don't even know where he is!'

'Have no fear,' said Mr Cummings. 'I will not let any ill befall you.'

How young we were! I suppose that it seems laughable, now, but I felt like Juliet. It never occurred to me that a talent for enjoying oneself was hardly the bedrock for a successful union, or that Mr Cummings was not *necessarily* the man with whom I was destined to find eternal happiness. As we drew closer and closer to my family's house, I became more and more convinced that I should die without him. For had he not agreed to accompany me directly into the Lion's Den?

You may scoff at our feelings. You may see nothing admirable or romantic about a silly young girl with windblown hair and a dirty gown making sheep's eyes at a freckled youth wearing tattered ribbons on his hat. I concede that we were not the stuff of Shakespeare. Yet we were as much star-crossed as any Montagu or Capulet, and I know that *my* heart was beating double-quick time when we gained the picket fence encompassing my mother's house. In the setting sun, it looked not unlike a row of bared teeth.

My mother was at home. I discovered this when I pushed open our front door, and stepped into the drawing room. For she walked straight up to me and slapped me hard across the cheek.

Behind me, Mr Cummings gasped.

'Loathsome creature!' my mother exclaimed. 'What? Are you *shameless*? Have you brought him *with* you?'

I burst into tears. It was not a weakness in which I frequently indulged; perhaps I was a little sun-struck. In any event, it touched a nerve with Mr William Cummings.

340

'Mrs Barton,' he protested, shielding me, 'this is hardly fair or reasonable.'

'Mr Cummings,' said my mother, 'get out.'

'You've not heard what I have to say—'

'Nor wish to,' my mother spat. 'Will you leave, sir, or must I summon the police?'

'I will not leave until you calm yourself.'

At this, my mother threw herself against him, trying to push him back across the threshold in a foolish and undignified manner. It certainly must have struck *him* as an absurd response; he was, after all, at least a foot taller than she was. I noticed that he began to smile as he braced himself.

'Mrs Barton . . . please . . .' he protested. 'What good will come of this?'

'You are not welcome here!' my mother cried. 'You are corrupting my daughter!'

'Indeed I am *not*.' His smile faded, to be replaced by a very grim look. 'Ma'am, if you will allow me to explain—'

'I got *lost!*' was my hurried contribution. 'Mama, I could not find you! Mr Cummings *rescued* me!'

'Nonsense.'

'Mrs Barton—'

'Leave him alone!' I tried to pull her off Mr Cummings, conscious all the while of Emily and Louisa staring from the hall doorway. 'You are ruining *everything*! You always ruin everything!'

'If I may say one thing, Mrs Barton—'

'No! Get out! You weasel! You rogue!'

'Mrs Barton, *I wish to marry your daughter!*'

After a moment's shocked silence, my mother ran from the room.

Thirty

I f you had glanced at the *Sydney Morning Herald* on the sixth
of March, 1844, you would have seen the following item of
domestic court news.

'Atkinson v Barton on Petition

*This was an application to the court to refer it to the Master to
enquire and report whether Charlotte Elizabeth Atkinson, aged about
sixteen years, and now residing with her mother, Mrs Barton, might
be married to William Cummings junior of Liverpool, and if so that
arrangements might be made for her marriage settlement out of the funds
and property in which she is interested, and which is under control of
the Court. It was also stated that Mrs Barton and several other parties
interested had given their consent, some to the marriage and others to
the reference, provided the costs of the same, and of the application,
were not taken out of the funds under the control of the Court.*

*The Court granted the application, at the same time remarking
that it would be a very important part of the Master's enquiry to
ascertain as to whether the young gentleman who proposed as a husband
for the young lady named on the petition was a man of
substance . . .'*

It makes me smile now. A 'man of substance'? Mr William Cummings was as insubstantial as a ray of sunlight; he had hardly any weight to him at all, and this was what endeared him to me. Yet with regard to property and reputation, I suppose that he was well enough endowed. Certainly there was nothing shabby about him—not that leapt to the eye. Even my solicitor could see no clear objection to the marriage, though he droned on about my 'inexperience' and my 'tender years'. 'If your mother has doubts,' he said, 'perhaps you should reconsider your intentions. For Mrs Barton *is* a good deal older, and knows what is best for you.'

'My mother has approved the marriage,' I rejoined stoutly. 'She will not stand in my way.'

'Yet she *has* expressed certain reservations . . .'

'When?' I glared at him. 'When were you speaking to my mother?'

'Miss Atkinson, it is my duty to protect your interests—'

'Then you will kindly listen to *me* instead of my mother. Mr Cummings is a good, respectable man who will take care of me for the rest of my life. And I fail to see why there has to be all this fuss, simply because I intend to marry him! He has money of his own, you know! He is not chasing after mine!'

If you are shocked at my bluntness, please consider my family's past experience with the legal profession. Though Mama and I were barely on speaking terms by this stage, I was fully aware that lawyers had made her life a misery with their astronomical fees and outrageous demands. That I was now required to parade myself through the Courts in order to marry the man I loved seemed to me yet another example of the Law's unreasonableness.

All the same, I used it to my advantage. Had my mother not been in such a precarious position, I might never have carried the day. The very fact that I was obliged to petition the Courts meant that she could not forbid me to marry without running the risk of yet more tedious and expensive litigation. And she was tired of it. She could not summon up the energy to fight.

So she submitted, with as much ill grace as she could muster.

I shall not describe the many, many arguments that we had regarding my decision to accept Mr Cummings's proposal. Some of them flared up at moments of great anxiety—when we were discussing my *trousseau*, for instance—and some were reasonably civil, with both of us sitting down to explain our positions in a vain attempt to win the other's support. My mother thought me too young to marry, especially in light of my 'restless' disposition. She distrusted any man who had made his way in the world by selling spirits, however sunny and good-natured he might appear. She also pointed out that Mr Cummings and I were not well suited, since there was a great disparity of age, education, rank and temper. 'How well do you know him really?' she once asked. 'And how well does he know *you*?' Whereupon I was driven to retort: 'How well did you know Mr Barton, Mama?' And the exchange became heated, and nothing useful was accomplished.

Perhaps, if my mother had been frank with me, she might have achieved her purpose. I would have listened to her then. Despite all the noise and fuss—despite the fact that most of my attention was fixed firmly on William Cummings—in one still, small corner of my mind I was waiting for an explanation. And every time my mother and I locked horns over my betrothal, I was expecting an illuminating remark about marrying in haste, or matches made in Hell, or unfortunate choices. It seems incredible to me that she never let slip a single piece of advice that might have had at least some bearing on her own situation. My mother had married the wrong man, for what must have been precisely the wrong reasons. Yet for all that we conversed endlessly about my falling into a trap of my own making, she never *once* claimed that her hard-won experience gave her valuable insight. She never took me aside and said: 'Charlotte, I do not want you to make the same mistake that

I did.' She never tried to show me how, in jumping to certain conclusions, or in submitting to certain threats, or even (who knows?) in accommodating certain social conventions, my mother had spoiled all our lives.

Perhaps it was something that she could not bear to acknowledge, even to herself.

As for me, my thinking was so muddled by emotion that I did not seize the opportunity as I should have. I did not use my betrothal as a lever, to pry open the sealed places in her heart. Though I tried once or twice, in a clumsy way, it was not done with sufficient skill or determination. My passions always seemed to distract me, blowing me off course. Perhaps I was too young to know my own mind.

At any rate, you must imagine a household in turmoil during the late summer and early autumn of 1844. There were, as I have described, various legal questions to be settled: money would be due to me from my father's estate when I came of age, and how exactly that might be disposed upon my marriage was something that concerned a great number of Sydney lawyers. The estate itself was still the subject of much wrangling. (Its management continued to be investigated, though a receiver had been appointed just a few month before, at my mother's request.) Furthermore, we were plagued by other difficulties of a more humdrum nature. Louisa caught a chill, and had to be removed from Mr Rennie's school for some weeks. Our milking cow broke through the fence and went wandering off down the road to Darling Point, where she met with an unknown fate—possibly involving wild dogs. My mother and I bickered incessantly. Betsy left us for a better-paying position, to be replaced by a graduate of the Female School of Industry, who—though manifestly good-hearted—was so distressingly stupid that she could not be trusted with the ironing or the shopping.

The only misfortune that we did *not* suffer, at this time, was an unexpected visit from George Barton. My stepfather had been invisible for months. His absence might have been the result of a sudden windfall; the Equity Court had decreed that Mr Alexander Berry should pay George Barton ninety-five pounds, and my mother had been informed that her husband would be using this money to take over a farm near Bathurst. George Barton did not tell her this himself, not even in writing. He had abandoned us. Or at least, this is what we profoundly hoped.

But we made no assumptions. It did not do to make assumptions where George Barton was concerned. And as you will see, we were right to be wary. For George Barton had not quite disappeared from our lives.

He resurfaced in March, around the same time as the *Sydney Morning Herald* made mention of my betrothal. I cannot help thinking that the newspaper report may, in fact, have influenced his decision to return. Though I have forgotten the *exact* date, it was on the same afternoon as the match between the Australian and Cumberland Cricket Clubs in Hyde Park. I know this because I attended the match myself, with the Rickards family and Mr Cummings.

Neither my mother nor my siblings joined us. Despite the fact that I was still spending a good deal of time with the Rickards, my mother was nowhere near resigning herself to their company. She avoided them wherever possible, just as she did her best to dodge William Cummings. Whenever he paid a call, there would be a domestic crisis, or a headache, or an appointment, and she would make her excuses in a hurried fashion—if, that is, she actually appeared at all. I do not know if she was protecting herself or Mr Cummings; it is possible that she distrusted her own temper, and wished to spare him any offence that she might cause by her tendency to outspokenness. At any rate, she usually left us alone.

And since we had no quarrel with that, I never upbraided her for her conduct. Though impolite, it was not unwelcome.

On the day of the cricket match, my mother took the rest of the family to Balmain. She was driven to such an extreme measure by the Rickards' invitation. Not wanting to accept it, she had used the trip to Balmain as an excuse; James, she said, had long been wishing to ride the new Balmain steam ferry, and she had promised to indulge him on the very day of the scheduled match. I doubt that anyone believed her. But it was a face-saving pretext, and appeared to be accepted by the Rickards. So my family went off to collect molluscs at Balmain, and I went off to cheer cricketers at Hyde Park.

I seem to recall that the Australian team lost, though I cannot be certain. I paid very little attention to the proceedings on the field. For this was yet another of those festive occasions at which the Rickards seemed to excel; there was endless laughter, and an excess of champagne, and quantities of delicious food, some of it eaten and some (it must be confessed) thrown about in imitation of a cricket ball. Fanny was in her element, thanks to the presence of Lieutenant Wren. William Cummings made us laugh with a great many absurd and spurious rules of the game, declaring in the most solemn manner that if a stump should fall, custom decreed that the batsman should be beaten around the head with it, briskly, a total of seven times. He even tried to demonstrate—using Fanny's parasol and Thomas's head—until brought to the ground by Fanny's burly lieutenant. We all drank the health of both teams, and walked around the park several times. Fanny and I discussed the blossoms that would crown her when she served as my bridesmaid. Many fond jokes were made about my wedding, some of which caused me to blush. For I was not wholly inured to the broad humour of the Rickards' set.

It was a pleasant picnic, and I enjoyed it immensely. But towards four o'clock the weather failed. A biting wind sprang up, raising dust and penetrating shawls. Faced with such an unpromising turn of events, the party quickly scattered. The Rickards walked back to their house, which was just across the park. Lieutenant Wren and his companion sauntered away in search of further amusement. And Mr Cummings escorted me home on the omnibus.

There are probably still today English ladies of good birth who would blanch at such a confession. To have gone off with a single gentleman! On a public conveyance! With no one else to attend me! I daresay the Macleays would not have approved, but I was past caring. I had no mind to model myself on the Macleays—not when I had Mr Cummings to guide my steps. Whatever Mr Cummings thought acceptable, I was ready to accommodate. And in his defence let it be said that he never took advantage of me. On the contrary, I think that he enjoyed playing the shepherd to my lamb—as men often do who are a little unnerved by the opposite sex. I cannot be sure, but I wonder now if his profoundly respectful demeanour, like his playful conversation, suggested a lack of confidence. After all, he was a man of twenty-six. Why did he want to spend his time frolicking with a mere child, unless he found older girls intimidating?

You must understand, he gave no obvious indication of this. I never saw him tongue-tied in the presence of any lady; he sported with all females alike. Yet I am puzzled. And it occurs to me that my mother might have been puzzled as well. Perhaps *that* is why she warned me so fervently against the union.

Perhaps I have done her an injustice.

In any event, for whatever reason, Mr Cummings's conduct was faultless. That is why I had no qualms about inviting him into the house when we reached it. I knew that our servant had been given the afternoon off. I knew that, in all probability, Mama and the others had not returned home. Yet I trusted Mr Cummings in a way that seems almost absurd, looking back. How naïve I must have been! Or was there something about the man—something peculiarly unsusceptible—that precluded any possibility of risk?

Maybe so. Still, I am appalled at my own stupidity. No girl as well acquainted with the dreadful history of John Lynch should have put herself in such a vulnerable position. For if Lynch taught us one lesson, it was that an amiable manner can disguise a Devil's heart. And as my mother had said: how well did I really know Mr Cummings?

Fortunately, in my case, God tempered the wind to the shorn lamb. Though I *did* meet with a Devil upon entering that house, it was not a Devil in the form of William Cummings. When I pushed open the front door, and called out 'Mama!', I heard a noise from out the back. It was a scuffling noise, followed by the creak of a board, as if somebody was creeping around in one of the bedrooms.

'Peggy? Is that you?' Peeling off my gloves, I walked briskly towards the rear of the house, across the drawing-room carpet and through the library door. Mr Cummings followed me, pausing to lay down his hat and stick. 'Mama? Mr Cummings brought me home. If Peggy has not returned, I can make the tea mys—'

I froze, breaking off in mid-sentence. For there, in my mother's bedroom, stood George Barton.

We discovered afterwards that he must have climbed in through the kitchen window, which had not been properly secured. He was unshaven and dishevelled, and a most unhealthy colour. But the first thing I noticed about him was the tangle of chains and trinkets in the palm of his hand. I realised straight away, without so much as a pause for reflection, that he had been rifling in my mother's jewel-case.

He thrust his spoils immediately into the pocket of his coat.

'Is it you, is it?' he rasped, trying to be appear unconcerned. 'Aye, and sneaking yer fella home too. *Fine* behaviour, I must say.'

He pushed past me, heading into the hall. He smelled sourly of liquor. 'I allus said you'd turn out wild, Charlotte.'

'What do you think you're doing?' was my very natural retort. Having recovered from my initial shock, I hurried after him. 'Stop! Stop at once!'

'Does yer Ma know what you're up to?' he growled, without turning or pausing. By this time he had almost reached the front door; his heavy tread, as he made his escape, seemed to shake the whole house. Both of his pockets bulged with ill-gotten gains.

'Who is that?' said a bewildered Mr Cummings, behind me. But I ignored him. Instead of replying, I snatched up his cane from my mother's writing desk, rushing across the room as Barton closed his fingers around the door-knob.

'*Stop!*' I cried, bringing the stick down hard on Barton's outstretched arm.

You must understand that I was not thinking very clearly. My only intention was to retrieve our belongings—it *outraged* me that a cur like Barton should regard them as his own, or even touch them with his filthy hands. The sight of him, moreover, affected me like a slap in the face. I had thought myself rid of him. Now, once again, he had crawled out from whatever cess-pit he had been occupying, and smeared his dirt all over my mother's lace and letters and mourning lockets—all over my beautiful autumn day in Hyde Park. The anger that engulfed me had more to do with revenge than reason.

'*Thief! You thief! Give it back!*' I yelled, as he cried out in pain. My next blow struck him across the ear, and he staggered, trying to shield himself. I was very foolish. Had he not been slightly drunk, I might have run a grave risk in assaulting him thus. But rum had slowed his responses. He was only able to use one arm, since I had briefly paralysed the other. When he reached for my cane, I dodged him easily. And showered more blows upon his head and neck.

I shall never forget the sensation. It seemed to shoot down my wrist straight to my heart; neither before nor since have I ever felt the same peculiar sense of *contact*. I have chopped a lot of wood in my day, and whipped a few beasts, and boxed a few ears. I have even thrown one or two tantrums involving walls and furniture, when I was very much younger than I am now. And never has the object of my attack yielded in quite the same way as Barton did on that autumn afternoon. His flesh and bone offered up almost no resistance. Mr Cummings's cane did not spring back, as it would have from a table or a log of wood. It seemed practically to bury itself in Barton's skin, though no blood was visible.

Dropping to one knee, he snatched at my legs, hoping to bring me down. Whereupon I fetched him a kick that nearly upended *me*. (Hoop petticoats might as well have been specially designed to prevent ladies from kicking, I have found.) He grabbed a handful of skirt, swearing horribly, and I struck him again.

'Let go!' I screamed. 'Get your stinking hands off me!'

Then he caught my stick. He yanked it away, still hiding his face, and hurled it in my direction. In avoiding it, I lost my advantage. Though I clawed at his scalp, he managed to rise; he was bent and unsteady, but upright again. I was lucky that his thoughts were all bent on escape. Had he been prepared to fight, I would have been badly injured at this point.

Instead he pushed me, hard. There was so much weight behind his push that I went straight over. As I struggled with my voluminous petticoats, he tugged open the door.

I lunged for his over-stuffed pocket.

'Stop!' I screeched, hooking three fingers into it. Alas—it did not tear. The stitching was too fine and strong.

He freed himself with a flailing kick, which landed on my elbow. The pain was immense. I was still battling it when I got up again, bawling imprecations after his retreating figure. He went straight down the front path on ankles like jelly, stumbling and reeling and holding his head. I might have caught him then, if not for my petticoat. I had ripped it while falling, you see, and now I tripped on the tear. So I fell again, and grazed my palms, and jolted my injured elbow, and by the time I had righted myself he was through the gate, running.

'*Thief!*' I picked up a stone and hurled it, missing him. '*I'll call the police, you thieving pig! Stop, thief!*'

Had there been anyone about, he might yet have been apprehended. Unfortunately, the street was a windswept void. You could have shot a musket-ball down almost its entire length without hitting so much as a goat. There was nothing else to be seen except rocks, fences, gardens, a sprinkle of browsing livestock and a few widely spaced houses between clumps of trees.

As I looked about for help, my stepfather must have ducked behind one of these trees. At any rate, he disappeared suddenly. Stamping my foot, I yelled for William Cummings.

'William!' I called from the front gate. 'William, quick!'

Mr Cummings had not even crossed my mind since my first glimpse of George Barton. But now it occurred to me: *William* might catch him! William was young and strong and uninjured. Moreover, he was not wearing skirts. Barton would *never* outrun William Cummings.

'*William, hurry!*' I shrilled. '*Or he will escape!*'

I moved clumsily back towards the house, clutching my elbow and panting like a sunstruck cow, my petticoat trailing, my palms smarting, all red and ruffled and wild-eyed. I had not much consideration for my own plight. Then Mr Cummings appeared, framed in the doorway, and I stopped.

The look on his face told me all that I needed to know. It sent every thought connected with George Barton straight out of my head.

Two days later Mr Cummings withdrew his suit, and returned to Liverpool. I have never seen nor heard from him since. As

I said before, he was not reckless enough to risk his own comfort by marrying a crazed termagant. Certainly not a termagant who was prepared to beat her own stepfather to death in her mother's drawing room.

He had not the bottom for that.

Thirty-one

An interlude

My mother did not have George Barton charged with theft. She may have found it a difficult case to prove, since he was, after all, her husband. Had he claimed that the trinkets in his possession were given to him freely—as tokens of affection, or for the purpose of raising money—she would have been hard put to refute it. Moreover, she had no wish to drag her name and character through the courts yet again.

So she let the matter rest. And this despite the fact that Barton had made off with my brother's silver fob-watch, which James had inherited from my father, and which bore my father's name. 'I know you have suffered a terrible loss,' Mama said to James, 'but with the watch in his custody, he will be frightened to return, I am sure. And even your dear watch is not too high a price to pay for the removal of Mr Barton from our lives.'

I am not convinced that James entirely shared this view. He mourned the watch, much as my mother mourned the locket containing miniatures of her own deceased parents, painted long ago in London. But Mama's instincts were correct. Mr Barton did *not* return. Neither she, nor James, nor my sisters ever saw him again.

To the best of my knowledge, I was the only member of my family who had anything more to do with the monster. And I was granted a long reprieve, because it was not until 1857 that I met with George Barton for the very last time. I have never spoken of this to anyone. I hardly like to do so now. But at my age I have little to lose, and nothing much to regret. Besides which, this is a private memoir. It is not intended for *public* consumption.

I have undertaken to illuminate the dark corners of my past—and cannot fulfil that promise without reference to the winter of 1857.

I was then living at Cutaway Hill, on the farm that we were later obliged to sell. At the time, it was a fairly prosperous concern. We had enlarged it by several acres only a few months previously; my husband had bought an adjoining block of Crown land, and cleared nearly half of it. The weather had favoured us, too, for we had not yet been brought low by the drought of '58, nor yet by the fatal floods of 1860. Flora, at nine, was old enough to help around the house. Ernest had not yet been conceived, so I was free of *that* burden, at least until the following year. As for our health, it was remarkably good considering the season. Past illness had brought about some tragic losses—losses from which I shall never fully recover, no matter how long my life might prove to be. Nevertheless, our family had survived them. We had not been overcome. And by the winter of '57, I was beginning to feel more confident of the future. I allowed myself to hope. I tempted Fate, perhaps, in assuming that we had faced the worst and come through it. My arrogance was unpardonable.

No wonder I was punished.

Do not mistake me; I should emphasise that we were not living easily, even then. The work never ceased. In winter my husband went off to his labours directly after breakfast, and was absent until the light began to fail, at around five o'clock. In summer his day was even longer. Having no help but that which Flora could provide, I myself was just as busy. I toiled from dawn until dusk and beyond, cooking and cleaning, mending, feeding, ensuring that the milking was done, the water fetched, the woodpile replenished. Without Flora, I should have been lost. Nor would I have accomplished all my allotted tasks had there been more than two or three children to mind, for it is a hard thing keeping them out of the fire and away from the well. So you must not believe that I led an existence made pleasant by idle pursuits. When I say that I was feeling confident in the future, it was not because we were considering the purchase of a carriage, or the employment of new staff. I mean only that our prospects seemed better than they had been, since we now owned our own land, and were working it well enough to supply ourselves with more than the basic necessities.

On the day of which I speak, the prospect from Cutaway Hill was as grim as I had ever seen it: grey and lowering, with a threat of sleet in the air, and a stiff wind from the south. What a bitter wind it was! I remember wrapping myself in two layers of shawl every time I left the house, however briefly. I remember the whistling draughts that penetrated every chink in our slab walls, and made the fire leap on the hearth, and tugged and banged at the shutters, though we had secured them as tightly as possible. It had been damp for some days, and the weather was still uncertain, so the kitchen was hung with wet laundry. Charles was in a dreadful mood, as a consequence of being so much penned up. I had a sick turkey on my hands, and a pudding on the boil, and an insufficiency of butter to contend with. I was also worried about my husband. Every day, while he was out, I worried that he would not return. I worried that he would cut himself mending fences, or be crushed while clearing timber, or contract a deadly chill in the process of rescuing a calf from a muddy wallow. It was only when he became a carrier that I stopped worrying, no longer having the strength to waste on such a fruitless activity. There was nothing to be done about a man on the drays, you see. He might be shot, trampled, crushed or robbed, but worrying could not help him. It was better to direct one's thoughts away from such troubling possibilities, and get on with one's life as if the worst had already happened.

I was up to my elbows in flour when the knock came. You must understand that a knock was the rarest of noises, at Cutaway Hill. Who, after all, would have bothered to make the toilsome trip up from the Old South Road? It required crossing all that dirty, boggy ground near the creek, then climbing a raw-looking track through a lot of partly cleared land and over numerous jagged outcrops. We were on the very edge of settlement, in those days, with nothing much between us and the Wollondilly. Why, even the Joadja Mines had not been thought of.

So we were unaccustomed to receiving visitors, and jumped when the knock sounded.

'Who can that be?' I said aloud. '*One moment, please!* Flora, see who it is. No—not the door, child, the window.' I was being cautious, because we had no grown men about to protect us. And although bushrangers were no longer quite the threat they had once been, they could still be found here and there. Why, Ben Hall himself was in the district no more than eight years later. 'I doubt that anyone would knock who meant us harm, but—'

'It's an old man, Mama,' Flora interrupted. She was peering through a crack in the shutters. 'A ragged old man with a bundle on his back.'

This was unwelcome news. Not being directly positioned on a main road, we were spared many of the itinerant men who roamed about looking for work, or begging for money. Such men were, in any event, more likely to approach big houses like Oldbury or Mereworth, where tradition decreed that they should receive some sort of hospitality (unless there was an inn nearby).

Yet even modest huts like ours were subject to visits from wandering men with empty bellies. Their number had grown, in fact, since the opening of the goldfields. In the old days no bush homestead would have turned away a stranger, but times had changed. It seemed to me that I could not be expected to feed and accommodate every vagrant who came along, especially in light of my own reduced circumstances.

'Give him some bread and cheese,' I snapped, 'and tell him there's water in the well.'

'Yes, Mama.'

'Tell him it's not so far to Berrima, but if he wants to rest here, he must take his ease in the barn. We have no room in the house, tell him. Charles, *leave the turkey alone!*'

I was not eager to abandon my pastry for the sake of an old beggarman, so I continued to knead away as Flora collected the bread and cheese. I heard the door creak, and glanced over my shoulder to check that no one tried to push past her into the house. I remember taking comfort from the fact that a big iron pot lay within easy reach, should I find that it was needed.

But the vagrant made no attempt to invade my kitchen. Instead he announced, in loud, hoarse accents: 'Tell yer Ma I'll be wanting more than that, or she'll regret turning me away, by damn—you tell her.'

Even then, I had no idea. His voice had changed, you see. It was a ruined instrument, cracked and worn down, its back broken by drink or smoke or illness, or perhaps just the miseries of incarceration. Not until I turned and approached him (much alarmed by his choice of words) did I glimpse his face under the slouch hat.

Then I stopped. I stopped moving, I stopped breathing—for a moment I even stopped thinking.

'Hello, Charlotte,' he wheezed, with a ghastly grin. 'Reckernise me, do you?'

Though my hands were caked with dough, I had snatched up my iron pot in response to the threat that he had voiced previously. Now I dropped the saucepan and slammed the door in his face.

This was done without proper consideration. I acted instinctively, making no conscious choice. For I wanted only to block out the sight of my very worst nightmare.

'Flora!' I gasped. 'Fetch Papa, hurry!' As she blinked at me in astonishment, I almost cursed aloud. 'Go and find him! Take your brother! Use the other door!'

'But—'

'*Now! Quick!* Put your shawl on! *Run!*'

She ran. Flora was no fool, and she knew better than to argue. She took Charles and went, even as Barton addressed me through the kitchen door.

'If you turn me away, there's others hereabouts will take me in,' he rasped. 'And they'll hear what I have to say, Charlotte. You know how folk relish a good tale in this part of the world.'

'Go away!' I could hardly speak. 'You're not welcome in my house!'

'Never was, was I? Though I had every right to be there.' He coughed wetly. 'But I wasn't good enough for any of *you*, oh no . . .'

'I have a gun!' (This was a lie—we could afford nothing so costly—but *he* would not have known it.) 'And I'll fire if you make trouble!'

'I know *that*, by damn!' He gave a short laugh. 'Shall I tell yer little lass how you tried to shoot me? Maybe I'll show her all the scars you left on my poor old bonce, eh?'

'What do you want?' I was shaking as I leaned against the door, fumbling to bar it. 'Why have you come here?'

'I came on account of yer Ma,' he replied. 'I thought as how she might pay me to go away again. But I find that she's gone herself—and the rest of 'em, too.'

'What do you mean?' My mind was racing. 'James is still at Oldbury.'

'Not now, he ain't. Rode off to a station, or some such thing. I asked after you, and was told how you married down. Didn't surprise me.' He gave another rattling chuckle. 'In the family way, were you? I allus knew you'd end up hot-blooded. Just like yer Ma.'

'Be off!' I spat. 'Or I'll thrash you again, *old man*, don't think that I wouldn't!'

'Oh, aye? And have yer children's Pa come upon you? I've not forgot the other one. Frightened him off, so I heard. Nothing a man likes less than a woman with a temper on her.' He hawked and spat. 'Open the door, girl, it's bitter out here. Do you want me to die on yer doorstep?'

'There's nothing I should like more!'

'Is that so? Now, I'd have reckoned different.' I could hear his tortured breathing through the thick planks of wood. 'See, if you was to kill me, or send me away empty-handed, I might end up in the papers, like as not. I might be driven to desperate measures—a little thievery, say—and I'd be brought before the magistrates (since I've not the wind to leg it) and there'd be questions asked. About me and yer Ma, and why I was away so long, and why I came back only to be treated like a dog by my wife's own family. And old tales might be told, and things might be said that yer Ma wouldn't like.' He coughed again. 'For pity's sake, will you let me in? I won't be leaving without a drop of the creature in me, so what would you prefer when yer loved ones return? A dead man on the doorstep, or a happy man long gone? I'd not want to tarry, Charlotte. Just give me what I came for, and I'll be off.'

'You want money? Is that what you want?' It was hard to swallow my fury. 'Does this *look* like a house with money to spare?'

'I'll need only enough to send me on my way, lass,' he wheedled. 'You'd not want me beached here, rambling on about the past in yer children's hearing? Just a coin and a crust, and a drop of something to moisten it. Or I'll be forced to throw myself on the mercy of the vicar—what's his name? One of them Hassalls, ain't it? I'd have to tell him how I'd found no charity at Cutaway Hill—'

I opened the door then, cutting him off. You may wonder at this decision, but it was reached by careful reasoning. I had put aside my anger and despair in order to make some stone-cold calculations regarding the time, the weather, and the amount of liquor in the house—among other things.

'Don't spit on the floor,' I instructed. 'And take off your boots.'

His boots were in such a parlous state that it must have been hard to keep them *on*. He peeled them away almost like scabs, before collapsing onto a stool in front of the fire. When he removed his hat, I saw that his hair had thinned a good deal, and turned a dirty silver.

You could have bred up twin joeys in the pouches under his eyes.

'Aah, now there's a fine blaze,' he croaked. 'Best I've seen in many a long day.'

'Where did you come from? Parramatta Gaol?'

'No, no. Been out of *there* a while. Tried my luck in Bathurst, first, but my friends have all deserted me.'

I snorted. Whereupon he fixed me with a baleful look, dimmed somewhat by tears. He was sniffing, too, but not from an excess of emotion. It was the cold that affected him.

'What have you got?' he asked abruptly. 'Rum? Gin?'

'Brandy and rum.'

'I'll take the rum in hot water.'

He requested no food, and I gave him none. It did not suit my purpose. With a generous hand I poured him his drink, and he threw it down like a dose of medicine.

'A drop more of that would ease the pain,' he said.

I took the cup and kept it filled, though he was not slow to drain it. All the while, I kept him talking. This was easily accomplished, since the spirits had loosened his tongue. He was disposed to talk, in any case. He was curious about my family.

'They told me in Sutton Forest that yer sister had died—the middle one. What was her name?'

'Emily.'

'Emily. That's it. I allus thought the other would go first. The sickly one.'

'Louisa is safe with my mother.'

'So I heard. Up in the Mountains, is it?'

'I'll not tell you where they are. You'll not be bothering *them*.'

'What—you mean you wouldn't care to see 'em wriggle?' He looked around my dingy kitchen. 'Seems as if they've thrown you off same as me, my girl. There's yer brother, now, living in that great house, with staff a-plenty, and yer sister with leisure enough to be writing for the papers—aye, they all know it, down at Sutton Forest—and here's you, living like this.'

'Better than *you* are living, old man.'

'True. Very true.'

'At least *I* have a clear conscience!'

'Is that what you call it?' He gave a spluttering laugh. 'Tried to kill me once, I seem to recall.'

'*That* does not trouble me, I assure you!'

'No. I daresay. But you were allus a wild one.' His eyes glinted up at me from beneath wiry grey brows. Though rheumy and bloodshot, they were still the eyes of George Barton. 'Just like yer Ma. As wild as they come. You were bound to make trouble—yer Ma had a taste for felons, too.'

I glared at him. 'My husband was not a convict,' I hissed.

'Is that what he told you? It's not what *I* heard.'

'If you continue in this vein, I'll not answer for what he might do.'

'Rough'un, is he? I thought as much. Yer Ma allus liked a bit o' the rough and tumble. And gave as good as she got—I've the bite-marks to prove it.' Barton was slurring his words by now, though he was still clear-headed enough to stay upright. The liquor had acted quickly, thanks to his empty stomach and frail constitution. 'She got a real taste for heavy handling at Belanglo. Remember? They flogged me bloody, but never touched a hair on her head. And there's a reason for that.'

'I don't want to hear it.'

'She made the offer herself, you know. Practically begged 'em. Took 'em both on, one after the other, to save her own skin. Enjoyed it, too.'

'Shut your filthy mouth.'

'After that, she couldn't stay away from the assigned men. Barnett had her. Rogers. Stanley—'

'*Shut your filthy mouth!*' I picked up my big pot. 'You know I'll do it! Give me a cause, and I'll do it!'

'No need for violence.' (The gall of the man!) 'A pound or two will shut my mouth. And I'll not come back, neither—not to you.' Clumsily, he tapped his nose with one finger. 'I know lean pickings when I see 'em. Give me something to be going on with, and no one will ever find out what a whore yer Ma was.'

'*My mother was not a whore!*'

'Thass not what the folk around here think. They saw her ride out time and again. With every horny-handed rascal in her employ.' He gave a braying laugh, and the force of it nearly unseated him. 'She married *me*, didn't she? They think her a whore for that, if nothing else.'

'I have no money. Don't you understand? *There is no money here.*'

'There must be something . . . treasure you c'n dig up.' This time, when he flashed me a look, he seemed to have some difficulty focusing his eyes. 'Trinkets. A watch, mebbe . . .'

'Damn you.' My hand was clenched around the pot-handle. 'What did you do with my brother's watch?'

'What do you mean?' he mumbled. 'I never took no watch.'

'Liar. Thief.'

'You want me to tell yer children about yer Ma and what she did? Make me stay, and I will . . .'

I went to the bedroom and fetched my silver pencil-case—the one that Fanny had given me so many years before. It took several minutes to find the thing. By the time I returned, Barton had emptied the rest of the rum down his gullet.

I was astonished to see him standing.

'Aye, that'll do,' he said, with a hiccough. He took the pencil-case, turning it in front of his slightly crossed eyes. 'Solid silver? Good girl. Don't reckernise it . . . where'd it come from?'

'None of your business!'

'Favours in exchange, eh?' he leered.

'Get out. You have what you came for. Now get out!'

'I'll take the brandy bottle,' he said, swaying perilously. 'Whassat? Silk slops?'

'Silk? Is it likely?'

'I'll take the brass, too . . . might be a shilling in it . . .' He grabbed a candlestick on his way to the door, stuffing it into his pack. When he swung this bundle over his shoulder, the weight of it nearly toppled him.

He had to steady himself against the door-jamb.

'Compliments to the lad who took you on,' he muttered thickly. 'Brave man . . . brave man . . .'

'Where are you going? Berrima?'

'Uh . . . aye.' He made an obvious effort to gather his thoughts as the cold air hit him. 'Aye, Berrima. Aye.'

'It's that way. Head straight for that hill. And don't come back.'

'Wouldn't want to. Not worth the trouble. Mingy bitch.'

I pointed. Whereupon he set off, weaving slightly, the brandy bottle clutched to his chest, his unbuttoned coat flapping in the arctic wind. He had forgotten his boots, and was too drunk to notice. Later, I threw them into the fire.

I had no fear that he would encounter my family. You see, my husband was working down near Cutaway Creek, which lay to the east, between our house and the road to Berrima.

George Barton was heading west, into the wilderness. As I closed the door, I took note that the light was fading, and that the brooding grey clouds held a promise of snow.

I never saw the man again. I cannot be sure exactly what befell him.

Your guess would be as good as mine.

Thirty-two

1846

We returned to Oldbury in the winter of 1846.

It was a miserable homecoming, dictated by necessity. My mother's income was by this time a mere two hundred pounds per year. She had decided that we could no longer afford a town house, nor the expense of buying most of our food. Circumstances decreed that we pursue a cheaper mode of existence, in accommodation for which no rent would be charged. Oldbury was therefore the only option left to us.

We had no illusions as to what we would find upon our return. The house had stood empty for three years. The insolvency of our former tenant, Thomas Humphery, meant that no repairs had been undertaken since at least 1841. Our pastures and fences were in a slightly better condition, thanks to Mr Alfred Welby; he was a respectable farmer from Sutton Forest, and in 1843 had been entrusted with the task of administering my brother's inheritance. By letting land and collecting rents, he had ensured that at least a portion of the estate was still productive.

But make no mistake, Oldbury's days of glory were long past. It stood 'defaced by time, and tottering in decay'. If you have read *Cowanda*, you will have some inkling of the pitiful sight that greeted us when we renewed our acquaintance with the old homestead, which, though it belonged to James, was being managed by my father's executors. Louisa drew from her own experience in describing the typical estate belonging to a youth still in his minority, who is unable to take proper care of his inheritance; like her fictional Aloe Hill, Oldbury was all cracked walls and broken glass, mouldy rooms and untended gardens.

Mr Welby had tried to prepare us. In his letters he had made mention of collapsed huts, stained plaster and unpruned vines. He had urged the need for a species of advance guard to clear and clean, and had supervised the employment of these servants on my mother's behalf at least three weeks before our arrival. There were other matters to arrange as well: the purchase of feed and livestock; the replacement of items filched by my stepfather; the transportation of furniture, plate and linen. The outlay was enormous, or so it seemed to me. I asked my mother how she could possibly justify such an expense.

'We will spend far more in removing from Sydney than we would if we stayed,' I said, pouting. 'I have never seen such a fine example of false economy in my life. Why, the horses alone will cost as much as our rent! We had much better stay.'

But my mother ignored me. I was not surprised, having grown accustomed to such treatment. Since the end of my engagement we had found ourselves perpetually quarrelling, and were sometimes unable to sit together in the same room. I do not know why we tried each other's tempers so horribly. Perhaps we were too much alike. Mama complained of my strident manner, but her own was not very different. She expressed her opinions just as forcefully as I did, and spoke no more softly when roused. Our arguments were loud and vicious affairs that must have poisoned the lives of those around us. As the old proverb says, '*It is better to dwell in the wilderness than with a contentious and an angry woman*'. Possibly my mother had this in mind when she decreed that we should return to the wild country where I was born. She may have hoped that, free of the city's constraints, I would wear out my restlessness in long walks, hard rides, and the demanding daily round of a working farm.

She was wrong, however.

It would be impossible to exaggerate the extent of my aversion to Oldbury. My blackest memories were associated with that place; I had no wish to revisit its dark-panelled vestibule, its haunted cellar, or its scarred landings. I shrank from the brooding prospect of Gingenbullen, which had inhabited my dreams for so long that it seemed invested with an almost spectral menace. In the six years that had elapsed since my last glimpse of Oldbury, I had refashioned it into a dark and sinister repository of all that was bad, bloody and Godforsaken.

Besides which, I was eighteen years old. I had no desire to bury myself in the remote 'back runs', away from all possibility of civilised amusement. I wanted to dance. I wanted to hear good music, and watch colourful crowds. Even in Sydney the variety of our social intercourse was restricted, but at least there was always hope of a chance meeting, or an unlooked-for introduction. You never knew who might accost you in a milliner's shop. I was desperate for company, and not only because I was bored. At eighteen, I was beginning to panic. I was beginning to wonder if I would die an old maid.

No doubt you think me foolish. Eighteen is not such a great age, after all. Yet it seems incredibly advanced when one has been forced to endure the unspeakable shame of being thrown over. I assure you, I hardly set foot outside the house for months after William Cummings rejected me. My life seemed utterly blighted. As for my friends, they offered me no comfort. How could they? Though Fanny Rickards declared herself 'disgusted' with Mr Cummings, he nevertheless remained her brother's confidant. And when Fanny became engaged to Lieutenant Wren, my pride could not endure the contrast between her happy prospects and my own. I felt utterly demoralised, and could see only one remedy: namely, another betrothal. Without an eager swain by my side, I was unable to hold up my head, for it seemed as if I was branded by my own failure. I was sure that people gossiped about me whenever I left the room.

In the circumstances, you might wonder at my reluctance to quit Sydney altogether. It might seem to you that a girl in my position would have been better off abandoning the feverish atmosphere of Sydney's drawing rooms in favour of more tranquil domestic occupations among the fields and flowers. Why remain, when it meant facing so much whispered speculation and false sympathy?

The answer is simple. Even flawed social intercourse was better than none. Though Sydney offered me little, Oldbury would offer less. I would lose all hope of varied acquaintance if I returned to Oldbury. For the few families worth knowing in its immediate neighbourhood had exhibited no particular interest in knowing *us*. And the Sunday service at Sutton Forest was not fertile ground for striking up friendships with young men.

It surely cannot surprise you that I dreaded the thought of a rustic existence? That I refused to submit quietly, and was most unhelpful during the tedious process of packing, sorting and cleaning? Fanny promised to write, but I knew that she would not. Miss Rennie raised the possibility of a future visit, but in the vaguest possible way. I was in a state of black despair even before arriving at Oldbury—where a heavy mist, a chilling drizzle and an assortment of unpacked crates occupying the clammy, unaired rooms cast me into such a fit of despondency that my mother ordered me from the house.

'Out,' she said, with grim resolution. 'Get out. I can't stand your moping any longer.'

'But it's raining!' I said.

'Precisely. It will suit your mood. If you cannot cheer up and make yourself useful, I want you out there where you belong.'

'The servants should have done all this!' I protested. 'At least they should have seen that the chimneys were cleaned! We'll all suffocate from breathing this smoke!'

'Then go and take a turn in the fresh air. Now. Go and don't come back until you are fit for company.'

'I suppose you don't care that I could catch my death?'

'Not particularly,' my mother snapped. 'At least it will stop you from making everyone's life miserable.'

I must acknowledge that I was at a trying age. All girls can be difficult as they approach womanhood. There is something in the blood that starts to affect them when they enter their fifteenth or sixteenth year. Even my Emily Louisa, the most docile child imaginable, was married at sixteen. As for Eva, by the time *she* had turned eighteen, she was already the mother of an illegitimate child.

In 1846, I needed a husband. That is the truth of the matter. Somewhere deep inside, I knew that I needed a husband. And I also knew that my chances of finding a suitable one, so deep in the bush, were remote.

Doubtless that is why I stormed from the house, slamming doors behind me.

'You might as well bury me six feet under, and have done with it!' I cried.

Had I been of a more amenable nature, I might have repaired to the kitchen. Here I would have found a dry seat and a warm fire. But being in a contrary mood, I decided that I *would* catch my death—there being nothing much to live for. My first inclination was to march off into the bush. Then it occurred to me that I would ruin my good kid boots if I went walking on such a dirty, wet day.

So I turned into the stables.

Like the house, this building had suffered many sad reverses. Where once it had accommodated all of half a dozen fine horses in style and comfort, it was now a dank and echoing shell, with a leaky roof and many deserted stalls. Nevertheless, it was partially occupied. An estate the size of Oldbury requires at least some horseflesh, no matter how reduced its flocks and herds. My mother had therefore been obliged to purchase a hardy gelding and a rough grey cob, the former as a stockhorse, the latter to pull our gig. The resurrection of the old gig had come as a surprise to me. I had assumed it long gone, with the rest of our more luxurious possessions. Yet Mr Welby had rescued it from some dark, forgotten corner of the barn, and had had its upholstery restored, and its wheels oiled, and its brass polished. With the result that, upon alighting from the mail-coach at Berrima, we had found ourselves confronted by two vehicles: Mr Welby's gig and our own.

Our gig had been driven by one of the new servants, Thomas, whom my mother persisted in calling a 'coachman'. There being nothing in the least coach-like about our gig, I had privately designated him the ostler. Unlike Henry (our former ostler) he was a young man in possession of both eyes.

I found him in the stables when I entered them.

'Oh,' I said, not well pleased. 'Are *you* here?'

'Far as I can make out,' he replied. He appeared to be attending to our cob, which—in my view—had been a very poor bargain. I am firmly of the belief that mares do not make ideal harness horses, and this cob was a mare. It was furthermore the squattest, thickest, roughest little beast you ever saw, lacking any vestige of quality, and a bad colour. Mama had got it cheap, I suppose. She may even have been intending that it should serve a double role, since we had no pony, and it was small enough for Louisa to ride.

I was determined, however, that I should never be seen on top of such an ugly animal. The stockhorse would do for me.

'I should like to go for a ride,' I said. 'You need not trouble yourself, for I can saddle my own mount.'

In fact, it had been several years since I had saddled my own mount, and even then I had done so only under Henry's supervision. But I was disinclined to ask favours of an insolent Irishman. I was quite sure that I would manage perfectly well, for all that it was so dark in the stables.

'Ye'll not be ridin' in this weather?' said Thomas.

'Why not? I have never yet dissolved in the rain.' Imperiously, I gestured at the stockhorse. 'Is this hack temperamental? I have heard that golden chestnuts can be very skittish.'

The ostler raised his brows. They were thick and dark, as was his hair. But his eyes were blue.

'Sure, and ye're not lookin' to wear them boots, are ye?' he queried. 'Yer heels are too high for a slipper stirrup, Miss.'

'Then you can take off the slipper stirrup.'

'Not with them old-fashioned saddles. There's only the two pommels on 'em. Ye'll have a sad time of it wit'out some support to yer left foot.'

He was right, I knew. Yet it irked me to be baulked at every turn.

'Perhaps you'd care to tell me what *else* I may not do?' was my waspish retort, whereupon the ostler tapped his chin and cocked his head.

'Pitch an egg at t'Queen?' he suggested.

I turned on my heel, and began to retrace my steps. 'Well if I may not ride, then I shall walk! Since you are so reluctant to entrust me with one of your precious horses,' I snapped. But I was on the verge of tears, and he might have heard it in my voice. At any rate, he called after me in far more winning tones.

''Tis the horse I don't trust, Miss,' he wheedled. 'This fella's right hard in the mouth for a lady, never mind his colour. He's a man's hack, by my reckonin', though he's under fifteen hands. Ye'll need a good seat to hold him back, and ye'll never have that wit'out the slipper stirrup.'

'Then I shall walk,' I said. For Thomas was right: I could not use our side saddles wearing city heels, nor sit astride in my brown merino. And even if I had been willing to return to the house, my chances of finding a single pair of low-heeled boots among the confusion of crates and trunks and boxes were remote, to say the least.

'Ah, now, don't be walkin' in this weather,' Thomas protested, as I hunched my shoulders against the rain. 'Miss! Wait! If ye're wantin' to pay a call, I'll get out t'gig.'

Pay a call! I would have laughed a bitter laugh, had I not been afraid that it might turn into a sob. In whose house would my family be welcome? I was quite sure that our return would be viewed as an embarrassment by all those who had, in the past, been pleased to entertain my father—but whose relations with my stepfather had been less than cordial. They would not want to mix with us. So what did it matter that the yard was dirty? What did it matter that my boots would soon be spoiled beyond redemption? No one would ever see them. No one who *mattered*.

I squelched along, dragging my skirts through the mud, determined to find a lonely place where I could mope and mourn in private. Remembering the high rock on Gingenbullen, where I had many times sat pondering the mysteries of my fraught existence, I turned towards the old convict huts. I had a vague idea of punishing my mother with a prolonged absence. If I stayed out very late, she might even organise a search party.

'Ye'll not find nothin' up that way, Miss,' the ostler remarked behind me. 'Lessen ye're plannin' to walk back to Berrima.'

He had followed me into the yard, and now had the gall to read me a lecture on the geography of the estate. It enraged me, for some reason. I swung around and upbraided him with quite unnecessary venom.

'I *know* where I'm going! I grew up here! I know every inch of this wretched place, and could draw you a map if I chose to!'

'Oh, aye?' He seemed impervious to my fury. 'Well, now, that'd be right helpful. If it could be managed.'

'What?' I was confused. 'If what could be managed?'

'A map.' He stood with his hands in his pockets, his coat hanging open and his eyes screwed up against the misty rain. 'See, it seems to me there's folks hereabouts like to run their stock through yer fields—since no one's bin around to stop 'em. And the fences not bein' what they should be, it's hard for the likes o' me to know when to take a stand. I'd not be wantin' to throw stones at any strange beast unless I knew't were on yer land, Miss.'

Trespass! This was news. 'You mean someone has been using Oldbury as a back run?' I asked, my interest piqued.

'Aye.'

'Who?'

The ostler shook his head. 'That I cannot say,' he replied, 'not bein' well acquainted with yer neighbours' stock.'

'One of the tenants, perhaps?'

He shrugged. 'Thing is, Miss, I cannot be sure they've strayed— not wit' so many fences gone.'

'Gone? *Completely* gone? Or just collapsed?'

'Taken away.' His lip curled at the expression on my face. 'Oh, aye. Some folks'll stoop so low, ye'd have to dig to find 'em.'

'But this is unacceptable.' As much as I loathed Oldbury, it was still my family's estate. It offended me to think that low-bred neighbours were taking advantage of my mother's absence to plunder our meagre property. 'This must be stopped. Have you told my mother?'

'No, Miss. Though I mentioned it to Mr Welby.'

'Then *I* shall tell Mama. And she will take you on a tour of the estate, and show you where the boundaries lie.' These words were barely out of my mouth before a picture leapt into my head:

a picture of my mother, riding out beside George Barton on that January day in 1836. She was ten years older now, and greyer, and heavier—but her spirit was still high. I was sure that, given the opportunity, she would have no hesitation in ruining her reputation all over again.

A flush rose to my cheeks as I looked at the ostler. For suddenly it had become apparent to me that he was just the sort of man who might easily give rise to gossip, what with his trim waist and broad, white smile.

The thought was hugely unpalatable.

'I must go,' I said, and found myself walking back to the house. Though my mother had evicted me, I felt that I should acquaint her with the facts as soon as I could. Or would it be better to wait until she was less preoccupied?

I hesitated, one foot on the back veranda.

'Go on, Miss,' said Thomas. 'This is no weather for walkin'. Ye'll spoil yer clothes and ruin yer health, and Mrs Barton'll tear strips off me.' He was still standing bare-headed in the middle of the yard, hands buried deep in his trouser-pockets. 'Go on back inside, and I'll saddle up a horse when t'rain clears.'

So I went inside. Only much later did I realise how clever he had been, in distracting me from my purpose.

It was not the last time he would do so, by any means.

Thirty-three

My mother did not appoint an overseer when we returned to Oldbury. We had no real need of one, because our permanent staff was so small. We kept a housemaid, a cook, an ostler (Thomas), a gardener and a black boy. My mother had to supervise the cook in the dairy, while my sisters and I helped the housemaid with our washing, ironing and mending. Occasionally we hired a ploughman or carpenter, or even a team of bullocks. But we no longer ran a dray or bred up heifers. We could not afford to. Especially in view of the fact that not one of our servants had been assigned to us.

They were free men and women, who required fair wages.

I know that there were land-owners in New South Wales who regretted the passing of the old assignment system. But my mother was not among them. Though cheap labour is all very well, it can come at a hidden cost; under the assignment system one was generally obliged to take what was given, no matter how raw and unrepentant, while at the same time enduring the constant scrutiny of Government officials. Living out in the bush, my mother felt more secure surrounded by staff who could be dismissed for bad service, rather than flogged for it. She once confessed herself well pleased to be 'relieved of the job of a turnkey'.

Not that our servants were all of stainless character. The boy was, naturally; he was hardly old enough to have committed a multitude of sins. Our cook had never faced a magistrate's bench either. She had simply followed her husband to Australia upon his emancipation, displaying the truest and most devoted conjugal attachment. Her husband was Richard Prince, our gardener. He had been transported for theft, but was not corrupted by the experience, and had quickly won himself a ticket-of-leave. Though diligent and hard-working, however, he was not quick-witted. His attempt to farm land of his own had been a failure; he had run up debts, and bad weather had finally sunk him. You *could* say that his ill luck had been our good fortune, because he was a reliable gardener without a vicious bone in his body. His wife, on the other hand, had not her husband's happy temperament, so their presence was a mixed blessing. Her nerves had been overthrown by the loss of three children on the voyage out. She also pined, I think, for undisputed ascendency in her very own kitchen. Of all the servants, Sarah Prince gave Mama the most trouble.

Our housemaid, in contrast, was a treasure. Her name was Mary Ann, and she seemed to view Oldbury as a safe harbour in an uncertain world. As far as I am aware, her history was one of great misfortune. Having been seduced by a rascal and cast out by her parents, she had subsisted on the streets until arrested and transported for theft. Upon arriving in Australia, she had been most unfortunate in her assignments, which had exposed her to the kind of attention that played upon her undoubted weaknesses. Twice she was confined, once in the Female Factory and once under the aegis of the Dorcas Society. The first child died at birth; the second was raised chiefly at the Orphan School. I believe that Mary Ann contributed as best she could to the expenses of raising this little girl, and might have done more had the child survived her twelfth birthday. But this was not the case, and Mary Ann had fled the city soon afterwards. She preferred the country, she said. And the country around Sutton Forest reminded her of her own home in Oxfordshire.

She was a short, sturdy, middle-aged woman, plain-faced but sweet-voiced. While not as highly skilled as she might have been, she took instruction with the utmost goodwill, and always worked steadily. I do not think that I have ever met with such a good-hearted soul. Louisa was her particular favourite. No doubt my sister reminded Mary Ann of her own daughter, who had died at exactly Louisa's age. There was a definite bond between the two. If you consult the book *Cowanda*, you will find a portrait of Mary Ann, disguised as one 'Aunt Nancy'. According to Louisa, Aunt Nancy was *'such an everyday character, only unusual in the excess of her homely worth—not the remotest selfishness or unkindness in her composition. A peculiarly square, flat face, of a pale hue, and a pair of small, quiet grey eyes, were indexes of her abundant goodness, but utter absence of imagination: her house was her world, and all her honest, steady principles led her to an unaffected and sincere Christian faith in life.'*

This description touched me. It surprised me too, for I had no idea that Louisa was so attached to Mary Ann. But my sister's affections always ran quiet and deep. It was just like her to remember our housemaid in her book. Mr James Calvert was a lucky man to win such a heart as Louisa's.

By now you must be wondering at my own lengthy portrayal of the Oldbury servants. Why these detailed descriptions? Why have I lavished so much time and attention on my mother's domestic staff?

The answer is simple. My account of them is so thorough because I knew them so well. And I knew them so well because I mixed with almost no one else. Day in and day out, I was confined to the society of family and servants. Mr Welby was an occasional visitor, but he generally came on business, and never brought his wife. At church we exchanged platitudes with our more respectable neighbours, but nothing came of *that*. The Throsbys were still busily breeding, and far too preoccupied to waste any time on us. The same was true of the Badgerys. The Morrices, being Presbyterian, were rather exclusive. As for the Wilmots, my mother preferred not to communicate with them at all. It was said that Mr Thomas Wilmot had been transported for horse-stealing, though he was a generous benefactor of the church, and had acquired a large property not far from our own. Indeed, Mama would not even attend his funeral in the spring, for all that it was practically the event of the season, with two hundred people paying their respects and an account of it appearing in the *Sydney Morning Herald*. 'A whited sepulchre' was how my mother described Thomas Wilmot. Certainly he was a bigamist—though it was not until after his death that we learned of his first wife, still living in England. She tried to claim his property, you see.

The only neighbours who made even a token effort on our behalf were the Nicholsons. The reason, I believe, is that they were very intimate with the Reverend Stone and his family. Owing to Reverend Stone's sense of pastoral duty, we were invited to the parsonage a number of times, and to Newbury twice. I remember how it pained me to see the flourishing condition of Newbury, in contrast to Oldbury's decrepit state. Perhaps my mother felt the same, and quietly turned down any subsequent invitations that may have been extended to her. Or perhaps there *were* no invitations. Though Captain Nicholson was a bluff old sailor with a heart of gold, and his wife an agreeable lady of no pretensions whatsoever, they were not the type of people to fret themselves over matters outside their immediate purview. Energetic and cheerful, they were dutiful landlords, generous parishioners and loving parents. They were even sporadically kind neighbours, sending us the occasional new book or basket of produce. But they were not of a temper to feel the weight of tenuous moral obligations, and would have been nagged by no feelings of guilt at the thought of my family, alone on our isolated farm. Since they got through their own days easily enough, they probably expected that we were of a similar disposition.

They were wrong, however. We were not content. How could we be? My mother was perpetually short-tempered. She was struggling with the lawyers for money, while at the same time labouring over the sort of domestic tasks that should rightfully have been entrusted to a housekeeper, a laundress, or a dairywoman. I know how *I* used to feel at the beginning of my married life, when I looked up from my washboard to see grubby infants playing in a dirty yard. Mama must have felt the same. She must have wondered how a fifty-year-old matron of gentle birth, once the mistress of a score of servants and a flourishing estate, had been reduced to ironing flounces or plucking fowl.

James was not much happier. At fourteen, he was of an age to begin his apprenticeship as a country squire, though he had only my mother to instruct him. It was rather an abrupt transition. From a schoolboy excelling at geography and mathematics, among peers whose interests tended toward the naval and mercantile, he was abruptly cast into a strange world of tillers and reaping hooks, draught cattle and hurdle-making. Where once he had been pleased to pore over Latin epics, his evenings were now given over to what remained of my father's library of farming works, which included an encyclopaedia of horticulture and a book on agricultural chemistry. I believe that his strengths lay more in the field of abstract thought than in the practical application of theoretical knowledge. At any rate, he must have felt the full weight of his inherited responsibility, for it showed in his face. His brow acquired an almost permanent pucker of concern. I would see him questioning the gardener, or receiving instruction from our ostler, and always that slight contraction of the forehead would be present.

He sought advice from other quarters as well. Sometimes he would shut himself away with Mr Welby. Sometimes he would ride to Newbury, unannounced, and make inquiries of Captain Nicholson. Sometimes he would corner Mr Throsby after church. I think that, of all our family, he was the member most sympathetically received. For there was something especially poignant about an earnest stripling made prematurely old by the manifold cares of proprietorship.

Louisa seemed far more satisfied with her lot. She had always been the keenest student of Nature among us, and pursued her interest with zeal when we returned to Oldbury. She discovered the nest of a wedge-tailed eagle on the crest of Gingenbullen, and made pets of two curlews, whose antics were a perpetual delight to her. Emily enjoyed them too, though not with such wholehearted enthusiasm. Indeed, poor Emily became more and more subdued. Rural life should have suited her very well, for she was naturally amenable, and shy of company. But she was also an impressionable soul, as sensitive to the feelings of others as she was to the atmosphere engendered by memories of past distress. She could not forget George Barton—not in that place where he had once reigned supreme. Nor could she disregard the short tempers and weary impatience that characterised our home. Discord was an absolute punishment to Emily. It gave her headaches, and made her cry. When I picture this period of my life, and turn my thoughts to the sitting room at Oldbury, I see James scowling at an essay on drainage, Mama sighing fretfully over a begging-letter, Louisa shelling peas in a cloud of abstraction, and Emily snivelling beside a great heap of darning, which was as much my burden as it was hers.

I need hardly add that my own presence at this scene would not have improved it. I was miserable during the latter part of 1846. Though spring came, and the buds opened, and the cows calved, and the fruit trees flowered, I took no solace from any of this. Wherever I looked, I saw evidence of fertility and a promise of rich abundance. Yet I remained barren stock. I regarded myself as a flower 'born to blush unseen,/and waste its sweetness on the desert air'. News of Fanny's wedding reinforced this view. I felt cast aside, like a seed fallen upon stony places.

My mother sympathised, but only to a degree. She had no patience with my 'tragic airs', as she called them. 'You are more fortunate than many,' she would say. 'Look how ill Louisa has been.' Then she would add something to the effect that hard work was the cure for low spirits, and send me to milk the cow or bring in the laundry. At eighteen, I could no longer excuse myself from domestic tasks by claiming that I had to finish my lessons. Mama had decided that my formal education was complete. Though I might read, write and draw for my own amusement, henceforth such pursuits must always yield to more pressing demands.

I had played the housemaid in Sydney, of course. We had none of us lived like aristocrats there, either. But in Sydney we had bought most of our food. We had sent our laundry out, and had had our fuel delivered. The Sydney winters had also been much warmer, and the streets not so dirty as the yards and roads that turned to mire with every heavy rain at Oldbury. In the country, moreover, one seems surrounded by dung. It must be swept continuously from the yard and stables. It must be collected and distributed over the crops, though not before it has become 'well-rotted' after a lengthy sojourn against a wall in the sun.

As for the flies, they are never as bad on the coast as they are inland.

When I look back now, I am grateful that I was so well prepared for my married life. Had I but known it, Mama was continuing my education in the most practical way, and did me no disservice with her scoldings and demands. At the time, however, I was full of resentment. I considered my home a dreary cage, staffed by despondent gaolers.

Is it any wonder that I tried to escape?

To flee! To lose myself! That is what I most desired. Sometimes I thought that I should burst with all my pent-up longings and fettered fury. Yet I did not seek freedom in an acceptable way, as my sisters did. Emily found hers in the pages of her books. Louisa used her paints and brushes, carrying them with her on walks up to the heights of Gingenbullen. My own technique was more dangerous. I found my escape on horseback.

I had always been fond of riding. As a child I had played on my father's ponies, and at Budgong had begun to learn the proper technique of riding side-saddle. We had all of us improved our horsemanship at Budgong—James in particular. But our removal to Sydney had put paid to any further study of equestrian matters. In town, wherever we did not walk, we took an omnibus.

So it was both strange and invigorating to find myself once again mounted, and mistress of an almost limitless space. I do not know if I can convey to you the pleasure of a good, hard, unhampered bush ride. It is so utterly absorbing, for one thing. When you are going pretty sharp, and your way is blocked here by a fallen tree, or there by a rivulet—when you must dodge encroaching boughs and descend a hill plentifully scattered with loose stones—then your arms and legs and eyes must be constantly active. There is no time for mournful reflection. Your mind becomes wonderfully concentrated, and all other thoughts simply fly out of your head. Nor do they return very quickly, since after the ride you are generally much too tired to mope. I remember dozing at the dinner table more than once, during this period. Two or three hours in the saddle would leave me so thoroughly exhausted that I had not even the energy to argue with my mother. No doubt this pleased her, though she *did* complain about the horses. She felt that I was too greedy with them.

'A little exertion is all very well,' she said, 'but if you ride those horses into the ground, how will Ida draw the gig, or Sovereign bear a trip to the Post Office? They are not hunters, Charlotte. They are not being kept for your personal amusement. You should be more sparing with them.'

'But they must be exercised,' I pointed out. 'Thomas says so.'

'Exercising a horse does not mean exhausting it.'

'I never tire Sovereign. He tires me. He drags like an ox. He is a man's hack, Thomas says, though he's barely fifteen hands.'

'That's true,' said James, looking up from his mutton. 'He may not be all that big, Mama, but he has hocks down to the ground.'

'Then perhaps you should be using Ida, Charlotte, in that case.'

'Ida!'

'She is a perfectly useful little horse, and if it weren't for your silly prejudice—'

'It is not prejudice, Mama!' (Though of course it was.) 'Thomas says that a lady should always ride a gelding in preference to a mare.'

'Oh, Thomas, Thomas, Thomas!' My mother spoke crossly. 'Is Thomas such an oracle, that he must be quoted at every turn?'

'You have told me that I should mind what Thomas says, lest I take a tumble. Have I permission to ignore him now?'

'Don't be clever. You know perfectly well what I mean.'

'Really, Mama, I do not.'

'These days you talk about nothing but cruppers and galls and pole-straps and suchlike. It is *immensely* tedious, and not the least bit useful. You sound like a stockman, Charlotte. And you know how I feel about stockmen. They might be sturdy fellows, but you would hardly call them intellectually developed. If you're not careful, you will find yourself unable to make cultured conversation at all.'

'Cultured conversation!' I cried. 'What purpose will *that* serve, when we never see any cultured people?'

'Do not raise your voice at me.'

'It is your fault, Mama, if I talk about nothing but galls and pole-straps! In Sydney there were books and fashions and lectures to discuss, and people to discuss them *with*! What have we to remark on here, except manure and milk-veins?'

'Once again, you are grossly exaggerating your plight—'

'I am not! I am *not*! What would you have me do, converse about the Linnean Society with Mary Ann?'

'It would be better than conversing about snaffle bits with Thomas McNeilly. You spend too much time in the stables, Charlotte, it is a dreadful waste of a perfectly good education. Thomas is an excellent coachman, I appreciate his talents, but they are not wide ranging. There is more to life than horses. Rather than frittering away your time in Thomas's company, you should apply yourself to an improving book. *Historical and Miscellaneous Questions*, perhaps. Emily has just finished with it.'

She was no fool, my mother. Nor was she inexperienced. She must have sensed that all was not as it should have been in the stables.

But her warnings came far too late.

Thirty-four

It was a struggle between us from the very first.

We differed in our opinions. I was perhaps over-confident in my abilities, while Thomas wanted me to 'start slow' on the cob. When I protested, he would not yield. Side-saddles were dangerous enough, he said, and ours particularly so. For they were not made to measure. 'What's yer height?' he queried. 'Five foot six? This saddle's too short by a good inch, Miss. It'll pay to learn a few tricks afore ye try yer strength on Sovereign.'

'I shall not ride that cob,' was my stubborn reply. 'I don't care what you say. She is the ugliest, squattest creature I ever saw, with the very worst proportions.'

'Sure, and she's no beauty. But she's serviceable.' He looked at me with a twinkle in his eye. 'For meself, I'd always pick a broad chest and ragged hips over a handsome, round-barrelled, gaudy-lookin' high-stepper any day. On account o' when a creature's bred for ornament, two hours' work is all she's fit for.'

I glanced at him sharply, wondering if I had just been offered some kind of insult. But his expression was too bland to read.

'If *you* will not saddle Sovereign then *I* shall girth him up,' I declared, and proceeded to do so. While Thomas watched, I worked myself into quite a fluster trying to lay the saddle on Sovereign's back—for it was monstrous heavy, and rucked up the saddle cloth every time I heaved it over his ribs. When at last I triumphed, however, it was only to endure yet another blow.

Ideally, a lady should mount with two people in attendance: one to help her, and one to hold the horse. Otherwise she will find herself in a pretty pickle attempting to position her right thigh between the pommels without sliding ignominiously off. With one assistant, or even a mounting block, it *can* be done. With neither, her success depends entirely on her level of expertise.

It may not surprise you to learn that I embarrassed myself thoroughly, and was forced to ride the cob.

After that defeat, I was hard pressed to prove myself worthy of the stockhorse. For when it came to riding, Thomas McNeilly was of an acutely cautious temperament. Though he seemed rather more concerned about the comfort of the horse than of its rider, his fanatical attention to the quality of my seat, and the disposition of my hands, stemmed from a perfectly justifiable emphasis on safety. 'If ye persist in hangin' off the pommels like that,' he warned, 'then ye'll be goin' over backwards wit' every sharp turn.'

'It's not *my* fault,' I protested. 'How can I help slipping, when the saddle is worn smooth?'

'Smooth my—' He caught himself just in time. 'Beggin' yer pardon, Miss,' he went on, with elaborate courtesy, 'but that there's good doeskin, not leather. And doeskin don't wear. Ye're not sittin' square, nor usin' yer back, is yer problem.'

'I am!'

'Then why's yer left knee out there flappin' in t'wind? It should be close in, heel down, toe raised.'

'It is!'

''T'isn't.'

'Well, what would *you* know about it? I haven't heard that *you* trained up any duchesses to the hunt.'

'Nor you have, neither. So mind me, if ye please. Lessen ye fancy a broken nose.'

'What do you mean by that?' I exclaimed in alarm, and he burst out laughing.

'Oh, Miss. Ye'd not be thinkin' I'd throw a punch? No, no.' He shook his head, still grinning. 'I'm only feared ye'd take a tumble, is all.'

'Well I won't. You watch.'

'Aye. I will.'

He did, too. Whenever I was on horseback, he would not let me out of his sight—at least not for some weeks. He was especially loath to give me free rein with Sovereign, who had an iron mouth and a slightly wilful character. My word, but he was a tiring horse! And he resented the side-saddle too, for which I cannot blame him. Side-saddles are wretched things. If ill-fitting, a side-saddle is far more likely to gall a horse than a man's saddle will. A side-saddle is also very uncomfortable for both the rider *and* the mount, when ascending or descending a hill. Furthermore, its effect on the spine can be most unfortunate. I have known women with one hip higher than the other as a result of riding side-saddle.

When I put these arguments to Mama, however, she would not allow me to don men's clothing of any description. She had 'never heard of such a thing', she said. Fifteen years later, Louisa freely looped up her riding habit to form trousers when she was exploring the Blue Mountains, but no such latitude was granted to me. Again and again I pointed out that I should not be seen by anyone of importance. My mother replied that Thomas would see me, and Richard Prince, and perhaps one of the tenants, if I rode too far afield. 'You would be thought a disgraceful object, not worthy of the protection that is normally afforded our sex,' she declared. 'At any rate, I have ridden to Budgong and back on that same saddle. It never hindered me.'

'Because it was *made* for you, Mama! You are shorter than I am! If you had only seen me today, wriggling about like a worm on a hook—'

'What a disgusting comparison, Charlotte.'

'Not nearly as disgusting as my posture. Thomas says he wouldn't trust me on a steep slope.'

'Then you must stay on the flats,' said my mother, firmly. She would not be drawn into any further discussion on the matter. And since Thomas was in her employ, he was obliged to enforce her ruling. Though he distrusted side-saddles, and was utterly bemused by the voluminous folds of my habit (which had to be 'trayned up' like a theatre curtain, and carried over my arm when I dismounted) he was immovable on the subject of riding astride. 'Mrs Barton would have the hide off my back,' he insisted, quite incorrectly. 'I'd not be wantin' to lose my place, Miss.'

'You would not lose your place! How absurd! She would not even *know*, if you didn't tell her!' Seeing him shake his head, I added: 'You could take him for a ride yourself, and meet me at the creek. She never goes down there anymore. And when I have finished, you could ride him back again!'

'No, Miss.'

'It would work! It would, I tell you! Oh, bother it all!' Frustrated past bearing, I actually stamped my foot. 'This is ridiculous, what harm can it possibly do?'

'I dunno about harm,' Thomas replied. 'But it'll do no good—leastways not to me. What would *I* gain from such a ploy? If ye'll pardon me for askin'.'

It was an unexpected question, phrased with peculiar emphasis. I frowned up at him.

'What do you mean?' A sudden thought struck me. 'I hope you're not wanting *money* from me?'

He gave a crooked smile. 'No, Miss. That I'm not,' he murmured.

'Because you must see that I have absolutely none at all! If I had any money, I should have bought my own saddle! *And* my own horse! As it is, I suppose I shall have to crush myself into that nasty object, and haul away at the reins as if I were a seaman hoisting the mainbrace!' As he grinned again, I snapped: 'What are you laughing at?'

'Ah, ye've a way wit' ye, Miss Charlotte.'

'Have I? Well, I'm glad you find my distress so amusing! Next time you're nipped or trodden on, I'll be sure to enjoy the spectacle just as thoroughly!'

I cannot count the number of times I stormed out of those stables, deprived yet again of some dear wish. Thomas would not allow the horses in his charge to be tired out or overpaced. He had an aversion to cantering, which 'knocked a horse's hoofs to pieces', and brought it home too hot; he did not seem to care that trotting for any length of time can be agonising to the back when one is riding side-saddle. We were forever at loggerheads on the subject of martingales, and he refused to let me gallop. 'Not yet,' he would say. 'Ye're not safe enough yet, Miss.'

I thought that I was, however. *And* was ready to prove it. But Thomas slept in the stables, and spent a good deal of time there. When he was not about, he entrusted the horses to his mongrel, Bennett. Bennett was the perfect guard-dog. I have never encountered a more snappish, low-bred, sour-tempered animal. He would mind only Thomas, and eat from no one else's hand. If left to watch the horses, he would remain by them indefinitely until his master instructed him to 'git down'. Though generally feared, he was also much admired. 'There's nowt would get past that ould gentleman,' Richard Prince once remarked, as the noise of Bennett's hysterical yapping announced the approach of Mr Welby's gig. It was felt that, with Bennett about, we had nothing to fear from horse-thieves. Nor, indeed, from marauders of any description.

I loathed Bennett. More than once, when I quietly approached Sovereign with a saddle and a mounting block, Bennett confronted me with his hackles raised and his savage teeth bared. He could not seem to understand that the horses were more mine than Thomas McNeilly's. And I could hardly request that Thomas explain the matter to him. For in doing so I would surely expose myself.

In the end I grew desperate, and stooped to underhanded methods.

You may recall that my mother kept a small supply of laudanum at Oldbury. In Sydney, there had always been doctors close at hand—and dispensing chemists also. In the country, however, this was not the case. So my mother stocked her medicine chest with useful doses and unguents, all of them carefully locked away. Since she still wore her keys at her waist, gaining access to laudanum was a matter of careful planning. I saw my opportunity one afternoon when she sent me down to the cellar, unaccompanied, with her keys. On my way back, I made a short detour to unlock the medicine chest, which she was not in the habit of checking very frequently. After that it was just a question of waiting.

I waited until Thomas took the gig to Berrima. He went to collect the mail, and James and my mother went with him. Because the gig could accommodate no one else comfortably, my sisters and I were left at home. Louisa was recovering from a nasty cold, and Emily had been designated her nurse; they consequently kept to the house, where they were very attentive to the sitting-room fire. I was not. I made myself busy, bustling in and out with wet clothes and dry clothes and wood and water and anything else that struck me as convincing. During one of these trips, I put a few drops of laudanum in Bennett's water-bowl. Then I returned it to its customary place, from which I had secretly filched it early that morning, when word of the trip to Berrima had first reached my ears.

Poor Bennett, being thirsty, was soon unconscious. (I wonder if I was a trifle generous with the laudanum, for he was not himself for a week afterwards.) By ten o'clock he had collapsed in the dirt, and my way was clear. Having already smuggled my riding habit into the stables, piece by piece, during my morning's rounds, I dressed myself in Thomas McNeilly's little sleeping alcove, away from prying eyes. Then I saddled Sovereign. It was the trickiest task that I had set myself, for Richard Prince was always about, and the black boy moved everywhere like a shadow, soundlessly. Side-saddles, moreover, are heavy things, festooned with all kinds of jingling buckles and slapping straps and creaking seams. I had to smother my grunts as Sovereign whinnied and tossed his head. Even with the mounting block on hand, he was difficult to control. No doubt he sensed something untoward.

Horses can be very canny, in that way.

I had decided to take him west, past Mereworth. East would have brought me to Sutton Forest, where I would have attracted unwanted attention, riding around on my own. Northwards lay Berrima, and I had no wish to encounter Mama. By heading west I would see no one—unless dogged by a singular misfortune—and would have the chance to enjoy several wide, clear meadows before striking thick bush. I was seeking cleared land because I wanted to gallop. I had an all-consuming picture in my head: I saw myself flying along like a spirit of the ether, utterly unrestrained. It was an alluring fancy.

I had just passed the front fence when Richard called my name. Glancing back, I saw him standing quite bemused, with his hoe. But I did not tarry, nor reply to his hail. Instead I rode on in a determined fashion, using my stick to apply pressure. Sovereign, I should point out, was still not wholly comfortable with the absence of a leg across his right flank. He was accustomed to cross-saddle riders; yielding to a stick instead of a right leg made him nervous. Therefore we were both in a somewhat jittery state when we set out, notwithstanding the stillness of the morning. Had I been more experienced, I would not have attempted too much. I would have known better than to over-excite the horse with a headlong gallop on a loose rein—especially in light of the fact that, once left even briefly unchecked, Sovereign was a difficult animal to regain control over.

Not that I wholly disgraced myself. The gallop was a fine one. Sovereign did not fall foul of any wombat holes or hidden logs, but flew across the crisping pasture as if airborne, beating a rapid tattoo on the hard ground as I held on for dear life, employing every muscle of my body. How the old stumps rushed past! A brisk wind stung my face, dragged through my hair, whipped tears into my eyes. I remember repeating to myself Thomas McNeilly's useful adage: 'Head and heart up, hands and heels down.' Though we started with an easy, swinging gallop at three-quarters' speed, I soon lost my head with the thrill of it, and we must have got to twenty-odd miles an hour at one point. Then the forest loomed up, and I was forced to wrestle with that iron mouth. It was like pulling at the side of a house. In fact *I* cannot take credit for the way he eased off. His own horse-sense guided him, and we entered the woods at a far more sedate pace, though he was sweating and snorting already.

For a time we wove a pattern through the trees. We followed a stock-trail and a creek-bed. We skirted rises and crossed clearings over fallen trees. My enjoyment of my liberty was absolute. Though my heart bounded with every bright parakeet that shot across my path, trilling, I was not in search of flora or fauna. It was freedom that I sought. Up high on that powerful brute, I feared nothing. I felt as if I were riding a loaded cannon, and was therefore careless of my own safety. I let my mind wander. I let my grip slacken. I was stupid.

The result was inevitable. A bounding wallaby, flushed from the scrub, startled Sovereign. He shied, and before I could turn his head away or otherwise steady his nerves, executed a couple of rough pig-jumps. As Thomas had foreseen, I went straight over backwards. But I was fortunate. Instead of falling onto a rock, or getting my leg caught in the saddle and being dragged for half a mile, I took a roll straight off Sovereign's rump, head over heels. This meant that my feet hit the ground first. And though I did some fine damage to one of my ankles in consequence, my brains stayed safe in my skull.

It was later determined that I did not break a single bone. At the time, however, I assumed that I had. For I had come down awry, turned my right ankle, and torn the ligament. I thought that I should die from the pain. I remember rolling about in agony, groaning and squealing, oblivious even to the pulled muscle in my shoulder. Almost certainly it was the spectacle of my distress, with its attendant noises, that drove my horse away. For when at last the sharper pangs abated, and I was able to look about me, he had gone.

At first I was not greatly troubled. Being still rather preoccupied, I noticed only that he was not in the immediate neighbourhood, and felt sure that he had strayed but a short distance, perhaps in search of a mouthful to eat. So I sat nursing my injured ankle, waiting for the pain to subside and never thinking that I had been abandoned. Such a prospect did not occur to me even after fifteen minutes had elapsed, and I was ready to move again. Putting my weight on the affected foot was an excruciating manoeuvre that drove every other consideration from my head; I realised at once that I would need a crutch of some kind, and cast about me for a large bough to serve as a walking stick. This done, I was able to prop myself up with a fair degree of success. I also discovered that I could hop along, though it was heavy work, and liable to send a spurt of pain shooting up my leg with every jolt. What a mercy, I decided, that my right foot was the injured one! For if it had been my left, I would have had no chance in the world of remounting.

It was at this point that I scanned my surroundings more anxiously. Where was Sovereign? I called his name without eliciting any response. I peered into the thickets of woolly gum that ringed me. I staggered forward, changing my perspective in the hope that I might espy the swish of a tail behind an acacia.

At last I came to the awful conclusion that Sovereign had gone. My heart sank almost to the level of my torn ligament. For if I had lost the horse, my mother would never forgive me.

I had no concerns about finding my way home. It was a bright day, and not long past noon; even crippled, I was fairly confident that I would be able to reach Oldbury before night fell. I had a vague idea of where I was, despite all the encroaching bush. And once I had retraced my steps to the cleared pastures—with their sweeping, uninterrupted views of nearby hills—there would be no difficulty in fixing my exact position. Had I been at Budgong, I might have worried, for the Shoalhaven is rarely kind to lone wanderers. Even around Wollondilly or Belanglo I would have been in some peril. But I was familiar with the terrain near Sutton Forest, which was partly settled even then. No; it was not the journey itself that I feared. It was what lay at the end of that journey.

'Stupid fool! Stupid fool!' I kept repeating, as I began to head in an easterly direction, retracing Sovereign's steps. Here and there I found his hoof-prints in the soft earth, and hairs from his tail caught in spiny leaves. My memory of our approach was quite good, and I was relieved to encounter many a familiar stone or tree as I hobbled along. It was the distances between them that surprised me. For Sovereign had been very quick, and I was by then appallingly slow. I had to place my stick quite carefully before attempting to hop. And after a few falls, I knew better than to attempt crossing jagged or uneven ground. Instead I had to work my way around each obstacle—a procedure that lengthened the trip by many weary minutes.

Faced with such challenges, I could spare little thought for what lay ahead at Oldbury. But after a time I felt a growing unease, which at first I could not account for. I suppose that when the shadows lengthened, it crossed my mind that the woods were not entirely safe; that while there were no bears or wolves to threaten me, I was only a short ride from the Belanglo gully, where bushrangers were known to congregate. Certain black memories began to scuttle about like cockroaches in my head. In 1836, my mother had been riding to Belanglo when the infamous meeting had occurred. How far was I from Belanglo now? Five miles? Six? Ten?

I became conscious of little noises arising in the silence of the bush around me: rustles and chirrups, creaks and flutters. My own breathing was loud. My clumsy progress broke many sticks and scattered many tumbling stones. I must have sounded like a wounded bullock or an hysterical sheep, vulnerable to whatever pack of native dogs might decide to stalk it. My mind began to run on predators. No one had ever been charged or arrested for the attack on my mother. It had occurred ten years previously, and in all likelihood the perpetrators were long since dead, or departed. But their very facelessness gave them an indestructible quality. To my way of thinking, they seemed almost to merge with the trees and the rocks. I wondered if they were still wandering around Belanglo, those anonymous men. I wondered if they had been preying on other women in the hushed, unfriendly bush.

And then I heard a distant 'Coo-ee!'

I knew instantly that I was being sought. Nothing else seemed as likely. So I 'Coo-eed' back with all my strength, and sat down on a tussock. The trees were thinning, by this stage. Glimpses of grassy flats were visible through a fretwork of limbs and boughs.

I saw the approaching rider before he spotted me.

'Coo-ee!' I cried, waving my stick. At that moment I recognised the horse, and my heart leapt into my mouth. I thought: 'Have I been foolish? Has Sovereign been caught by a man of vicious intent, who would take advantage of a lonely woman?' I did not for one instant believe that the horse could have returned to Oldbury in such a short time. At least not until his rider brought his head around.

Even from that distance, the careless flick of the rein against Sovereign's off-side was all that it took. I knew Thomas McNeilly at once, though his face was shadowed by his hat-brim. The blue striped shirt was also familiar.

Slowly I lowered my stick, wondering if I *wanted* to be found. The prospect of being vigorously upbraided was suddenly too much for me to bear. I was tired, and in pain, and ever so slightly ashamed of myself.

But it was far too late for misgivings. Thomas had seen me; he urged Sovereign forward with what must have been a barely discernible tightening of the thigh muscles. (His horsemanship was immensely restrained, as if he were reluctant to waste a single drop of energy on anything quite so unremarkable as riding a horse.) When he removed his hat, I saw that he was frowning. My own expression cannot have been much more attractive.

'Are ye hurt?' was his initial inquiry.

'No. I mean—yes. A little. My foot. It's nothing.'

The gap between us gradually closed as Thomas guided Sovereign between patches of crumbling rock and low scrub. He said nothing more until he was near enough to speak without raising his voice.

'What in hell were ye playin' at?' he said at last, his jaw stiff, his dark brows knotted.

'It was a wallaby. You would have fallen, too.'

'Mrs Barton's sent Richard off in t'gig, for more men. She's all but gutted, seein' this horse come back alone.' He began to shake his head. 'Jaysus, Mary and Joseph, ye could have broken yer neck, *and* yer mother's heart. Are ye mad? Don't ye care? Christ, we thought ye were *dead*, dammit.'

I sniffed, and looked away. Had I spoken, I would have burst into tears.

I was in no state to defend myself.

'Lucky our Rick saw ye ride away,' Thomas continued. 'Meant that I knew where to start.'

Still I said nothing.

''Twas dire hard for me. Keepin' an eye on the ground . . .' He sighed, and rubbed his eyes with the back of his hand before replacing his hat. 'Well—better get back 'fore the whole county's raised,' he added. 'Can ye get up in front o' me? Ye'll never keep yer seat if I lead, not on a cross-saddle in that dress. Ye'd break yer other foot.'

'It's not broken.' My voice was hoarse. 'It's sprained.'

'Which one?'

'This one.'

'Can ye get over here, or not?'

I rose, and lurched towards him. When Sovereign jibbed at my approach, Thomas quietened him with a steely calm. I was instructed to drop my stick and face away from the horse, with my left heel wedged into the stirrup. I felt Thomas reach down to grip me under the armpit.

Next thing I was sitting in his lap, my shoulder having been practically wrenched from its socket. I whimpered at the pain in my foot.

'There, now. There, now,' said Thomas. Tears pricked my eyes—before I realised that he was speaking to the horse, which had staggered under our combined weight. 'We'll take it slow. One step at a time, poor lad.'

I do not know if I can properly convey to you the shock of that moment. For I was hedged about by Thomas's arms, and my nose was level with his scrubby chin. I found myself staring straight at his throat, which was as finely moulded as any marble statue's, in those days. Since his collar was open, I also saw the black hair creeping up from hidden places. And I felt the supple length of him along one side, and the strength in his well-knit shoulders, and the rise and fall of his chest. He seemed all about me, like a rough woollen cloak. I sat wedged between his torso and the pommel; is it surprising that I was shaken to the core?

'Hold on,' he said, turning Sovereign. So I groped for the pommel, too startled to speak. It was like riding a rowboat on a heavy swell. Thomas cursed to himself, quietly, when the jolting made me grunt. But he uttered not another word during the entire journey back, which might have been accomplished in the snow, for all that I can remember. My recollections are limited to the texture of his shirt, and the warmth of his breath on my cheek.

As you grow older, you lose all shame. It becomes a luxury that you cannot afford when you must nurse infants, and tend invalids. At nineteen, however, I had my fair share of it—despite what was later said. I knew not where to look nor what to say, when Thomas held me. I was utterly unprepared, no matter what the world might think. And if you want my honest opinion, I was a victim of circumstance.

Had my thoughts not been running in a certain direction, I might never have been alerted to the quickened pulse beneath his skin, or the vague promise embodied in every neat, unhurried movement. An unlucky conjunction of factors overthrew me; old memories opened the door to new sensitivities.

Simply speaking, none of it would have happened, if my mother had not already led the way.

Thirty-five

I did not walk for a week. Instead I spent my time in bed, or propped in a chair with my injured foot raised. My ankle itself received every attention, from feather pillows to mustard poultices. But the rest of me was practically ignored. For I had revealed myself as a headstrong, selfish, careless young fool, who had received far less than her just desserts. Even Emily was resentful. 'You cannot imagine how upset we all were,' she explained at one point, slamming down a cup of tea in the most grudging manner.

Mama would not speak to me at all. When she chose to communicate, she did it through her agent, Mary Ann. I was made to eat apart from the family, and could not accompany them to church. The Reverend Stone, however, did pay me a visit. At my mother's request, he came to read me a lecture on the cruelty of wilfulness. ('Obedience is the crown of womanhood' was how he put it.) Otherwise, I was left alone with my books and my needlework, to reflect on how badly I had behaved, and to consider the best means by which I might make amends.

Normally, I would have been enraged at this. I would have sulked and snapped and refused to cooperate. Indeed, my mother probably expected something of the sort, and was perplexed at my stunned acquiescence. It was simply not *like* me, she admitted to the Reverend Stone. 'I am beginning to worry about Charlotte's general health,' I overheard her saying, 'for she seems remarkably listless. But she has no fever, and complains of no great discomfort.'

'Perhaps it was the shock,' William Stone rumbled.

'Perhaps. Unless she . . . you don't think . . .' My mother faltered, clearly uncertain as to how she should proceed.

'Go on,' said the Reverend Stone.

'I am very concerned that something might have happened. Out there in the bush,' my mother gasped.

'Oh.' There followed a brief silence. When our rector spoke again, his tone was rather constrained. 'Oh, I think not, Mrs Barton. She would have mentioned it, surely? And there would have been . . . well, traces left behind. Torn clothing, and so forth. Scratches. Bruising.' He hesitated once again. 'I have had some experience with such crimes, alas. There is generally violence involved, and it always leaves its mark,' he concluded.

My mother said nothing. I myself quailed, hoping and praying that she would never know that I had eavesdropped on this conversation, which made me writhe in my seat. How dismayed I felt! It was bad enough that I had been stripped of all my defences, and left as fragile and exposed as a newborn kitten. It was bad enough that my mind boiled with unanswered questions and confused fancies, until I could hardly sleep. It would be infinitely worse if my mother decided to approach me and make gentle, veiled inquiries about my 'purity' and 'maidenhood'. For what could I say in response? That my thoughts were as corrupted as my person was stainless? That I understood, now, why she had married my stepfather?

During the long watches of the night, I had been visited by an intensely vivid, profoundly disturbing vision. I had seen my mother watching George Barton as he tightened a girth, his sleeves rolled up and his strong arms gleaming. It had made me so ill, I had nearly brought up the contents of my stomach. Whenever it flashed into my head subsequently, I would wince and shut my eyes. What comfort could there be in such an explanation? If our miseries were all derived from these base yearnings of the flesh, then I was no better than my mother. And my prospects looked similarly hopeless.

It occurred to me that the bush itself might cast some kind of spell—that the spicy scent of eucalypts and the drowsy warmth of the sun might combine with fatal consequences for a healthy female constitution. I did not know. I could hardly make inquiries. All I could do was fret, and wriggle, and catch my breath every time the door opened. For I had not seen Thomas since my return to Oldbury; I had been confined to the house, which he rarely entered, and hardly knew how I felt about meeting him. Being quite sure that I would turn pale, or lose the power of speech, or in some other way disgrace myself, I feared our next encounter as much as I longed for it.

Little wonder that my innards lurched with every approaching footstep.

'This is foolish,' I would tell myself. 'I was affected by the fall, and have not yet recovered. I am not Mama. I would not marry a servant. Why, he cannot even write! No—it was a touch of the sun. When I see him again, he will be dirty, and awkward, and shabbily dressed, and he will hold his hat in his hands, and the scales will fall from my eyes, and everything will be as it was before.'

That was my prayer. But it went unanswered. I had anticipated that he would visit me one day in the sitting room, where he would no doubt have looked out of place in his grubby clothes and heavy boots. Every morning I expected it, and every evening I clumped off to bed disappointed. My heart sank lower as I judged him disgusted with me. Nothing else could account for his rudeness, I decided. At the very least he could have asked after my health.

Then one morning Mama had my chair carried outside. Mary Ann informed me that I was looking peaky; my mother had decreed that I should spend a little time in the fresh air, before the sun got too hot. Certainly I must have been as white as snow when I hobbled onto the back veranda. For I knew that I was bound to see Thomas if I stayed there long enough, and the prospect drained every drop of blood from my cheeks.

Sure enough, I saw him. He crossed from the kitchen to the stables, pulling on his hat. At one point during his brief journey Sarah called to him from the kitchen door, so that he checked in mid-stride, swinging around. Then he laughed as he caught the carrot that she tossed at him (for the horses, no doubt). He was wearing his blue shirt, tucked into the narrow waist of his dusty cords, and a dark neckerchief tied at his throat.

When Sarah withdrew into the kitchen, Thomas turned and spotted me. He froze. I swallowed. When I lifted a trembling hand, he jerked at the brim of his hat. Then he walked on, head down, and disappeared into the stables.

I almost cried. The sight of him had done nothing to ease my overburdened heart. On the contrary, it had shaken me all over again. For the first time I realised that he was beautiful. I had always admired the condition of his teeth, but how could I have disregarded his warm skin, his perfect proportions, or the way his glossy hair tumbled over his brow? His voice was beautiful too, with its rough edge and Irish lilt.

I had to cover my eyes. He is a *servant*, I reminded myself. He cannot read or write. You know absolutely *nothing* about him—why, he might have been a convict! At least George Barton was never a convict.

The memory of my stepfather catapulted me once again into a slough of murky speculation. I tried to shake him off. Throughout

403

the rest of the day, my feverish brain seemed constantly to bounce between thoughts of George Barton and Thomas McNeilly, until I was driven almost mad. My mother noticed it. She actually addressed me, saying, 'Are you not well, Charlotte? You look dreadful.' Since this was not something that I wished to hear (for what if I had looked dreadful to Thomas McNeilly?), I snapped at her, causing much offence. We parted on bad terms outside our bedrooms that evening.

Later, in bed, I formed no coherent plan for the future. I did not think: 'He is a poor prospect, and therefore must be avoided at all costs.' Nor did I decide that I would defy the world, marry for love, and stand fast against the consequences. I simply indulged myself in filmy, romantic dreams, or chewed on my nails when my dreams became contaminated with more disquieting elements. In my defence, let me say that I did make *one* resolution. I resolved that I would inquire about Thomas McNeilly, without, at the same time, revealing myself hopelessly smitten.

This was more easily said than done. To begin with, it meant that I could not betray myself with leading questions. I had to be oblique, and careful. I had to find a legitimate excuse for placing myself in the kitchen, where the servants tended to congregate and where confidences were often exchanged. Though the state of my ankle did not allow me to stand, I was by then capable of shelling peas, chopping vegetables and kneading pastry. This I did, in the manner of a humble penitent; my mother, I think, was cheered to see me so eagerly playing the role of domestic handmaid. Her icy mien thawed considerably at this time. No doubt she believed that I was trying to atone for my sin.

Alas, however, my industry was entirely self-serving. I listened intently as Sarah gossiped with Mary Ann, and Richard reminisced to Sarah, and Thomas made inquiries of Richard. Thomas ate in the kitchen, and would wander in and out occasionally in search of goose-grease, or twine, or some other necessity. I knew this, and was prepared for it. I did not blush the first time he sauntered in, doffing his hat and running his hand through his hair. He had come to collect his boiled barley, which he sometimes gave to the horses as a restorative. Having cheerfully greeted Sarah, he crossed the floor towards the stove before catching sight of me.

Then he hesitated.

"Mornin', Miss,' he said at last.

'Good morning.' Desperately I racked my brain for something to add, without success.

'I hope yer foot's improved?' he continued, in a stilted and formal fashion.

'Yes. Thank you.'

Shameful as it is to admit, my very bowels yearned. As he peered into the bubbling pot, I had to drag my gaze from his lean and graceful form, lest my eyes betray me. 'This not done yet?' he asked Sarah, who was banging her pots around with irritable emphasis.

'You tell *me*,' she snapped. 'I ain't no horse-doctor.'

'Ten more minutes,' he judged, stepping away from the stove. 'What's for dinner, then?'

'Half a pound o' nothing, if you don't leave me be!' Sarah responded. Thomas caught my eye, and seemed to rally a little. 'Ye mustn't be a skivvy to 'er, Miss, for she'll take advantage,' he said, with a half-smile. Whereupon Sarah shook her ladle at him.

'That I will *not*!' she exclaimed. 'What are *you* doin', I should like to know, that you can spend your day roamin' in and out o' my kitchen?'

'Why, Mrs Prince, I cannot keep away from ye,' said Thomas, blithely. I had the impression that he was accustomed to teasing her in this suggestive way, and had let drop the remark without thinking. For he then recalled that I was present, and glanced at me, and looked confused. 'Aye . . . well,' he muttered, donning his hat. 'Good day t'ye, Miss.'

I nodded, being all but speechless. No sooner had he walked out than Sarah began to complain about him. He was a Godless, smarmy, indolent Irishman, she muttered, with no respect for her married state and an unhealthy fondness for hard liquor.

'Oh,' I said, my spirits sinking, 'does Mr McNeilly drink?'

'Drink!' Sarah snorted. 'Is there an Irishman who don't, Miss?'

'But have you *seen* him drinking?'

'No need to see 'im, is there? Not when you can smell it on 'im. With all them 'otels in Berrima, no one need ever run short of a nip. And 'e's not backwards in comin' forwards, not when there's mail to be collected.'

'Maybe he is simply anxious to collect his *own* mail,' I remarked. But Sarah frowned, and shook her head.

'McNeilly never gets no mail,' she said, reaching for a knife. 'Couldn't read it even if 'e did. You ready with them taters, Miss? Only I'll need 'em soon.'

As you may imagine, I was dismayed to learn that Thomas McNeilly might be a secret drinker. At our next meeting, the following day, I watched him closely. He was finishing his breakfast when I entered the kitchen, and I searched his face for the kind of symptoms that had once been evident in my stepfather's of a morning: the bloodshot eyes, the slight list, the short temper and sensitivity to light. I noticed none of these things, however. Thomas McNeilly's demeanour was brisk and firm. Though his chin was unshaven, his eyes were bright. He spoke clearly, without a trace of hoarseness, and his brown hands were as steady as his gaze.

"Mornin', Miss Charlotte,' said Mary Ann, as the servants all rose to greet me. 'Can I help you, Miss?'

'No, no.' I was limping, but not incapable. 'I shall sit over here, on the stool. Is there anything I might help *you* with, Sarah?'

'Well, now . . . let's see . . .' Our cook surveyed the room, eager to supply me with some menial task. 'When Mrs Barton gives the orders, Miss, I'll have a better notion, I'm sure . . .'

'You ought not o'erstretch yersel', Miss,' said Richard Prince, in his kindly way. Thomas said nothing. He simply sat down again and addressed himself to his tea.

The others followed his example, awkwardly, as if my presence made them self-conscious.

'Mrs Barton warnt askin' fer me, were she, Miss?' said Mary Ann.

'No. I don't think so. She is writing letters, at present.'

'Then she'll not be wantin' the gig?' Thomas inquired, wiping his mouth. I shook my head, unable to reply—for his voice took my breath away. 'If not, I should exercise Ida,' he added. 'The gig won't be needed this afternoon, I daresay?'

'I doubt it,' was all that I could croak out in response. Whereat Thomas put down his cup, and rose.

'I'll be away, then,' he said, and nodded politely in my direction. When he left the room, it seemed to me as if the sun had gone behind a cloud.

Being of fairly regular habits, he was accustomed to exercising the horses at around the same time every morning, as long as they were not required for other duties. I therefore arranged to leave the kitchen just before nine o'clock, when I was bound to find the stables empty. Bennett was there, but he was not himself still; I found him sleeping in Sovereign's empty stall. Thomas McNeilly's meagre possessions had therefore been left unguarded.

He slept on a mattress made of canvas ticking stuffed with dry grass, which was placed behind a linen curtain. In the light that seeped through cracks in the wall I saw a four-legged stool covered by a stained damask towel, on which reposed a tin mug, a shaving brush, a comb, a small, speckled mirror, a couple of blue earthenware plates and a grubby picture of a Catholic saint. From a hook positioned over his pillow hung more Popish implements: a crucifix and a rather fine amber rosary. His Sunday clothes dangled from another hook. A colza lamp stood on top of a battered hatbox, in which I discovered no hidden bottle of gin, but only a seashell, a set of fishing hooks, an ancient missal with a silk ribbon (not much used), a fine linen cravat, a carved trinket box, and a bundle of yellowing papers. None of these papers was a ticket-of-leave, I was pleased to learn. One was an engraving torn from a book or newspaper, showing 'A View of Cavan'. One was something that *may* have been a pawn ticket. There was also a signed 'pass' of the type often granted to free or freed men by persons in the commission of the peace, lest they (the recipients) be arrested as vagrant bushrangers while travelling. Finally, there was a letter. It may come as a surprise that I hesitated to read this letter—that I possessed, in fact, even a modicum of common decency. I was sitting on my heels, the letter in my hand, pondering its possible contents, when I heard a noise.

I turned just as Thomas McNeilly pushed back the curtain.

We simply stared at each other for the longest time. I sprang to my feet, red and speechless, still clutching the tell-tale letter. Thomas's gaze travelled from the letter to the open hatbox to the bed (which had not yet been explored), before returning to my face.

'Well now,' he drawled at last, propping himself against one of the supporting beams, 'here's a pretty sight.'

I opened my mouth, but no sensible excuse sprang to mind. What could I possibly have said? With a faltering movement I placed the letter on the nearest horizontal surface, and edged towards the door.

'What might ye be lookin' for, Miss?'

'N-nothing,' I stammered, and he raised his eyebrows.

'No?'

'I wasn't going to *take* anything! I just . . . I wanted . . .'

'Did ye think mebbe *I* took somethin'?'

'Oh, *no!*' I was aghast. 'Not at all!'

'There's not much here, but ye're welcome to any of't.'

'No, I . . . I'm sorry, I . . . excuse me.' I felt almost suffocated by my own sense of acute shame, and had to get out—immediately. When I tried to push past him, however, he caught my arm.

'Whatever it is ye want,' he said quietly, 'I'll give it to ye.'

'No, don't—I mean . . .' I could hardly draw breath, for his face seemed very close in the dimness. 'Let go, please . . .'

'Is this what ye're lookin' for?' he murmured.

Then he bent his head and kissed me on the corner of my mouth.

Thirty-six

An interlude

It seems to me that my upbringing was tainted. I should have slapped Thomas when he kissed me. I should have run, and never looked at him again. Yet I did not.

Instead I reached for him, and sealed my own fate. I returned his kiss with ardour. In my defence let it be said that I broke away almost immediately—but that was not the end of the story, as you must surely realise. Therefore I cannot offer up the excuse that I was carried away by the moment, and deeply regretful afterwards. The fact is, I was somehow corrupted. No doubt it was owing to George Barton's influence, or to my mother's. *She* went into the forest at Belanglo with George Barton. As a consequence, perhaps, *I* threw myself into the arms of Thomas McNeilly. And the impurity endures, because I have been punished through Eva. What else can be the reason for her perverse and destructive recklessness? To have one illegitimate child is wicked enough, but *four?* It smacks of an inherited defect.

Perhaps I erred. Perhaps I should have kept Eva here, exposed to the ridicule of our friends and neighbours, from the very first. At the time, however, I was not thinking clearly. I was not myself. Eighteen-eighty-five was such a terrible year that this third blow

410

was altogether too much for me to bear. I can only be thankful that Thomas never knew. It was not, after all, Eva's disgrace that killed him.

On the contrary, I have always believed that Emily Louisa's passing brought about his own.

He died exactly three months after my darling daughter expired, and the first symptoms of his malady appeared within days of her interment. Had I known, I would have engaged a doctor much more quickly. But I was beside myself with grief—as was Thomas. We both of us lost our appetites. We both of us became thin. How was I to know that, whereas my own wasted appearance was the natural outcome of a broken spirit, my husband's sprang from an even grimmer cause?

We were at Byng Street, by then. Edwin was with us—and Ernest too, God rest his soul. Eva was only eighteen. Flora was living in Molong with George, and we saw her from time to time. Her eldest, Emily Susan, had just set up as a dressmaker, though the other two girls were still at school. *My* Emily had married Henry David in 1877. So she had her own house and her own life, on the other side of Orange.

It was as well, perhaps. When poor Charles died in 1873, he was laid out in my bedroom. I did not sleep well for a year after that, and had to buy a new bed. After Emily's death, I was not so haunted. This may have been because I had not see her slack and colourless face adorning my pillow. On the other hand, it may have been because my fears for the living soon overwhelmed my concern with the dead. Though not soon enough, I regret to say.

I intend to be frank, here. I shall spare myself nothing, and may hurt others in the process. For the fact is that my marriage was not always a happy one. And if you should read this, Edwin and Flora, then I am sorry to pain you. But it surely cannot come as a surprise. You yourself witnessed many a bitter exchange between your parents. Why, Flora must have been all of five years old when your dear brother Thomas died, and I was mad with anger, and blamed your father for it. I was unjust in doing so, because he *did* bring a doctor, and drank himself stupid only after the dear child had already gone. At the time, however, I was in search of someone to punish. And when I considered our humble life, with all its attendant miseries, I was convinced that poor little Thomas had fallen victim to it. I was sure that, had I been well supplied with trained nurses, fine food, woollen blankets, sealed walls and clean water, my darling would never have perished as he did.

Perhaps it was true. Perhaps not. Whatever the case, I was wrong to blame my husband, for all that he seemed so helpless in the face of unfriendly circumstance. He did his best, though it seemed (at times) inadequate. I wince when I consider the accusations that I made against him. He had lost his only son, and I stood over him like some avenging Fury, heaping censure upon his bowed, dishevelled head. You may remember it, Flora. You may recall that at last he lashed out, not with his tongue but with a tankard, drenching me in brandy-and-milk. Certainly *I* shall never forget it. I shall never forget how I hit him, and he fended me off, and how, as we grappled shamefully there in the kitchen, I happened to look away—while shielding my face—and caught a glimpse of your own grave, wide-eyed stare in one corner.

It was one of so many disgraceful incidents. There was a furious argument about baptism, which stemmed from my own disillusionment; for while Flora was christened a Catholic, I was adamant that the rest of my children would be received into the Anglican Church. There was chronic bickering about liquor, and how much of it should be permitted in our house. There were disagreements about literature. When Louisa's first novel was published, in a series of short 'numbers', Thomas began to resent the effect that it had on my spirits.

'If ye're findin' it such a strain,' he advised, somewhat impatiently, 'then stop readin' it.'

'How can I? When everyone *else* hereabouts will know what she has said?'

'Everyone else?' He snorted. 'Who else? Who else cares?'

'The Throsbys, for a start. *And* the Reverend Stone.'

'Oh, aye. Well, next time we're takin' tea at t'Throsbys, I'll be sure and ask 'em what they thought o' yer sister's grand book.'

'It means nothing to you, of course,' I snapped. 'Since you cannot read, and your friends cannot read. You have no *idea* what it is like among literate people. You cannot understand the importance of the written word.'

This was said to wound, and it did. His face darkened. He turned on his heel. But he said nothing else on the subject for some time, save (once or twice) to complain about the cost of buying up all Louisa's 'numbers'. Then, towards the middle of the book, I stumbled upon the wedding of Mary O'Shannassy. And it cut me to the quick.

If you have read *Gertrude*, you may recall this scene. It takes place on the estate of Murrumbowrie, which bears a very close resemblance to Oldbury. The domestic staff sweep out the largest wool-shed, and festoon the walls with green boughs, and lay long planks on stones and blocks of wood to form benches. They cover a table in rough fare, and tie scarlet and yellow handkerchiefs to the uprights to serve as flags. For illumination, they use tallow candles thrust into the necks of gleaming black bottles. When the dancing begins, it is 'real, active, violent exertion, such as a lot of spirited horses at play take'. This jumping, bounding and stamping is fuelled to some degree by quiet visits to a two-gallon keg of rum, smuggled into the shed by the 'slyest means'.

This was my wedding dance. There can be no question about it. I recognised every inclusion, down to the costume of the bride. My mother had refused to buy me anything even remotely resembling white silk, and I had been forced to wear a green *muslin de laine* gown—just like Mary O'Shannassy's—with white hose and glazed shoes. The only difference lay in the fact that I possessed a serviceable bonnet, and was therefore not required to attach my veil directly to my head.

Now, you may ask: why take offence at this? Why should a factual representation of my wedding day make me seethe and splutter? In return, I would answer that, while factual, the sketch is not truthful. It makes the whole occasion comic. For Mary is portrayed as a silly girl, forever changing her mind, and Father Patrick O'Connor, the portly priest—with his taste for brandy and genealogy—is no more admirable. At one point, when he emerges from the big house, Mary rushes forward and flings her arms around his feet, kneeling before him and begging him to perform the ceremony. At first he refuses. But as he shuffles across the yard she clings to him, stopping when he stops, moving when he moves. At length, 'sundry titters' swell into 'scarcely suppressed laughter', and Father Patrick agrees to preside over the marriage of that importunate girl. The wedding takes place five minutes afterwards, in the wool-shed.

For many years, I could not entirely forgive Louisa. She had turned my wedding into a feast of fun, larding it with fictitious events (like the scene that I have just described) and condemning it with the faintest praise. 'It was universally declared an "illigant" affair,' she jokes, adding with the utmost condescension, 'we rather suspect a dance in a wool-shed, or barn, is more enjoyed than the most *recherché* ball among the elite'. Only in later years has it occurred to me that she may have been struggling to do me a small service. My wedding was not the most joyous occasion, you see. Though there *was* dancing, and music, and hilarity, it was of the somewhat violent type that stems from ragged nerves and stubborn defiance. It is possible that Louisa was attempting to drain the event of its poison. A comic wedding, after all, is better than a tragic one.

This possibility never even crossed my mind in 1857, when I first read Louisa's novel. On the contrary, I was so distressed that I tore into pieces the little booklet containing this festive chapter. Upon seeing the result, Thomas was unimpressed.

'What the hell are ye playin' at?' he demanded. 'That book cost sixpence, and ye ripped it up!'

'It is not a book, it is a brazen insult!' I cried. 'I shall never forgive her, never!'

'I told ye to stop buyin' 'em,' he said. 'Mebbe next time ye'll heed me.'

'She has made a mockery of our wedding!'

'Let her. There's no one round here will care.'

'I shall write to her. I shall tell her what I think of her betrayal!'

'That ye won't. Where are they now—up Richmond way? That's a fair whack in postage. Sure, and I'll not be spendin' good money on a family row.'

As it happened, the letter was never sent. I had barely enough time to read, let alone write. But I could not prevent myself from purchasing the next instalment of Louisa's sprawling tale, and Thomas soon discovered this. Our residence was not so large that a new publication could remain concealed in it for long.

'I thought ye said ye'd finished wit' this?' he demanded.

'I changed my mind,' was my sullen response.

'Then ye'll change it back. I can have yer temper for free—I'm not inclined to pay sixpence for it!'

'Why not? We pay far more than sixpence for the rotgut that sours *your* mood.'

'It'll end up kindlin', just like the last,' he warned.

'No it will not.'

'Lass—it'll do ye no good. Ye said yerself, 'tis all of 't lies.'

'I was wrong, then.'

'What?'

'Louisa is quite right. Our wedding *was* a joke.' Much pent-up bitterness began to flow from me at this point, for I was mortally tired, having only recently recovered from an early miscarriage. 'I have come to think her very shrewd, as a matter of fact. Why, her portrait of *you* is a perfect likeness!'

'What d'ye mean?' Thomas snatched at the booklet that I was holding. 'She's not put *me* in't?'

'Oh, I think so. I recognise the tin mug. And the blue plates. And the four-legged stool, with one leg too short.'

'But she's never used me *name*?'

'She doesn't need to. It is all there. You are the "distracted lover". The "disconsolate bridegroom".' Seeing him flip helplessly through those yellowish pages, unable to read a word, I was visited by a cruel impulse. '*Anyone* could see through such a thin disguise. Dick McMaster, she calls you, and you're cast as a sawyer, but the resemblance is clear enough. She has captured exactly your way of putting off demanding tasks. He is such an eager swain, this sawyer, that he will not travel thirty miles to fetch a priest to marry him.' This was a true account of Louisa's fictional sawyer, as it happened, but I immediately began to embellish it with lies of my own. 'And she has included Bennett, who is shown as being *far* more intelligent than his master. Oh—and let us not forget good old Dick's pressing inquiries about his bride's inheritance, or the fawning, obsequious compliments that he is continuously paying to the owner of the estate . . .'

Thomas, who had slowly been turning red, uttered a gasp of rage. Before I could stop him, he ripped my booklet in two and cast it at the wall.

'*That's a bloody lie!*' he roared, the veins standing out in his forehead.

'Oh! You beast!' I pounced on the literary remnants. 'You have ruined it! Just *look* at what you've done!'

'Hands off that!'

'You savage—'

'Give it here!'

'I shall not!'

'*Give it here!*' He tried to wrench the torn pages from me. 'How can ye read such muck, and want t'keep readin'?'

'Let go!'

'What did ye tell 'er? What lies were ye spreadin'?' He began to peel my fingers away from the cheap binding. 'That I had a mind for yer money, is that it? When I never once asked, nor cared, God damn it!'

'Ouch!' I kicked him, and hit out with my free hand. But his grip did not loosen. Grimly, he tucked my arm beneath his own and continued to work at releasing *my* grip, jerking his head free of my fingernails from time to time.

When at last the tattered booklet was in his possession, he gave me a shove that sent me reeling into the kitchen table.

'No decent wife would have paid sixpence for this,' he spat, and threw a fistful of crushed paper into the fire.

I burst into tears, then. I tried to retrieve the offending pamphlet with the tongs, and was prevented, and there was a scuffle. I cannot tell you how many scuffles there were, over the years. Is it any wonder that, after we lost our farm, Thomas eventually became a carrier? I can say with some confidence that I drove him onto the drays. And if I sometimes lamented his long absences, when he was transporting bacon to Sydney or cloth to Goulburn, I knew even then that I had only myself to blame. For though he had a taste for breaking in horses, he came to discover that domestic conflict yielded little in the way of excitement, after a while.

I suppose that I wore him down. He certainly tried *my* patience. I thought him overly generous to his mates when his family were wanting. I did not like his spells of drinking, nor his sentimental attachment to a host of unhelpful things: Irish superstitions, grisly Popish martyrdoms, a succession of ill-tempered dogs, his dead mother, the colour green, and Arab horses. (I began to regard the Arab horse as a serious rival for his affection.) He was cagey about his past, too. Though he convinced me that he had indeed come to Australia as a free emigrant, I was not so sure that an innocent desire to make good had actually driven him here. Despite all his denials, I have a suspicion that he left Ireland only a few steps ahead of the Law. For there was a good deal of unrest in his country at the time. And Thomas was just the sort of man who might have become embroiled in some illegal political activity at the behest of a good friend. God knows, he was inclined to overlook the many failings of his fellow draysmen and labourers. 'Oh, there's nothin' wrong wit' Murtha that a spell o'luck won't fix,' he would say. Or 'just a little drap o'the creature for poor Bob, lass, he's that old and cold, 'twould be a pity to turn 'im away yet'.

He was a good man, was Thomas. I cannot deny it. He was naturally generous, and intrinsically honourable. Though he must have regretted our marriage often, he never abandoned me. Sometimes he stayed away for long periods of time, and once I almost despaired, but he always returned. Then, after we moved to Orange, he finally found a vocation that suited him. He was fifty years old by then, and perhaps reluctant to travel; at any rate, he became a dealer. As a dealer he employed his easy nature to our advantage. He could charm the business out of all but the stuffiest men. And though he was not a *wild* success—being far too open-handed—I was at least able to give up my school, eventually.

It must be confessed that Edwin is very much his father's son. Though wiser and more morally upright than Thomas, he has inherited his father's keen delight in varied company. It is no accident that Edwin became an auctioneer and stock agent. In Edwin's nature are happily combined my own fierce determination to account for every penny, and my husband's appreciation of informal social intercourse.

Thomas was not at his best on more formal occasions, however. His speech at Flora's wedding was uncharacteristically stiff, as he stood awkwardly in his brand new dress-coat. At funerals he was a broken reed. Though he never went so far as to shed tears freely, he was liable to lose the power of speech, and had to be kept away from strong spirits. It seemed at one point that he might be unable to attend Emily Louisa's funeral at all—not, at least, in a dignified manner. I had to comb his hair and shave him, for I could not have asked his sons to do it. No son should witness his father in such a state.

'You must not shame us, Thomas McNeilly,' I told him. 'If you cannot hold up your head, then you must stay here.'

He shot me a frantic look, his eyes glazed and bloodshot.

'To say goodbye . . . to me own little girl . . .' he mumbled hoarsely.

'Say nothing. Do you hear? Say nothing, for it will only upset you to speak. I shall speak for us both.'

And I did. And he never once shamed me. But I believe now that the effort of it killed him, for when he returned home he was a different man. Death had marked him out. He recovered neither his spirits nor his health.

If only I had realised sooner!

At first, as I have said, he seemed to be grieving. He lost his appetite and became thin. I thought little of it, until Edwin pointed it out to me. He asked if his father was ill.

'Ill?' I repeated.

'He is so thin.'

'We are all thin, Edwin.'

'But I think that his stomach may be affected. I heard him bringing up his breakfast.'

'Nervous symptoms,' I declared. For Thomas had always been cursed with a tendency to vomit when under emotional strain. He had done so on the morning of his wedding day, and the birth of his children had affected him in a similar fashion. Sometimes our more punishing fights had been cut short by his need for a basin or bucket.

Still, I thought it only decent to make inquiries.

'Is your gut troubling you?' I asked him that evening, as we prepared for bed.

'A little,' he admitted.

'Edwin heard you bringing up your breakfast.'

'I cannot seem t'keep things down,' he complained.

'You couldn't when Charles died.'

'Aye, that's true.'

'Are you costive?'

'A little.'

'I'll get you a dose.'

But the dose had almost no effect. By the middle of June it had become apparent to me that something was genuinely wrong. For while Thomas remained haggard around the face, his belly began to bloat. This puzzled me a great deal. Though I had been bombarding him with constipation cures of every description, I could see little improvement. On the contrary, he was not himself. He seemed constantly tired. He ceased to visit his local public bar of a Friday evening. He had trouble keeping things down, and developed a pain in his abdomen. When he started to vomit blood, I insisted that he visit a doctor.

'It might be Typhoid fever,' I fretted.

'If it was the Typhoid fever, I'd be dead by now,' he rejoined weakly.

'Not at all. My father died of Typhoid fever, or so they say. He lingered for weeks.'

'How could it be Typhoid fever? I've *had* no fever,' Thomas insisted. And despite my pleas, he would not allow me to summon medical help for the longest time. I believe that he was afraid to hear the truth. He must have had some inkling, you see, and preferred to shield us from the worst of it—at least until the last possible moment.

Finally, on the second of July, I took matters into my own hands. I called in Doctor Hemmerman, who had the gravest news to impart. Thomas, he said, was very ill indeed. And all the symptoms indicated that he was suffering from cancer of the stomach.

'You are a strong and capable woman, Mrs McNeilly,' he continued. 'I know of your recent loss and you have my sympathy, but I don't believe that platitudes will satisfy someone of your character. There can be no hope for a victim of this disease. It is already well advanced, and will act swiftly. I would be amazed if Mr McNeilly survived the month.' Though he paused for a moment, I made no comment. I simply sat there, straight-backed, like a marble statue. So he went on. 'The pain can be treated. We have powerful drugs that will ease his passing. The underlying condition, however, cannot be cured. I am really very sorry.'

Some memories are unbelievably excruciating. I hate to think of that day, and of what came after. Four weeks it took, and every hour was torture to me. You children cannot understand, perhaps—not fully—that I had to be strong for all of us. I know how much you loved your father. He was a loveable man. He made you laugh, and bought you silly trinkets, and sang all those pretty Irish songs that I could never master, though I tried at first. The fact that he was away so much made you love him all the more, *I* know. And the pity of it is that you hardly ever saw him on a horse. You would have loved him even better, if you had. He knew just how to handle a horse, and was blessed with a natural seat. When you see someone doing what he was born to do—what God *intended* him to do—there is nothing more worthy of admiration. Yet your father gave up his birthright. He gave it up for me. You cannot support a family on an ostler's wage, not if your wife is bred to higher things.

I used to sit beside him all night towards the end. Poor Edwin—you could not bear to look at him. But I used to look at him for hours and hours. I could hardly believe that he was the same man. He was so frail and wasted, as if that luxuriant hair of his (grey, though still thick) was draining the strength from his body. And his teeth were still so good! Yet all the rest was yellow and shrivelled, and his big, broad hands were like claws, and his eyes were sunk back in his skull as if their light had already been extinguished.

He was often restless at night, when the effect of the morphine began to wear off. Sometimes there were good spells, when he would drink a little broth, and ask about his children (you meant the world to him), and have me read from the newspapers. As time went on, however, there were no good spells. When he was not sunk in a deathly sleep, he was in agonising and unremitting pain. You must remember what it was like—that dreadful noise, which he tried to stifle when he was conscious of his situation at all. And I could do nothing, absolutely nothing, except to remain at his side. No doubt you assume that I felt less, because I was so stoic. But that was not the case. I owed him at least my tendance, and was determined not to falter in my duty. What good would it have done *him*, had I shrunk from his torment and covered my ears when he cried out? It seemed to me that, deficient as I had been as a wife, I would at least not fail him in his final hours. Certainly not through a morbid excess of sentiment.

This was my most earnest prayer. However, there was one moment, on the second-last day, when my heart nearly failed me. I was sitting at his bedside, holding his hand. My eyes were so dry that they felt as if they had been sandpapered. My limbs were as stiff as broom-handles, and I seemed to myself all wrung out, like a parched and twisted old rag. Even when he began to moan and twitch, I sat there regarding him with all the sympathy that you would expect from a chair or a table. I felt that perhaps I had reached my end—that I had no more to give.

Then he came to himself for a moment. 'Charlotte?' he croaked, clinging to my hand with all his little strength. I looked down and met his gaze. There were tears in his eyes, which were fixed on me in the most helpless and pitiful entreaty. His lip trembled. He whimpered like a child. Suddenly, beneath the strong bones of his face and the virile stubble on his chin, I saw a tender soul in desperate need—of *my* care, and *my* aid, and whatever poor solace I could offer. And the carapace around my heart dissolved, and I was all at once moved practically beyond the limits of human endurance. To see this sturdy man, so reduced and broken—I can hardly convey the pathos of it—the *unbearable poignancy*. And I loved him to my very depths: for the first time, perhaps, I loved him as I ought to have loved him, all those many years. I said to him: 'Have no fear, my darling, for I shall never leave you.'

He appeared to derive some comfort from my words, and soon fell asleep again. Afterwards, as the room slowly darkened, I listened to his breathing and thought about my mother. I thought of how she had been forced to watch as George Barton was flogged until his back was a bloody pulp. I thought of how she had begged that he not be flogged a second time—my mother, who did not beg for anything. Though I have never, thankfully, witnessed a flogging, I have once or twice seen the dreadful damage that a scourge can inflict if applied without a qualm. I have read accounts of fleshy fragments scattered across the raw earth, and dogs licking at pools of blood. I have heard my mother describe the sufferings of certain convicts on board the *Cumberland*, when she was travelling to New South Wales. 'It is weak, I know,' she once said, 'but had I stayed on deck during the entire proceedings, I would have been forced to run to their aid. No one with a spark of human feeling could have felt anything except the most profound and visceral sympathy. When the pain is that extreme, one would do *anything* to relieve it. One almost enters into their torment—it is quite unavoidable, though undesirable. I suppose,' she added, 'on some basic level, distress of that kind makes us all kin.'

'Whoso shall receive one such little child in my name receiveth me.' If God is love, then to receive Him is to receive the love that removes all doubt. When I looked at Thomas McNeilly on his deathbed, I saw him in his very essence, and his essence was that of a child. And I could do nothing else but open my heart, for God worked upon it, and tore open all the locks. Only suffering can arouse such love, which is the love of Christ in his agony.

I wonder, now, if my mother felt such love for George Barton when she witnessed his suffering. Can it be that, in my own life's twilight, I have stumbled on the truth? Can it be that her marriage was founded on a pity so tremendous, so stainless and irreproachable, that I have done her a terrible wrong? Or was it their shared suffering that forged the bond between them? For it is common knowledge that when a band of soldiers face death together, they will always be brothers of the heart henceforth. My mother faced death in the company of George Barton. She could not have been sure that they would survive—not when that pistol was placed against her head. Can it be possible that this common experience, so profound and heart-wrenching, made them in some way strangers to everyone except each other? That a kind of dark sympathy held them in its thrall?

If so, I hardly know how to feel. Good or bad? Rewarded or condemned? Excluded, certainly. For I expect that I shall never know the truth. Not, at least, until I appeal to that eternal tribunal, before which everyone may receive the things done in his body, according to that he hath done, whether it be good or bad.

Thirty-seven

1847

My marriage to Thomas McNeilly was not a foregone conclusion, even after our first kiss. Only consider the objections to such a match. Thomas was an Irish Catholic groom, whereas I was a Protestant lady of English extraction, ten years younger than he was. To contemplate so unlikely a union was to foresee all manner of insurmountable difficulties.

Perhaps that is why I shut my eyes to the future, living wholly in the present until circumstances forced me to do otherwise.

With a purpose to my existence, I no longer spent all my time sulking and raging. Instead I was careful not to flout any rules, since this would inevitably have led to further restrictions. I was helpful, meek and industrious. I avoided the subject of Belanglo, at least in my mother's hearing, and did not go riding off on my own. I had no desire for solitude. My longing now was for Thomas's company, though it was not easily assuaged. Oldbury seemed a hive of people; I would be going to accost him when someone—a relative or servant—would suddenly emerge from a room or outbuilding, compelling me to swerve off course. Thomas, moreover, was rarely invited into the house. And I could find very few legitimate reasons for visiting the stables.

Oh, but we were star-crossed lovers! In more ways than one, too, for we did not understand each other in the least. How could we? I hardly knew whether to trust him. He, in turn, did not feel sure of me. 'I could not understand what ye wanted,' he once confessed. This is hardly surprising, since I did not know myself.

Certainly he must have been on tenterhooks after kissing me. There was every chance that he might lose his job. A day passed, and then two, during which we exchanged only intent looks as we passed each other in the yard. Gradually it must have become apparent to him that I had not run and told my mother. Whereupon his wary expression became more speculative, and the muscles in his shoulders relaxed.

I was up and about, limping slightly but otherwise capable, when at last he approached me again. That was in the dairy, one drowsy afternoon. It was the luckiest thing that I should have been alone, and in such a secluded spot; normally my mother skimmed the cream, while it was Sarah's job to churn the butter. My duties tended to keep me either inside the house or somewhere that admitted of no concealment. (The vegetable garden, for example.) And though I was often in the kitchen, so was Sarah. Traffic through the kitchen was such that one could not be sure of a minute's solitude among the cooking pots.

The dairy was a different matter. Because it was generally kept locked, this little stone building was not much frequented. Milk and butter being such precious commodities, my mother was extremely protective of the dairy and its contents. James, for example, was never allowed in. For James could not be trusted with cream.

'If that is you, James, Mama says you mayn't even cross the threshold,' I announced, when I heard the creak of hinges. Then I looked up, and my heart bounded.

'Tisn't yer brother, Miss,' said Thomas, quietly pushing the door shut behind him. 'I came on account o' yer Ma. She says that, if ye start ridin' agin, it must be on Ida. At least 'til ye're well ready for the hack.'

'Oh,' I said. He smelled of horse, and his hair was damp with sweat, and his boots were filthy. Yet I did not care in the least. I thought him in every way admirable.

'Are ye puttin' much weight on that foot?' he inquired, taking a step forward.

'I—I don't know,' was my stammered response.

'Will ye take a turn around the room, Miss? So as I might see how ye're farin'?'

I laid down my skimmer, prepared to comply. But my pride then came to my rescue.

'You want me to parade up and down like a horse, in order to check my gait? I think not.'

'Then I suppose I must examine yer fetlock,' he said, cocking his head and taking another step forward.

'You will do nothing of the kind!' I exclaimed, with a delicious thrill. 'Really, what an idea!'

'Then how am I to judge ye fit?' he said plaintively.

'*I* shall be the judge, not you.'

'Oh, aye?'

'As a matter of fact, I am perfectly fit to ride side-saddle. And was planning to do so tomorrow.'

'If ye cannot dance, ye cannot ride.'

'I beg your pardon?'

'I'll not be lettin' any lass up on a horse who cannot show a trim pair o' heels on a dance floor, beggin' yer pardon, Miss.' He folded his arms. 'Thing is, if yer foot cannot take a sturdy polka, 'twill baulk at a stirrup.'

'You want me to dance a polka?' I could hardly believe my ears. 'And then you will allow me up on a horse?'

'Aye.'

'Is that a promise?'

'Word of honour.'

I promptly executed a quick polka step, somewhat hampered by my voluminous Holland apron.

'There,' I said.

'Ye winced.'

'I did not!'

'I saw't clear as day.'

'Nonsense.' I was growing annoyed. 'We had an agreement. I shall not dance again.'

'Not even wit' me?'

I looked up at him, suddenly breathless. He had drawn very near, and seemed all at once immensely tall.

'If ye can manage a waltz, I'll not say another word about that foot,' he said. 'Once around the room, eh? Slow time.'

Though I made no reply, my expression must have betrayed me. I did not object as he put his arm around my waist. His hand found mine without any help, but without encountering any resistance either. 'One, two, three; one, two, three . . .' he counted, and we were off.

I watched his feet at first, because I did not have the courage to raise my head. His close proximity was almost dizzying; his warmth seemed to enclose me, much as it had before. Soon, however, I was distracted by his awkward gait. It had surprised me that he should have known *how* to waltz, for in those days the waltz was still very much a gentleman's dance, and not one of which my mother's generation thoroughly approved. I myself had learned it in Fanny's drawing room—and Thomas, I later discovered, from watching a ball on board ship. As a consequence, he was not wholly accustomed to the steps, and was inclined to perform a kind of modified mazurka unless firmly restrained.

After a short time, I found that I had to stop.

'I'm sorry, this will not answer,' I said. 'We are not well matched.' The words had barely left my mouth when I grasped their full import, and glanced up in alarm.

His face was gloomy.

'Sure, and weren't we always a poor fit?' he replied, without relaxing his hold. 'Only a fool would think otherwise. And we're neither of us fools.'

My eyes filled with tears, which must have glittered in the dim light. For he clicked his tongue, and shook his head.

'Ah, don't,' he begged. 'I'd not want ye to be unhappy. Not on my account.'

'I am not unhappy on *your* account,' I snivelled. 'In fact—oh, I don't know *what* to think!' My voice broke on a sob, as I ducked my head. 'I am so miserable!'

'Aye, 'tis mortal hard.' Still he would not release me. In fact his grip tightened. 'When I first laid eyes on ye,' he said, and his voice was hoarse, 'I thought to meself: there's the finest, fairest lass I ever saw, though she'd need a firm hand.'

'Oh, no!'

'Just so it's said. I'll never say one word again, if ye'd rather I didn't. Would ye rather I didn't?'

An unfair question! I gloried in such praise, and would have been delighted to hear more. Yet I could not for one moment have admitted it. Instead, I had to dissemble.

'I am miserable because I hate it here,' was my oblique response. 'I hate it here so much! I—I wish I could go away and never come back. Ever.'

'From a spread such as this?' He spoke gently, as if to a child. 'There's worse places than this, lass.'

'You wouldn't understand,' I said, trying to pull away. 'You must think it all very fine, but it is poisoned for me!'

'Then what can I do to make it better?' he asked, with a warm, almost fraternal smile. I hardly knew where to look. My confusion was disorienting.

He seemed to sense this, and did not press his advantage. Rather he backed down, dropping my hand and relinquishing my waist.

'At least let me be a friend to ye,' he said. 'For it seems to me ye're in sore need o' one.'

'Oh, I am! It is so *lonely*, here, and my mother hates me!'

'Ah, no—'

'She does! It's true! You don't understand! Everything is ruined, and I cannot—it's so *wretched*—I might as well be dead!' Glimpsing the quizzical look in his eye, I turned on him. 'You don't know what happened here! You know *nothing* of what happened! I was once fed manure in that very yard outside, and now must live here as if it were all forgotten!' Seeing his brows snap together in sudden shock, I clapped my hands over my mouth and ran for the door. I was full of tumultuous emotions: shame and desire, fury and despair.

Thomas caught me before I could escape.

'Wait,' he said. 'Not yet. Wait till ye're settled.'

'I can't—I can't—'

'Listen. What if someone sees ye come out o' here like this, and me followin' along behind? 'Twill do neither of us no good.' Seeing me wring the tears from my eyes with my knuckles, he released my elbow, and wound an arm around my shoulders. 'There now, don't fret,' he crooned, squeezing me hard. 'There might have bin bad times, but ye'll face 'em down well enough. I've seen ye face down that old cock when ye're collectin' eggs, and there's no one else hereabouts can do it! The way ye raise yer chin and straighten yer back as if to say: "I'm Miss Charlotte Atkinson, and ye'll not forget it in a hurry!"'

This elicited a watery smile. 'Is that really what I do?'

''Tis.'

'When I'm collecting the eggs?'

'And leadin' a horse. And fightin' wit' yer Ma.'

'I like the way *you* pat the horses. And talk to them,' I said shyly. Whereupon he swallowed, and looked away.

'Aye . . . well . . .' he mumbled. 'It gets so as you have to talk, no matter who ye're talkin' to.'

'You can talk to me.'

We looked at each other for an extended moment. I do not know what might have occurred, had we not heard a voice close by. It was Richard's voice, raised in the yard. He was calling for Thomas.

Thomas and I sprang apart as if we had been scorched.

'Aye! Comin' directly!' Thomas cried, and flashed me a curious, sheepish little grin. Then he departed the dairy, carefully closing the door behind him.

I did not speak to him again that day, though I thought about him often. And the next morning, when I presented myself at the stables clad in my riding habit, our conversation was stilted and formal, owing to the close proximity of Richard in the garden.

You must understand that circumstances were against us. Though my dream was to ride off with Thomas into the bush, I had as much hope of attaining it as I had of reaching the moon. We could ride together around the yard or the paddocks, exercising our horses at a gentle trot. We could snatch a few stolen moments in the stables, while saddling Sovereign or brushing down Ida. But there would never be any rambling rides for *us*—not if I was to keep my unsullied reputation. 'Oh no,' my mother remarked, when I raised the subject. 'What would people say? Riding off into the forest with the groom? Oh no.'

'But you told me that I must not go riding alone, Mama.'

'And you shall not. You may take James with you. Or one of your sisters.'

'But my sisters cannot ride Sovereign. And *you* have insisted that I must use Ida!'

'Only as long as your foot continues to trouble you. When it is better, you may ride Sovereign—though never at a gallop—and take Emily or Louisa on the cob.'

'But—'

'I will not be defied, Charlotte. You are not a child any longer. You know perfectly well what people would think, if you were to be seen riding alone with the likes of Thomas McNeilly.'

'Yes, I know what people would think!' Denied my dearest wish, I became reckless in my anger. 'No doubt they thought the same thing when *you* were seen riding alone with the likes of *George Barton*—though it never seemed to trouble *you* in the least!'

My mother reddened, but did not strike back. Instead she studied me pensively over her fancywork, slowly unpicking an errant stitch. She seemed distracted by some troubling thought.

'It seems to me,' she said at last, 'that you are already spending a little too much time in Thomas's company. I have said so before, and I shall repeat my warning—nothing good will come of it. I understand that you both share an interest in horseflesh, but he is not your equal, and you should bear that in mind.'

I swallowed, my flash of temper suddenly extinguished. It occurred to me that my mother must have some inkling of how I felt, since she herself had followed a similar path. But did she truly understand the depth of my devotion to Thomas McNeilly?

I sincerely hoped not. For once the truth came out, she would make sure that Thomas and I were forever sundered. And that would be unbearable.

'Really, Mama,' I said, deciding that the best defence was a vigorous offence, 'I wonder why you are continually dwelling on such sordid, indelicate subjects. Could it be because you yourself have been a martyr to unsavoury gossip? Perhaps that accounts for your acute sensitivity, and your suspicious mind. Next thing you will be putting ideas in my head.'

'Charlotte—'

'I really do not see why you are so concerned about the neighbours. They think the worst of us already, owing to certain *incidents* in the *past*. How can I possibly disgrace myself in their eyes when our whole family is already disgraced?'

'That is *not true!*'

'Then why do we never see anyone, except at church? I think it most extraordinarily hypocritical to scold me for talking to the groom, when you yourself married your overseer, and used to ride out to Budgong with convicts—'

'*That is enough!*'

'—which fact happened to be dragged through the public courts, thanks to George Barton, so that the whole *world* came to know it—'

'Are you trying to punish me for the past? Is that what this is all about?' My mother had shot to her feet, and was gathering up her workbox as a prelude to leaving the room. 'Because if it is, Charlotte, then let me point something out. While you might punish *me* with your indecorous behaviour, you will punish yourself far more. You will regret it *for the rest of your life!*'

'As you have?'

'Augh!' She slammed down the lid of her workbox. 'You are *impossible!*'

And she left me there, in possession of the sitting room. I thought myself rather clever for having thrown her off the scent. While she might once have suspected a love affair, she would now view my dalliance with Thomas as an elaborate attempt to wring some sort of admission or apology out of her. And this, I decided, could only work to my advantage. Why, her response might be to ignore me entirely! To show herself unaffected by my conduct!

It never occurred to me that she might be correct.

It never crossed my mind that I would indeed come to regret my indecorous conduct, which—as she so acutely promised—would punish me far more than it had ever punished her.

Thirty-eight

During the next few months, my attention was fixed on Thomas McNeilly. I do recall one or two events unconnected with my own affairs: in April, for instance, Bishop Broughton laid the foundation stone for a new church at Berrima. But on the whole, I remember nothing of early 1847 except those shining moments that I spent with Thomas. *They* remain as clear and bright as stars in a night sky.

Mostly we met to exercise the horses. Thomas would mount Sovereign, and I would mount Ida, and we would walk or trot in a genteel fashion around the property, always within sight of the house. On these occasions we were very self-conscious, and rarely spoke of anything except equestrian matters.

Sometimes, when the gig was required, there would be no need to exercise the cob. If Thomas was sent to Berrima or Sutton Forest, I would usually secure a place beside him. I never enjoyed the good fortune of having Thomas to myself during any one of these trips. But at least I could watch him, surreptitiously, as I conversed with Louisa about nesting, or with James about wool. It was a strange and poignant pleasure. Though I was convinced that someone must surely notice how conscious we were of each other, nobody ever did. Once, at Berrima, I had the good fortune to accompany Thomas to the Post Office while my mother was buying ribbon. Unfortunately, however, there were so many people about that we were unable to converse freely.

Our most precious moments together occurred in the stables, where I insisted on helping him with the saddles and harness. We stole a few kisses there (under Bennett's baleful eye) and talked as lovers generally talk, of beauty, and sadness, and when next we might meet. We spoke of the distant past, but not of the distant future. I found it comforting to describe scenes that were never discussed within my family; on one memorable occasion I confessed that I had tried to shoot George Barton, and that Barton had then tried to shoot me. It all came spilling out in a rush, like bile, and Thomas held me to stop me from shaking. He rocked me back and forth, with my head tucked under his chin. 'Ah, Jaysus,' he sighed. 'That's a hard thing t'carry in yer heart.'

He, in turn, would make reference to his own straitened childhood—to potato blight, and empty bellies, and stealing apples, and the money spent on clothes for dead infants. Though it was not a very coherent picture that he painted, I heard enough to understand that he was haunted by his own ghosts. Nevertheless, he seemed more generally content than I was—perhaps because, in his own words, he had 'left most of his troubles in Ireland'.

I replied gloomily that there were no vast oceans dividing me from George Barton. The last I'd heard, he was farming near Bathurst. But that was not to say he wouldn't return.

'If he does, I shall kill him,' was my heartfelt promise. 'I shall get the gun from the study, and shoot him in the head.'

'That ye won't,' said Thomas.

'I will!'

'No, no. There'll be no need for that. Not while I'm here. Ye've nothing to fear while I'm here.'

'Oh, Thomas.' We were sitting together on the mounting block, so I was able to fling my arms around his neck without undue effort. 'Don't ever leave! I'll die if you leave!'

'Now, why would I want to do that?' he replied tenderly, smoothing the hair from my forehead. 'Unless I was to take ye wit' me.'

'I wish we *could* go somewhere! Just the two of us, with no one else to pry and scold . . .'

'Aye.' His voice was suddenly glum. 'That would be a fine thing.'

'Somewhere Barton would never find us. Somewhere *Mama* would never find us.' And I would make my fanciful suggestions, without for one moment thinking seriously about the future—which frightened me so much that I had no wish to confront it. For if I married Thomas, it would be in the face of such opposition as I had never endured, and might never survive. Whereas if I did *not* marry Thomas, then I would surely perish.

Thomas, I think, was more practically minded. He must have taken at least a little time to consider his options, perhaps because he was less inclined to live in a dream of romance. Men rarely are, I have found. It has always surprised me that Eve gave the apple to Adam, since in my experience it is never the woman whose thoughts first drift towards sins of the flesh. Certainly it is never the woman who takes the first, definite step in that direction. Poor Thomas; it must have been very hard for him. He was a passionate man, and kisses are rarely enough for passionate men. All those childish embraces must have driven him halfway to distraction. During the course of our long and volatile marriage, he compared me unfavourably to at least three other women of his acquaintance whose favours were bestowed on him long before we met. (I even have a suspicion that there was another, some time in the '60s, when he was working on the drays.) At any rate, he was not inexperienced. At least not with women of his own class.

But I was another proposition entirely. I have no doubt that he was far more tentative with me than he would have been with

Sarah or with Mary Ann. This was partly because he lacked confidence, and partly because he could foresee no happy resolution. Thomas knew that I had not reached my majority. As a consequence, I would be unable to wed without my mother's permission. And even *with* her permission, he was not sure that I would actually stand by him if it came to the point. 'A young lass livin' on a cloud' was how he described me, long afterwards. I rather fancy that the women of his class learn to abandon their illusions at a far younger age than I did. Thomas therefore never felt utterly confident of my attachment. 'I did wonder if I were buildin' my castle on a bed o' smoke,' he once confessed.

All the same, he was willing to build his castle. And that meant making plans. I am absolutely convinced that he never, at any time, intended to play the heartless seducer. Nor was he trying to marry money. He loved me—of that I am sure. But he did not *know* me, any more than I knew him. We each fashioned our own idol in the shape of our beloved, and invested it with all manner of improbable virtues. We could do this so easily because we had such different backgrounds. And while I do not believe for an instant that he was motivated by greed, it cannot have escaped his notice that I would receive at least a small sum on attaining my majority.

For this reason alone, he would have been a fool to aim for anything *but* marriage.

Not that he pressed his suit with any great vigour. He was, as I said, very tentative. When I spat out my violent tales of George Barton, he would gravely inquire as to whether I thought all matches 'of that kind' were doomed from the start. Or he would make vague reference to other, more successful unions between ladies and their overseers. (Had not Mrs Samuel Hassall married *her* overseer after the death of her first husband?) When I praised my father, Thomas would observe that to be a good husband and father must constitute the finest ambition of any Christian man.

'Though it were poor and hungry, there weren't never no fightin' in my home—not between my Ma and Pa,' he assured me. 'And there's many a wealthy marriage that's never so blessed.' By means of such cunning little hints, he probably hoped to win me over before broaching the subject more openly. I do not know. We never discussed it. Because events overtook us long before he made up his mind as to how he should proceed.

It was all on account of that wretched flower.

You may not be surprised to learn that Thomas McNeilly sometimes picked flowers for me. These were not lavish bouquets, but modest single blooms which he found occasionally among the paddocks and scrubland of Oldbury, or along the road to Berrima. Though he had no particular interest in botany, he had been raised to regard the Floral Tribute as a correct and acceptable gift to bestow on his sweetheart. And I received them in the same spirit, taking care that they did not attract too much attention.

One day he brought me from Berrima a fine example of *Banksia spinnulosa*, which he thought 'most wild and fierce', and not unlike his 'fiery darlin''. If you are familiar with the Banksia plant, you will know that its blooms do not lend themselves very easily to concealment, being large, exuberant and often highly coloured. This particular specimen, though not a bright and vibrant yellow (as they so often are), was rather an unusual shade of reddish purple, and easily as big as my hand. I saw at once that I should not be able to press it for a keepsake, as I had with his kangaroo-apple blossom. So I decided, rather foolishly, that I would sketch it in watercolours.

Not being *utterly* brainless, I chose a secluded spot for this undertaking. I set up my easel out near the stockyard, beneath a mighty eucalypt, where I hoped to remain undisturbed. From a distance, it would surely look as if I was attempting a landscape, or perhaps a view of the house.

My mistake was to borrow Mama's camel-hair pencil.

Inspired by my industry, perhaps, she soon came in search of it—surprising me before I had a chance to conceal anything. 'Oh!' she exclaimed. 'A botanical drawing! I thought you must be painting Oldbury.' Her gaze then alighted on the Banksia flower. 'What a *very* unusual tint!' she exclaimed. 'I don't believe I have ever seen anything comparable. Where did you find it?'

'Oh . . . um . . .'

'Louisa will want to see it. You know that she takes a particular interest in that *genus*. Is the bush anywhere nearby? It must be, I suppose, since the head is fresh-cut.' She glanced about her, eyes narrowed. But as I remained silent (struck dumb, if you want the truth) her wandering regard was drawn back to my face. 'Is the bush nearby?' she repeated.

'I—I—'

'You have not been out *riding*, Charlotte?'

'No!'

'No, of course not. I've seen you about.' She frowned. 'Where *did* it come from? Show me.'

Inextricably trapped, I had to resort to a careless, indifferent tone that cannot have been altogether convincing.

'Oh, Thomas found it, not I. You must ask him,' I said.

'Thomas found it?'

'He knows how interested we are in native flora. I told him to watch for unusual specimens.'

Whereupon I applied myself vigorously to my sketch, conscious of Mama's searching gaze. 'I see,' she said at last, before quietly withdrawing. Her restraint on the topic made me very uneasy. I was on edge for the rest of the day, expecting some form of interrogation that never, in fact, occurred. My mother's preoccupied air at dinner made me doubly anxious. I therefore refrained from approaching the stables, keeping to the house and applying myself diligently to petticoats and dusters until the next morning, when I was instructed to go riding with Louisa.

I forgot to mention my rides with Louisa. They had begun soon after my ankle mended, when I was given permission to mount the hack. Because I complained bitterly at being restricted to the yard and paddocks, my mother had made a suggestion. Though I was not to go riding by myself, she had no objection to my accompanying Louisa, who also liked to explore the bush roundabout. 'Sustained and gentle exercise will do your sister the world of good,' my mother remarked. 'Only you must promise not to leave her and go galloping off to indulge some whim, Charlotte. If I ever hear that she has been left alone, you will never sit on a horse again, is that clear?'

Bound by half-a-dozen promises, I was finally allowed to flee Oldbury—at least for short periods. During the autumn of 1847, Louisa and I explored Gingenbullen, the eastern end of Black Bob's Creek, and some of the wild country around Berrima. These were largely wordless excursions, since we rarely dismounted, and Sovereign was so much higher than the cob. But we fared pretty well together, despite the fact that I was always slightly discontented in any company other than my sweetheart's, and Louisa's fascination with even the humblest woody nut far outstripped my own. Occasionally she would get down to make a quick sketch, during which time I would take the opportunity (if the terrain was sufficiently accommodating) to kick Sovereign into a brief gallop, from which I would return breathless, sweaty, and very much improved in spirits. Louisa and I made a pact regarding these episodes. We each promised not to tell Mama that we had separated, even for so short a spell. 'For if we do, she will forbid us to go out again,' Louisa acknowledged, 'and I shall *never* find a native cherry.'

On the morning after the Banksia episode, Louisa came to inform me that, the day being very crisp and fine, Mama wanted us both to take some exercise on the horses. Such a command, though unusual, was not unprecedented; my mother had once or twice before made a similar request, since she was always careful of Louisa's health, and was determined that my sister should not spend too much time 'hunched over her desk', ruining her posture and cramping her lungs. Nevertheless, I was suspicious. It occurred to me that Mama might wish to observe my behaviour towards Thomas, whose own response might also be of some interest to her. I was therefore quite surprised when she did not follow me to the stables. The thought crossed my mind: could she be hiding somewhere? Then I wondered if she had enlisted Louisa as her spy.

For Louisa came with me, laden down with her sketchbook and pencils and magnifying glass. She was thirteen, by then, but still quite small, with a pale face, a sylph-like form, and hands that seemed permanently blue with cold. I remember her as always wearing my cast-offs, which did not suit her colouring as well as they had mine. Though not exactly shy, she had little to say on subjects outside her scope of interest, and rarely spoke to Thomas unless he addressed her. This he did rather gently and nervously. Her delicate health was a subject so endlessly discussed about the place that he had got into the habit of regarding her as one might regard an expensive crystalline vessel, liable to break at the slightest mishandling. For this reason, I think, he avoided her wherever possible—much as he avoided having anything to do with our snowy table-linen and fine English tea-service.

But Louisa was far more robust than her appearance suggested. She sprang up onto Ida without difficulty, and with only the smallest degree of assistance. I myself mounted Sovereign in a similar manner, hardly daring even to *look* at Thomas, who had the wit not to let his hands linger at my waist. Something about my demeanour warned him off; we exchanged just a few, terse remarks as I prepared for my ride, and were indeed so brusque with each other that anyone watching must have wondered at our curious conduct.

Louisa did, I am sure. Though she said not a word during the first portion of our ride, she threw me a number of pensive, sidelong glances, each of them calculated to raise an ominous tumult in my breast. We had agreed to head towards Mereworth, if only because a westerly course would ensure that the sun was not in our eyes. You may recall this route. I have already described the flat stretch of cleared land that intervened between Oldbury and Mereworth. It made the area quite a favourite with me, and provided Louisa with an incomparable source of butterflies during the summer. In winter, of course, the pickings were not so various—and at first, upon gaining the meadow, we saw nothing that merited stopping or even pausing. Only as we drew near to the unbroken mass of trees on the other side did a flash of black tail mark the abrupt departure of a wallaby. (Possibly a *Petrogale penicillata*, though it was far too quick to be sure.)

'We shall never catch up,' I remarked, as it vanished into the trees. 'You would not want to chase it, would you?'

'No,' said Louisa.

'Though we *could* take that path. We might flush out something else if we do.' Reining in Sovereign, I turned to my sister. 'Wherever we go, I want to return this way and get in a bit of a gallop. If you have no objection?'

Louisa shook her head.

'It won't be more than five minutes,' I added, 'and I shall wait for you at the other side. There is absolutely nothing else around here except the road. And you know how bad *that* would be for the poor boy's hooves. Thomas would never stand for it.' I saw her gaze slide away, and was immediately unnerved. 'Is something wrong?' I inquired, too sharply. 'Are you feeling ill?'

'No.'

'If you are feeling ill, Louisa, we had best head back straight away, or Mama will have my hide.'

'No, no. We cannot. I mean—' To my immense surprise, Louisa began to rub her forehead. She only rubbed her forehead during moments of acute anxiety. 'What time is it?' she asked. 'How long have we been out?'

'How long?' I had been entrusted with Mama's little jewel-encrusted watch, which was pinned to my tucker on every one of these mounted excursions. Usually, the watch was accompanied by a stern lecture regarding the necessity of being back within two or three hours. 'We have been out for fifty-five minutes,' I said, upon consulting the instrument. 'Why? She told me that we had two hours—three, if we were inclined.'

'At *least* two hours,' Louisa corrected.

'What?'

'She told *me* that we must not return before the end of two hours. Three, if possible.' As I stared at her in utter perplexity, Louisa rubbed her pale, puckered forehead again. 'She even told me to head west.'

'*She* told *you*?'

'Yes.' Louisa's voice was very small. 'I am so sorry, Charlotte. It didn't occur to me, until just now. Of course, this would give her the perfect opportunity, with you out of the way . . .'

Still I was at a complete loss. She must have seen it, because her colourless little face became a positive mask of anguish.

'Oh, Charlotte!' she quavered. 'I think it so *very* wrong! And in such an underhanded fashion, too! But I had *no idea*—you must believe me—'

'No idea about *what*?' I exclaimed. 'What *are* you talking about?'

'Why, Thomas McNeilly, of course.' Seeing me flush, Louisa blinked back tears, and croaked: 'She wants to have him dismissed.'

Every muscle in my body must have tightened, because Sovereign suddenly lurched sideways. Bringing him back into

444

line kept me preoccupied for a few seconds, while Louisa rushed to explain herself.

'She never said as much to *me*, but I overheard her speaking to Emily last night. She was asking if Emily had ever witnessed . . . well, anything. Because you were spending too much time in Thomas's company, Mama said. And when Emily told her no, she said that she would have to dismiss Thomas before matters became too serious.' Gazing up at me with brimming eyes, she added: 'You do like him, don't you, Charlotte? I saw it at once, this morning. I never noticed, but—oh dear! I saw it at once, and I thought how cruel—how wrong—I don't want you to hate me for the rest of your life—ah!'

I had reached out and grabbed her wrist, so abruptly that even peaceful, plodding Ida started.

'*What else did she say?*' I hissed.

'Ow—'

'What did she *say?*' I shook the poor girl's arm. 'Tell me!'

'Nothing! I mean—I don't know! I didn't hear! Charlotte, be *careful!*'

I released her before she could lose control of her horse. My mind was racing. What should I do? Ride back to the house? But what if Thomas had already been expelled? Which road would he take? The road to Sutton Forest or the road to Berrima? Whichever way he took, he would be walking. That much was certain.

'She *told* you to go west?' I gasped. 'Are you sure?'

'Yes, but—'

'Then he must be heading east.' I was sure of it. 'If he were heading north, she would have told you to go south.'

'I suppose so.'

'And it makes sense, if he's walking. Berrima is too far away. The Crossroads, too. Perhaps she sent him off with a letter for the Throsbys, or someone else along the Argyle Road. Someone who will take him on. Do you think?'

'I—I don't know.' Louisa was barely audible. 'Perhaps. Charlotte, what are you going to do?'

'What do you think?' I tapped Sovereign's flank and turned his head. But before I could bring him around, Louisa caught at my reins.

It was a brave act, since she had never found Sovereign easy to handle.

'Wait,' she said.

'Let *go*!' I raised my whip, fiercely. 'Don't you *dare* interfere!'

'I shan't! I haven't! I told you, didn't I?' She took a deep breath as she relinquished her grip. 'It was wrong of her, Charlotte, but you must forgive her. She only did it for your sake, I *know* she did.'

'Hah!'

'She is worried about you. Can you blame her? She wants you to be happy. She wants us all to be happy.'

If I had been less enraged, I would have pitied Louisa. As it was, I possessed just enough self-restraint to realise that she was speaking from the heart, and was thoroughly well-intentioned. What immense courage she had! For she put her case clearly and gravely, though I held a whip in my hand, and had every advantage over her in height, weight and reach.

Louisa never betrayed me. All her life, she bowed to my mother's every whim—though not where I was concerned. With her immense powers of penetration, formidable even in her earliest youth, Louisa saw exactly who I was, and respected me for it.

I honour her. I miss her. And I wish that I had thanked her, all those years ago.

But I did not.

'If Mama had wanted us to be happy,' I spat, 'she would never have married George Barton.'

'Charlotte—'

'You'll have to make your own way back. She will have your head when she finds out.'

'Wait! Charlotte!'

'I can't. I'm sorry.' With a nudge and a slap, I urged Sovereign forward. 'I have to go.'

'But where? Charlotte? *Where are you going?*'

I made no reply. How could I, when I did not know myself?

All I knew was that I had to reach Thomas.

Thirty-nine

Of all the rides that I have ever taken, none remains with me as clearly as my sprint towards Sutton Forest. The day was clear but cold, with an occasional chill breeze. The landscape for the most part wore the dull, unvariegated mantle of winter, save for here and there a dusting of early grevillea blossom or the sudden splash of a Banksia flower. White cockatoos soared overhead, and a scrub wren burst from the undergrowth as I thundered past. Four or five wandering cattle, dotted around the pastures like glossy brown anthills, raised their heads in unison at the sound of my approach.

Apart from these few creatures—and the snorting, sweating hack beneath me—I seemed alone in the universe. Though vaguely worried that I might encounter someone before reaching Thomas, this concern was not foremost in my mind. On the contrary, I was obliged to fix almost my full attention on the horse, and on the terrain opening out in front of him. For having crossed the cleared land, I had to thread my way through a thick stretch of shrubs and trees before I hit the road to Sutton Forest. I have already described your typical bush-ride, with all its attendant perils. Even a stockman's training is no certain defence against the unexpected obstacle that might bring a horse down on a headlong charge through wooded country: the sudden, steep slope; the hidden wombat-hole; the rearing outcrop of boulders. Commonsense decreed that I slow down during this leg of my journey, and I did. But even at a more deliberate pace I was nearly thrown when Sovereign wheeled unexpectedly, his poor nerves jangled by an explosive flurry of wings.

I lost my hat at one point. It was dragged off by a clawing branch, and I surrendered it without a second thought. The whip was another matter. I dropped my whip as I fumbled with both hands to wrench Sovereign's head around when he shied. And this was not to my discredit, let me assure you. But I could not dismount, knowing how difficult it would be to regain my seat unassisted. So I had to press on, snatching at twigs until I secured one supple enough to serve as a decent goad.

I make no complaint about the hack, incidentally. He was perfectly amenable, though somewhat confused. With a stronger, more experienced hand on his reins he would no doubt have proven a steadier mount. When we reached the road, moreover, he accelerated with only the mildest encouragement, despite the dreadful condition of what was really no more than a goat-track. I tried to keep him on the grass verges, of course. One would hardly *choose* to canter over ruts and pebbles, no matter how eager one might be to cover a distance. And a lady's weight cannot compare to a gentleman's, when all is said and done.

Nevertheless, I made some unreasonable demands on Sovereign, who rose to the occasion most nobly. Perhaps he was calmed by the familiar surroundings. Perhaps the clear delineation of his route, or the absence of encroaching foliage, invigorated him. Whatever the cause, he seemed all at once to sense my desperation, and threw his whole heart into a fervent but disciplined burst of speed.

We fairly flew down the road, unhindered and unobserved. I can still feel the power of it. Nowadays, in my last decline, I would exult at such a rhythm beneath my hands and my feet, but I was then engulfed by a terrible fear. As the road unfurled beneath us, and every crest that we gained revealed only another empty stretch of hard-baked dirt, I asked myself: Was I wrong? Has he gone another way? Have I *missed* him?

I knew that, if I had miscalculated, I would have to confront my mother. I would have to *force* directions out of her—since there could be no other way of finding Thomas in all that far, wide country. If he was not heading east, then he could be anywhere.

And then I saw him.

We were approaching the more settled district at the edge of Sutton Forest. The roof of All Saints was in clear sight. Fences were beginning to replace thickets and groves. A faint smell of wood-smoke distracted me for an instant, like the buzzing of an importunate fly; I had to shake off a sudden pang of hunger to fix my attention on the shuffling silhouette ahead of me.

I would not have recognised him by his gait, which had lost all of its fluid confidence. His head was bowed. Each step looked hesitant. He would stop, then move on, only to stop again.

The angle of his jaunty slouch hat, however, was unmistakable.

'Thomas!' I screamed, and it was as if all my strength left me with that cry. Sovereign felt it. He began to slow immediately, while my hands dropped and loosened on his neck.

Thomas spun around. There was not one second's pause; he discarded his swag and rushed forward to catch me on my way to the ground, so that I slid straight into his arms. We clung to each other without a thought for anyone who might be watching among the fields and gardens. Thomas seemed impervious even to the horse.

'She threatened to set the dogs on me,' Thomas panted, in tones of despair. 'What could I do?'

I was breathless from my energetic ride, and could only clutch at him even more frantically, gulping down lungfuls of air. My knees were beginning to shake.

'I wouldn't have failed ye,' he croaked. 'I swear, I would have found some way—someone to write a letter, or bring a message . . .'

I burst into tears.

'Ah, don't—don't.' He kissed my hair repeatedly. 'It breaks my heart.'

'You said you would never leave me!' I wailed, causing him to clasp me so tightly that he almost crushed my ribs.

'Jaysus, Charlotte, I don't want to leave ye!' His voice cracked. 'I love ye so much—ye're the finest lass in all the world—I'd marry ye now, if I could, but how can I? Ye're not twenty-one—t'wouldn't be legal.'

'You shan't go.' I was absolutely determined, though I sobbed and shuddered. 'You *shan't go!*'

'I'll stay close. I won't desert ye. I'll find work at t'Crossroads, or—or down on a station, by here. I'll come visit whenever I can—'

'No.' I wiped my damp cheeks as he caught his breath.

'Darlin', I'll wait. I swear, I'll wait. 'Twouldn't be more'n two years, and I'd wait forever.'

'No,' I repeated, with a set jaw. 'I shall *not* wait. Why should I?' Peering up into his haggard face, I drummed my fists on his chest. 'We don't have to wait! Not if my mother agrees.'

'But—'

'She will if she has to. We can *force* her to agree. It wouldn't be hard.' His stunned expression made me impatient. 'Don't you see, Thomas? We can do it now. If we get away from here quickly, and go somewhere for the night, do you think she would object to a wedding afterwards? She will have us married off so quickly, it will knock the breath out of you!'

'Get away?' he repeated, in utter perplexity. 'But—'

'Together! The two of us!' I wanted to shake him, I was so distraught. 'Isn't that what you *want*?'

'Aye.' He still seemed dazed, however. 'Only—where could we go? There's no one about would take us in, not like this.'

'I know *exactly* where to go. Except that we must ride there and . . .' I craned my neck to study Sovereign, who was still heaving like a pair of bellows '. . . and we have but one horse,' I finished.

Thomas studied me, then the horse. The knot between his brows was beginning to unravel.

'Sovereign's stout enough,' he said in a reflective manner. 'Provided we take it slow. But Charlotte—'tis downright thievery, takin' this horse.'

'It is *not*!' I insisted. 'Sovereign is as much mine as he is hers. *She* does not own the estate! In any event, she will know that I have him. And she would rather die than tell the police, I assure you. My only concern is the side-saddle. It will not support both of us.'

'Then I will take it off,' Thomas decided. And without further ado he began to unfasten the girth and crupper, while I held Sovereign's bridle. The contents of my saddlebags were transferred to his own modest bundle, which he slung over his shoulder. The bags themselves, and the saddle attached to them, were left abandoned at the roadside.

'You mean to say that we shall be riding bareback?' was my nervous inquiry, when it became apparent that this would in fact be our only option. At which point I received a smile so warm and tender, I almost melted away in its beam.

'*I'll* be doin' the ridin',' Thomas answered. 'Yer only concern'll be to hold on tight. Can ye do that for me?'

'Yes.'

'And not slide about, nor fret the poor beast wit' any twitchin' or squeakin'?'

'No.'

'Up ye get, then.'

It is no easy task, mounting a bare-backed horse, especially when one is clad in long skirts. Thomas had to lift me and follow on behind; even with my feeble assistance, he struggled and heaved as if he were climbing a sheer brick wall. Sovereign was *most* unimpressed, jibing and staggering and rolling his eyes. The weight must have been considerable, for all that I was so thin, and Thomas as trim as a man of his height could be. I was sure that the creature would baulk. Though Thomas calmed him with a firm hand and a soothing voice, I was convinced that we were courting disaster.

'He will throw us,' I gasped, perched precariously in front of Thomas, who promptly shook his head.

'Nay, he'll do us proud. Long as we don't press 'im too hard, nor take 'im too far.'

'And how far is too far?' I twisted my head to look my beloved straight in the eye. 'It is no small distance to Belanglo, Thomas.'

The word hit him like a slap. His head jerked back, and his mouth dropped open.

Beneath us, Sovereign shifted uneasily.

'Belanglo!' Thomas exclaimed.

'Mama will never go there. She will *never* look for us there, believe me. I know.'

'But Charlotte—Belanglo—that's a perilous place.' He reached around me, steadying Sovereign with a pat on the neck. 'There's any number o' thieves in them gullies. Why, I've heard tell that yer own mother—'

'What about her?' I nearly jumped out of my skin. 'What do you know about my mother?'

'Well—weren't she bailed up at Belanglo?' He frowned at me. 'There's bin talk of't.'

'That was a long time ago.' Somehow, I could not relinquish this notion of mine. It had taken hold of me with an obsessive force. 'She was visiting our station there. It is deserted now. We can shelter in the old hut, and no one will ever find us. There is a creek, and I have dried fruit with me. We shall want for nothing.'

'Charlotte—'

'Then tomorrow we shall ride back to the house! It can be no more than ten or fifteen miles! Even if we travel slowly, we should reach it by nightfall!'

'Have y'ever bin there?'

'To Belanglo? No, but there is a road. We must follow the road.'

'Past all o' them thieves and cutthroats?'

'Well, what do *you* suggest?' I was beginning to lose my temper. 'Put up at an inn? Or at some settler's house? It will defeat the purpose, don't you see? We shall find ourselves sleeping in a room with all manner of people, and that will give my mother the perfect excuse! She will say that we were chaperoned—why, she would swear in *witnesses* to stop us from marrying!'

'Aye, but Charlotte—'

'What do we have that any thief would want, except the horse? And we can always *walk* back.' I glared at him. 'Or perhaps you think the prize is not worth the risk?'

'Ah, no.'

'In which case I shall say goodbye and return to Oldbury! Since I can offer no *other* solution!'

My voice cracked on a sob, for I was in a great deal of nervous distress, and quite prepared to launch myself to the ground. I even began to wriggle about in preparation for an impassioned departure. Whereat Sovereign tossed his head in protest, and Thomas grabbed my waist.

'Don't be a bloody fool!' he barked. 'Sit still, or ye'll fall!'

'What do *you* care? If I'm such a bloody fool?'

It was, I think, the first time that I had ever used vulgar language. Certainly it surprised Thomas. He blinked, and raised his eyebrows, and cracked a reluctant smile. 'Ah, Charlotte,' he said. 'Them bad words sound so pretty, a-comin' out o' yer little mouth.'

'Let me go!'

'Not I. Not ever.' And he planted a kiss on my lips that left me light-headed.

Then he clicked his tongue, and nudged poor Sovereign into a brisk walk.

'To Belanglo, then,' he declared. 'And I pray to all the holy saints and martyrs that we don't get lost.'

We did not, as it happened. Our route to the Old South Road was simple enough, if risky for being well frequented. We went out of our way to avoid Mereworth. On the Old South Road itself we stayed well clear of the Kentish Arms (which no longer belonged to my uncle) but encountered a pair of teamsters on a loaded dray, heading for Sydney. They saluted us with speculative looks, their attention caught by Sovereign's bare back. 'They'll report us to the first trap they come across,' Thomas observed with a sigh. 'We'd best get off this road right sharpish.' There was no need for us to tempt fate by passing close to the Wilmots' handsome spread, or the tumbledown convict stockade closer to Berrima. Instead we rode south for a short distance before reaching a rough track that plunged into the brooding forest to the west. 'This is it,' I said. 'Mama pointed it out once, do you remember? We were on the gig—'

'Aye.' Thomas slowed our pace as we approached the intersection, which was distinguished by some of the most cavernous ruts and gouges that I have ever seen. It looked as if the world's heaviest dray had taken a right-hand turn during a thunderstorm of Biblical proportions. 'I do recall mention of all t' fine, new work bein' done to open up this part o' the country.' He eyed the jagged folds and corrugations of dried mud. 'Though I'd have to say, this looks to me as if someone dragged a log through them trees, chained to a team o' bullocks.'

'Please, Thomas, let us quit the main road. People are always riding along here—the Gordons and the McPhersons and the Morrices. And they all know me by sight.'

'Sure, and we shouldn't linger,' Thomas agreed. 'Last thing we want is the Reverend Stone flaggin' us down, on his way out to the Crossroads.'

So we set off, 'through tangled forests, and through dangerous ways', with only the vaguest notion of where we were going. It astonishes me to think that we should have been as bold and foolhardy as we were. Believe me when I say that the woods around Belanglo are not easily penetrated. Even now, they present a formidable challenge; something about them repels invasion, and there still exist no thriving communities dotted among the dour stands of shadowy timber, which seem to absorb all light and sound. Do not assume that my impression of the country is tainted by early associations. Do not doubt my ability to describe without prejudice the sombre, sapless hues and implacable falls of rock. I assure you, that landscape has an identical effect on all those who traverse it. Though the sun might beat down like a hammer, and gentle zephyrs might tease at the glum foliage and long, pendant ribands of ragged bark, and unseen birds might flit and chirrup, still the soul of that forest remains unmoved and disengaged. Not hostile, exactly, but coldly unhelpful. One seems to be labouring perpetually beneath a hard, level stare.

Even Thomas felt the chill of it.

'Sure, and this is an ill-favoured patch,' he muttered. 'As bad as the Bargo Brush, and twice as airless. How long before we reach the station?'

'I don't know.'

'Eh?' He sounded startled.

'There will be a track. The more overgrown it looks, the more likely it is to be connected with our property.' I gazed around at the disheartening prospect of endless, impenetrable growth.

'You can see why no one wanted to lease it. Though I daresay our neighbours have been running their stock through it, occasionally.'

'Not to mention the gully-rakers and footpads,' Thomas muttered. 'I wish we had a pistol wit' us.'

I was beginning to wish the same thing. For this reason I scanned the roadside intently, watching for the slightest break in all that scrub and timber. How slowly it unfolded, as Sovereign trudged along! How wearying it became, to see nothing but the same screen of eucalypt for what felt like miles and miles!

Then, at last, we stumbled upon a kind of tunnel through the brush, perceptible only as an absence of trees and a slight depression in the earth.

'Here,' I said. 'This must be it.'

Forty

I shall tell you something very strange.

As you know, my mother almost never spoke of her ordeal at Belanglo. Certainly she never furnished me with any details. So it was not until I read George Barton's statement, when I was a grown woman on my way to Goulburn, that I was afforded even an inkling of exactly what might have occurred. Or *where* it might have occurred.

According to the newspaper report (which I have here now, beside me), the incident took place when my mother and her overseer were 'going down a steep mountain' about ten miles from Oldbury. There is mention of a rock and a tree. It must have been a large rock, to conceal the body of a bushranger. It must have been a sturdy tree, to withstand the force of Barton's whole strength as he pulled at the ropes that bound him against it. This much, at least, can be deduced.

But nothing else in the statement gives any clue as to the precise location of the hold-up. I still cannot tell you where it happened. I can only hazard a guess. And knowing what I know now, I would guess that I passed over the very spot about half a mile from our destination, when Thomas and I were picking our way down the side of a gully.

We were on foot, by then. The parlous condition of the track demanded it. Had we remained on horseback, we would have been unseated a dozen times by low boughs, and blinded into the bargain. Thomas was carrying his bundle, there being no means of attaching it to the horse. He was also leading Sovereign, while I walked behind them both. Thomas would not let me lead. He insisted on treading down all the encroaching undergrowth ahead of me, lest my trailing skirts become entangled in it.

As the ground rose, the foliage thinned out. From dense bush we emerged onto a gentle slope more thinly scattered with stunted trees. At first we were grateful for the change. Upon climbing the ridge, however, we learned that this new terrain was covered in loose stones and twigs, often concealed by sliding patches of leaf litter. It made for an awkward, unstable surface, which was not improved by the headlong drop that we encountered on the other side of the crest. Our path became so precipitous, at this point, that I really wondered if it was navigable.

It seemed to plunge straight down into the gully, where it lost itself beneath a canopy of trees before re-emerging further on, by the edge of a dry and stony watercourse.

'Well, now,' said Thomas. 'Here's a fine thing.'

'You can see where it goes,' I hastened to point out.

'Aye, but this poor lad'll have a pretty time of 't.'

'Not if we take care. We must be very, very careful, and watch where we tread.'

Good advice, you might think. And it certainly was. Yet as we descended further and further—as the trees became thicker and the sunlight more filtered—Thomas began to exhibit symptoms of increasing unease. His pace slowed. He kept stopping and raising his head, distracted from the task of plotting his course by other, more ominous considerations.

These did not even cross my mind, at first. I was fully occupied keeping my balance until he suddenly stretched out his hand and said, 'Shh!'

'What?' Skidding to a halt, I grabbed at the nearest rock-ledge.

'*Shhh!*'

I listened, but heard only Sovereign's noisy breathing.

At last Thomas lowered his hand.

'I don't like the feel o' this here,' he muttered. 'Straight down into a bloody pit, wit' all eyes on yer feet and none to spare for what's round about. It won't pay to linger. We must get on.'

He was right. As I became more aware of my surroundings, I realised that we were well placed for an ambush. Yet I never once made the connection. Though I kept close to Thomas, unnerved by the stillness, and the silence, and the cliff-walls looming above us on either side, I had briefly forgotten my mother. In my conscious thoughts, the past and present never converged. Not having read George Barton's statement, I knew nothing of a mountain, or a tree, or a rock. It did not occur to me that George Barton's blood might have soaked into the stony soil over which I stumbled. For I had somehow got it into my head that my mother was attacked at the old sheep station. And it was this unseen station that dominated my reflections at the time, filling me with a curious kind of anticipatory dread.

Nevertheless—and here is the strange thing—I must have felt it. I must have *sensed* the truth, by some mysterious means beyond all rational explanation. Because the relief that I experienced upon emerging from that gully was overwhelming.

Even my fear of what the station would reveal was dissipated somewhat by a glorious awareness of *release*, as if taut strings binding my breast had suddenly unravelled.

'It cannot be far now,' I declared. 'There is part of a fence, see? We must be very close.'

And we were. Within another twenty minutes the old hut was in sight. Within half an hour we were pushing open the door. If you are unacquainted with sheep stations as we knew them back in the early days, let me assure you that they were by no means large or magnificent. Commonly, they comprised a simple slab hut and accompanying fenced yards, together with a water source and perhaps (if the two or three shepherds assigned to the place were of an industrious bent) a modest kitchen garden. This particular property was no exception to the rule. It had been hacked out of the forest, which was rapidly reclaiming its own. Though the hut was still standing, its bark roof looked the worse for wear. Many of its fence-posts had collapsed. Its wood-pile was utterly overgrown. Yet from heaps of dry dung and black embers in the hearth, we deduced that passing stockmen must have made use of the facilities not long before.

Even so, the accommodation left a lot to be desired. It stood in the most half-hearted of clearings, hard up against a lowering hill; I did not like the way those invasive trees seemed almost to be jostling each other as they slowly, invisibly, advanced towards the hut. One had an eerie sensation that the path behind us would rapidly disappear, if left unwatched—that the hut itself would be engulfed and stifled by the forest overnight, trapping us there forever.

To escape these unnerving fancies, I quickly went inside. Here I found reality in all its starkness. There was only one big room, little better than a cow-byre. A stone fireplace at one end of the room was the sole concession to comfort. The floor was hard-packed earth. The walls were unsealed. Canvas had been tacked across the ceiling, but even this hung here and there in tatters. The wooden frame of a bed had been rendered useless by the rotting of the ropes that would have supported a mattress. The rickety table stood deserted; no doubt every bench or stool had been chopped up for firewood.

I cannot fully convey to you the desolation of that scene. It was not simply poor and dilapidated. It was deficient in every trace of animation or activity: even the flies were avoiding it. Torn ribbons of canvas fluttered in the draughts that penetrated through every crack. The pattern of sunlight on the floor shifted slightly as a stray breeze punched at the flapping, creaking door. Yet these slight movements seemed only to accentuate the sheer emptiness of what was, in effect, a lifeless shell. Everything was grey: the walls, the floor, the ceiling. Everything was weathered to the point of petrification.

I looked around, and saw only a dry husk. I could not imagine that the place had ever been occupied. It conveyed to me not the slightest hint of human emotion. There were no ghosts in that flimsy structure—no faint echoes of past torment. There was nothing. Nothing spoke to me at all.

It was dead.

Slowly I lowered myself onto the table-top, which was the only available seat. Though it wobbled dangerously, it did not disintegrate. The same cannot be said for my spirits, however, which were profoundly and peculiarly affected. Even then, I realised that I must have been expecting some sort of solution—some sort of answer to a question that was never properly formulated. But I found no solace of enlightenment within those four walls. The perpetual, chafing discomfort within me was not eased.

Overwhelmed by a black tide of bitterness, I dropped my face into my hands and wept.

'Why, what's this?' said Thomas, upon entering the room. 'There's no call for this, lass, we can fix ourselves a royal bed for the night.' He came over and wrapped his arms around me, without risking a seat on the table. He must have seen at a glance that it would not bear his weight. 'Shh, now,' he continued. 'Once we have a fire lit, and a bed o' heath put down under my blanket—why, we'll be happy as kings!'

I shook my head, unable to express the cause of my despair.

'Aye, that we will, I swear. There's an old potato patch out by the creek, and a board I can use to dig it. I'd be right flummoxed if I couldn't find a pair o' tubers under all o' them weeds.' He dropped a bracing kiss on my brow. 'What wit' my tea and sugar, and yer raisins, and a couple o' roast potatoes, we'll be t'envy o' many a poor Irishman,' he said. 'So dry yer tears. Sovereign needs tendin', poor lad.'

'I thought it would be different,' was my muffled response. 'I thought—I don't know what I thought . . .'

'Darlin', ye've no cause to fret.' Thomas pushed the hair from my eyes, fixing me with a serious and tender look. 'I'd not offend ye for the world. If it's two beds ye'll be wantin', I'll make 'em up. But I've only one blanket, and the night'll be a cold one.'

'No, I—it's not that.'

'If we're to be married, lass, I want it done right. So we can face the priest with a clear conscience, though everyone else might wag their tongues.' He hesitated briefly. 'It'll be Father McGinty, won't it, Charlotte? Ye'll not be wantin' a Protestant to wed us?'

'I don't know. I never thought.' And I was appalled at my own lack of foresight. 'Mama will be angry, but—it's really not so *very* different, is it, Thomas? Not for me. My family has always been quite high church, you know.'

'Ye'll never regret it. Not while I have breath left in my body.' He kissed me again and again. ''Tis all the same God, Charlotte,' he whispered.

'Oh yes. I know. I do believe that.' Though I was not quite sure about my mother's opinion. 'And times have changed, have they not? There is much less uncivilised prejudice, and—and misunderstanding.' Nevertheless, I quailed before the prospect of what I would endure upon marrying into the Roman church. To defy my class was one thing; to defy my religion, entirely another. 'Oh dear,' I quavered, 'how unpleasant it's going to be!'

'Nay! Unpleasant? It'll be glorious!' Thomas placed his hands on either side of my tear-stained face. 'We'll be together always. We'll make a new home for ourselves. A new life. If we stand together, nothin'll defeat us. I do believe that. As long as we love each other, we can be happy.'

'A new life . . .' I breathed. And at that instant, I threw in my lot wholeheartedly with Thomas, beguiled by a golden vision. It was the vision of a new life. Make no mistake, a new life was what I desperately, passionately wanted. In one fell sweep, I would reject all my past. I would turn my back on old associations, and on the memories embedded in every space, object and personal exchange at Oldbury. I would embrace a new style of existence, far away from the influence of unmentioned torments that dragged perpetually on my spirits like a dark undertow.

Looking around me, I saw desiccated wood, and vacant corners, and a complete absence of information. I thought to myself: the past is dead. I can be free.

But I was wrong.

Oh, make no mistake: my plan succeeded well enough in one sense. Thomas and I spent the night together chastely, huddled beneath a single blanket. We returned to Oldbury the next day. And we bravely weathered the storm that broke, and the insults that were flung at us, and the tears that were shed on our behalf. I am even inclined to believe that my family's resistance only strengthened our attachment. In the face of so much opposition, we clung to each other as never before. We were married within the week, quickly and quietly, though not without the commonplace celebration that Louisa described so many years later in her book. Suddenly I found myself plunged into a very different world: a world of shrieking housemaids, thundering dance-steps, and extremely salacious jokes. (A new life, indeed!) I went to my nuptial bed quite shaken by it all, and my experience when I got there was no less disconcerting.

Yet, despite the fact that I spent the first month of my marriage in a virtual daze, it soon became apparent that I had not really escaped the past. Initially, I blamed our physical circumstances. For Thomas and I were still living on the Oldbury estate, trapped in one of the tenant farms until I received my small inheritance at the age of twenty-one. I was convinced that a removal would change everything—that once free of Oldbury, I would also be free of its dismal legacy. For years I believed it. Until, that is, I was forced by sorry experience to acknowledge the truth.

'Remembrance wakes with all her busy train/Swells at my breast, and turns the past to pain.' I know now that I shall never escape. Not 'while mem'ry yet/holds fast her office here'. Those early scars remain with me still; there is a hidden canker that eats away at every new bud on my wizened stem. A long, long shadow has been cast across my life, and I can feel its chill even now. For as Milton so truly said, he that hides a dark soul walks benighted under the midday sun: himself is his own dungeon. And even *that* would not be so intolerable, if those close to me were not likewise affected.

With my own poisoned tongue and grievous actions, I have darkened many lives. I rent apart the fabric of my own family, which was never fully mended thereafter. I almost smothered my husband's love for me. As for my children—my beloved children— they have fallen, one by one, as if infected by the black rot at my centre. My precious ones. My babies. How can it be that I sit here now, slowly withering, when they are cold in their graves? How can God allow such a perversion of the Natural Order?

I have failed all my children, even those who survive. Even Edwin, who loves me. For he has made his way alone, when he might have had assistance. When I could have spoken, and illumined his path, I chose to remain silent. I allowed him to walk away, in sheer ignorance, from his own cousin. Fear and selfishness drove me to leave him shallow-rooted, in dry, impoverished soil.

I must ask forgiveness for this, and for all my other sins and omissions. I must make some small amends for the bitterness in my blood.

There is a time to every purpose under heaven: a time to rend, and a time to sew; a time to keep silence, and a time to speak. The time has come to sew. The time has come to speak.

With this testimony, I pray that I shall give light to them that sit in darkness. I pray that by my words, at long last, we shall all have some measure of peace. For there cannot be perfect peace without truth—since the truth, in all things, will set us free.

'Behold, thou desirest truth in the inward parts:
And in the hidden part thou shalt make me to know wisdom.'

I ask your forgiveness. I thank you for your attention. And I would have you, at every turning, make better and wiser choices than I have.

'Bouka', Byng Street, Orange
October, 1905

December 16th, 1905

Dear Aunt Charlotte,

I was so delighted to receive your letter! How *kind* of you to write. As you say, it is *high time* our two branches of the family became better acquainted. I fear that my own is sadly reduced, now that my dear parents are both deceased. But I *do* have a little daughter, Janet, who is eager to meet your many grandchildren. She has so few cousins, poor thing, especially now that your brother's sons are gone to Western Australia.

In response to your inquiry, I am sorry to tell you that few of my mother's papers have survived. This is because all her possessions remained at Oldbury. I do not know why my father left them there when he moved to Sydney from Swanton. It may have been because your brother refused to give them up. I regret to say that my father and your brother quarrelled dreadfully when I was about two—did you know?—and I never laid eyes on Oldbury again until I was orphaned. Then, as I mentioned in my last letter, I returned for a short time. But I trust you will not be offended if I confess that I was never very *happy* there. Though my uncle was a kind man, he was also extremely quiet and melancholy. As for his wife, she was *not* a nice woman. I hate to speak ill of a relative, and one who must have been sorely tried by the symptoms of such a violent stroke, but I *cannot* forgive Aunt Sarah for what she did to my mother's papers. In addition, might I say that I had a *great deal of trouble* with her eldest son, and firmly believe that his difficult nature arose from the example she set.

When your brother died, I was immediately expelled from Oldbury. I went to live with the Reverend Joseph Mullens and his family in Sutton Forest, where I could *not* have been happier. I had already moved to the rectory when Aunt Sarah and her sister put Oldbury up for auction in 1887. In preparation for this event, those two wretched women decided to *burn* all of my mother's possessions! All her manuscripts, her paintings, her specimens—even her collection of stuffed birds and animals! I barely heard the news in time, and had to *run* all the way from Sutton Forest to Oldbury (which must be at *least* three miles) in order to save what I could. I was given no assistance whatsoever, and was able to rescue only as much as I could carry back with me. That was little enough, I'm afraid, and none of it refers to an incident at Belanglo involving my grandmother. My mother *did* write a brief memoir of her own mother's life shortly before she died, which happily escaped destruction. I treasure it greatly, because it was written for my benefit, but it does not refer to Belanglo. Even so, it makes me wish that I could have known my grandmother. She must have been a remarkable person!

If you would like a copy of the memoir, I could easily make one for you. Be assured that it does nothing but justice to its subject. '*At the age of 2,*' according to my mother, '*she* (that is, *your* mother) *could read well and professed throughout her life brilliant talents and great clearness of mind. No words could too highly paint her excellence and worth. Warm in disposition and affections, she was too marked a character not to meet with persons to whom her uprightness and courage made her obnoxious.*' It fills me with pride when I think that I am descended from such an excellent and formidable lady!

I'm so sorry that I could find nothing among the papers that was addressed to you. But I have enclosed something that must have *belonged* to you. Apparently, when my parents were living at Swanton, some remains were discovered in the forest beyond Berrima, near Cutaway Hill. There was nothing to indicate who the dead man might have been, but the police returned to your brother a gold watch which bore the name 'James Atkinson', and which was found amongst the bones. Since the watch had mysteriously disappeared some time previously, it was concluded that the bones belonged to a *thief*. One can only assume that the thief must have robbed Oldbury at some point, because the silver pencil-case that I have enclosed was also discovered in his possession. And I was informed by your brother that it was originally yours.

You should know that your brother spoke of this pencil-case *specifically* before he died. He said that it had been identified as your own by Aunt Louisa, who had recognised it instantly when the police showed it to her. And Aunt Louisa had always *vowed* that it should be returned to you, because you were always so attached to it, and would never have sold it or freely given it away. But no one knew where you were living at that time, and so the pencil-case was kept in trust.

I took it when I last left Oldbury, knowing that Aunt Sarah would not bother to restore it to you. I do think that my uncle felt *very strongly* that he had a duty to return the case, or why mention it to me at all? He actually called me into his study, and said: 'If you should ever come across your Aunt Charlotte, then you must tell her about this little silver case. Because she ought to know when it was found, and where. She ought to know that your Aunt and I realised how sorely she must have grieved to have been parted from it. But at least the thief has received his just desserts, however much we may pray for his unredeemed soul.' I remember his exact words, because I recorded them directly afterwards in my journal. (I kept a journal in those days, though not any longer—I have far too much *else* to do!)

It therefore gives me great pleasure to return this precious article, which I hope will not be unwelcome. I think I can say, without exaggeration, that it comes to you with the loving regards of your brother and sister—and of myself, naturally! If you would like a copy of the memoir as well, please send me word, and I will take up my pen at once.

Until then I remain, most respectfully yours,

(Mrs) Louise S.A. Cosh

Extract

from the Conservation Report on Oldbury, Berrima
Written by Kim Johnston of Bennet Fox Designs, 2003

'. . . In the centre bedroom, the name Atkinson is scratched in the softwood. Roughly done, its direction bumped by the late growth/ early growth ridges, the "o" clumsily like an "a". Beneath it, there appears "James". This room was probably the children's bedroom. James's son, also a James, with his three sisters, endured a childhood of a mad stepfather, corrupt or incompetent executors of his father's estate, and repeated attempts to remove the children from the custody of their mother. It may not be carved by James but still the house bears the name of Atkinson . . .'